ONE
Summer
AT THE CASTLE

ANNE
MATHER

PENNY
JORDAN

JULES
BENNETT

ONE Summer COLLECTION

June 2016

July 2016

July 2016

August 2016

August 2016

September 2016

ONE
Summer
AT THE CASTLE

ANNE
MATHER

PENNY
JORDAN

JULES
BENNETT

MILLS & BOON

First Published in Great Britain 2016
By Mills & Boon, an imprint of HarperCollins*Publishers*
1 London Bridge Street, London, SE1 9GF

ONE SUMMER AT THE CASTLE © 2016 Harlequin Books S.A.

Stay Through the Night © 2006 Anne Mather
A Stormy Spanish Summer © 2011 Penny Jordan
Behind Palace Doors © 2013 Jules Bennett

ISBN: 978-0-263-92231-8

09-0716

Printed and bound in Spain
by CPI, Barcelona

STAY THROUGH
THE NIGHT

ANNE MATHER

Anne Mather and her husband live in the North of England, in a village bordering the county of Yorkshire. It's a beautiful area and she can't imagine living anywhere else. She's been making up stories since she was in primary school and would say that writing is a huge part of her life. When people ask if writing is a lonely occupation, she usually says that she's so busy sorting out her characters' lives, she doesn't have time to feel lonely. Anne's written over 160 novels, and her books have appeared on both the New York Times and *USA Today* bestseller lists. She loves reading and walking and browsing in bookshops. And now that her son and daughter are grown, she takes great delight in her grandchildren. You can email her at mystic-am@msn.com

CHAPTER ONE

IT WAS COLD. Much colder than Rosa had expected, actually. When she'd arrived the night before, she'd put the cold down to the drizzling rain, to her own feelings of anxiety and apprehension. But this morning, after a reasonably good night's rest and a bowl of Scottish porridge for breakfast, she didn't have any excuses.

Where was the heatwave that was supposed to sweep all of the UK through July and August? Not here in Mallaig, that was definite, and Rosa glanced back at the cosy lounge of the bed and breakfast where she'd spent the night with real regret.

Of course part of that unwillingness to part with familiar things was the knowledge that in the next few hours she was going to be stepping into totally unknown territory. An island, some two hours off the coast of Scotland, was not like visiting some local estate. That was why she was here in Mallaig, which was the ferry port for the Western Isles. In an hour she'd be boarding the boat—*ship*?—that would take her to Kilfoil, and she still didn't know if that was where Sophie was.

Fortunately, she'd brought some warm clothes with her, and this morning she had layered herself with a vest, a shirt and a woollen sweater. Feeling the chill wind blowing off the water, she guessed she'd have to wear her cashmere jacket as well for the crossing to the island. She just wished she'd packed her leather coat. It was longer and would have kept her legs warm.

Still, at least it was fine, and she could survive for two hours, she told herself, leaving the guesthouse behind and walking down the narrow main street to the docks. Crossing the already busy car parking area, she went to the end of the jetty, wrapping her arms about herself as she gazed out over the water.

For all it was cold, the view was outstandingly beautiful. The island of Skye was just a short distance away, and she wondered if those purple-tipped mountains she could see were the famous Cuillins. She didn't know. In fact she knew very little about this part of Scotland. Despite the fact that her grandfather Ferrara had been imprisoned near Edinburgh during the war, she had never been farther north than Glasgow. She did have aunts and uncles and cousins there, but her visits had been few and far between.

Now, she realised she should have been more adventurous when she had the chance. But she'd gone to college in England, married an English boy and lived in Yorkshire for most of her life to date. It was easy to make the excuse that she hadn't ventured very far because of her widowed mother and younger sister. But the truth was she wasn't an adventurous sort of person, and Colin had always been happiest spending holidays in Spain, where he could get a tan.

Of course she couldn't make Colin an excuse any longer. Three years ago, when she'd discovered he'd been cheating on her with his boss's secretary, Rosa hadn't hesitated before asking for a divorce. Colin had begged her to

reconsider, had said that she couldn't destroy five years of
marriage over one solitary lapse. But Rosa knew it hadn't
only been a solitary lapse. It wasn't the first time she'd suspected him of seeing someone else, and she doubted it
would be the last.

Fortunately—or unfortunately, as far as Rosa was concerned—they'd had no children to be hurt by the break-up.
Rosa didn't know if it was her fault or Colin's, but she'd
never been pregnant. Of course during the turmoil of the
divorce Colin had blamed her for his unfaithfulness. If
she'd spent more time with him, he said, and less at that
damn school with kids who didn't appreciate her, their
marriage might have stood a chance. But Rosa knew that
was only an excuse. Without her salary as an English
teacher Colin would not have been able to afford the
frequent trips to the continent that he so enjoyed.

Anyway, it was all in the past now, she thought ruefully.
And, although sometimes the things Colin had done still
hurt a little, on the whole she was getting on with her life.
That was until the phone call yesterday morning that had
brought her on this possibly wild goose chase to Kilfoil. But
her mother had been desperate, and frantic with worry, and
Rosa had known she had no choice but to do as she wished.

She sighed, resting her hands on the bars of the railings,
staring out across the water as if the view might provide
the answers she sought. What if her mother was wrong?
What if Sophie wasn't on the island? Would there be some
kind of inn or hostelry there where she could spend the
night until the ferry returned the following day?

She'd been told the ferry booking office opened at nine
o'clock, and that she should have no trouble getting a ticket
to Kilfoil. Apparently the majority of the traffic from

Mallaig was between there and Armadale, the small port on Skye where they all disembarked.

But that wasn't the ferry Rosa needed. She would be boarding the one taking tourists and backpackers to islands farther afield. Dear God, she thought, it sounded so remote, so inaccessible. For the first time she half wished her mother had come with her. It would be so good to have someone she knew to talk to.

Liam drove the Audi into the car park and swung his legs out of the car. Then, holding on to the roof with one hand and the top of the door with the other, he hauled himself to his feet and looked around.

The wind off the water was knife-sharp, but he didn't notice it. He'd been born in Hampstead, but he'd lived in Scotland for the past ten years. Ever since his first book had been such an astounding success, actually, and he was used to the climate. A famous Hollywood director had read his book and liked it, and had optioned it for the iconic blockbuster it had become. But that had been when his life in London had gradually—and ultimately violently—become impossible to sustain.

He ran a hand down over his thigh, feeling the ridge of hard flesh that arced down into his groin even through his worn jeans. He'd been lucky, he reflected. Of the many wounds he'd had that one could have killed him. Instead, although the knife had severed his femoral artery, causing an almost fatal loss of blood, and sliced through enough nerves and sinews to leave him with a permanent weakness in his left leg, he'd survived. It was his attacker who'd died, turning the knife on himself when he'd been confident he'd achieved his objective.

Liam grimaced, determinedly shoving such thoughts aside. It had all happened a long time ago now, and since then none of his books had aroused such a frenzied response in his readers. He took a deep breath of cold sea air, glad that he'd chosen to drive back from London overnight to catch this morning's ferry to the island. There wouldn't be another ferry until Thursday, and he was impatient to get back to Kilfoil and to his work.

Locking the car, he flexed his shoulder muscles and stretched his legs, feeling the stiffness of driving almost non-stop for ten hours in his bones. He had pulled off into a service area around 3:00 a.m. for coffee, and slept for twenty minutes before resuming his journey. But it wasn't the same as sleeping in his bed.

His attention was caught by the sight of a lone woman leaning on the railings at the end of the jetty. It was her hair that had drawn his eyes: deep red and wildly curly, it refused to be controlled by the ribbon she'd tied at her nape. But she seemed hardly aware of it. She was gazing out towards Skye, as if she hoped to find some kind of answer in the mist gathering over the rain-shrouded hills.

Liam shrugged. She was obviously a visitor, dressed for summer in the Highlands, he thought ironically. But, while they had been known to have temperatures well into the eighties, at present the northerly breeze was creating a more predictable sixty-five.

Jack Macleod, who ran a fleet of sailboats that he hired out to tourists, hailed Liam as he left the car and started across to the ferry terminal. 'Now, then, stranger,' he said, grinning broadly. 'We were beginning to think you'd changed your mind about coming back.'

'You can't get rid of me that easily,' said Liam, hooking

his thumbs into the back pockets of his jeans, his chambray shirt parting at the neck to reveal the dark hair clustered at his throat. 'I got back as soon as I could. Spending too long in overcrowded cities doesn't appeal to me any more.'

'Didn't I hear you'd gone to London to see the medic?' Jack asked, regarding his friend with critical eyes. 'Nothing serious, I hope.'

'A check-up, that's all,' said Liam quickly, not wanting to discuss his private affairs in public. He was aware that their voices had attracted the attention of the woman at the quayside, and she was looking at them over her shoulder.

She sensed their awareness of her interest and looked away, but not before Liam had registered an oval face and unusually dark eyes for a woman of her colouring. Of course her hair colouring might not be natural, which was probably the case, and although she was tall she was much too thin.

'You'll be getting this morning's ferry,' Jack was continuing, unaware of Liam's distraction, and he forced himself to concentrate on what the man had said.

'If I can,' he agreed, accepting Jack's assurances that Angus Gallagher would never turn him away, and when he looked back towards the jetty the woman was gone.

Rosa went back to the bed and breakfast, collected her things and was back at the terminal building in time to book her passage to Kilfoil. She supposed she looked like any other tourist, in her jeans and trainers, with a backpack over her shoulder. The other backpackers, queuing for their tickets, didn't give her a second glance. Unlike the two men she'd seen earlier in the car park. Well, one of them, anyway. He'd certainly given her a thorough appraisal.

And found her wanting, she was sure. She'd definitely

sensed his disapproval. But whether that was because he'd found her watching them, she couldn't be absolutely sure.

Whatever, he had been attractive, she conceded, remembering his height—well over six feet, she estimated—and the broad shoulders filling out his crumpled shirt. She guessed he was one of the fishermen who, in increasingly smaller numbers, trawled these waters. He hadn't looked like a tourist, and the man who had been with him had been wearing waders, she thought.

Still, she was unlikely to see either of them again—unless one of them was the captain of the vessel she was hoping to sail on. Maybe someone on the ferry would remember a pretty blond girl travelling out to Kilfoil the previous week. Dared she ask about Liam Jameson? She didn't think so. According to his publicity, the man was reputed to be a recluse, for goodness' sake. So why had he been attending a pop festival in Glastonbury? For research? She didn't think so.

Her mind boggled, as it always did when she thought about what her mother had told her. Sophie had pulled some stunts before, but nothing remotely resembling this. Rosa had thought her sister was settling down at last, that she and Mark Campion might move in together. But now that relationship was all up in the air because of some man Sophie had met during the pop festival.

Rosa got her ticket and moved outside again. The rain that had been threatening earlier seemed to be lifting, and the sun was actually shining on the loch. A good omen, she thought, looking about her for the ferry she'd been told would be departing in three-quarters of an hour. Pedestrian passengers would be embarked first, before the vehicles that would drive straight onto the holding deck.

She saw the man again as she was waiting in line at the quayside. He had driven his car round to join the queue of traffic waiting to board. Unexpectedly, her pulse quickened. So he was taking the same ferry she was. What a coincidence. But it was unlikely he was going to Kilfoil. According to Mrs Harris at the guesthouse, Kilfoil had been deserted for several years before a rich writer had bought the property and restored the ruined castle there for his own use.

Liam Jameson, of course, Rosa had concluded, unwilling to press the landlady for too many details in case she betrayed the real reason why she was going to the island. She'd told her that she planned to photograph the area for an article she was writing on island development. But Mrs Harris had warned her that the island was private property and she would have to get permission to take photographs.

She lost sight of the man when she and her fellow passengers went to board the ferry. Climbing the steep steps to the upper deck, Rosa shivered as the wind cut through even her cashmere jacket. God, she thought, why would anyone choose to live here if they had the money to buy an island? Barbados, yes. The Caymans, maybe. But Kilfoil? He had to be crazy!

Still, she could only assume it gave him atmosphere for his horror stories. And, according to her sister, they were shooting his latest movie on the island itself. But was that feasible? Had the story Sophie had told Mark any truth in it at all? Rosa wouldn't have thought so, but her mother had believed every word.

If only Jameson hadn't involved Sophie, she thought unhappily. At almost eighteen, her sister was terribly impressionable, and becoming a professional actress was her ambition. But although she always maintained she was old enough to make her own decisions, she'd made plenty of bad ones in the past.

If she had met Jameson she would have been impressed, no question about it. His books sold in the millions. For heaven's sake, Sophie devoured every new one as soon as it came out. And all his films to date had been box office successes. His work had acquired a cult status, due to an increasing fascination with the supernatural. Particularly vampires—which were his trademark.

But would he have been attending a rock festival? Stranger things had happened, she supposed, and Sophie had certainly convinced Mark that this was a chance she couldn't miss. Why she hadn't phoned her mother and told her, why she'd left Mark to make her excuses, was less convincing. But if she had been lying, where in God's name was she?

Thankfully, there was a cabin on the upper deck where passengers could buy sandwiches, sodas and hot drinks once the ferry sailed. Rosa stepped inside gratefully, finding herself a seat near the window so she could watch the comings and goings on the dock.

It didn't take long to board the remaining passengers, and the queue of automobiles soon disappeared below. They must be loaded in the order they would disembark, Rosa reflected, wondering if the man she'd seen was familiar with the routine.

The ferry was due to sail to Kilfoil first, then the other islands on its schedule. Rosa was glad. It meant that Kilfoil was the nearest, and as the boat slipped its mooring lines and moved out into the sea loch she hoped it wouldn't be too far.

The island of Skye seemed incredibly close as they

started on their journey, and for a while other islands hemmed them in, giving an illusion of intimacy. But then the body of water widened and the swell caused the small vessel to rise and fall more heavily on the waves.

Rosa hunched her shoulders and glanced back at the group of people gathered at the snack bar. She wished she'd bought herself a drink before it got busy. As it was, she wasn't totally sure she could walk across the cabin without becoming nauseous. She'd never been a good sailor, and the bucking ferry was much worse than the hovercraft she and Colin had once taken to Boulogne.

'Are you feeling okay?'

Guessing she must be looking pale, Rosa turned her head and found the man from the car park looking down at her. So he *had* boarded this ferry, she thought inconsequentially, noticing that the rolling vessel didn't seem to bother him. Apart from donning a well-worn leather jacket over his shirt and jeans, he looked just as big and powerful as she'd thought earlier. The shirt pulled away from the tight jeans in places, to expose a wedge of hair-roughened brown skin.

Sex on legs, she mused, momentarily diverted from her troubles, but he was waiting for an answer and she forced a rueful smile. 'I didn't expect it to be so rough,' she confessed, wondering if he was aware that her eyes were on a level with his groin. She endeavoured to look anywhere else than there. 'I suppose you're used to it?'

His eyes narrowed, thick black lashes veiling irises that were a clear emerald-green. God, he was good-looking, she thought, noting his tanned skin, his firm jaw and his mouth, which was oddly sensual despite being compressed into a thin line. But then he spoke again, his voice harder than before, and she was diverted from her thoughts by the re-alisation that he didn't have a Scottish accent.

'Why do you say that?' he demanded, and Rosa blinked, unable for a moment to remember exactly what she had said.

But then it came back to her. 'Um—I just thought you seemed familiar with the area,' she confessed awkwardly, wondering what was wrong with that. 'Evidently I was mistaken. You're English, aren't you?'

Liam scowled, cursing himself for the impulse that had driven him to ask if she was all right. She'd looked so damned pale he'd felt sorry for her. She was obviously out of place here. No waterproof clothing, no boots, even the pack she'd dumped beside her looked flimsy.

'We don't all speak the Gaelic,' he said at last, and she shrugged her slim shoulders.

'Okay.' Rosa quelled her indignation. At least their con-versation was distracting her eyes from the restless sea outside. 'So,' she said at last, 'do you live in the islands?'

'Perhaps.' He was annoyingly reticent. And then, discon-certingly, 'I hope you don't intend to go hiking in that outfit.'

Rosa gasped. 'Not that it's any of your business.'

'No,' he conceded ruefully. 'I was just thinking out loud. But I couldn't help noticing how cold you looked earlier.'

So he *had* noticed her. Rosa felt a little less antagonis-tic towards him. 'It is much colder than I'd anticipated,' she admitted. 'But I don't expect to be here long.'

'Just a flying visit?'

'Something like that.'

Liam frowned. 'You've got relatives here?'

Rosa caught her breath. He certainly asked a lot of ques-tions. But then she remembered she'd been going to ask if anyone had seen her sister. If this man used the ferry on a regular basis, he might have seen her. And Liam Jameson. But she preferred not to mention him.

'As a matter of fact, I'm hoping to catch up with my sister,' she said, trying to sound casual. 'A pretty blond girl. I believe she made this crossing a couple of days ago.'

'She can't have,' he said at once. 'This ferry only leaves every Monday and Thursday. If she made the crossing at all, it had to have been last Thursday.'

Rosa swallowed. Last Thursday Sophie had still been in Glastonbury with Mark. It had been on Saturday night that he'd phoned to tell her mother what had happened, and that had resulted in Mrs Chantry phoning Rosa in such an hysterical state.

'Are you sure?' she asked now, trying to assimilate what she'd learned, wondering if Liam Jameson had a plane or a helicopter. He probably did, she thought. Why should he travel with the common herd? He might even have a boat that he kept at Mallaig. It had probably been naïve of her to think otherwise.

'I'm sure,' her companion replied, his gaze considering. 'Does this mean you don't think your sister's here, after all?'

'Maybe.' Rosa had no intention of sharing her thoughts with him. She took a deep breath. 'Is it much farther, do you know?'

'That depends where you're going,' said Liam drily, curious in spite of himself, and Rosa decided there was no harm in telling him her destination.

'Um—Kilfoil,' she said, aware that her words had surprised him. Well, let him stew, she thought defiantly. He hadn't exactly been candid with her.

CHAPTER TWO

LIAM WAS SURPRISED. He'd thought he knew everything about the families who had moved to the island after he'd first acquired it. Having been uninhabited for several years, the cottages had fallen into disrepair, and it had taken a communal effort on all their parts to make the place viable again. In the process of rewiring the cottages, reconnecting the electric generator and generally providing basic services, they'd become his friends as well as his tenants. These days Kilfoil had a fairly buoyant economy, with tourism, fishing and farming giving a living to about a hundred souls.

He wanted to ask why she thought her sister might be on the island, but he knew he'd asked too many questions already. Okay, she intrigued him, with her air of shy defiance and the innocence with which she spoke of his island. Unless he missed his guess, there was something more than a desire to catch up with her sister here. Had the girl run away? Or eloped, maybe, with a boyfriend? But why would she come to Kilfoil? As far as he was aware, there was no regular minister on the island.

Rosa saw him push his hands into the back pockets of his jeans, apparently unaware that the button at his waist had come undone. She was tempted to tell him, except that

that would reveal where she was looking, and she hurriedly averted her head.

'About another hour,' he said, answering her question, and then, as if sensing her withdrawal, he moved away to approach the bar at the other end of the cabin. It was quiet now, and, watching with covert eyes, she saw him speak to the young man who was serving. Money changed hands, and then the young man pushed two polystyrene cups across the counter.

Two?

Rosa looked quickly away. Was one for her? She dared not look, dared not watch him walk back to where she was sitting in case she was mistaken.

'D'you want a coffee?'

But no. He was standing right in front of her again. 'Oh—um—you shouldn't have,' she mumbled awkwardly, but she took the cup anyway. 'Thanks.' She levered off the plastic lid and tasted it. 'Why don't you sit down?'

Liam hesitated now. This wasn't his usual practice, buying strange women cups of coffee, letting them share his space. But she looked so out of place here he couldn't abandon her. She might be a journalist, he reflected, eager to get a story. But, if so, she'd been very offhand with him.

Nevertheless, she seemed far too vulnerable to be alone, and much against his better judgement he dropped down into the empty seat beside her. Opening his own coffee, he cast a sideways glance in her direction. Then he saw her watching him and said hastily, 'At least it's hot.'

'It's very nice,' Rosa assured him, not altogether truthfully. The coffee was bitter. 'It was kind of you to get it for me.'

Liam shrugged. 'Scottish hospitality,' he said wryly. 'We're well known for it.'

She gave him a sideways look. 'So you *are* Scottish?' she said. 'You must know this area very well.' She paused. 'What's Kilfoil like? Is it very uncivilised?'

Liam caught his breath, almost choking on a mouthful of coffee. 'Where do you think you are?' he exclaimed, when he could speak again. 'The wilds of Outer Mongolia?'

'No.' Despite herself, her cheeks burned. 'So tell me about the island. Are there houses, shops, hotels?'

Liam hesitated, torn between the desire to describe his home in glowing detail and the urge not to appear too familiar with his surroundings. 'It's like a lot of the other islands,' he said at last. 'There's a village, and you can buy most of the staple things you need there. The post and luxury items come in on the ferry. As do the tourists, who stay at the local guesthouses.'

Rosa felt relieved. 'So it's not, like—desolate or any-thing?'

'It's beautiful,' said Liam, thinking how relieved he'd be to be back again. 'All these islands are beautiful. I wouldn't live anywhere else.'

Rosa's brows arched. 'Where do you live?'

He was cornered. 'On Kilfoil,' he said reluctantly. And then, deciding he'd said quite enough, he got to his feet again. 'Excuse me. I need to go and check on my car.'

When he'd gone, Rosa finished her coffee thoughtfully. She wasn't totally surprised by his answer, but she couldn't help wondering what a man like him found to do there. Could he be a fisherman, as she'd speculated? Somehow that didn't seem very likely. A thought occurred to her. Perhaps he worked for Liam Jameson. Or the film crew, if they were making a film on the island.

She should have asked if there was a film crew on the

island, she chided herself. But then, if she had, she'd have had to explain why she was really here. No, it was wiser to wait until she got there before she started asking those questions. She didn't want to alert Jameson as to who she was.

She couldn't help the shudder that passed over her at the thought of what she had to do. Her *mission*, she thought wryly. Goodness, what was she letting herself in for? But surely if there was a film crew on the island the people in the village would know about it. Whether they'd tell her where Liam Jameson lived was another matter.

The journey seemed endless, even worse than the three train journeys she'd had to make to get to Mallaig. Then at least she'd had some scenery to look at. Apart from a handful of mist-strewn islands, all she could see now was the choppy water lapping at the sides of the ferry.

She sighed and glanced at her watch. If what the man had said was true, it shouldn't be long now. Glancing towards the front of the vessel, she glimpsed a solid mass of land immediately ahead of them. Was that Kilfoil? She hoped so. She'd call her mother as soon as she stepped onto dry land.

Lucia Chantry would be desperate for news. Sophie was her baby, and although she knew as well as anyone that her daughter could be selfish and willful at times, Rosa had never been left in any doubt as to who was her mother's favourite. Sophie could do no wrong, whereas Rosa was constantly making mistakes. Not least when she'd married Colin Vincent. Her mother had never liked him, and she hadn't hesitated to say *I told you so* when Colin turned out to be such a jerk.

The ferry was slowing now, cutting back on its engines, preparing for its arrival at Kilfoil. As it eased into its berth,

Rosa got to her feet, eager for her first glimpse of her destination. It was certainly unprepossessing, she thought,
just a handful of cottages climbing up the hillside from the
ferry terminal. But the overcast sky didn't help. She was
sure it would look much more appealing in sunlight.

Fifteen minutes later she was standing on the quay,
watching as the few cars heading for the island rolled off
the ferry. Glancing about her, she saw the road that wound
up out of the village and the dark slopes of a mountain
range behind.

The island suddenly seemed much bigger than she'd anticipated. But what had she been expecting? Something the
size of Holy Island, off the coast of Northumberland,
perhaps? And if she did find Sophie here, if she hadn't been
lying, how was she supposed to get her to come home? If
her sister was starstruck, she wouldn't be influenced by
anything Rosa said.

Rosa had just located a sign that said 'Post Office' when
she saw a dusty grey Audi coming up the ramp towards her.
The man who'd bought her coffee was at the wheel and she
turned abruptly away. She didn't want him to think—even
for a moment—that she was looking for him.

To her relief, the big car swept past her, but then it
braked hard, just a dozen yards up the road, and she saw
its reversing lights appear. It stopped beside her and a door
was pushed open. The man thrust his legs out, got to his
feet with an obvious effort and turned towards her.

She noticed he was favouring his left leg, something she
hadn't observed on the ferry. But then, the rolling of the
vessel would have precluded any observation of that kind.
She'd been decidedly unsteady on her own feet.

Liam, meanwhile, was cursing himself for being all

kinds of an idiot for stopping the car. But, dammit, she still looked as if a puff of wind would blow her away. And she certainly wasn't interested in him. He'd noticed the way she'd deliberately turned her back on him. So what was he doing playing the knight errant again?

'Got a problem?' he asked, forcing her to turn and face him.

'I hope not,' she said tightly, wishing he would just go away. But, on the off-chance that he might be able to help her, she ought to be more grateful. 'Um—I was looking for the Post Office, that's all. I wanted to ask where Kilfoil Castle was.'

'Kilfoil Castle?' Liam was wary now. 'Why do you want to know where Kilfoil Castle is? It's not open to the public, you know.'

'I know that.' Rosa sighed. Then, giving in to the urge to trust him, she added, 'Do you happen to know if there's a film crew working there?'

'A film crew?' Now Liam was genuinely concerned. Had he been wrong about this woman all along?

'Yes, a film crew,' repeated Rosa. 'I understand they're making a film of one of the Liam Jameson's books on the island.'

Like hell!

Liam stared at her, trying to decide if she was as naïve as she looked. 'Why would you imagine Liam Jameson would allow a film crew to desecrate his home?' he demanded bleakly. 'Movies have been made of his books, I know, but they're not filmed *here*.'

Was it just his imagination or did her shoulders sag at this news? What was going on, for God's sake? Had she expected to find her sister on the set? 'I think you've made a mistake,' he said gently. 'Someone's given you the wrong information. I can assure you there's no production team at Kilfoil Castle or anywhere else on the island.'

Rosa shook her head. 'Are you sure?'

'I'm sure.'

'You're not just trying to put me off?'

'Hell, no!' Liam gazed at her compassionately. 'I realise it must be a blow, but I don't think your sister's here.'

Rosa's brows drew together. 'I don't remember saying that I thought my sister was with the film crew,' she retorted defensively.

'No, but it doesn't take a mathematician to put two and two together.'

Rosa bit her lip. 'All right. Perhaps I did think Sophie might be with them. But if she's not, then perhaps she's somewhere else.'

Liam gazed at her. 'On the island?'

'Yes.' Rosa held up her head. 'So perhaps you could direct me to Kilfoil Castle, as I asked before. Is there a taxi or something I could hire if it's too far to walk?'

Liam blinked. 'Why on earth would you think your sister might be at Kilfoil Castle?' he asked, trying not to sound outraged at the suggestion, and his companion sighed.

'Because she apparently met Liam Jameson a few days ago, at the pop festival in Glastonbury. He told her they were making a film of his latest book in Scotland and he offered her a screen test.'

To say Liam was stunned would have been a vast understatement. It was as if she'd suddenly started talking in a foreign language and he couldn't make head or tail of what she was saying. For goodness' sake, until Sunday morning he'd been in a London clinic having muscle therapy to try and ease the spasms he still suffered in his leg. Besides which, he'd never been to a pop festival in his life.

Realising she was waiting for him to say something, Liam tried to concentrate. It was obvious she believed what she'd just told him. Her look of uncertainty and expectation was too convincing to fake. But, dammit, if her sister had fed her this story, why had she believed it? Anyone who knew Liam Jameson would know it was untrue.

But perhaps she didn't. Certainly she hadn't recognised him. And, taken at face value, it wasn't so outrageous. Two of his books *had* been filmed in Scotland. But not on Kilfoil. He'd made damn sure of that.

'Liam Jameson does live here, doesn't he?'

Rosa was wishing he'd say something, instead of just staring at her with those piercing green eyes. They seemed to see into her soul, and she shifted a little uncomfortably under their intent appraisal. He probably wasn't aware of it, but they were making her feel decidedly hot.

'Yes,' he said at last, when she'd finally managed to drag her gaze away from his. 'Yes, he lives at Kilfoil Castle, as I assume you know. But there's no way he could offer your sister a screen test. He isn't involved in film production. If she told you he was, she was wrong.'

'How do you know?' Although Rosa was prepared to accept that he might be right, she was curious how he could be so certain about it. 'Do you know him personally?'

Liam had been expecting that. 'I know of him,' he said, curiously reluctant to tell her who he was. 'He's— something of a recluse, and to my knowledge he's never been to Glastonbury. Your sister sounds quite young. Jameson is forty-two.'

'Forty-two!' If he'd expected her to know his age, too, he'd been mistaken. She hunched her shoulders. 'That old?'

'It's not so old,' muttered Liam, unable to prevent a twinge of indignation. 'How old is your sister?'

'Almost eighteen,' answered Rosa at once. 'Do you think Liam Jameson likes young girls?'

'He's not a pervert,' said Liam sharply, and then modified his tone as he continued, 'And, let's face it, you don't have any proof that it was Jameson she went off with.'

'I know.' Rosa blew out a breath. 'But where else can she be?' She wet her lips, her tongue moving with unknowing provocation over their soft contours. 'Anyway, if you'll give me those directions to the castle, I'll go and see if Mr Jameson has an answer.'

That was when Liam should have stopped her. He should have explained who he was, and how he knew Jameson had never been to Glastonbury, but he chickened out. He'd gone too far with the deception to simply confess that he was the man she was looking for. And his innate sense of privacy made him a victim of his own deceit.

'Look, I think you're wasting your time,' he said carefully. 'Jameson has never been to a pop festival.' He caught her eyes on him. 'As far as I know.'

'You know an awful lot about him,' said Rosa curiously. 'Are you sure you're not a friend of his?'

'I'm sure,' said Liam, wishing he'd never started this. 'But I do live on the island. It's a small place.'

'It doesn't seem very small,' said Rosa unhappily. 'And I'm not really looking forward to meeting this man, if you want the truth. He writes about horrible things. Ghosts and werewolves—'

'Vampires,' put in Liam unthinkingly.

'—stuff like that,' she muttered, proving she hadn't been listening to him. 'That's probably why Sophie was so impressed by him. She's read everything he's ever written.'

'Really?'

Liam couldn't help feeling a glow of satisfaction. No matter how often he was told by his agent or his publisher that he was a good writer, he never truly believed it.

'Oh, yes.' Rosa sighed again. 'Sophie's mad on books and TV and movies. She wants to be an actress, you see. If this man has been in contact with her, she'll be like putty in his hands.'

'But he hasn't,' said Liam. And then he amended that to, 'You don't really believe he has?'

'Perhaps not.' Rosa had to be honest. 'But, if you don't mind, I'd rather hear that from Liam Jameson himself.'

Liam scowled, scuffing the toe of his boot against a stone, aware that at any moment someone could come up and speak to him and then he wouldn't have any choice in the matter.

'Look,' he said reluctantly. 'Why don't you just get on the ferry again and go home? If your sister wants to tell you where she is, she will. Until then, it would probably be wiser for you not to accuse people of things you can't know or prove.'

Rosa shivered. 'Get on the ferry again?' she echoed. 'I don't think so.'

'Well, it doesn't call here again until Thursday, like I said.'

Rosa tried not to show how dismayed she felt. 'Oh, well, there's nothing I can do about it now. And Liam Jameson's the only lead I've got.'

Liam blew out a breath. 'Okay, okay. If that's your final word, I'll take you.'

'Take me where?'

'To Kilfoil Castle. That is where you want to go, isn't it?'

'Well, yes. But do you think Mr Jameson will agree to see me?'

'I'll make sure he does,' said Liam drily. 'Let's go.'

'But I don't even know who you are,' Rosa protested, the idea of getting into a car with a strange man suddenly assuming more importance than it had before.

'I'm—Luther Killian,' muttered Liam ungraciously, waiting for her to recognise the name of his main character. But there was no reaction. Her sister might read his books, but she definitely didn't.

CHAPTER THREE

ROSA hesitated. 'Um—is it far?' she ventured, drawing a sigh of impatience from the man beside her.

'Too far to walk, if that's what you're thinking,' he said shortly. 'There's always old McAllister, of course. He runs a part-time taxi service, if it's needed. I can't vouch for the reliability of his vehicle, though.'

Rosa glanced down at her bag which, even looped over her shoulder, was heavier than she'd expected when she'd packed it the previous day. 'Well, all right. Thanks,' she said, not without some misgivings. 'If it's not out of your way.'

Don't do me any favours, thought Liam irritably, reaching for her bag and opening the rear door of the car. He tossed it onto the seat and then gestured for her to get into the front. His leg was aching from standing too long and he couldn't wait to get off his feet.

'You didn't say if it was far,' she ventured, after he'd coiled his length behind the wheel, and Liam shrugged.

'The island's not that big,' he said, which wasn't really an answer. 'Don't worry. It won't take long to get there.'

Rosa hoped not, but the island did seem far bigger than she'd imagined as the Audi mounted the hill out of the village. They emerged onto a kind of plateau that stretched away ahead of them, very green and verdant, with small lakes, or lochs, glinting in the intermittent rays of the sun.

Away to their left, the mountains she'd seen from the quayside looked big and imposing. Their shadowy peaks were bathed in cloud cover, but the lower slopes changed from grey to purple where the native heather flourished among the rocks. Here and there the scrubland was dotted with trees, sturdy firs that could withstand the sudden shifts in the weather.

'This is Kilfoil Moor,' said her companion, nodding towards the open land at either side of the road. 'Don't be fooled by its look of substance. It's primitive bog in places. Even the sheep have more sense than to graze here.'

Rosa frowned. 'Are you a farmer, Mr Killian?'

A farmer! Liam felt a wry smile tug at his mouth. 'I own some land,' he agreed, neither admitting nor denying it. Then, to divert her, 'The island becomes much less hostile at the other side of the moor.'

'And have people—like—walked onto the moor and been swallowed up by the bog?' asked Rosa uneasily.

Liam cast her a mocking glance. 'Only in Jameson's books, I believe.'

Rosa grimaced. 'He sounds weird. I suppose living up here he can do virtually as he likes.'

'He's an author,' said Liam irritably, not appreciating her comments. 'For God's sake, he writes about monsters. That doesn't mean he *is* one!'

'I suppose.'

Rosa acknowledged that she was letting the isolation spook her. A curlew called, it wild cry sending a shiver down her spine. A covey of grouse, startled by the sound of the car, rose abruptly into the air, startling her. She made an incoherent sound and her companion turned to give her another curious look.

'Something wrong?'

Rosa shrugged. 'I was just thinking about what you said,' she replied, not altogether truthfully. 'I think I agree with you. Jameson wouldn't have brought Sophie here.'

'No?' Liam spoke guardedly.

'No. I mean—' She gestured towards the moor. 'I can't imagine any man who lives here going to somewhere frantic like a pop festival.' She paused. 'Can you?'

Liam's mouth compressed. 'I seem to remember saying much the same thing about half an hour ago,' he retorted.

'Oh. Oh, yes, you did.' Rosa pulled a face. 'I'm sorry. I think I should have listened to you.'

Liam shook his head. He didn't know what she expected him to say, what she expected him to do. But if she hoped that he'd turn the car around and drive her back to the village she was mistaken. He was tired, dammit. He'd just driven over five hundred miles, and there was no way she was going to add another twenty miles to his journey. If she wanted to go back, Sam would have to take her. Right now, he needed breakfast, a shower and his bed, not necessarily in that order.

Or that was what he told himself. In fact, he was curiously loath to abandon her. He felt sorry for her, he thought. She'd been sent up here on a wild goose chase and she was going to feel pretty aggrieved when she found out he'd been deceiving her, too.

The awareness of what he was thinking astounded him, however. This had always been his retreat, his sanctuary. The one place where he could escape the rat race of his life in London. What the hell was he doing, bringing a stranger into his home? For God's sake, *she* wasn't a teenager. She was plenty old enough to look out for herself.

'Anyway,' she said suddenly, 'I'm still going to ask him if he knows where she might be. I mean, if they are making a film up here, he will know about it. Where it's being made, I mean. Don't you think?'

Liam's fingers tightened on the wheel. Why didn't he just tell her who he was? he wondered impatiently. Why didn't he admit that he'd kept his identity a secret to begin with because he'd been half afraid she had some ulterior motive for coming here? She might not believe him, but it would be better than feeling a complete fraud every time she mentioned his name.

'Look, Miss—er—'

'Chantry,' she supplied equably. 'Rosa Chantry.'

'Yes. Miss Chantry.' Liam hesitated now. 'Look, I think there's something I—'

But before he could finish, she interrupted him. 'Oh, God!' she exclaimed in dismay, and for a moment he thought she'd realised who he was for herself. But then she reached into the back of the car, hauled her pack forward and extracted a mobile phone. 'I promised I'd ring my mother as soon as I reached the island,' she explained ruefully. 'Excuse me a minute. I've just got to tell her I'm all right before she begins to think she's lost two daughters instead of just one.'

'Yeah, but—' he began, about to tell her that there were no transmitters for cellphones on the island when she gave a frustrated cry.

'Dammit, the battery must be dead,' she exclaimed, looking at the instrument as if it was to blame for its inactivity. Then she frowned. 'That's funny. There's no signal at all.'

'That's because we don't have any mobile phone masts on Kilfoil,' said Liam mildly. 'The place was deserted for years—apart from a few hardy sheep—and although things have changed a bit since then, we prefer not to litter the island with all the detritus of the twenty-first century.'

'You mean I can't ring my mother?'

'No. There are landlines.'

'So do you think Liam Jameson will let me make a call from the castle?'

'I'm sure he will,' muttered Liam, aware he was retreating back into the character he'd created. 'Don't run away with the idea that the island's backwards. Since—since its modernisation, it's become quite a desirable place to live.'

Rosa arched brows that were several shades darker than her hair. 'Is that why you came here?' she asked. 'To escape the rat race?'

'In a manner of speaking.'

'And you like living here? You don't get—bored?'

'I'm never bored,' said Liam drily. 'Are you?'

'I don't get time to be bored,' she replied ruefully. 'I'm a schoolteacher. My work keeps me busy.'

'Ah.' Liam absorbed this. He thought it explained a lot. Like how she was able to come up here in the middle of August. Like why she seemed so prim and proper sometimes.

The moor was receding behind them now, and they'd started down a twisting road into the glen. He pointed ahead. 'There's the castle. What do you think?'

Rosa caught her breath. 'It's—beautiful,' she said, and it was. Standing square and solid on a headland overlooking the sea, its grey walls warmed by the strengthening sun, it was magnificent. 'It's very impressive,' she breathed.

And not what she had expected at all. 'But how can anyone live in such a place? It must have over a hundred rooms.'

'Fifty-three, actually,' said Liam unthinkingly. And then, with a grimace, 'Or so I've heard.'

'Fifty-three!' Rosa shook her head. 'He must be very rich.'

'Some of them are just anterooms,' said Liam, resenting the urge he had to defend himself, but doing it just the same. 'I'm fairly sure he doesn't use them all.'

'I should think not.' Rosa snorted. 'Is he married?'

'No.' Liam had no hesitation about telling her that. It was in the potted biography that appeared on the back of all his books, after all.

'Well, does he live alone?' Rosa was persistent. 'Does he have a girlfriend? Or a boyfriend?' she added, pulling a face. 'These days you never know.'

'He's not gay,' said Liam grimly. 'And he has household staff who run the place for him, so he's hardly alone.'

'All the same...' She was annoyingly resistant to his opinion. 'I bet he has to pay his employees well to get them to stay here.'

Liam clamped his jaws together and didn't answer her. He could have said that several of the people he employed were refugees from London, like himself. He did employ locals, where he could, but the islanders only wanted part-time work so they could pursue their own interests. The Highlanders were an independent lot and preferred fishing and farming to working indoors.

They approached the castle through open land dotted with sheep and cattle. Rosa saw shepherds' crofts nestling on the hillside, and more substantial farm buildings with whitewashed walls and smoking chimneys. A stream, which evidently had its source in the mountains, tumbled over rocks on its way to the sea. And in the background the shoreline beckoned, the sand clean and unblemished and totally deserted.

Rosa knew that anyone who'd never seen this aspect of Scotland wouldn't believe how incredibly beautiful it was. The sea was calm here, and in places as green as—as Luther Killian's eyes. And just as intriguing. Though probably as cold as ice.

The castle itself looked just as splendid as they drew closer. Although obviously renovations had been made, they'd been accomplished in a way that didn't detract from the building's charm and history. Only the square windows, that had replaced the narrow lattices once used for firing on the enemy in ancient times, were out of character. But the heavy oak front doors looked just as solid a defence.

There were outbuildings set back from the main house, with a cobbled forecourt edging the stone steps in front. They approached over a wooden bridge spanning a dry ditch, which might once have been a moat, and parked on the forecourt to one side of the studded doors.

One of the doors opened immediately and a man and several dogs stepped out into the sunlight. The dogs—two golden retrievers and a spaniel—bounded down the steps to greet them, their tails wagging excitedly.

To the accompaniment of their barks of welcome, Liam swung open his door and hauled himself to his feet. Once again, his leg had stiffened up and he cursed its weakness for spoiling one of the true pleasures of his life. He had always enjoyed driving and had a handful of expensive cars in his possession. He preferred them to the helicopter that his agent had insisted was essential, and leased the aircraft to the local air ambulance service more often than he used it himself.

Steeling himself against the pain, he left the car and strode towards Sam Devlin, the man who ran Kilfoil for him with such consummate skill and efficiency. 'Liam—' began Sam, only to break off when his employer raised a warning finger to his lips. 'It's good to see you again,' he amended, his grey brows drawing together in confusion. 'Is something wrong?'

Liam glanced back significantly, and now Sam saw Rosa getting out of the car. 'Do we have a visitor?' he asked in surprise. He knew, better than anyone, that Liam never brought strangers to Kilfoil.

'We do,' said Liam in a low voice, after shaking hands with the older man. 'She's here because she wants to ask *Liam Jameson* where her sister is.'

'What?' Sam stared at him. 'But you're—'

'She doesn't know that.' Liam sighed. 'It's long story, Sam, but now's not the time to share it. Just play along, will you? I intend to tell her who I am, but—not yet.'

Sam grimaced. 'But why bring her here—?' he began, and then broke off when the young woman left the car and started towards them. She was slowed by the snuffling of the dogs, but she was too near now for them to continue their conversation. He collected himself with an effort. 'Welcome to Kilfoil, miss.'

'This is Sam Devlin, Liam Jameson's second-in-command,' said Liam smoothly. 'Sam, this is Miss Chantry. Rosa Chantry, isn't that right?' He looked to her for confirmation. 'Perhaps Mrs Wilson would be kind enough to provide Miss Chantry with lunch.'

'I'm sure she'd try,' Sam agreed drily, but Rosa couldn't impose on her host in that way.

'Actually,' she said, 'if I could just have a quick word with Mr Jameson—?'

'Mr Jameson's—tied up at present, Miss Chantry,' said Sam, with a wry look at his employer. 'If you'll come with me, I'll show you where you can wait.'

'Oh, but—do you think he will see me?'

Rosa addressed her words to Sam now, even though Liam had assured her he'd arrange it himself.

Sam looked at his employer blankly. 'I think it's— possible,' he said, gaining a nod of approval. 'Um—why don't you follow me?'

Rosa hesitated, turning to the man who'd driven her here with a grateful smile. 'Thanks for the lift,' she said. 'Goodbye, Mr Killian.'

Liam inclined his head, aware that Sam was staring at him, open-mouthed. 'My pleasure,' he replied, realising he meant it. He turned away as Sam pulled himself together and led her into the castle. She wasn't going to be so pleased when she discovered who he really was.

Meanwhile, Rosa was experiencing an unwarranted feeling of regret that she wouldn't be seeing Luther Killian again. He had been kind, in spite of her ingratitude. She wished she'd asked him where he lived now. After all, whatever happened later, she was going to be stuck on the island for at least another couple of days.

She followed Liam Jameson's man into the castle with some reluctance. Despite her desire to speak to Jameson and get this over with, it was a little daunting being faced with such surroundings. Although the hall they entered via an anteroom was brightly lit by several wall sconces, and the huge fire that was burning in the grate, it was intimidating. With its lofty ceiling and tapestry-hung walls, it reminded her that the man she'd come to see made his living from scaring his readers.

'We only use the hall as a reception room,' Sam Devlin offered, as she hovered just inside the door. 'The rest of the castle is much more cosy. It would be impossible to keep the place warm otherwise.'

Rosa could believe it. 'Does Mr Jameson live here all the year round?'

Sam seemed to consider his words before replying. 'Mostly,' he said at last. 'Except when he's away on business or pleasure. Now, please come this way.'

To Rosa's surprise, and trepidation, they crossed the hall to where a winding flight of stone stairs led to an upper floor. Although the stairs were carpeted, Rosa viewed them without enthusiasm. She'd assumed the man was going to show her into one of the rooms that opened off the hall.

'Wouldn't it be easier if I just waited here for Mr Jameson?' she asked.

'I'm afraid not.' Sam was polite, but resolute. 'This floor of the castle is given over to kitchens and storerooms, as well as providing living quarters for the full-time staff.'

'I see.' Rosa was reassured by the idea that there were other people living as well as working here. Luther Killian hadn't told her that.

With no alternative, she followed the man up the stairs, realising as she did so that this must be one of the towers she'd seen from the road. She wasn't good with spiral staircases, but happily it opened out onto a narrow landing, with windows in an outer wall that gave an uninterrupted view of the bay.

'Oh, isn't that wonderful!' she exclaimed, pausing at a window embrasure and gazing out at the view. The windows overlooked the front of the castle, with the little bridge they'd driven over just below her. And she saw, with some surprise, that Luther Killian's car was still parked in the same spot. Frowning, she glanced round at Sam Devlin. 'Um—Mr Killian's still here.'

'Is he?' Sam didn't sound particularly interested, and then Rosa remembered Killian had said he'd speak to Liam Jameson himself. He might be explaining the situation. If so, that would be something else she had to thank him for. Maybe she'd ask Sam Devlin where Killian lived before she left.

But thinking about leaving reminded her that she still hadn't phoned her mother. 'Er—do you think I could make a phone call while I'm waiting?' she ventured, and Sam shrugged.

'There's a phone in here,' he said, opening a door into what appeared to be a library. 'Make yourself at home. I'll ask Mrs Wilson to provide some refreshments.'

'You will tell Mr Jameson I'm here?' Rosa reminded him, wondering about the rather curious look that crossed his face at her words.

'I'll tell him,' he agreed, remaining on the landing. 'If you'll excuse me...?'

Rosa nodded, trying not to feel apprehensive when he closed the door rather firmly behind him. Well, she was here. She'd reached her destination. And if the circumstances were not what she'd expected, it wasn't her fault.

Turning, she surveyed the room with determined confidence. One wall curved, as if it was part of the tower she'd just climbed, but all the walls were lined with bookshelves. There was a granite-topped desk, strewn with papers and a laptop computer, and several leather chairs.

Rosa wondered if these were Liam Jameson's books, but there were obviously too many for that to be so. Approaching one of the shelves, she drew out a bulky tome, hand-carved in leather. But the title, *Vampire Myths of the Fifteenth Century*, made her hastily push it back again.

But she was wasting time, she thought, noticing the neat black instrument set at one end of the desk. She had to call her mother. Mrs Chantry would probably be biting her nails by this time. Particularly if she'd tried to ring Rosa herself.

As she waited for the connection, Rosa perched on the edge of the window seat. The walls were thick and the sills were broad, plenty broad enough to provide a comfortable seat. Glancing down, she saw that from this angle she could see the gardens at the back of the castle, and a couple of huge glasshouses, set into the lee of the tower.

Obviously the place was self-sufficient, she thought. And, despite her initial reaction, Rosa quite envied Jameson for living here. It was peaceful in a way very few places were these days.

Then, her mother answered. 'Rosa? Rosa, is that you? Have you found Sophie? Is she all right?'

'I haven't found her.' Rosa decided there was no point in prevaricating. 'There isn't a film crew on the island, Mum. Sophie must have been making it up.'

'Oh, she wouldn't do that.' Mrs Chantry was so gullible where her younger daughter was concerned. 'If she's not there, then Mark must have made a mistake. Scotland's a big place. They must be filming somewhere else.'

'But where?'

'I don't know, do I? That's for you to find out.'

'Perhaps.' Rosa was non-committal. 'I may know more after I've spoken to Liam Jameson himself.'

'You mean you haven't spoken to him personally?'

'How could I?'

'Well, for heaven's sake, Rosa, what have you been doing?'

'Getting here,' retorted Rosa indignantly. 'It was a long journey, you know.'

'So where are you now? Sitting in some bar in Mallaig, I suppose. And who told you there's no film being made on the island?'

'As a matter of fact, I'm on the island at this moment. I'm at Kilfoil Castle. And I'm pretty sure that nothing's going on here.'

Her mother snorted. 'So if Jameson's not there—'

'I didn't say that,' Rosa interrupted. 'Haven't I just said I'll know more after I've spoken to him?'

'So he's not with the production?'

If he ever was. 'It would appear not,' said Rosa trying to be patient. She heard the sound of someone opening the library door. 'Look, I've got to go, Mum. I'll ring you later. As soon as I have some news.'

She rang off before Mrs Chantry could issue any more instructions. Then, getting up from the window seat, she turned to find Luther Killian standing just inside the door. He'd evidently changed. The crumpled shirt and jeans he'd worn to travel in had been replaced by a long-sleeved purple knit shirt and drawstring cotton trousers. Judging by the drops of water sparkling on his dark hair, he'd had a shower as well.

Rosa knew her jaw had dropped, and she quickly rescued it. 'Oh, hi,' she said, a little nonplussed. 'I thought you'd gone.'

Well, she'd thought he would have by now.

Liam's smile was guarded. 'Is everything all right at

home?' he asked, guessing what had been going on. He pushed the tips of his fingers into the back pockets of his pants. 'You look—surprised to see me.'

'I am.' Rosa didn't think there was any point in lying about it. 'Have you spoken to Liam Jameson? Has he agreed to see me?'

'He has,' said Liam drily, finding this harder than he'd expected. 'I'm sorry to disappoint you, Rosa, but I'm Liam Jameson.'

Rosa stared at him aghast. 'You're kidding!'

'No.' Liam pulled a face, and then, abandoning his awkward stance, he crossed to the desk and went to stand behind it. 'I didn't intend to deceive you. Not initially. It just worked out that way.'

CHAPTER FOUR

'YOU'RE NOT SERIOUSLY going to allow her to stay here until she can get a ferry back to the mainland, are you?' Sam Devlin was dismayed. 'Man, you know nothing about this woman. How do you know this wasn't just a ruse to get into the castle?'

'I don't.' Liam finished the plate of bacon and eggs Mrs Wilson had cooked for him and reached for his steaming mug of coffee, sitting on the gleaming pine table beside him. He took a mouthful of the coffee, the third cup he'd had that morning, and sighed his satisfaction. 'But, in answer to your first question, she's leaving this morning. As soon as she can get her belongings packed.'

'Well, that's a mercy,' said Sam briskly. 'I could hardly believe it when Edith told me she was staying the night. Not but what the lassie seems honest enough. It's just unlike you to invite a stranger into your home.'

'I know.' Liam could hear the edge in his voice, but he didn't appreciate Sam telling him what he already knew. 'Anyway, I doubt if you'd have wanted to drive her back to the village last night.'

Sam sniffed. 'You could always have called McAllister out. He gets little enough work as it is.'

'Well, I didn't,' said Liam shortly. 'And, for your information, I don't think she has an ulterior motive for being here. For God's sake, she didn't know who I was until I told her.'

'So you say.'

'So I know.'

'All right, all right.' Sam backed down. 'But I'm always suspicious when supposedly innocent strangers turn up out of the blue. I mean, who would be stupid enough as to believe you'd allow anyone to make a film on Kilfoil?'

'Her teenage sister, perhaps?'

'But you have nothing to do with film production.'

'I told her that,' said Liam mildly.

'So why did you bring her here? Couldn't you have convinced her you were telling the truth and sent her on her way?'

'She wanted to come,' said Liam flatly. 'She insisted on speaking to Liam Jameson in person.'

Sam shook his head. 'This was when you were masquerading as Luther Killian?'

'If you want to put it that way, yes.'

Sam snorted. 'Well, I don't know what you were thinking of, Liam. For God's sake, you're not a teenager. You're a middle-aged writer of horror fiction. You should have known better.'

'Gee, it's so good to know what you think of me,' drawled Liam drily. 'Why didn't you add with more scars than Ben Nevis and a gammy leg into the bargain?'

Sam's gnarled cheeks had gained a little colour now. 'Och, you know what I think of you, man. Surely there's no need for me to mince my words.' He paused, and when his employer didn't say anything he continued fiercely, 'If you were the type who played around with the lassies, Liam, it would be different. But you're not. You never have been. Sure, I know you've had the odd fling now and then, but you've never brought your conquests home. Not since Kayla—'

'Don't go there, Sam.'

Liam came to life now, and the older man hunched his shoulders at the reproof. It was years since he'd even thought about Kayla Stevens, thought Liam grimly. The woman he'd been intending to marry before the disastrous attack that had almost killed him.

They'd met at a launch party his publisher had thrown for him when his first book had made number one on the bestseller lists. Kayla had been a struggling model, hired out by her agent for such occasions to add a little glamour to the mix. She'd seemed out of place there, too innocent to be forced to earn a living in that way. Liam had felt sorry for her—much as he'd done for Rosa Chantry, he thought now, scowling at the memory. But he'd eventually learned that Kayla had always had an eye to the main chance.

Although she'd hung around the hospital for a while after the attack, the idea of getting hitched to a man who was badly scarred, who might be impotent or paralysed, and who would definitely need a lot of care and under-standing to recover, hadn't appealed to Kayla. Six months after returning Liam's ring, she'd married a South American polo player with enough money to keep her in the style to which she'd become accustomed. The fact that without Liam she'd never have had the opportunity to meet such a man didn't even compute.

Sam was looking dejected now, and Liam took pity on him. 'Look, this isn't about what Kayla did, right? It's about helping someone out. Rosa's mother doesn't know where her younger daughter is. I expect she's pretty worried by now.'

'So why doesn't she go to the police?'

'And say what? That her daughter's gone off with another man and her boyfriend's jealous? Sam, teenagers are notoriously unpredictable. She'll probably turn up in a couple of days and deny the whole thing.'

'So why did you get involved?'

Good question. 'I've been asking myself that,' admitted Liam sagely. 'I don't know. Because my name was mentioned, I suppose. According to Rosa, her sister's a big fan. Maybe I was flattered. In any case, she's leaving today.'

It was the sunlight that awakened her. When she'd finally gone to bed—some time after midnight, she thought—she'd been sure she wouldn't sleep and the moonlight had been comforting. But she must have been more tired than she'd thought, both mentally and physically. Otherwise, why would she have accepted that man's help?

Discovering that the man she knew as Luther Killian was really Liam Jameson had knocked her off balance. And angered her, too, she admitted. He'd had no right to lie about his identity, however desperate he was to retain his anonymity.

The fact that he must have been equally stunned to learn that he was supposed to have met her sister at a pop festival and offered her a screen test made it marginally excusable. But she wouldn't have come here at all if he'd been honest with her from the start.

Pushing back the duvet, Rosa swung her legs out of bed and padded, barefoot, to the windows. The floor was cold beneath her feet, but she thought she'd never get tired of the view. She was on the second floor of the castle and her windows looked out over the headland. She had an uninterrupted view of the restless sea that broke against the rocks.

It was so beautiful, the sun already tingeing the tips of the waves with gold. But there were clouds on the horizon, brooding things which threatened rain later. Perhaps this afternoon, she considered, wondering where she'd be sleeping tonight.

The realisation that it must be later than she'd thought occurred belatedly. Or perhaps it was the appetising aroma of warm bread drifting to her nostrils that reminded her she hadn't eaten much the night before. She turned with a start to find there was a tray resting on the chest of drawers standing by the doorway. Someone had evidently put it there. Was that what had woken her?

She'd been resting her bare knee on the wide sill, but now she straightened and headed back to the bed, where she'd left her watch. Snatching it up from the nightstand, she saw it was already half-past-nine. Good heavens, she must have slept for at least eight hours.

She hesitated, torn between getting washed and dressed or investigating the contents of the tray. The tray won out, and, deciding that whoever had put it there deserved to be compensated, she picked it up and carried it back to the window seat.

A flask of what was obviously coffee invited her to try it. There was milk and cream in small jugs, brown sugar, and a basket of warm rolls. These were what she'd smelled, she realised, touching them reverently. Warm rolls, giving off the delicious scents of raisin and cinnamon.

Had Liam Jameson arranged this for her? More likely

Mrs Wilson, she thought, remembering how rude she'd been to her host the afternoon before. But learning that he had been Liam Jameson all along had been so humiliating. When he'd told her he was the man she'd been waiting to see, she'd felt hopelessly out of her depth...

'You?' she'd said stupidly. '*You're* Liam Jameson?' She shook her head. 'You can't be.'

He was annoyingly laconic. 'Why not?'

'Because you don't look anything like your picture,' Rosa protested, remembering the young man with a moustache and goatee beard she'd seen on the back cover of one of his novels. This man's face was clean-shaven, if you didn't count the shadow of stubble on his chin.

'Well, I'm sorry to disappoint you, but I really am Liam Jameson,' he said. 'The picture I think you're referring to was taken about twelve years ago.'

'Then you ought to have it updated,' she snapped.

As if!

Liam shrugged. 'As I believe I told you earlier, I'm a fairly reclusive soul. I prefer not to be recognised.'

'That's no excuse.' Rosa was trying hard not to feel too let down. 'So, what about Sophie? Do you know where she is?'

'Of course not.' The exasperation in his voice was unmistakable. 'If I did, don't you think I'd have told you?'

'I don't know what to think, do I?' Rosa's nails dug into her palms. 'You bring me here under false pretences...'

'Now, wait a minute.' Liam didn't know why her words stung him so much. That *was*, in effect, what he'd done. Taking a different tack, he went on, 'Would you have believed me if I'd told you who I was? You've just accused me of not looking anything like my picture.' He paused. 'If you must know, I felt sorry for you. You'd obviously been sent on a wasted journey, and whatever I'd said you would still have been stuck here for three more days.'

Rosa lifted her chin at this. 'There was no need for you to feel sorry for me, Mr Jameson.'

'Wasn't there?' Liam couldn't help but admire her courage. He'd obviously judged her too harshly when he'd thought she had no spirit. 'So—what? If I'd told you who I was, you'd have just booked into a bed and breakfast and waited for Thursday's ferry? You wouldn't have been at all suspicious that I might not have been telling you the truth?'

'Well, I would have asked you about Sophie,' said Rosa, her shoulders slumping. 'You should have told me who you were,' she added again. 'Who is Luther Killian anyway? Someone who works for you?'

'You might say that.' A trace of humour crossed his face, and she was annoyed to feel herself responding to his charm. 'Luther Killian is the main character in all my novels. Which just proves that you're not a fan.'

'I've told you, Sophie is the one who reads your books.' She shook her head bitterly. 'You must think I'm such a fool.'

'Why would I think that?'

He had the nerve to look indignant, but Rosa was way past being understanding. 'Because I was too stupid to suspect anything,' she retorted. 'Even when it became obvious that you knew too much about him not to be involved.' She took a deep breath. 'Why did you do it, Mr Jameson? Were you just playing a game? Did making a fool of me turn you on?'

Now, where had that come from?

Rosa was still gazing at him, horrified at what she'd said, when someone knocked at the door. There was a

moment when she feared Liam Jameson was going to
ignore it, but then he turned and strode across the room.
Once more, he was dragging his leg, but Rosa was too
dismayed to feel any compassion for him. God in heaven,
he would think she was no better than her sister.

The housekeeper was waiting outside. She was carrying
a tray of tea and sandwiches, and Liam let her into the room
with controlled politeness.

'This is Mrs Wilson,' he said, his voice as cold as she'd
heard it. 'Enjoy your lunch. I'll speak to you later.'

But in fact he hadn't. When Mrs Wilson had come in to
collect the tray again, she'd offered the news that Mr
Jameson was resting. He'd apparently asked the housekeeper to provide a room for her, where she could freshen
up and so on. And that was how Rosa came to be here,
almost twenty-four hours after her arrival.

Not that she'd ever expected to stay the night. When
she'd had as much of the tea and sandwiches as she could
stomach, with her conscience making every mouthful an
effort, she'd ventured downstairs with the tray, hoping to
run into her host. But the only person she'd encountered
was Sam Devlin, and he'd taken some pleasure in telling
her that Mr Jameson was indisposed and wouldn't be able
to speak to her that afternoon after all.

Naturally, Rosa had blamed herself for Jameson's condition, sure that her behaviour had contributed to his malaise.
But when she'd asked how she could get back to the village,
Devlin had reluctantly admitted that his employer didn't
want her to leave until he'd spoken to her again.

'Mr Jameson suggests that you might like to spend a
little time exploring the grounds of the castle,' he'd said

tersely. 'I can come with you, if you like? Or, if not, you're free to relax in the library. There are plenty of books to read, and Mrs Wilson can supply anything else you need.'

In the event, Rosa had agreed to go for a walk, though not with Sam Devlin. She'd a managed to convince the dour Scotsman that she wouldn't get lost, and she'd spent a fairly pleasant hour wandering through gardens bright with late summer flowers, with only the dogs for company.

Back at the castle, and not knowing what else to do, she'd retreated to the library. Though not to read. She'd seen what manner of books were on the shelves, and, while she was sure Jameson only used them for research, she'd had no desire to give herself nightmares.

She'd been a little disturbed when Mrs Wilson had informed her that supper would be served at seven in the dining hall. She'd never expected to stay for supper and she hadn't been wholly surprised when she'd ventured downstairs again, after washing her face and combing her hair, to find that she was eating alone.

'Mr Jameson has suggested you spend the night,' Mrs Wilson had explained gently, much less antagonistic than Sam Devlin had been. 'He says he'll see you in the morning. Will that be all right?'

Of course Rosa knew she should have refused, that accepting anything from Liam Jameson was putting herself in his debt. Which was definitely something she didn't want to do. But she also knew that she owed him an apology, and much against her better judgment she'd agreed to stay.

She sighed now. Whether she'd wanted to or not, she'd accepted his hospitality, and sooner or later she was going to have to make her apologies and take her leave. So, was her reluctance just embarrassment, or was she, as she suspected, curiously unwilling to say goodbye?

She shivered. How ridiculous was that? Liam Jameson meant nothing to her, and she'd made sure he would be glad to see the back of her. And what a way to repay his kindness. Okay, he should have told her who he was right off—but would she have believed him as he'd said?

She considered. On the ferry, she'd told him very little about why she was coming to the island, and even after they'd disembarked she hadn't exactly welcomed his help. By the time she'd confessed why she was really here, he'd already let her think he only knew Liam Jameson, not that that was who he really was.

The situation had definitely not been conducive to confidences, and she had to admit she'd been too anxious to get to her destination to listen to reason. Was that really why he'd kept his identity from her, as he'd said? It certainly made more sense than what she'd accused him of.

Not wanting to think about that scene in the library, Rosa finished her coffee and one of the warm rolls, and then went to get a shower. A glimpse of her tumbled hair convinced her that she couldn't face Jameson in her present condition. She needed to have herself firmly under control before she encountered him again.

The bathroom was just as elegant as the bedroom where she'd slept, with a free-standing claw-footed tub and mirrored walls. The fluted glass shower could have accommodated at least three occupants, and the windows were made of clear glass.

The idea that anyone could look into the bathroom as she had her shower sent Rosa immediately to the windows. But there, on the second floor of the castle, there was no danger of being observed by anyone. Open spaces stretched in all directions, the nearest dwelling at least a mile away.

Stripping off the man-sized tee shirt she'd brought to sleep in, Rosa was caught for a moment by her reflection in the mirrored walls. Long legs, small breasts and a bony frame did not make for beauty, she decided ruefully. Okay, her complexion was fair, her eyes were dark and she didn't suffer from freckles. But her mouth was too wide, her nose was too long and at present there were frown lines between her brows.

She sighed, losing patience with herself and stepping into the shower. What did it matter what she looked like? Liam Jameson was not going to be attracted to her. Goodness, she'd thought he was gorgeous when she'd believed he was Luther Killian. Now she knew who he really was, she would not have been surprised if Sophie had fallen for him.

Sophie!

Rosa felt ashamed of herself. Here she was, thinking about Liam Jameson, when she still had no idea where her sister was. She would have to phone her mother again, she thought, knowing Mrs Chantry would be waiting for her call. Hopefully her mother would realise that Rosa wasn't free to use Liam Jameson's phone at random. Particularly when the call she needed to make was long distance.

Emerging from the shower a few moments later, she quickly grabbed one of the luxury towels from the rack and wrapped it about her. Then, after cleaning her teeth, she went back into the bedroom to dress.

To her surprise, and dismay, the tray had disappeared in her absence. Remembering that she hadn't bothered closing the bathroom door, Rosa hoped she hadn't been seen. But if she had it would only have been Mrs Wilson,

she assured herself. There was no way Liam Jameson
would have collected the tray himself.

And if he had, what of it? she asked herself bitterly. It
wasn't as if she was the kind of woman men spied on.
Unlike Sophie, who, with her spiky hair and rounded
figure, was always being pursued by one man or another.
And it now seemed as if her involvement with Mark
Campion was on the skids as well.

Thankfully, there was a hairdryer lying on the period
dressing table in the bedroom. Like the bathroom, the
bedroom was an attractive mix of ancient and modern. The
cheval mirror was Victorian, and the chest of drawers was
even older. But, although the bed was a four-poster, the
mattress was reassuringly twenty-first century in design.

It took a little while to dry her mass of hair, and then
even more time to secure it in a French braid. If the severe
style and the high-necked navy sweater she chose to wear
with her jeans owed anything to a desire to stifle any trace
of femininity, she refused to acknowledge it. It was important to appear confident, however insecure she might feel.

She was quite familiar with the stairs that led down to
the lower floor by this time. The dining hall was on the floor
below, not far from the library. But the dining hall, with its
mahogany-lined walls and long refectory table, was empty,
the epergne of roses in the centre the only sign of life.

She wondered if it was worth going down into the reception hall, but she doubted she'd encounter her host
there. If, indeed, he was up and about. But she remembered
there had been a desk and a computer in the library.
Perhaps that was where Jameson wrote his books.

She tapped at the library door first, before venturing
inside. But, although she listened intently for any move-

ment from within, the room seemed eerily quiet. Now, why had she used that adjective? she chided herself. She hadn't felt any unusual presence in the castle. It was just her imagination working overtime because there was nobody about.

There was only one way to find out. Reaching for the handle, she turned the knob. She sensed she wasn't alone only seconds before someone spoke behind her. 'Looking for me?' enquired Liam Jameson in a hollow voice, and she almost jumped out of her skin.

CHAPTER FIVE

'I—YES. YES,' she said, dry-mouthed, her breathing quickening uncontrollably. She swung round to find him propped against the wall to one side of the heavy door. Then, seeing his mocking smile, she forgot all about the promises she'd made herself. 'Did you do that on purpose?' she demanded hotly.

'Do what?' Liam adopted an innocent expression, but he could tell from her face that she knew he had.

'Try to frighten me,' she exclaimed, pressing a hand to her chest, where her heart was beating wildly. 'Honestly—' she endeavoured to calm herself '—you almost gave me a heart attack.'

'I'm sorry.'

But he didn't sound particularly sorry, and Rosa recoiled instinctively when he leant past her and pushed open the door. 'After you,' he said, apparently unaware that his hand had brushed the side of her breast as he did so. Her breast tingled, and Rosa stiffened, but he seemed indifferent to her response.

However, Liam wasn't indifferent, and he was glad when she turned and went ahead of him into the room. For God's sake, he thought, annoyed with himself as much as her. She was behaving like an outraged virgin and he was experiencing the kind of reaction that would have been pathetic when he was a teenager.

What was wrong with him, for pity's sake? He had no interest in repressed spinsters. Women who knew little about sex, and what they did know scared them rigid. When he needed a woman, he preferred one who knew the score.

All the same, a little voice inside him taunted, it might be amusing to see how she'd react if he came on to her. It was years since he'd used sex as anything more than an infrequent necessity, with good reason. And just because Rosa Chantry intrigued him, it was no reason to think anything had changed. She'd be just as horrified as Kayla had been when she'd seen his injuries. But it would have been so nice to pull the pins out of her hair and feel all that fiery silk spilling into his hands...

Once again he steeled himself against that kind of madness. Despite the ache between his legs, he was determined not to give her another reason to accuse him of upsetting her. Hell, he didn't need that kind of aggravation, but if that childish plait and masculine outfit were intended to deter any thoughts of a sexual nature they were having quite the opposite effect.

He closed the door behind him, leaning back against it, struggling to gain control of his sudden need. Rosa had hurried across the room, meanwhile, obviously wanting to put a safe distance between them. Then, when she felt she'd achieved her objective, she turned to face him.

'I—*was* looking for you,' she said, linking her hands together at her waist, unaware that it was a particularly protective stance. 'I wanted to thank you.'

'To thank me?' Liam couldn't think of anything she'd want to thank him for, but Rosa's lips had tightened.

'For allowing me to stay the night,' she informed him primly. 'You didn't have to do that.'

'Ah.' Liam was relieved to feel the restriction in his trousers easing, and he straightened away from the door. 'No problem.' He waited a beat. 'Were you comfortable?'

'Very comfortable, thank you.'

'Good.' Liam came further into the room. 'I'm sorry I had to leave you on your own all evening. I'm afraid I fell asleep, and didn't wake until after midnight.'

Rosa was tempted to say, *How appropriate* bearing in mind his occupation, but she didn't. She was still intensely aware of him, and inviting that kind of intimacy wasn't sensible. 'It's all right,' she said instead. 'Your housekeeper looked after me. I slept really well.'

'You weren't afraid I might turn into a vampire in the night and ravish you?' Liam couldn't resist the urge to tease her and she flushed.

'Only briefly,' she retorted, surprising him again. 'But I'm fairly sure vampires don't ride ferries or drive cars in broad daylight.'

'Luther Killian does,' he said at once, and Rosa gave him an old-fashioned look.

'Luther Killian doesn't exist,' she said. 'Or only in your imagination, anyway.'

'You think?'

Rosa shook her head. 'You're not telling me you believe in vampires, Mr Jameson?'

'Oh, yes.' He nodded. 'There have been too many reports of sightings, both here and in Eastern Europe. And if you went to New Orleans—'

'Which I'm not likely to do,' she said tightly, realising she was letting him distract her from her purpose. She ought to be asking him if she could use his phone again, instead of indulging in a discussion about mythical monsters. Shrugging, she made a face. 'I know very little about such things, Mr Jameson. But I imagine it makes good publicity for your books.'

Liam caught his breath. 'You think that's all it is?' He was indignant.

'Well, I don't know, do I? I know nothing about vampires.'

'You know they don't normally go out in sunlight,' he reminded her, and she sighed.

'Everyone knows that.' And then, unable to resist it, 'Except Luther Killian, apparently.'

'Ah, but Luther is only *half* inhuman. His mother was a witch before she met Luther's dad.'

Rosa couldn't help smiling. 'And he converted her, I suppose?'

'Vampires always convert their victims,' agreed Liam, closing the space between them. 'D'you want me to show you how?'

Rosa backed up. 'I know how, Mr Jameson,' she mumbled, not sure if he was teasing her now or not. 'Please—' She held out her hand in front of her. 'I'm not a character in one of your books.'

'No,' he conceded flatly, aware that he was in danger of allowing their relationship to develop into something it was not. He turned back towards his desk, hearing her sudden relieved intake of breath as he did so. 'You're obviously not a believer.'

Rosa sighed now. She didn't want to offend him, for

heaven's sake. 'A believer in what?' she asked, much against her better judgement, and he turned to rest his hips against the granite surface.

'In the supernatural,' he said carelessly, folding his arms. 'What was it you said on the way here? Ghosts and were-wolves—we call them shapechangers, by the way—and things that go bump in the night.'

Rosa shrugged. 'And you are?'

'Oh, sure. Anyone who has encountered evil in its purest form has to be.'

Rosa frowned. 'Are you saying *you've* encountered evil?'

Oh, yes.

For a moment Liam thought he'd said the words out loud, but the expectant look on her face assured him he hadn't. Thank God!

'I suppose we all encounter evil in one form or another,' he prevaricated, having no intention of discussing his experiences with her. He'd already stepped too far over the mark, and he backtracked into the only avenue open to him. 'Luther certainly has.'

'Oh, Luther!' She was disparaging. 'Who's only a character in your books.'

'The main character,' he corrected her. 'He's what you'd call an anti-hero. He kills, but his intentions are always good.'

'Isn't that a contradiction in terms?' she exclaimed at once. 'How can anyone—or anything—that makes a living killing people be regarded as good?'

Liam shrugged, and as he did so Rosa caught a glimpse of something silvery against his neck. It was either a birth-mark or a scar of some sort, and her mouth went dry. It occurred to her that it might have been made by some-one's—or something's—teeth.

Oh, God!

'I suppose that depends on your definition of good and evil,' he replied, diverting her. 'Isn't ridding the world of genuinely wicked individuals worthy of some respect?'

Rosa struggled to regain her objectivity. 'And that's what your books are about? Some—some vampire bounty-hunter working to make the world a better place?'

'A safer place, anyway,' agreed Liam drily. 'Don't knock it. You never know what you'd do if you were faced with primal evil.'

'And you do?' She sounded sceptical, and Liam had to bite his tongue not to tell her exactly what had happened to him. 'Come on, Mr Jameson. We both know you've lived a charmed life.'

Liam had to tuck his fingers beneath his arms to prevent himself from tearing his clothes aside to show her the kind of evil he'd encountered. 'Maybe,' he managed tersely. 'But I haven't always lived in Scotland, Miss Chantry.'

'I know.' She'd relaxed a little now. 'I read about you on the Internet. Didn't you used to work at the Stock Exchange, or somewhere?'

'It was a merchant bank, actually.'

'Whatever.' Rosa shrugged, glad of the return to reality. 'I imagine you had a fairly good salary. Then you made a lot of money with your first book and bought your own castle. How difficult was that?'

Liam pushed himself to his feet. 'If that's what you want to think,' he said, turning to shuffle the papers on his desk. 'Which reminds me, I have work to do.'

Rosa felt ashamed now. It wasn't anything to do with her how he lived his life. 'Look,' she said, taking a step towards him, 'I'll admit I know nothing about you, really.

And—and if you say you know how it feels to face real evil, then I believe you. But—'

'But you don't believe me,' said Liam sharply, swinging around again, and Rosa was uneasily aware that there was barely a hand's breadth between them now. 'You're humouring me, Miss Chantry, and I don't like it. I don't need your endorsement.'

Rosa licked her dry lips. 'I was only being polite,' she protested. 'It's not my fault if you're touchy about the veracity of your books.'

'Touchy about the veracity—' Liam gazed at her angrily. 'You haven't the first idea what you're talking about.' He dragged a calming breath into his lungs and tried to speak naturally. 'Let's just say I have had some firsthand knowledge of evil. But I'd rather not discuss it. Okay?'

Rosa lifted her shoulders. 'I had no idea.'

'Why should you?' Liam wasn't at all sure he liked the look of sympathy in her eyes any better than the disbelief he'd seen before. 'Forget it. I have.'

Though he doubted he ever would.

Rosa hesitated. 'I didn't mean to suggest your books weren't believable,' she persisted, laying a reckless hand on his sleeve. 'I'm sorry if I've offended you.'

Offended me?

Liam expelled a strangled breath. Although he was wearing a warm sweatshirt, he could feel the touch of her fingers clear through to his skin. The muscles in his arm tightened almost instinctively, the tendons heating and expanding much like those other muscles between his legs.

'It's not important,' he muttered harshly, concentrating on anything but the feminine scent of her skin. But then he lifted his lids and encountered those anxious brown eyes, and he felt as if he was drowning in their soft depths.

Hardly aware of what he was doing, he lifted his hand and brushed his thumb across her parted lips. Moisture that had gathered there clung to the pad, and he didn't think before bringing his thumb to his mouth to taste her.

For her part, Rosa was almost paralysed by his actions. She'd never dreamt that an innocent attempt to comfort him might have such a disturbing result. Her whole body felt hot and trembly now, and she was aware of him in a way that she hadn't been before. Or was she only kidding herself? She'd been aware of him right from the start.

When her tongue emerged to circle her lips it was because they'd suddenly gone dry, not to absorb any lingering trace of his scent. Although she did. She heard him suck in a breath and wondered what he was thinking. Dear God, this wasn't meant to happen. But she knew that Colin had never made her feel anything like this.

When he spoke, however, his tone was harsh. 'I shouldn't have done that,' he said shortly. 'I'm sorry.'

Now it was Rosa's turn to take a gulp of much-needed oxygen. 'It—doesn't matter,' she said, glancing behind him at the telephone. 'Um—' She had to calm down, she told herself. 'I was wondering if—'

But that was as far as she got. 'It does matter,' he said, raking back his dark hair with a frustrated hand. 'For God's sake, you must think I'm desperate for a woman!'

Liam saw the way his words affected her almost before he'd finished speaking. The fact that he'd been trying to reassure himself that his emotions weren't involved here was no excuse. He realised, belatedly, that what he'd said could be taken two ways, and he wasn't at all surprised when she turned on him.

'I'm sure you're not,' she retorted stiffly, wrapping her arms tightly across her slim body so that her small breasts were pushed upward in an unknowingly provocative way. 'And I'm not that desperate for a man, either.'

Liam suppressed a groan. Didn't she realise he hadn't intended to offend her? Evidently not. He scowled. Now it was up to him to defuse the situation he'd created, and one look at her face convinced him that it wouldn't be easy.

'Look,' he said persuasively, 'that wasn't intended as an insult. On the contrary. I wouldn't like you to think I expected any payment for my hospitality, that's all.'

Rosa gave him a disbelieving look. 'We both know what you meant, Mr Jameson,' she said tightly. 'I'm not a fool. You don't have to tell me I'm not the type of woman someone like you would find appealing.'

Liam felt a twinge of indignation. Despite the warning voice of his conscience, which was telling him not to continue with this, he resented the contempt he'd heard in her voice. Who the hell did she think she was, making un-informed judgements about him? She didn't know him. She knew nothing about him or his tastes in women. Yet she was implying he was some moron who could only think with his sex.

The fact that that *was* what he had been doing was not something Liam chose to consider at that moment. 'Be careful, Miss Chantry,' he said unpleasantly. 'I'll begin to think you were disappointed that I stopped when I did.'

'How dare you?'

Rosa didn't think she had ever felt so furious. Her hand

balled into a fist almost automatically, connecting with the hard muscles of his stomach before she had time to reconsider. She suspected she'd hurt herself more than she hurt him, but it didn't matter. He had no right to ridicule her. Not when, for a heart-stopping moment, he'd made her feel so good.

Liam was surprised at the fierceness of her attack. 'You need to control that temper of yours, Miss Chantry,' he panted, annoyed at his shortness of breath. 'What the hell's the matter with you? What did I say to warrant that response?'

'You know what you said, Mr Jameson.' Rosa was trembling, but she refused to back down.

'Yeah?' Some evil demon was urging him on. 'And wasn't it true?'

Rosa stared at him, wondering how she could ever have been attracted to this man. 'You have a much inflated opinion of yourself, Mr Jameson,' she said icily, keeping her voice down with an effort. It would have been so much more satisfying to shout at him. 'If I allowed myself, just for a moment, to give in to you, it was simply because I felt sorry for you. I mean, it can't be much fun living here on your own, with only your female staff for diversion.'

The outrage Liam felt at being unknowingly but callously reminded of Kayla's defection brought a crippling wave of anger sweeping over him. Forgetting that he'd been in the wrong here, that her insults were just a counterattack to his sarcasm, he grasped her wrists and twisted them behind her back. 'You're just a mine of bitterness, aren't you, Miss Chantry?' he chided scathingly. 'It's no wonder you've never been married. No decent man would put up with a spiteful bitch like you.'

Rosa gulped, the instinct to correct his bald assumption overwhelmed by the alarm she felt at finding herself

locked in his savage embrace. She tried to break free, but
with his hot breath almost stifling her, and his thigh
wedged aggressively between her legs, she was helpless.
They were both breathing rapidly, and for several seconds
a silent battle ensued.

But it wasn't really a battle, Rosa acknowledged weakly.
She was at his mercy and he knew it. Though, strangely,
he didn't appear to appreciate his good fortune. On the
contrary, when his eyes encountered hers, she saw they
were filled with a mixture of confusion and regret.

'Hell,' he said harshly. 'This was not meant to happen.'

'So let me go,' said Rosa a little breathlessly, not entirely
immune to the appeal of those green eyes no matter what
he'd said.

This close, she could also see that silvery scar she'd
noticed earlier. She quivered in spite of herself. How had
he really got that?

'Yeah, I should,' he agreed, distracting her, his gaze
dwelling on her mouth with an intensity that felt practically
physical. 'But you know what?' He shifted against her and
she was almost sure she could feel him hardening. 'I don't
want to. Now, isn't that the damnedest thing?'

A knot twisted in Liam's stomach as he watched her
reaction to his admission. Had she any idea that a wave of
heat and need was drumming through him, making what
had begun as a desire to punish her into an insane urge to
show her what she was missing? He could feel her trembling, even though she was doing her best to hold herself
away from him, and the breasts he'd admired earlier were
now surprisingly urgent against her woollen sweater.

'Please,' Rosa said unsteadily, probably hoping to
appeal to his better judgement. But Liam only heard what

she said as if from a distance. He'd captured both her wrists in one grip now, and brought his free hand round to rub his knuckles against one of those button-hard nipples. He felt her shuddering recoil with a pleasurable rush of blood to his groin.

God, she was responsive, he thought incredulously, wondering how long it had been since she'd had a man. If she'd ever had one, he appended, though he didn't quite believe she was a virgin.

Nevertheless, he wished he'd met her in other circumstances—wished he hadn't antagonised her by being cruel about her unmarried state. Because he was attracted to her, no matter how he might deny it. She wasn't beautiful, of course, but she had a fey charm that appealed to the romantic in him. And there was no denying that he could imagine, only too easily, all that glorious hair spread over the pillow on his bed.

Rosa's legs were beginning to feel as if they wouldn't support her weight for much longer. Liam had turned his attention to her other breast now, covering it with his hand so that the hard peak butted against his palm. The sensation it caused made her feel dizzy, though not as dizzy as getting naked with him would feel, she thought crazily.

Wetness pooled between her legs and she was disconcerted. What was wrong with her? She'd always known, even when Colin was making passionate love to her, that some part of her had stood apart and watched what was going on with a certain objectivity.

But she couldn't be objective with Liam. When he looked at her as he was looking at her now, she couldn't even think straight, let alone anything else. She felt weak, possessed, consumed by needs she'd hardly known existed, so that when he bent his head towards her, her lips parted instinctively for his kiss.

However, although his mouth skimmed the curve of her neck, and the roughness of his jaw grazed her cheek, he didn't kiss her. Well, not on the mouth, anyway. With a feeling of dismay she felt his sudden withdrawal. He let go of her wrists and she stumbled, hardly aware she'd been relying on his support until it was taken away from her.

Then, as she struggled to regain her balance, he turned his back on her and leant on his desk.

CHAPTER SIX

LIAM, MEANWHILE, was hoping she hadn't realised why he'd had to turn away from her. Letting her go hadn't been easy, and his body still wouldn't accept what his mind was telling it to do. Instincts as old at time were demanding satisfaction, but, although the temptation was great, common sense insisted that he had to take control.

Dammit, he reminded himself, apart from the fact that he hardly knew the woman, did he really want to expose himself to ridicule again? Yet when she'd been in his arms, when he'd been breathing her scent, feeling her slim body moving against his, it had been all too easy to delude himself that this might work. All the pheromones in his body had responded to her and he'd so much wanted to bury himself inside her. To find out if she was as tight there as he imagined she would be.

Which, he acknowledged grimly, was crazy. Did he want her to go away from here and tell all her friends what a monster he was? A monster who couldn't keep his pants zipped, he thought bitterly. Yeah, the tabloids would have a field-day with that one.

Of course eventually he had to look behind him. Without the slightly unsteady sound of her breathing he wouldn't have known she was still there. But she was, and she deserved some explanation. Though what he was going to say he wasn't sure.

After checking himself to make sure there was no embarrassing bulge in his pants, he turned to face her again. Her face was still flushed, he noticed, giving her an unexpected beauty, but she was doing her best to behave as if he hadn't just made a complete prat of himself. God, he thought, he didn't need this. He had a book to write, for pity's sake.

Rosa steeled herself as he turned. If he intended to blame her for what had happened, she had her answer ready. She hadn't asked him to touch her, and he'd had no right to treat her with so little respect. Heavens, he still thought she'd never been married. Goodness knew what he might have done if he'd known the truth.

If only there was some way to get away from here. If she had a car, for instance—or the use of a phone—she wouldn't have had to stand there like a fool, waiting for him to remember he had a guest. As it was, she was dependent on him for a phone, both to ring for transport and to call her mother. She disliked being beholden to him for anything after what had happened.

Liam sighed. This was a new experience for him, and he didn't like it. He didn't like it one bit. When he needed a woman, he found one who knew what she was doing. He'd never brought any woman here before, never done anything to violate the atmosphere of his home.

Until now.

Swallowing his pride, he said stiffly, 'I know you're not going to believe me, but I don't do this sort of thing—'

He would have continued, but Rosa broke in before he

could say anything else. 'You're right,' she said tersely. 'I don't believe you, Mr Jameson. I may be naïve, but you can't tell me you've never taken advantage of a woman before.'

'Dammit!' Liam caught his breath. 'I didn't take advantage of you,' he exclaimed impatiently. 'If I had, you'd know it, and you don't.' He paused. 'And call me Liam, for God's sake. You don't know how ridiculous you sound, calling me Mr Jameson after what just happened. You may still be a virgin, but I'm not.'

That was unforgivable, but he'd had it with trying to humour her. And it wasn't as if she hadn't played some part in the affair. Some part in his downfall, he amended grimly. He wasn't going to forget this in a long time.

'Oh, I'm sure everything about me seems ridiculous to you,' Rosa retorted, stung by his unfair criticism. 'But for your information I *have* been married, Mr Jameson. I divorced my ex-husband over three years ago.'

Liam stared blankly at her. 'You've been married?' he echoed disbelievingly.

'For five years,' she agreed, glad she'd been able to shock him at last.

'You don't look old enough.'

'Well, I am. I'm thirty-two, Mr Jameson. Quite old enough, I assure you.'

Liam was surprised. And disgruntled. He'd put her down as being no more than twenty-five. But he was most disturbed by the way this news affected him. If he'd known how old she really was, and that she'd been married...

But he mustn't go there. Wasn't it enough that he'd made a bloody fool of himself and created an awkward situation for himself into the bargain?

'Look,' he said, tight-lipped, 'let's agree that we've both made some mistakes here. I shouldn't have grabbed you, I admit it. But you shouldn't have made me so mad that I forgot what I was doing.'

Rosa wanted to argue that she hadn't been the one who'd brought her here, that if he'd been honest right from the beginning none of this would have happened. But a reluctant awareness that she hadn't exactly put up much of a fight kept her silent, and when she finally spoke it was to say, 'Would it be all right if I used your phone, then?'

Liam knew a most inappropriate desire to laugh. Her words were so unexpected, so prosaic, as if all they'd been doing for the past half-hour was discussing the weather. But he had the sense to realise that humour would definitely not go down very well at this moment, and with a careless lift of his shoulders he said, 'Why not?'

'Thanks.' Rosa hoped she sounded sincere. 'I just want to ring my mother again.'

Liam arched dark brows. 'And tell her your sister's not here?'

'Yes.'

'Okay.' He nodded towards the desk where the phone was situated. 'Be my guest.'

Rosa hesitated for a moment, feeling awkward now. 'Um—perhaps I could ring for a taxi at the same time?' she ventured. 'What was it you called that man?'

'McAllister?'

Rosa nodded.

'No need.' Liam started for the door, trying to hide the fact that his leg was protesting at the sudden activity. 'Sam's driving over to the village later this morning. You can go with him.'

Rosa wasn't sure she wanted that. Sam Devlin hadn't exactly welcomed her here. 'If it's just the same to you, I'll call McAllister,' she murmured, wishing she didn't have to ask. 'I don't want to put anyone out.'

Liam paused now, half turning to face her, his brows drawing together above those piercing green eyes. 'What's Sam been saying to you?'

'Oh—nothing.' And it was true. 'I'd just—prefer to make my own arrangements.'

Liam regarded her broodingly. 'So you don't want any advice on where to stay?'

'Well—yes.' Rosa hadn't thought of that. 'That would be useful.'

'Okay.' Liam reached for the door. 'I'll have Sam give you an address.' He pulled the door open, trying not to drag his foot as he moved into the aperture. 'Take your time. There's no hurry.'

'Oh, but—'

'Yes?'

His response was clipped, and Rosa, who had been about to ask if he'd injured his leg, changed her mind. 'You—haven't given me Mr McAllister's number,' she said, with sudden inspiration, and Liam frowned.

'I can't remember it off-hand. I'll have Sam give you that, too. After you've rung your mother.'

And wasn't Sam going to wonder why she'd refused to drive back to the village with him? But, 'Okay,' she said weakly. 'Thanks.'

'No problem.' Liam was eager now to put this unfortunate interlude behind him. 'Have a good trip back.'

'Oh—' Once again, Rosa detained him. 'I mean—I will see you again before I leave?'

It had been an inane question, bearing in mind that he'd just wished her a good trip, but, conversely, now that the time had come, Rosa was curiously loath to leave him.

Liam sighed, leaning heavily on the door for support. 'You're not going to tell me you'll be sorry to go, are you?' he asked flatly. 'Because, quite frankly, *I'd* find that hard to believe.'

Rosa met his mocking gaze defensively. Then, to her dismay, she found herself saying, 'I suppose you'll be glad to see the back of me?'

Liam took an audible gulp of air. How was he supposed to answer that?

'Pretty much,' he admitted at last. Then, seeing her expression, he added, 'You're too much of a distraction.'

'Oh, right.' She gave him a scornful look. 'What you mean is, I've wasted too much of your time already.'

Liam shrugged. 'I didn't say that.'

'You didn't have to.' Rosa turned towards the desk. Then, picking up the receiver, she said, 'I hope your leg's better soon.'

Liam blinked, but she wasn't looking at him now. And, although he was tempted to ask her what she knew about his injuries, he kept his mouth shut.

The door closed behind him and Rosa breathed a sigh of relief. The sooner she left here, the better. Despite what she'd thought before, he was dangerous to her peace of mind.

Her mother answered on the second ring, and when she did Rosa was instantly aware of the anticipation in her voice.

'Sophie?' Mrs Chantry said eagerly. 'Oh, darling, I hoped you'd ring back.'

Back?

Rosa was stunned. 'You mean you've heard from her?'

There was a moment's silence. 'Rosa? Rosa, is that you?'

'Who else?' Rosa could hear the edge in her voice but she couldn't help it. 'What's going on, Mum? I gather you've heard from Sophie?'

'Well, yes.' Her mother sighed. 'She rang yesterday evening.' She made a sound of excitement. 'You can't imagine how relieved I was.'

Rosa could. Sophie could do anything and their mother would forgive her. Even if, as in this case, she'd been telling a pack of lies.

'So where is she?' Rosa asked, forcing herself to be patient. 'Did she tell you that?'

'Of course.' Mrs Chantry sounded indignant now. 'She's in Scotland, as she said.' She paused, and then went on breathlessly, 'She's having a wonderful time. Everyone's been so kind to her, and there's every chance she'll get a part in the production. Isn't that amazing?'

'Unbelievable, certainly,' said Rosa drily, wondering if her mother was pathologically foolish where Sophie was concerned. For heaven's sake, who was going to employ a starstruck teenager with a very minimal acting talent?

'I might have known you'd say something like that, Rosa.' Mrs Chantry sounded irritable now. 'Just because Sophie isn't on the island, as you expected, you're taking your frustration out on me. Well, Scotland's a big country. It's natural that a production like this would need a less confined location.'

'It wasn't *my* idea to come to the island,' Rosa pointed out, aware that she sounded peeved. 'It was your idea, not mine.' She paused. 'Did you tell her where I was?'

'Not exactly.'

'You mean you didn't.' Rosa gritted her teeth. 'So where is she?'

'I've just told you. She's in Scotland,' said her mother testily.

'Where in Scotland?'

'Ah…' There was a pregnant pause. 'Well, I'm not precisely sure.'

'But you said you'd heard from her.'

'I have. I did.' Mrs Chantry sighed. 'But you know what Sophie's like, Rosa. She was so busy telling me all the exciting things that have happened to her that she forgot about giving me her address.'

'I'll bet.'

'Oh, don't be like that, Rosa. Can't you find out where she is?'

Rosa sighed. 'How am I supposed to do that?'

'Well, you said Liam Jameson was there, didn't you? He'll know.'

'Mum…' It was growing increasingly hard to be patient. 'There *is* no film production. Or, if there is, Liam Jameson doesn't know about it.'

'Have you asked him?'

'I—er—'

Belatedly, Rosa acknowledged that that was something that they hadn't discussed. When she'd found out Sophie wasn't on the island, that there was no film crew working there, she hadn't thought to ask if he'd given permission for a film to be made elsewhere.

But wouldn't he have told her?

Yet he hadn't told her who he was until he'd had to.

She'd been silent for too long, and her mother said sharply, 'You *have* spoken to him, haven't you?'

Spoken?

Rosa stifled the hysterical sob that rose in her throat at her mother's words. Yes, she'd spoken to him all right, she thought. Though that was a poor description of what had happened between them.

'Yes,' she said, her voice a little hoarse. 'I've spoken to him, Mum. He was very—nice, actually.' And that had to be the understatement of the year!

'And he insisted he'd never seen Sophie?' Mrs Chantry sounded anxious now, and Ross wished she hadn't been so brutal. 'Oh, I wish she'd taken her phone with her to Glastonbury. But Mark was taking his, and I was so afraid she'd lose it.'

'I—I don't think Jameson's seen her,' Rosa murmured weakly, hating the thought that her mother was going to start worrying all over again. 'I—I'll ask him again.'

'Oh, you're a good girl, Rosa.' Now that she thought her daughter was softening, Mrs Chantry was prepared to be generous. 'I knew I could rely on you. And don't forget to find out where the film is being made.'

Rosa put the phone down with a feeling of utter bewilderment. Speaking to her mother was like butting her head against a brick wall. Mrs Chantry only heard what she wanted to hear, and now that Rosa had agreed to speak to Liam Jameson again she was prepared to wait for developments.

Rosa swore—something she rarely did, but right now she felt it was justified. Wait until she got her hands on her younger sister, she thought. Sophie would regret putting them through all this trauma.

Yet if Sophie hadn't disappeared Rosa wouldn't have come here, wouldn't have met Liam Jameson for herself. And, while that was something she might live to regret, right now the prospect of seeing him again was causing her heart to beat so madly it felt as if it was in danger of forcing its way right out of her chest.

But where had he gone?

She crossed to the door and pulled it open, only to fall back in surprise when she found Sam Devlin just outside. Had he been listening in to her conversation?

But, no. Something told her that the burly Scotsman wouldn't be interested in anything she had to say, and this was confirmed when he said brusquely, 'Yon McAllister's on his way from the village. He should be here in about half an hour. Would you like me to carry your bag down for you?'

'Oh—no.' Rosa was taken aback. But she should have known that Sam would waste no time in sending her on her way. 'That won't be necessary.' She paused. 'Actually, I wanted to have a word with Mr Jameson before I go.'

'I'm afraid that's impossible, Miss Chantry. Mr Jameson is working, and it's more than my job's worth to disturb him.'

Rosa doubted that very much. From what she'd seen, the two men had a good working relationship, and it was extremely unlikely that Liam Jameson would risk that by threatening to sack Devlin if he was disturbed.

'It would only take a minute,' she said persuasively. 'I want to ask him something.'

'I'm sorry.'

Sam wasn't budging, and Rosa stared at him in frustration. If only she knew where Liam's office—*den*?—was. Evidently he didn't work in the library, as she'd thought at first. But in a place of this size he could be anywhere.

'Tell me what you want to ask him and I'll deliver your

message when he's free,' Sam suggested, but Rosa had no intention of trusting him.

'It's personal,' she said, but although she held the man's gaze for a long while, hoping to shame him into helping her, ultimately it was she who looked away.

Then another thought occurred to her. 'You could give me his phone number,' she said with inspiration. 'I'll ring him later.'

'I couldn't do that, Miss Chantry.'

'Why not?'

'Mr Jameson doesn't give his private number to anyone.'

'Then give me yours,' mumbled Rosa ungraciously. 'I'll let you know where I'm staying, and Mr Jameson can ring me.'

Sam looked as if he wanted to refuse, but perhaps he realised that that would seem unnecessarily anal. Besides, he couldn't really know that Liam wouldn't speak to her if he went and asked him.

However, when he spoke it wasn't what Rosa had expected. 'Mr Jameson knows where you're staying, Miss Chantry,' he said, and now Rosa noticed the scrap of paper in his hand. 'He asked me to give you this address.'

'Oh!' That stumped her. 'Thanks.' She took the paper from his outstretched hand and looked at it almost resentfully. 'Does Mr McAllister know where this is?'

'Everyone knows where Katie Ferguson's guesthouse is,' declared Sam scornfully. 'This isn't London, Miss Chantry.'

'I don't live in London,' retorted Rosa hotly. 'I come from a small town in North Yorkshire, Mr Devlin. Not some teeming metropolis, as you seem to think.'

'I'm sorry.' Rosa was sure he didn't mean it. 'I naturally assumed—'

'You shouldn't assume anything,' said Rosa, enjoying having him on the defensive for a change. She glanced down at the paper again. 'Thanks for this.'

Sam gave her a polite nod of acknowledgement. 'I'll let you know when the car arrives.'

'Thanks,' said Rosa again, and without another word Sam closed the door on her.

CHAPTER SEVEN

'HAS SHE GONE?'

It was later that morning, and Liam had just emerged from his study having spent a rather fruitless couple of hours trying to concentrate on characters who suddenly seemed as unconvincing as cardboard cut-outs.

He'd found Sam and Mrs Wilson in the kitchen on the ground floor of the castle, enjoying a coffee break, and he'd accepted a cup from the housekeeper with some gratitude.

He wasn't in the best of moods, however, and his temper wasn't improved when Sam said cheerfully, 'Aye, she's gone, Liam. Not but what she didn't ask to speak to you again before she left.' He gave his employer a knowing look. 'I told her you were working and couldn't be disturbed, but I don't think she was suited.'

Liam scowled. He'd just burned his mouth on the hot coffee, and Sam's announcement was the last straw. 'You did what?' he demanded harshly. 'Why did you tell her that?'

'Well, because you never like to be disturbed when you're working,' said Sam defensively. 'Don't tell me you expected me to come along to your office and break your concentration just because some lassie with more bluff than sense asked to see you?'

'I beg your pardon?'

Liam's scowl deepened, and Mrs Wilson made a hasty exit through the back door, murmuring something about needing some greens from the garden. Meanwhile, Sam stared at the younger man belligerently, although his face reddened with colour. 'I think you heard what I said,' he muttered defiantly.

'And who appointed you my guardian?' exclaimed Liam, equally unprepared to back down. 'I know you didn't like me bringing her here. You made that plain enough. But this is my house, Devlin, not yours.'

Sam straightened. He had been lounging against the drainer as he chatted with the housekeeper, but now he stiffened his back. 'I thought I was doing you a favour, man,' he protested. He lifted an apologetic hand. 'Obviously I was wrong. I'm sorry. Rest assured, it won't happen again.'

He turned and thrust his cup into the sink, but when he started across the room, evidently intending to leave Liam to it, Liam stepped into his path.

'No, *I'm* sorry,' he said roughly, ashamed at taking his frustration out on the older man. 'Forget what I said, Sam. It's not your fault I'm in a bloody mood.'

Sam hesitated, still looking upset, and Liam cursed himself anew for distressing him. Dammit, Sam was right. He probably *would* have complained if Sam had interrupted him. He was letting a woman he might never see again ruin the long-established relationship he had with his steward, and that was stupid.

'I mean it,' he grunted, holding out his hand. 'Take no notice of me. I've had a pretty useless morning, and I'm ready to blame anyone but myself.'

Sam's jaw clenched, but he took Liam's hand and shook

it warmly. 'Yon lassie's to blame,' he said staunchly, but Liam wasn't prepared to go that far.

'Well, she's gone now,' he said neutrally, taking another mouthful of his coffee and finding it more to his taste. 'McAllister turned up, I gather?'

'Aye. In that old rattletrap he calls an estate car,' agreed Sam, relaxing now. 'How it passes its MOT test, God knows!'

'I don't suppose it does,' said Liam, hoping it hadn't broken down between Kilfoil and the village. He was re-membering what Rosa had said about the dangers of the moor, and to imagine her walking into one of its treacher-ous bogs was enough to bring another scowl to his lips.

But he wasn't about to bring that up with Sam, and, fin-ishing his coffee, he said, 'I'll see you later. I'm going to take the dogs out.'

Sam arched his grey brows. 'Shall I come with you?' He eyed his employer's injured thigh with concerned eyes. 'You don't want to have another of those spasms when you're out on the cliffs.'

Liam hid his impatience at the other man's fussing, and said evenly, 'The physio says I should get plenty of exercise. He says that spending too long at my desk is probably the reason why I'm still having problems.'

'Even so—'

'I'll be fine,' Liam assured him tersely. 'But thanks for the offer.'

After collecting a coat, and the dogs, Liam emerged into the open air with a feeling of relief. The animals were just as glad to escape the confines of the castle, and they ran about excitedly, chasing every cat and bird in sight.

Liam didn't intend to go far. There were clouds massing on the horizon, and unless he missed his guess they'd have rain before nightfall. Knowing how quickly the weather could change in these parts, he had no desire to risk getting caught in a storm. He could be soaked to the skin in minutes. It wasn't as if he could run for cover, either. Thanks to his attacker, his running days were over.

Even so, he went out onto the cliffs, trudging through knee-high grasses that were an ideal hiding place for small rodents and birds of all kinds. The wind, blowing off the ocean, lifted the thick dark hair from his forehead and made him wish he'd worn something warmer than the ankle-length waterproof coat that flapped around his legs.

His thigh did move more freely as he exercised it, but he didn't think he was up to negotiating the cliff steps down to the cove this morning. Climbing down necessitated climbing up again, and that was probably a step too far.

He was considering turning back when Harley, the younger of the two retrievers, scared up a rabbit. The terrified creature must have been hiding in the gorse bushes that grew near the edge of the cliff, and when Harley started barking it shot away across the headland, making unmistakably for the gully that ran down to the beach.

Naturally, Harley gave chase, pursued by the other dogs, and although Liam shouted himself hoarse he soon realised he was wasting his time. The dogs weren't going to come back until the rabbit had been rousted, and it was at that moment that he felt the first heavy drops of rain.

He swore loudly, limping across to the edge of the cliffs. He could see all three dogs from this vantage point. The gully was a lot easier for a dog to negotiate than the steps, and, although there was no sign of the rabbit, the dogs were having a whale of a time racing along the sand, splashing in and out of the waves breaking on the shore.

'Dammit!' He swore again, but although he tried every way he could to get them to come back they weren't listening to him.

What price now his arrogant assertion that he didn't need Sam's help? he thought grimly. The man might be fifteen years older than Liam, but he wouldn't have thought twice about going after the dogs. And, unless he wanted to return home with his own metaphoric tail between his legs, Liam knew he'd have to do the same.

It wasn't too bad going down. Although the rain was getting heavier, his determination kept him going—until his boots sank into the damp sand. The dogs came to him eagerly now, barking and leaping around him, as if their aim had been to get him down there all along.

'Home,' ordered Liam grimly, ignoring their welcome, and at last his tone had some success. Or maybe it was the rain, he reflected wryly. It was certainly quite a downpour, and even the dogs preferred a dry coat to a wet one. Whatever the reason, all three of them obeyed his command, charging up the steps ahead of him, standing at the top, panting and wagging their tails with apparent pride at their achievement.

However, Liam found it much harder to follow them. The steps were slippery now, and every now and then, he was forced to clutch at handfuls of turf to prevent himself from sliding backwards.

His thigh ached, and halfway up he had to stop and allow the spasms in his leg to subside. God, he should have swallowed his pride and gone back to the castle for help, he thought bitterly. The way his muscles were feeling now, he'd probably undone all the good that treatment he'd had in London had achieved.

The dogs had disappeared by the time he finally reached the clifftop. Which was par for the course, he thought, panting heavily. He just hoped they'd gone back to the castle. If they hadn't, hard luck. He wasn't going looking for them. He was just relieved that Rosa Chantry wasn't still there. He'd have hated for her to see him like this. Dammit, he still had some pride.

It rained all day Wednesday.

Rosa, who was confined to Katie Ferguson's guest-house, stared out at the weather with a feeling of desperation. She felt so helpless. Where was Sophie? she fretted, the inactivity putting her at the mercy of her fears. All right, she'd said she was okay, and Rosa had to accept that. But something about this whole situation didn't add up.

Still, she could do nothing until the ferry arrived the following morning, she consoled herself, rubbing a circle in the condensation her breath had made on the glass. The guesthouse was cosy, her room small, but comfortable. But there were no other guests with whom she could have passed the time.

She glanced across the room at the table beside the bed. Two paperbacks that she'd bought at the post office-cum-general store resided there. One was a historical romance with a Scottish setting that she'd hoped might distract her from her troubles, but it hadn't. The other was a Liam Jameson.

The postmistress, a rather garrulous Scotswoman, had gone on at some length about the quality of Liam's writing. She'd read everything he'd ever written, she'd said, even though she didn't usually enjoy that sort of thing.

'But his characters are so good, aren't they?' she'd

enthused. 'That Luther Killian! My goodness, I'd never realised that vampires could be so fascinating.'

Of course Rosa had had to admit that she hadn't read any of Liam's books, and that was when she'd discovered how Sam had explained her presence on the island.

'Why, I was sure you'd have read all of them, seeing as you work for his publisher and all,' the postmistress had exclaimed in surprise. And when Rosa had looked confused she'd added ruefully, 'Och, old McAllister told us who you were. When Sam Devlin called him out to Kilfoil, he said a young lady from Pargeters had been visiting Mr Jameson.' She'd nodded at the rain. 'It's only a pity you're seeing the island in its worst light. It's really quite beautiful.'

Rosa had admitted then that it hadn't been raining when she'd first arrived. But, not wanting to contribute to any more gossip, she'd paid for the books and made good her escape.

However, she wondered now if Sam had told Mrs Ferguson the same story. It seemed possible, although her landlady was much more reserved, and she hadn't questioned why Rosa should have been visiting the castle.

Rosa sighed. Nevertheless, it was because of Liam that she'd found it impossible to read his book. She couldn't help associating Luther Killian with the man who'd created him, and the fact that Liam hadn't bothered getting back to her was a constant thorn in her side.

Not that she'd told her mother that. She'd rung Mrs Chantry on Tuesday evening to let her know where she was staying, giving her the phone number of the guesthouse as if she'd never stayed anywhere else. She'd promised she'd be speaking to Jameson again the following day, leaving her mother with the impression that another interview had been arranged.

Fortunately Mrs Chantry hadn't questioned that, and Rosa hadn't talked for long. Apart from anything else, she'd been conscious that Mrs Ferguson could come into the small hallway where the phone was situated at any time, and the last thing Rosa wanted was for her to suspect that her reasons for being here weren't what she'd heard.

All in all, it had been a miserable couple of days. The rain had started soon after she and Mr McAllister had left the castle the previous morning, and his old estate car had taken for ever to cross the moor. Then, coming down into the village, they'd skidded onto the grass verge, so that Rosa had been relieved when she'd arrived safely at her destination.

Leaving her seat by the window, Rosa crossed the room and picked up Liam's book. There was still an hour to fill before supper, which appeared to be served early in the Highlands. And another couple of hours after that before she could reasonably retire to bed. She had to do something.

Of course what she ought to do was hire old McAllister's cab again and drive back to the castle, if only to keep the promise she'd made to her mother. Liam wasn't going to ring her, either because Sam hadn't given him her message or because he chose not to, and this might be her last chance.

But the idea of chancing another ride in the elderly estate car filled her with unease. And, apart from that, she didn't really have a reason for seeing Liam again. Not a genuine one, at any rate. Wanting to spend a little more time with him just didn't cut it, particularly after he'd admitted that he'd be glad to see her go. So she might as well resign herself to another night at the guesthouse and a trip back to the mainland tomorrow afternoon.

But the following morning Rosa awakened to the sound of the wind howling round the walls of the old building. Snuggling under the covers, she wished she didn't have to get out of bed. It sounded more like a gale than anything, and she could just imagine being on the ferry in such a wind. Goodness, she'd felt sick coming here, and the water had been reasonably calm then. Now it was going to be as choppy as a bathtub. Or rather the ferry would be as helpless as a bathtub in a turbulent sea.

Rosa sighed, but there was no help for it. She had to get up. Mrs Ferguson had told her that the ferry usually arrived at about half-past-eleven and then left again at half-past-twelve, calling at the nearby island of Ardnarossa before returning to Mallaig.

Which meant at least another hour on her journey, thought Rosa dismally. Another hour in weather like this! She was going to be so seasick. She wished she dared feign illness and stay until the following Monday, when the ferry came again.

But it wasn't in her nature to lie, and she owed it to her mother to get back to the mainland and try and find out from the Scottish Tourist Office if they knew anything about the company Sophie professed to have joined. It was a doubtful proposition, but it was the only one she had at the moment. And right now the idea of being back on the mainland again sounded pretty good to her.

However, after washing and dressing and packing her bag, she went downstairs for breakfast to find Mrs Ferguson waiting for her.

'I'm afraid you won't be leaving today, Miss Chantry,'

she said apologetically. 'This storm has suspended all sailings, and the ferry won't be leaving Mallaig until it's blown itself out.'

The relief Rosa felt was paralysing. 'You mean, I'll have to stay here until the wind's dropped?'

'Well, until it moderates, at least,' Mrs Ferguson agreed with a regretful smile. 'I'm sorry.'

'It's not your fault.' Rosa was ashamed to realise she could hardly contain her relief. 'So—um, when do you think the storm will blow itself out?'

'Not before Saturday, at the earliest,' said the landlady sagely. 'And even then there's no guarantee that the ferry will come. We're just a small island, Miss Chantry. They may decide to wait until the regular sailing on Monday.'

'Monday!' Rosa thought ruefully that you really should be careful what you wish for. 'I see.'

'Of course, if there's an urgent reason why you need to get back to the mainland, you could always ask Mr Jameson. He might be willing to have his pilot take you in his helicopter. I mean…' Mrs Ferguson seemed to be considering the situation '…he *is* the reason why you're stuck here, isn't he?'

'Y-e-s.' Rosa drew the word out, knowing that her reasons for being here and the reasons Mrs Ferguson had probably been given for her being here were mutually exclusive. 'But I don't think that's a good idea.' As the landlady looked as if she was about to protest, she added swiftly, 'Don't helicopters have problems in bad weather, too?'

'Not like ferries,' Mrs Ferguson assured her. 'I'm sure that by tomorrow you'd have no trouble at all.'

Wouldn't she? Rosa doubted that. There was no way Liam would lend his helicopter—a helicopter, for heaven's sake!—to her. It was just another indication of how stupid she was being in wanting to see him again. His way of life was so incredibly different from hers.

However, she refrained from making any comment, and the landlady bustled away to get her guest's breakfast. Mrs Ferguson was probably thinking she was considering it, thought Rosa, with a grimace. When in fact what she was really thinking was that this might give her another opportunity to speak to Liam again.

CHAPTER EIGHT

FAT CHANCE, thought Rosa on Friday morning, having spent yet another day watching the rain. She had borrowed a coat from Mrs Ferguson and gone out for a while on Thursday afternoon, but it hadn't been much fun. The rain had been bad enough, but the wind had been unforgiving. It had torn back the hood of her coat and had left her hair at the mercy of the weather.

She'd even made another attempt to read Liam's book, and had been enjoying it until Luther Killian said something that Liam himself might say. It had brought back the memory of their encounter in all its disturbing detail, and she'd had to put the book aside and do something else.

Looking out of her window now, Rosa saw that it was going to be another wasted day. The wind hardly seemed to have eased at all, and although the rain seemed lighter, it was still coming down.

She could see the harbour from her window, the small boats that were moored there straining on their lines. No doubt the fishermen whose boats they were, were cursing, too. At least her incarceration didn't affect her livelihood.

Or Sophie's, she thought uneasily. But her sister would be all right, she assured herself. She was probably sitting in some luxury hotel at this moment, having a late break-fast with this man she'd taken off with. Okay, he wasn't Liam Jameson. But perhaps he'd told her that he was. Yet somehow she knew Sophie was too savvy to be taken in like that.

So where was she? Although Rosa was fairly sure Liam didn't know, perhaps he might have an idea. Anything was better than sitting here, twiddling her thumbs.

She shook her head impatiently, aware that she was only looking for excuses to go and see him again. After all, whatever happened, her mother expected her to do it. Pre-dictably, it was the first thing she'd asked Rosa when she'd phoned home the previous evening.

'But why haven't you seen him?' she'd demanded, and Rosa had explained about the storm. Then she'd hurried on and asked if Mrs Chantry had heard from Sophie—which she hadn't—to avoid the comeback. After all, it was her sister who was supposed to be in trouble here, not her.

Personally, Rosa thought her sister was keeping quiet deliberately. Now that she'd alerted them to the fact that she could phone, she was probably afraid they'd trace her call. Which left Rosa with the unenviable task of finding another way to locate her.

Her mother was woefully ignorant of her elder daugh-ter's circumstances, however. 'Surely there must be some other way to get back to the mainland?' she'd protested, when Rosa had told her that the ferries were suspended until further notice. 'What about aeroplanes? They're not grounded, are they? Or you could find another boat.'

Rosa had been stunned at her foolishness. 'There's no airport on Kilfoil, Mum,' she'd told her frustratedly.

'And what other boat would you suggest? A fishing trawler, perhaps?'

Mrs Chantry had tutted impatiently. 'So you're telling me there's nothing you can do until the ferries start running again?'

'As far as getting off the island is concerned, yes,' said Rosa shortly. 'Believe me, I don't like it any more than you do.'

But was that strictly true? Rosa asked herself now, aware that the knowledge that Liam was just a dozen miles away was some compensation. If the ferries had been running she'd have been several hundred miles away by now, and any chance of seeing him again would have been denied her.

She frowned. Well, she couldn't stay in her room all day. She'd had her breakfast, and once again the books she'd bought held no appeal. There must be some other way she could get out to the castle, she thought, her pulse quickening at the thought. At least it would give her something to do. Even if that old grouse Sam Devlin refused to let her in.

Mrs Ferguson was dusting the sitting room when she went downstairs and, feeling a little awkward, Rosa stopped in the doorway. 'Um—I was wondering,' she said, and the landlady looked up expectantly. 'I was wondering if there was a car I could hire for the day.'

'Do you not know McAllister's number?' The woman frowned and put her duster aside. 'I think I've got it here somewhere—'

'No.' Rosa interrupted her, and when the landlady halted uncertainly, she added, 'I didn't mean a taxi, Mrs Ferguson. I wondered if there was a car I could hire to drive myself.'

The woman frowned. 'Well, it's not much of a day for sightseeing.'

'I know that.' Rosa sighed. 'As a matter of fact, I'd like to drive over to see Mr Jameson again. There—er—there's something I forgot to ask him.'

'Ah.' Mrs Ferguson nodded. 'And you're not keen to have old McAllister drive you, is that it?'

'Well…'

Rosa felt her face turn red, but the landlady was smiling. 'Yes, I can see you're not impressed with his driving, lassie.' She laughed. 'I have to admit, I'd think twice about getting in his vehicle myself.'

Rosa relaxed. 'So—er—*is* there a car I could hire?' she asked hopefully. 'I'm willing to pay.'

'Och, you can take my car, Miss Chantry. It hardly gets used, anyway. It's not very grand, mind you, but it's roadworthy.'

Rosa gasped. 'Oh, that would be wonderful!'

Mrs Ferguson laughed again. 'Don't say that until you've seen it, lassie,' she advised. 'Come along. I'll show you where I keep it.'

The car, an ancient Ford, was kept in a shed at the back of the guesthouse, and Rosa saw at once that the landlady hadn't been exaggerating when she'd said it wasn't very grand. It had to be at least twenty years old, and was covered in dust into the bargain. Mrs Ferguson had to wipe away a handful of spiders' webs before she could open the door.

But the engine started after only a couple of hiccoughs, and Rosa stepped aside as the woman reversed it out onto the street. One good thing—the rain quickly cleared the dust from the chassis, and Rosa saw that the wipers worked. All in all, it was exactly what she needed, and she couldn't thank the landlady enough.

'Och, it's nothing,' said Mrs Ferguson, surrendering the

driving seat to her guest and stepping back into the shelter
of the shed, out of the rain. 'You drive carefully, now. The
roads can be treacherous in the wet. I wouldn't like you to
go skidding into a bog.'

Rosa thought she wouldn't like that, either, but she
refused to be daunted. She couldn't be a worse driver than
old McAllister if she tried. And there was no hurry. If she
took all morning to get there, it wouldn't matter.

The first indication that driving Mrs Ferguson's car
wasn't going to be a sinecure came when Rosa reached the
first corner and tried to turn. The wheel was like a dead
weight in her hands, and she realised that it had no power
steering. Of course, she thought impatiently, wrenching the
car round manually. The installation of power steering in
small cars like this was a comparatively recent innovation.

It made driving much harder, and her arms were aching
by the time she'd negotiated the twists and turns down to
the harbour. It was easier once she was driving up the road
out of the village, but she wasn't looking forward to the
journey across that lonely stretch of moor.

The rain hindered visibility, too, and once or twice she
was sure she saw ghostly figures rising out of the mist. But
it was only the skeletal trunks of trees worn bare by the
winds that raked the boggy scrubland. Nevertheless, she
was glad she didn't have to drive across here in the dark.

At last she reached the road that wound down into the
glen where Kilfoil Castle was situated. She couldn't see the
castle, of course. The driving rain made that impossible.
But now and then she glimpsed a farmhouse, and the unmistakable presence of livestock. She even saw a farmer
herding some cows into a barn.

She relaxed. She'd made it. The only problem now was

getting in to see Liam himself. She had the feeling Sam wouldn't be too pleased when she presented herself at the door. But he must know she hadn't left the island. Surely he might expect that she'd try to see his employer again?

She drove over the small bridge and parked in the same place Liam had used four days ago. Four days! She was amazed. Was that really all it was? She grimaced. Sometimes it felt as if she'd been here half her life.

She got out of the car, closing the door with care. No one had come to meet her, and she was curiously loath to announce her arrival in advance. Squaring her shoulders against the squally wind that blew in off the ocean, she crossed the forecourt to the double doors.

There was no bell, but she'd hardly expected one. Knights of old hadn't needed such things. In the books she'd read, the knight's lady would be watching for her spouse from one of the narrow windows in the solar, or perhaps a vigilant guard would warn of a stranger's arrival. The portcullis would be lowered to protect those within the castle—

'Miss Chantry!'

Rosa had been so absorbed with her thoughts that she hadn't heard the door being opened. But now the housekeeper stood there, regarding her with obvious surprise.

'Oh, Mrs Wilson.' Rosa knew she should have been better prepared for this encounter. 'Um—how are you?'

'I'm very well, thank you.' The woman cast a nervous glance over her shoulder. 'Is there something I can help you with, Miss Chantry?'

'I hope so, yes.' Rosa smiled. 'Is—er—is Mr Jameson about?'

It was a stupid question. Rosa knew that as soon as the words left her lips. Where else would he be?

'Mr Jameson?'

The housekeeper sounded doubtful, and she hurried on, 'Yes. I mean, is he working this morning? Or could I have a quick word with him?'

'Oh, I—' Once again Mrs Wilson looked back over her shoulder. 'I'm afraid that's not a question I can answer, Miss Chantry.' She hesitated, and then went on, 'You'd have to ask Mr Devlin.' She nodded. 'I'll get him for you.'

'No, I—'

Rosa started to say Sam Devlin was the last person she wanted to see, but it was too late. The woman had already turned and hurried away, leaving Rosa to cool her heels on the doorstep like some pushy double-glazing saleswoman.

She could have invited her inside, Rosa thought, disheartened. It wasn't as if she hadn't been inside the castle before. For heaven's sake, she'd spent a night here. Why was she being treated like an intruder?

Because that was what she was, she'd decided, when she heard Sam Devlin's footsteps crossing the hall. She'd just nudged under the overhang, in a rather fruitless attempt to keep dry, but she stepped aback almost instinctively when the man appeared.

However, Sam was surprisingly more charitable than the housekeeper. 'Och, come away inside, Miss Chantry,' he exclaimed, stepping back to allow her to enter the huge hall. 'It's a wretched morning, to be sure. You'll be wishing this storm would ease, no doubt. I dare say you're eager to get back to the mainland?'

'Yes.' Rosa had little option other than to agree. 'Um, I'm sorry to trouble you again, but I still haven't spoken to Mr Jameson.' She paused, and then went on rather recklessly, 'You did give him my message, didn't you?'

'What message would that be, Miss Chantry?'

Rosa sighed. She should have known his charity wouldn't stretch that far. 'Well, that I wanted to speak to him again,' she said stiffly. 'If the ferry hadn't been delayed, I'd be gone by now.'

'So you would.' Sam regarded her consideringly as he closed the heavy door. 'But, contrary to what you believe, Miss Chantry, I *did* tell Mr Jameson what you'd said.'

'Oh. Oh, I see.' Rosa felt foolish now, and her face burned with sudden colour. 'What you mean is, Mr Jameson didn't want to speak to me, is that right?' She swallowed her humiliation. 'Well, that's all right. I realise now I shouldn't have bothered him.' She turned back to the door. 'Thank you for telling me.'

'Wait!' As she fumbled with the latch, Sam spoke again. 'Look, Miss Chantry,' he said, and now he sounded a little embarrassed, 'I didn't mean to imply that Liam had refused to speak to you. As a matter of fact I don't know what he might have done if—if…' He hesitated, as if he didn't want to go on, but courtesy demanded it. 'If he'd been able,' he finished at last. Then, after another pause, 'He—er—he hasn't been too well since you left on Tuesday. And that's the truth.'

Rosa was dismayed at the effect his words had on her. 'Is it his leg?' she asked, realising she was stepping onto unknown ground, but anxious enough to take the risk. She linked her cold fingers, pressing them at right angles to her chest. 'Please—tell me.'

Sam frowned. 'You know about his injuries?' he asked warily, but Rosa wasn't brave enough to claim that.

'Just—just that he seems to be troubled at times,' she admitted, shifting from one foot to the other. She stared at him. 'Doesn't he?'

'Perhaps.' Sam was noncommittal. 'But as it happens he got soaked when he was out with the dogs on Tuesday afternoon, and since then he hasn't felt very sociable.'

'You mean he got a chill?'

Sam was evidently unhappy talking about his employer behind his back. 'Something like that,' he admitted at last. 'As you've learned to your cost, the weather here can be unpredictable.'

'You don't mean it developed into pneumonia?' exclaimed Rosa, aghast, and Sam gave a helpless shake of his head.

'Och, no,' he said half impatiently. 'Nothing so dramatic. Just a—nasty cold, is all.' He paused, and then added ruefully, 'Liam's no' a good patient, Miss Chantry.'

'Do you want to tell me what the hell's going on?'

The unexpected sound of Liam's voice caused them both to start in alarm, and Sam instantly looked as guilty as hell. 'God, man,' he protested in a shaken voice. 'Do you have to scare us half to death? I didn't hear you.'

'Obviously not.' Liam left his position at the foot of the tower stairs and walked heavily towards them. He noticed that Rosa was looking as if he was the last person she'd expected to see, and that annoyed the hell out of him. This was his house, dammit. Who had she expected to see? 'What's happening?'

Rosa gazed at him in total confusion. After what Sam had been saying, she'd imagined Liam weak and vulnerable, worn out by coughing and sneezing and blowing his nose.

But the reality was much different. In his usual tight jeans, the fabric worn almost white in places she wasn't supposed to look, and a long-sleeved silk shirt, the colour of which exactly matched his eyes, he looked darkly disturbing—and just as dangerous as Luther Killian, she was sure.

'Miss Chantry—' began Sam, but Rosa knew she couldn't allow the older man to take the blame for her intrusion.

'I came to see you,' she broke in quickly, allowing her arms to fall to her sides. 'Mr Devlin was just telling me that—that you hadn't been well.'

'I just told her you had a cold,' exclaimed Sam swiftly, and Rosa wondered at the look that passed between the two men at that moment. 'That's all.'

'Yeah.' Liam accepted his explanation. Whatever faults he might have, Sam was excessively loyal. He wouldn't talk about Liam's private affairs with anyone.

He returned his gaze to Rosa, noticing that she was shivering now. But whether that was because she was only wearing a light jacket or because he'd frightened her, he couldn't be sure. 'Well, Miss Chantry,' he said pleasantly. 'You'd better come with me.'

Rosa's eyes were wide and anxious. 'All right,' she said, giving Sam a grateful look. 'Thanks for your help, Mr Devlin.'

Sam stiffened. 'It was my pleasure, Miss Chantry,' he insisted. Then, as she started after Liam, 'Will you be wanting a lift later?'

'Oh, no.' Rosa gave him a tight smile. 'I borrowed Mrs Ferguson's car. But thanks, anyway.'

Sam nodded, then, addressing himself to his employer, he added, 'Will I ask Mrs Wilson to bring coffee?'

'Sounds like a plan,' agreed Liam, and Sam gave her another searching look before disappearing through a door below the tapestries at the side of the hall.

'You've made a conquest,' remarked Liam drily, gesturing for her to precede him up the stairs, and she frowned.

'I don't think so.'

'I do. Sam's not usually so talkative, believe me. Not with women, anyway.'

Rosa shook her head, starting up the stairs. Following her, Liam was intensely aware of the rounded curve of her bottom swaying with every step she climbed. She might be slim, but she was shapely, her legs long and graceful beneath the close-fitting woollen pants she was wearing.

He also noticed that she'd attempted to pile her glorious hair into a knot on top of her head this morning. But, as usual, the wind and rain had hampered her efforts. Already strands of dark red silk coiled seductively on the shoulders of her jacket, and he was tempted to pick one up and allow it to curl about his fingers.

But he refused to go there. The end result of such an action was not one he wanted to explore, however appealing his own satisfaction might be. Besides, although he was fairly sure she'd been a willing recipient of his attentions earlier in the week, once she'd seen the ugly scars that marred his body she'd probably run as fast as Kayla had done.

Rosa, meanwhile, hearing the sudden hoarseness of his breathing, decided that Sam hadn't been exaggerating when he'd told her Liam had had a cold. He sounded as if he was struggling for breath, and she felt ashamed for doubting him.

They reached the top of the stairs at last, and Liam went ahead along the narrow landing. They passed several doors, including the library and the dining hall that Rosa remembered from her previous visit, and stopped before a door at the end of the hall.

It opened into a large living room. Because of the lowering skies, lamps had been lit on tables and cabinets, several tall uplighters adding illumination to a room that was both beautiful and homely.

A pair of plush suede sofas flanked the carved façade of the fireplace, and bookshelves filled with novels and magazines filled the space beneath the long windows. Raw silk curtains, in the same warm caramel colour as the sofas, were drawn back to display the fury of the storm outside, but Rosa guessed that in fine weather the view would be breathtaking.

Underfoot, a huge Turkish rug in shades of blue and green complemented the heavy-textured wall coverings, which reminded her they were in a castle, not a millionaire's mansion. Though the distinction escaped her.

'Go ahead,' said Liam, stepping back to allow her to enter, and Rosa hesitated.

'My shoes are damp,' she murmured, glancing down, and Liam arched sardonic brows.

'I can see that,' he said with a shrug. 'So take them off.'

'You don't mind?'

'Why would I mind?' Liam queried mockingly. 'Take off anything you like.' He paused, aware that she was looking at him warily now, before adding smoothly, 'Your jacket? It's wet, too.'

CHAPTER NINE

ROSA didn't quite know how to take his flippancy, but she bent and removed her low-heeled shoes, placing them just outside the door. Her jacket she took off, but folded it over her arm. Then, with a strangely fatalistic feeling, she stepped into the room.

The carpet was soft and warm after her damp shoes. She hadn't realised how cold her feet were until she felt the warmth of the room enveloping her from head to toe. She was aware of Liam following her, and when the door closed behind him she swung round with an almost guilty feeling of relief.

'This is a beautiful room,' she said, needing to say something, if only to show he didn't intimidate her. 'The whole castle is beautiful. You're very lucky to live here.'

'Am I?' Liam lifted her coat from her arm and gestured towards the sofas. 'Well, why don't we sit down and talk about it?'

Rosa didn't have an answer for that, but, after watching him drop her jacket onto a chair by the door, she decided she had nothing to lose. Moving round the end of one of the creamy sofas, she perched rather nervously on the edge of the seat.

Liam came to join her, and once again she couldn't help noticing how he dragged his left leg. But she wasn't here to ask personal questions, she reminded herself, though her desire to keep her cool took a bit of a tumble when he chose to sit beside her.

'Okay,' he said, and she was forced to turn in her seat to face him, which caused her to slip a little further back on the cushions. 'So,' he said, 'you've changed your mind?'

'Changed my mind?' Rosa was nonplussed.

'About this place only being good enough for sheep and cattle,' remarked Liam mildly, his green eyes intent on her confused face.

'I didn't say that.' Rosa's cheeks turned pink.

'As good as. I seem to remember you asking me if it was even civilised.'

'That was before I'd seen it,' Rosa protested defensively. 'Anyway, that's not why I'm here.'

'I didn't think so.' Liam leaned back, resting his right ankle across his left knee. 'Sam told me you'd wanted to speak to me before you left on Tuesday morning.'

Rosa stiffened. 'But you didn't consider it important enough to get in touch with me?' she exclaimed impulsively. 'Even though you're evidently much better now.'

'Oh, I am. Much better,' agreed Liam drily.

Rosa regarded him warily. 'So—were you going to get in touch with me or not?'

'Not,' he declared softly. 'I thought it was for the best.'

Rosa swallowed. 'Whose best? Yours, I suppose?'

'Mine, yes. And yours.' Liam watched her with unwilling interest. He didn't need this, he told himself, even as he added, 'I don't think we have anything more to say to one another, do you?'

'Well, obviously I do.' Rosa knew it would probably be wiser if she got to her feet and got out of here before she said or did something unforgivable. 'There's something else I want to ask you about Sophie.'

Her sister!

Liam only just prevented himself from using a word that wasn't acceptable in mixed company. But hadn't they dealt with her sister's disappearance to distraction already? He didn't even know the girl, but he disliked her intensely.

Dropping his foot to the floor, he leant forward, allowing his hands to hang free between his spread thighs. Then, in a controlled voice, he said, 'What about her?'

Rosa moistened dry lips. 'I—forgot to ask you if it was possible that a film was being made in another part of the Highlands.'

Liam turned his head to give her an incredulous look. 'Well, sure,' he said. 'People are always making films in this part of the world. So what? You think now that your sister might really have hooked up with a guy from a film production?'

'It's possible.' Despite the disbelieving look in Liam's eyes, Rosa knew a twinge of optimism. 'And I think you might have told me about the probabilities of these other productions.'

'Say what?' Liam was indignant. 'What the hell do they have to do with me?'

'Well, they're your books, aren't—?'

'Whoa!' Liam halted her there. 'You think I'm talking about an alternative production of one of *my* books?'

'Well, aren't you?'

'Hell, no.' Liam gave an exasperated snort. 'I was talking about films generally. For God's sake, if I'd thought they were making a film of one of mine elsewhere in the Highlands, don't you think I'd have told you?'

Rosa's shoulders sagged. 'So they're not?'

'No.'

'You're sure?'

Liam gave a half-laugh. 'Well, let's put it this way, I've signed no contracts.'

'You mean they haven't paid you?'

'If you want to put it like that.'

Rosa gave a heavy sigh. 'What other way is there? I'm sorry I've wasted your time.'

'Hey, don't say that.' As suddenly as before, Liam changed his mind about her. 'You've certainly provided a pleasant distraction on a particularly dull day.'

'I'm glad I've amused you.'

Rosa's voice was thick, but when she would have pushed to her feet Liam's hand on her thigh prevented her from rising. 'Don't go,' he said, his fingers registering the warmth of her flesh beneath the fine wool trousers. She was quivering, and when her eyes widened uncertainly, he added swiftly, 'Mrs Wilson is bringing us some coffee.'

Rosa's mouth was dry. But, in spite of everything, she knew that this was really why she'd come here. Oh, she'd wanted to ask him about Sophie, too. But she hadn't held out much hope in that regard. What she'd needed to know was if the instant attraction she'd felt between them was just a figment of her imagination.

It didn't feel like it at this moment. The fingers gripping her leg were both strong and oddly possessive. And when she lifted her head and looked into his eyes she saw a reflection of her own thwarted desires.

Dear heaven, she thought incredulously, he *did* want her.

She just wished she had the first idea of what she was going to do about it.

The knock at the door was timely. Liam released Rosa at once, rising to his feet as the housekeeper obeyed his summons and came into the room carrying a tray.

'Sam said you wanted coffee, Mr Jameson,' Mrs Wilson murmured, her gaze flickering quickly over his guest's bent head. 'Where would you like it?'

Liam's lips twitched a little at the woman's unknowing innuendo, but he gestured towards the low table that was set between the two sofas. 'Just here's fine,' he said, wondering if her interruption was fate, trying to bring him to his senses. Mrs Wilson set down the tray and straightened. 'Thanks.'

The door closed behind the housekeeper with a definite click, and, because anything else would have looked strange, Liam subsided again onto the sofa beside Rosa. But he avoided looking at her, saying instead, 'Help yourself.'

Rosa made no move to do so. She merely stared at the tray as if it might provide the answers she sought. A steaming jug of coffee, two porcelain cups, a cream jug and a sugar basin. Such ordinary items, yet they represented the difference between an increasing awareness and the coolness she now felt from Liam.

'I'm not thirsty,' she said at last. 'And I think I'd better go, after all.'

Liam's jaw clenched, and before he could prevent himself he asked, 'Do you want to?'

No!

Rosa turned her head. 'I don't know,' she said weakly.

Liam groaned, and, forgetting what he'd told himself since the moment he'd laid eyes on her, reached out and slipped his hand behind her nape. Then, before he could change his mind, he pulled her towards him.

And she came, seemingly willingly, her lips parting beneath his with a sensuality he hadn't expected. He'd intended to keep this light, inconsequential, but when her mouth opened he plunged his tongue into that wet, heated cavern without giving himself time to think.

She tasted hot and sweet and immensely desirable. Before he knew what he was doing, his hand had slid from her neck to the sensitive hollow of her spine. She arched towards him and he felt her taut breasts nudging his chest. And, God help him, his hand slipped lower, cupping the provocative curve of her bottom.

She jerked uncontrollably, but she didn't draw away, and he urged her back against the cushions behind her. He was kissing her now with a wild abandon that he hadn't felt since who knew when. If he'd *ever* felt this way, he conceded with unwilling honesty, as he ravaged her mouth again and again.

But this was not what he'd intended, he thought, in a rare moment of coherency. Not what he'd intended at all. He didn't indulge in one-night-stands with needy divorcees who were looking for no-strings sex. Besides, he hardly knew her. And she knew nothing of the monstrous scars that lurked beneath the expensive civility of his clothes. Hadn't he learned to his cost that women were not to be trusted? If he didn't want to scare her half to death, he should stop this. Now.

Rosa, however, knew nothing of his private misgivings. And, while she doubted anything lasting could come of it, she was ready and willing to take whatever Liam had to give. Her marriage to Colin, the pain she'd suffered when she'd discovered he'd been cheating on her, seemed a distant memory. Colin had never made her feel like this. Their relationship had been one of convenience, she realised, not passion.

She moved, slipping her hands about his neck, letting her fingers curl in the hair at his nape. His hair was only lightly tinged with grey, but thick, and virile. Like the rest of him, she thought a little breathlessly, feeling the unmistakable pressure of his arousal against her stomach.

The fight Liam was waging against his own needs was rapidly fading. When her tongue came to twine with his, he felt the blood thundering through his veins. He sucked on her lips, bit her tongue, felt his head spinning with the gnawing hunger inside him. He wanted her, he thought savagely. He wanted to bury his aching shaft in her wet heat.

His hand stroked her jawline, and when he lifted his mouth to take a breath his thumb brushed sensuously across her swollen lips. Her tongue appeared, laving his thumb as he bent to bite her earlobe, and he felt his arousal straining at his zip.

Her hair had come loose during their lovemaking, and he couldn't resist twining the fiery strands around his fingers. He brought them to her lips and kissed her through the silky curtain, heard her give a moan of ecstasy as he did so.

God, this was getting heavy, he thought, dragging his hand away—but only as far as her chest. He couldn't resist cupping her breast through her sweater, but when he bent to take one hard nipple into his mouth she shook her head and guided his hand to the hem of the jersey.

Beneath the woollen garment her skin was smooth and unblemished. Unlike his own, he thought bitterly. When he peeled the sweater up to her chin, he found pert breasts, almost bursting out of her half-bra. The sight of all that creamy flesh was a harsh reminder of his own scarred torso, and with a groan of anguish he buried his face between her breasts and said hoarsely, 'I can't do this!'

Rosa was breathing rapidly, her chest rising and falling swiftly, matching the sexual cravings he was inspiring in her. There was a wetness between her legs, and a pain stirring deep in her belly. As well as electric shocks that sparked along her nerves and left her aching, restive and wanting.

'You want me,' she protested, not knowing where she found the courage to say such a thing to him. God, only a few days ago she'd been convinced he could never be attracted to her. Yet here she was, telling him he wanted her, when he might easily be playing her along.

However, he didn't deny it. 'That doesn't matter,' Liam declared grimly, but when he put his hands on the cushions at either side of her head to lever himself away from her she wouldn't let him go.

'It *does* matter,' she insisted, cupping his face in her hands and forcing him to look at her. 'I'm not expecting a lifelong commitment here. I just want to—be with you. Is that so wrong?'

Liam groaned. 'It's not wrong—'

'Well, then?'

'You don't understand,' he muttered, and this time he succeeded in pulling away from her. He drew her sweater down again, hiding those luscious breasts from his hungry gaze. 'I'm not what you think.'

Rosa gazed at him, narrow-eyed. 'If you're going to tell me you're not normal, then—'

'I'm not a vampire,' Liam assured her harshly. 'But just take my word for it. This would never work.'

'It doesn't have to work.' Rosa struggled into a sitting position and stared at him appealingly. 'I like you, Liam. I have ever since you spoke to me on the ferry. I know I'm not sophisticated or glamorous, but I thought—I really thought you liked me, too.'

'I *do* like you,' muttered Liam savagely. 'This has nothing to do with liking or disliking you. It has to do with me. Only me!'

Rosa knew when she was beaten. She'd given it her best and Liam had shot her down in flames. She didn't know what was going on here, but she didn't believe half of what he was saying. For some reason he'd changed his mind about her.

Was he afraid she might expect something he couldn't give? Even now? Hurting, she had to deliver one final taunt—if only to salvage something from the wreck of her self-respect. 'It's always about you, isn't it, *Mr* Jameson?' she demanded, wrapping her arms about her suddenly chilled body. 'You're completely self-motivated, aren't you? Self first, self last, self everything!'

The injustice of that statement almost choked him. He'd been thinking of *her*, for God's sake! And of himself, too, he admitted, and how he'd feel when she saw him and turned away. But mostly of her, mostly to spare her the ugly patchwork his attacker had made of his body. It wouldn't occur to her that the reason he wore long-sleeved shirts and sweaters was because the man had almost chopped his arms to shreds.

Realising he would regret this, he got to his feet and faced her. Then, as she gazed up at him in sudden alarm, he tore his shirt open. Buttons popped and danced across the floor, and he realised he'd probably torn them off. But he didn't care. In that moment all he wanted to do was show her the proof of what he'd been saying.

Rosa got to her feet as he dragged the shirt off his shoulders, her breath catching in her throat when she saw the scars on his arms and chest. Someone had attacked him—with a knife, she guessed—and he'd raised his arms to defend himself.

So this was what he'd been hiding, she thought, wondering if he thought they detracted from him as a man. The scars were old, and in many cases fading. But the memories they'd left with him were still strong enough to tear him apart.

Oh, Lord, she fretted, ashamed that she'd made him do this. Not to mention accusing him of having lived a charmed life. But did he really think she'd be repulsed by his appearance? For heaven's sake, she was ashamed of *herself*, not him.

'I—I didn't know,' she began, wanting to reassure him. 'I'm sorry, Liam, I—'

'Not half as sorry as I am, believe me,' he snarled harshly. 'But, as you say, you didn't know. I suppose that's some excuse.' He snatched up his shirt and shoved his arms into the sleeves. 'But now you do, and I want you to go. I'll get Sam to show you out.'

'But, Liam—'

'Don't,' he said, limping heavily to the door. 'Believe me, I've had all the sympathy I can take.'

Rosa fretted about what had happened all the way back to the guesthouse. She didn't think about the rain, or the fact that the roads were slippy and she had to be careful she didn't skid into a bog. Her own safety meant nothing to her at that moment. She didn't even notice the stiffness of the steering wheel. All she could think about was Liam's face when he'd wrenched off his shirt and shown her those awful scars. She didn't think she'd ever forget the torment in his eyes.

It was only when she pulled up outside the guesthouse that she realised it had actually stopped raining. Even the wind seemed to have eased a little, and she could actually walk up the path to the door without getting blown off her feet.

Conversely, the knowledge that the storm was waning didn't cheer her up. The ferry would come and she'd leave the island. She'd never see Liam again.

'Is everything all right?' Mrs Ferguson met her in the hallway of the guesthouse, her brow creasing when she saw how drawn Rosa looked.

'Yes. Yes, everything's fine,' lied Rosa, knowing she couldn't discuss what had happened with anyone. 'Thank you for the use of your car. I must pay for the petrol, though.'

'Och, that's not necessary.' Mrs Ferguson clicked her tongue dismissively. 'I don't want anything for the tiny drop of fuel you'll have used. Like I said before you left, it will have done the vehicle good to have an outing. When my husband was alive he used to like to go bird-watching all over the island, but since he died I've scarcely had a use for it.'

'You're very kind.' Rosa forced a smile. 'It—er—it seems to be brightening up.'

'Yes, I thought so myself,' agreed the landlady, glancing out of the door. 'But you're looking a little peaked, Miss Chantry, if you don't mind my saying so. Are you sure you didn't find the journey too tiring?'

Tiring!

Rosa stifled the sob that rose in the back of her throat.

'Just—a bit,' she said, hoping that would satisfy the woman. 'I'm used to power steering, you see.'

'Power steering?' Mrs Ferguson sounded impressed. 'And what would that be when it's at home?'

'Oh—' Rosa wished she hadn't said anything. 'It just makes it easier to steer,' she explained, without elaborating, and with that she headed towards the stairs that led to her room.

CHAPTER TEN

THE REST OF THE DAY was an anticlimax.

After refusing Mrs Ferguson's offer of lunch, Rosa holed up in her room, wondering if she'd ever feel normal again. The events of the morning seemed unbelievable in retrospect. Had she really almost been seduced by a man against his will?

She simply wasn't the kind of woman things like that happened to. Her marriage to Colin Vincent and his subsequent betrayal had left her distinctly suspicious where men were concerned. Yet from the beginning she'd not had that feeling with Liam. Perhaps because she'd never expected that he might be attracted to her.

Even now, she hardly knew what he felt about her. Not enough to trust her, she acknowledged, wishing she'd had a chance to convince him she didn't care about his scars. Were they the reason he lived here, miles from any of the people he worked with? She wished she knew him better, wished she could show him that she—

She—what?

Rosa shivered. What was she thinking? She wasn't in love with him, for heaven's sake. In lust, maybe, and she very much regretted the way she'd had to leave the castle.

But she hardly knew the man. Certainly not enough to trust him with her love.

Nevertheless, that didn't stop her from regretting what had happened. She still didn't know what he thought of her—if he imagined she was used to doing that sort of thing.

She wasn't.

Rosa quivered. She couldn't ever remember behaving so shamelessly before, even with Colin. But then, the feelings she'd had for Colin had been nothing like this, and that was something else she regretted.

But had she really *asked* Liam to have sex with her? Had she really promised him there need be no commitment on his part, other than to take her to bed and make mad, passionate love to her?

Her face burned at the memory. Burned, too, at the realisation that she'd meant it. That she meant it still. She wanted him. Wanted to be with him. And something told her it would have been an experience she would never forget.

But it wasn't going to happen. Liam had made sure of that. In one devastating move he'd shown her exactly how damaged he was. Not just physically. His physical scars had healed. It was the other scars he carried beneath the surface that worried Rosa.

Because it was that sensitivity, which seemed to be as raw now as when the attack had happened, that had caused him to turn away from her. She was no psychologist, but she'd gamble that someone else was responsible for the protective shell he'd built around himself. Someone had hurt him, and she didn't believe it was his attacker.

So who? It had to be a woman, she decided painfully. A special woman. A woman he'd been in love with. Someone he'd been relying on to support him through his ordeal…

The phone rang downstairs and Rosa tensed. Not that she expected it to be for her. Liam wasn't likely to try and get in touch with her again.

Nevertheless, her heart leapt when Mrs Ferguson called, 'It's for you, Miss Chantry.' And then sank again when she added, 'It's your mother.'

What now?

Rosa felt the weight of her own inadequacy descend on her as she hurried down the stairs to take the call. Yes, she'd asked Liam about the film, she rehearsed silently. But, no, she had no further news to give her mother.

'Hello, Mum,' she said, picking up the receiver, injecting a note of optimism into her voice. 'You'll be pleased to hear the storm's over at last. I'll be leaving the island on Monday at the latest.'

'Will you, dear?' Mrs Chantry sounded strangely agitated. 'Well, that's good.' She paused. 'Will you come straight home?'

Rosa frowned. 'I thought I might contact an information centre on the mainland and find out if they know—'

'Sophie's not in Scotland,' broke in her mother swiftly. And then, before Rosa could object, she added, 'She's been in London, but she's home now.'

Rosa was stunned. 'In London?' she echoed, blankly.

'Yes.' Her mother didn't sound as if she was enjoying this. 'She's been with some man she met at the pop festival. Some musician, I believe.'

'You're not serious!'

'I am.' Mrs Chantry sighed. 'I'm sorry, Rosa.'

'But why did she tell Mark she was going to Scotland?'

'I don't know.' Clearly her mother would have preferred not to go on with this. 'To put us off the scent, I suppose.

She knew I'd have worried if I'd known she was with some guitarist with a pop group. What with all the drug-taking that goes on and—'

'But you *were* worried, Mum,' Rosa reminded her. 'My God, when you rang me last Saturday night you were practically hysterical.'

'Oh, I wasn't, Rosa. You're exaggerating. Good heavens, we all know what Sophie's like. She's so impetuous!'

'So irresponsible,' muttered Rosa darkly. 'Is she there? Put her on. I want to speak to her.'

'You can't.' Before Rosa could argue, Mrs Chantry explained her reasons. 'Mark called a little while ago, and she's gone round to his house to try and patch things up with him.'

'Well, he's a fool if he believes anything she tells him,' said Rosa irritably. For heaven's sake, was she the only one in the family with a lick of sense? 'I can't believe you're letting her get away with this. If it had been me at her age, I'd have been grounded for a month!'

'Well, it's no good me going on at her, Rosa,' declared Mrs Chantry unhappily. 'She's going away to university soon enough, and if I play the heavy she's not going to want to come home at all.'

'Oh, Mum!' Rosa groaned. 'You can't let her blackmail you. She ran off with a musician, a man she'd only just met, who she knew nothing about. He could have been a—a white slaver for all she knew.'

'Oh, Rosa.' Mrs Chantry gave a little laugh now. 'White slaver, indeed!' She waited a beat, and when Rosa didn't say anything she added firmly, 'Anyway, she's learned her lesson. She says he dumped her when she refused to go to bed with him.'

And believe that if you will, thought Rosa cynically. But all she said was, 'Did she tell you why she went with him in the first place?'

'Oh, apparently he said he could introduce her to some people he knew in television,' said her mother, relaxing a little now that she'd delivered her news. 'She shouldn't have believed him. I told her that.'

'And where did Liam Jameson come in?' asked Rosa shortly. 'Or hasn't she told you that?'

Her mother hesitated. 'Oh—well, that might have been my fault.'

'Your fault?' Rosa was confused. 'How could it be your fault?'

'Well...' Mrs Chantry was obviously searching for words. 'I evidently jumped to the wrong conclusion.'

'I don't understand.'

'No.' Her mother sighed. 'No, you wouldn't.' There was another pause, and then she said reluctantly, 'Well, you know how much Sophie likes Liam Jameson's books?'

'Yes.'

'And how she'd said how great it would be to star in one of his films?'

'You're kidding!'

'No. No, I'm not.' Mrs Chantry spoke indignantly. 'She has said that. Heaps of times. And—and when Mark rang and said she'd run off to Scotland with some man she'd met at the pop festival—'

Rosa groaned. 'I don't believe this!'

'It—it's true.' Her mother sniffed pathetically. 'Mark did say that she'd told him that this man was going to introduce her to all the right people, and—'

'And you put two and two together and made fifteen,'

said Rosa shortly. 'Mum, why didn't you tell me this before I left?'

'Would you have gone if I had?'

No!

Rosa blew out a breath. 'Possibly not.'

'Probably not,' declared her mother tersely. 'I know you, Rosa. If you'd thought I was just clutching at straws, you'd never have approached Liam Jameson.'

And wasn't that the truth? thought Rosa, an unpleasant little pain making itself felt in her temple. 'Oh, Mum,' she said wearily, 'I wish you'd told me just the same.'

'And have you tell me what a stupid woman I am?' demanded Mrs Chantry. 'I thought you'd be glad to hear your sister was home, safe and sound. Instead all you can do is grumble about both of us!'

Rosa knew it was ridiculous. She was thirty-two, for goodness' sake. But her eyes filled with tears at her mother's harsh words. They were so unjustified, so unfair. She hadn't complained, not really. But Sophie was totally selfish and her mother refused to see it.

'I'd better go,' she said, hoping the catch in her voice wasn't audible to anyone else. 'Mrs Ferguson's probably waiting to use the phone.'

Which was unlikely, she conceded. Apart from this call, the phone hadn't rung at all while she'd been in the guest-house. Evidently people in Kilfoil tended to do their gossiping face to face.

'All right.' If Mrs Chantry suspected that the reason Rosa was ending the call was because she'd been a little unkind, she wasn't prepared to admit it. 'I'll expect you when I see you, then. Take care.'

'Bye.'

Rosa replaced the handset and scrubbed an impatient hand across her eyes. She was not going to cry, she told herself, even if the day had just gone from bad to worse. She had to focus on the future, on getting home to her little flat in Ripon, which suddenly seemed very far away. School would be starting again in a couple of weeks, and she had lessons to prepare before then.

Liam always stayed at the Moriarty Hotel when he was in London. It was a small, select establishment, known to only a few people, and they, like himself, reserved a suite of rooms year round, so that it was always available whenever it was needed.

It was one of the perks of being successful, he thought, as he drove south on the motorway. He could stay there completely anonymously, which suited him very well.

Not that he intended staying more than a couple of nights there on this visit. He was due to spend a few days at the Erskine Clinic in Knightsbridge, undergoing some further therapy on his leg.

Ever since August, when he'd been caught out in the storm because of the dogs, he'd been having an increasing amount of discomfort in his thigh. The local doctor thought he might have torn a ligament, and rather than wait for it to get better, which might not happen, Liam had been forced to seek relief.

Of course Sam thought he was crazy, driving to London. His opinion was that Liam should have used the helicopter. But helicopters tended to advertise one's arrival, and that was the last thing Liam wanted to do.

He'd left Scotland behind a little while ago, and now he was some miles beyond Penrith, heading towards the service area at Tebay. He might stop there, he reflected. He could do with a cup of coffee and the opportunity to stretch his legs. And to look at the map, he conceded, not prepared to consider why he should need to do so. His route was familiar enough, goodness knew. South on the M6 as far as the M5, then east on the M40 until he reached the outskirts of London. What could be simpler?

He parked near the service buildings at Tebay and went inside to use the facilities and buy a coffee. Then he carried it back to the car and pulled his map out of the glove locker.

Less than a mile farther on there was a turn-off for Scotch Corner. Well, for Kirby Stephen initially, but it eventually intersected with the A66 east, which in turn intersected with the A1 at Scotch Corner. And about twenty miles south of Scotch Corner was the small Yorkshire market town of Ripon.

Ripon!

Liam swallowed a mouthful of his coffee, wincing at its bitter taste. Now, why would he want to know how to get to Ripon? Okay, he'd found out from Mrs Ferguson that that was where Rosa Chantry lived, but so what? It was nearly two months since he'd seen her, and after the way he'd behaved he doubted very much whether she'd want to see him again.

He didn't even know why he was still thinking about her. He was too old to believe that their association had been anything more than a brief infatuation with sex. He'd wanted her, yes, but experience had taught him that you didn't always get what you wanted. There was no doubt that she'd been horrified when she'd glimpsed the ugly patchwork beneath his shirt. And she hadn't even seen the worst of it. It was a mercy he could still function as a man.

He tried to excuse his interest by telling himself he was concerned about her. Had she found her sister yet? Was she safe and well? Surely she must be. Despite searching the Internet, scanning every newspaper published in the Ripon area, he'd never read anything about a Sophie Chantry being missing. Wherever she was, she wasn't making news, and that was usually a good sign.

For Rosa's sake, he hoped so. He couldn't believe that in this day and age, with all the publicity there was about the dangers of young girls going off with men they knew nothing about, her sister should have behaved so foolishly. She was either completely naïve or completely stupid. Remembering what Rosa had told him, he'd put his money on the latter.

He folded the map and put it back in the glove box, and then sat for a while drinking his coffee. What now? Was he going to get back on the motorway and drive directly to London, as he'd told Sam? Or was he going to make a detour to the north-east?

He considered. A glance at his watch told him it was three o'clock on a Tuesday afternoon in October. By his reckoning, it would be five o'clock before he reached Ripon, if that was where he intended to go. How did he know she'd be home from work? Or even alone? Was he willing to take the risk just to satisfy a whim he'd probably regret later? He knew the answer, and he tossed the empty cup into a rubbish bin. If he didn't see Rosa again he'd never know how he really felt.

Happily, traffic was fairly light, and he arrived at the outskirts of Ripon soon after a quarter to five. There were plenty of cars heading out of town—probably commuters, making their way home, he decided. Now all he had to do was find someone who could tell him where Richmond Road was.

A policeman was patrolling the narrow street beside the cathedral, and although there were yellow lines warning him not to stop Liam pulled in beside him. Lowering the nearside window, he leant across the seat. 'I'm looking for Richmond Road,' he said ruefully. 'You couldn't help me, could you?'

The policeman looked as if he was about to point out that this was a no waiting area, but then seemed to take pity on him. 'Richmond Road,' he said thoughtfully. 'Yes.' He turned. 'You've just come past it. It's that way, just off Winston Street.'

Liam stifled a curse. This was a one-way street, and he'd already discovered that the town centre was a maze of similar thoroughfares. How the hell was he supposed to retrace his steps?

'It might be easier if you parked and walked back,' suggested the policemen, apparently aware of his dilemma. 'I could give you directions, but at this time of the afternoon—'

'I understand.'

Liam gave a brief nod and rolled up the window again. Was he being a damn fool? he wondered, driving back into the market square. All this fuss, just to find a woman who might not even be willing to speak to him. He dreaded to think what Sam would say if he found out.

He eventually found a car park just off the market square. And, because most people were heading home, he had no problem in finding a space. Then, hauling his woollen overcoat out of the back seat, he locked the car and pocketed the keys, pushing his hands deep into his coat pockets as he trudged back towards the cathedral.

A bell tolled and he realised it was already half-past five.

It had taken him longer to find her house than to drive from Scotch Corner to Ripon. And he still had about a five-hour journey ahead of him, if he was planning to reach London tonight.

Fortunately, it was a dry evening, though it was cold. The wind swept along these narrow streets, and his hip and leg became stiff and taut with pain. He should have stayed with the car, he thought. Walking any distance in his present state was madness. And all to see a woman he barely knew.

He found Richmond Road without much difficulty. It was a street of semi-detached houses, and it was still light enough for him to see number 24. He glanced at the note he'd stuffed in his pocket. It said number 24b. But there was no 24b. No 24a, either. Had she given Mrs Ferguson a false address?

He frowned. Then, deciding the only thing he could do was knock at number 24 and ask for directions again, he opened the front gate and walked up the path. That was when he saw the intercom pinned to the wall beside the door. It had been too dark for him to see it before. Evidently 24b was an apartment; likewise 24a.

He cast a glance at the windows. There were lights upstairs, so someone was home. But was that apartment 24a or 24b? He wouldn't know until he rang the bell.

'Yes?'

The voice that answered his summons was unmistakable. Liam disliked the way it danced along his nerves and curled its way around his heart. For God's sake, what was the matter with him? Even Kayla had never made him feel like this.

'Rosa?' His voice was a little hoarse suddenly. 'It's me, Liam Jameson. May I come up?'

Silence. Liam wondered what he'd do if she refused to speak to him. Break down the door? Walk away? He hoped he didn't have to make that decision.

'Push the door,' she said at last, and with a feeling of relief he heard the sound of the buzzer that released the latch.

Inside it was dark. He could just make out a hallway, leading to the back of the house, and a flight of stairs to the first floor.

As if she thought he might have some doubts about which apartment was hers, a light suddenly shone down from the top of the stairs. Rosa was standing on the landing above, looking down at him, and with a deep intake of air he closed the door and started up.

She looked different, he thought, and then realised she'd had her hair cut. Now it swung about her shoulders, still a fiery mass of curls, but softer, more feminine. She was wearing loose-fitting black trousers and a green blouse of some silky material that tipped off one shoulder as she moved. She looked good, he thought grimly. Too good to be spending the evening watching the television. Alone.

His leg stiffened as he mounted the stairs, and for a moment he couldn't move. Hoping she wouldn't notice, he said tightly, 'Sorry if I'm intruding.'

Rosa frowned, and he was almost sure she was going to comment on his momentary paralysis. But then he was able to move his leg again, and she stepped back into the lighted doorway behind her. 'You're not intruding. Come in.'

CHAPTER ELEVEN

'THANKS.'

Liam was very relieved to reach the landing. He didn't think he could have climbed another step, and he was already wondering how the hell he was going to get back to where he'd left his car. Perhaps he could call a cab? One thing was for sure: he didn't think he could walk all that way again tonight.

Meanwhile, Rosa was wondering what he was doing here. She tried to tell herself it could have nothing to do with what had happened before she left the castle, yet what else could it be?

He must have got her address from Mrs Ferguson. She could imagine that lady's surprise at such a request. She must have wondered why he hadn't contacted his publisher. Unless, for some reason, he'd told her the truth.

Her eyes darted about the room as he entered, trying to see it through his eyes. It was a comfortable room, a through dining and sitting room combined. But it was shabby, and nothing like the luxurious apartments he was used to.

She snatched up a discarded pair of tights she'd left draped over one of the dining chairs, and removed a magazine from the chenille couch. 'Why don't you sit down?'

she invited, aware of the laboured way he'd climbed the stairs. 'You look—tired.'

'Don't you mean beat?' suggested Liam drily, but he did subside onto the couch with some relief. 'I'm a bit stiff, that's all. I've been driving since early this morning.'

Rosa's eyes widened. 'But it's Tuesday!'

'So?'

'I thought the ferry only ran on Mondays and Thursdays.' She shook her head. 'Oh, of course. You probably used your helicopter?'

Liam slanted a glance up at her. 'How did you know I had a helicopter?'

Rosa straightened. 'Mrs Ferguson told me.' She paused. 'When—when I was stranded on the island, she suggested asking you if you could help.'

'Ah.' Liam nodded. 'The kindly Mrs Ferguson.' He shrugged. 'Well, I'm sorry to disappoint you, but I spent last night at Jack Macleod's.'

'Who?' Rosa had never heard of Jack Macleod.

'The man you saw me talking to that morning we took the ferry to Kilfoil,' he reminded her, resting back against the cushions and pushing his hands into the pockets of his coat. 'Or am I the only one who remembers that?'

Rosa moistened her lips. 'No. No, I remember,' she said defensively. 'Is he a friend of yours?'

'A good friend,' agreed Liam. 'He lives in Mallaig, and when I first bought the island he offered to put me in touch with the people I needed to renovate the castle and the cottages. His grandparents used to live on Kilfoil, and he was a great help. We've remained friends ever since.'

'Oh, I see.' Rosa absorbed this. Then, 'I suppose Mrs Ferguson gave you my address?'

'She did.' Liam regarded her from beneath lashes any woman would have died for. 'I hope you don't mind.'

'Why should I mind?' Rosa realised she was still holding the magazine and the tights she'd picked up when he arrived. With an absent gesture, she crossed the room to dispose of them into a drawer before turning down the gas fire. The room seemed overly hot suddenly, and with her back to him she added, 'Can I get you anything? A drink?'

'A beer would be good,' he said, not really wanting anything at this moment. The pain in his leg was just beginning to subside, and the last thing he wanted was to have to walk on it again. 'Um—did you find your sister?'

Rosa straightened and turned to him, the blouse sliding off her shoulder again to reveal the black strap of her bra. 'She was here when I got back,' she confessed wryly. 'She'd been in London all along.'

'London?' Liam was briefly diverted. 'What the hell was she doing in London?'

'Making out with a musician she met at the pop festival,' replied Rosa, with a grimace. 'He apparently dumped her when she refused to sleep with him.'

Liam looked doubtful at this, and Rosa had to continue. 'I know. Incredible, isn't it? But my mother believes everything she says.' She sighed. 'Sophie can wrap her round her little finger.'

Liam stared at her. 'So where did I come in?'

'Oh—' Rosa's cheeks reddened. 'That was my mother's fault. When Mark—he's Sophie's boyfriend—phoned her to tell her Sophie had gone to Scotland with some man who was going to help her get into the movies, she immediately thought of you.'

'Why, for God's sake?'

'Well, like I told you, Sophie's always been such a fan of yours. I suppose she needed something to focus on, and you were it.'

'So it was your mother who sent you to Kilfoil?'

'Mmm.' Rosa nodded. 'But Sophie had said she was going to Scotland. That part was true.'

Liam shook his head in disbelief. 'Dare I ask why?'

'To put us off the scent?' Rosa shrugged. 'Looking back, I must have been a fool to believe anything my mother said. But she is half Italian, and she was practically hysterical when she phoned me.' She pulled a rueful face. 'Now—a beer.' She started towards the kitchen. 'Is that all?'

Not nearly, thought Liam, but he assured her that it was, watching as she went into the adjoining room. She walked quickly, and he realised she was nervous. He wondered why. Was she expecting someone else. A man, maybe?

That thought irritated him beyond reason. God, he couldn't believe how much he'd wanted to see her again. It added to the sense of impatience he was feeling at his own weakness. Dammit, he hadn't come here for her sympathy. He'd wanted to test her, but not in this way.

Gritting his teeth, he hauled himself to his feet again and made his way across the floor to the open doorway. Then, propping his shoulder against the jamb, he said, 'Do you live alone?'

Rosa jumped. Having acknowledged how tired he was, she'd expected him to stay on the couch. She'd already extracted a bottle of beer from the fridge, and had been about to decant it into a glass, but his appearance had startled her.

'Um—yes,' she said, concentrating on unscrewing the cap. However, when she would have poured it into the tumbler she'd taken from the cupboard, Liam stopped her.

ANNE MATHER 133

'It's okay,' he said. 'I'll drink it from the bottle.'

Rosa looked doubtful. 'Are you sure?'

'I'm sure,' he said, holding out his hand, and with a shrug she passed the bottle to him.

He didn't move from the doorway, however, and she found herself watching as he carried the bottle to his lips and took a hearty swallow.

The muscles in his throat moved as he drank, the mark she'd seen when she was at the castle the only pale scar on flesh that was both brown and supple. And, just watching him, she felt again the flicker of desire—of awareness—that had been so unfamiliar to her until she'd met him.

Liam lowered the bottle suddenly, and turned to look at her. And, just like that, her limbs turned to jelly. It took an actual physical effort to look away from those jade-green eyes and say, albeit a little breathlessly, 'Why don't you go and sit down again? You can't enjoy anything standing up.'

'Don't you believe it,' said Liam provocatively, setting the bottle down on the unit beside him and holding out his hand. 'Come here.'

Rosa swallowed. 'Do you need some help getting—'

'No!' he exploded angrily. 'I don't need your help. Not in that way, anyway.' He gave her an exasperated look. 'Just come here, will you?'

Rosa hesitated, but eventually she left the support of the fridge behind and approached him. 'Now what?'

'Like you don't know,' he retorted softly, catching her wrist and bringing its sensitive network of veins to his mouth. 'Kiss me.'

Rosa's breathing faltered. 'Liam—'

'Just do it, dammit,' he demanded harshly, and without

another word she stepped closer and reached up to brush his lips with hers.

Liam gave a frustrated snort. 'Is that the best you can do?' He used his free hand to trace the shape of her jawline, allowing his fingers to move into the fiery glory of her hair. 'Kiss me, Rosa. Like you mean it. I didn't drive all this way just so you could give me a beer.'

'So why did you?' Rosa looked up into his strong face, resisting the urge to brush her own fingers across his lips. 'Drive all this way, I mean?'

Liam's eyes narrowed. 'Guess.'

Rosa took a breath. 'Because you wanted to see me?'

Liam's expression was sardonic. 'Gee, you have a real way with words.'

'So you tell me what to say,' she exclaimed, at once defensive and excited. 'Why did you want to see me? As I recall it, you couldn't wait to get rid of me before.'

'Yeah.' Liam made a mocking sound. 'That's what I let you think, didn't I?'

'Wasn't it true?'

'Hell, yes, it was true.' He tugged gently at a handful of hair. 'It's still true.' He grimaced. 'But I find I'm not quite as heroic as I thought I was.'

'Heroic?' Rosa was puzzled.

Liam sighed, shifting his weight from one foot to the other. 'If I had any sense at all, I wouldn't be here.'

Rosa drew back. 'Well, if you feel like that—' she began, only to break off in surprise when he bent and covered her mouth with his.

It wasn't totally unexpected. Goodness, they'd been edging towards this moment since she'd opened the door. But even Rosa was unprepared for the urgency with which he pulled her closer, and the groan that emanated from deep in his throat when he did so.

Her lips parted of their own accord, and Liam's tongue swept eagerly into her mouth. He found he wasn't immune to the temptation posed by her soft and yielding body pressed against his, or ashamed to take advantage of her obvious weakness. This was what he'd wanted since she'd let him into the apartment, and although his thigh was aching, a much more urgent ache was developing between his legs.

The kiss lengthened and deepened, draining them with its urgency, leaving them both breathless and trembling. Trying to hang on to his sanity, Liam left her mouth to seek the pulse beating behind her ear, biting the lobe feverishly, finding it increasingly difficult to keep his head.

Her blouse slipped off her shoulder again, and this time Liam tipped the bra strap aside, too, so that he could nuzzle the creamy slopes of her breasts. He nipped her with his teeth, sucked hungrily on her soft flesh, took pleasure in seeing his mark on her.

'You want me,' she exclaimed unsteadily, reaching up to grab the hair at the back of his neck in an effort to ground herself. 'You really want me.'

'You noticed.' His voice was rough with emotion. 'Yeah, I want you. Are you going to tell me you don't feel the same?'

'That would be pretty stupid, wouldn't it?' Rosa replied huskily. 'I think you know how I feel, or you wouldn't be here.'

'I know how you *think* you feel,' he said in response. 'But you don't know everything.'

Rosa quivered, feeling the thick pressure of his arousal building against her abdomen. 'I have been married,' she reminded him gently, but Liam only snorted at her words.

'That's not what I meant and you know it,' he muttered, releasing himself abruptly and turning aside into the living room. Then, not facing her, he said, 'You're not going to be horrified if I take off my pants?'

Rosa went after him then, sliding her arms around him from behind and pressing her face against the soft wool of his overcoat. 'You flatter yourself,' she whispered, trying to make light of what he'd said, but Liam only uttered a rude word.

'You think you've seen the worst of it, but you haven't,' he said harshly. 'You've had time to get over what you saw, but there are other scars—'

'Shh!' Rosa let go of him to come round and face him. 'Stop talking like that.' She paused. 'If you'd given me a chance to speak that morning at the castle, I'd have told you then that I don't horrify that easily.'

'But you were shocked—'

'Of course I was.' Rosa was indignant. 'For heaven's sake, who wouldn't have been in my position? I'd had no idea—' She broke off, and then went on more steadily, 'But I wasn't—repelled, repulsed, whatever ugly ideas are buzzing around in that head of yours. I thought it was a shame, that's all. That someone could have been evil enough to do that to you. If I felt anything, it was compassion—'

'I don't need your—'

'But I guessed you'd probably had all the compassion you could stomach.' She overrode him grimly. 'Besides, you must know you have so much else going for you. But you didn't give me a chance to say anything except goodbye.'

Liam's shoulders sagged. 'I didn't think there was anything else to say.'

'I suppose that depends on what you're going to do

now,' she replied, looking up into his troubled features. 'Whether you're going to storm off into the night or—take off your coat.'

Liam gazed down at her. 'You know, I want to believe you mean this.'

'Then do it,' she exclaimed fiercely. 'Take off your coat.' She stepped forward and slid her hands beneath his coat, slipping it off his shoulders. 'You must be warm in here, with all these clothes on.'

'I am warm—hot, actually,' he muttered. 'But it has hell all to do with what I'm wearing.' He let the heavy overcoat fall to the floor. 'Come here.'

'No, you come here,' she said, taking his hand and leading him across the room. Another door opened into a short corridor with two doors leading from it. One, he guessed, led to a bathroom. The other had to be Rosa's bedroom.

He was right. The room she led him into was small, but attractive, with honey-coloured walls and a creamy shag carpet underfoot. There was a bed—a single, he noticed, with a satisfied curl of his lip—a wardrobe and a chest of drawers. The curtains, which matched the pale green coverlet, were drawn, and Rosa bent to switch on a lamp beside the bed.

'I know this is nothing like what you're used to—' she was beginning, but he swung her round to face him, taking her mouth again in a kiss that left them both hot and panting for breath.

'I want to get used to you, not this room,' Liam told her when he could speak again. 'But could we lose the lamp? I don't think I'm up to being inspected.'

Rosa wanted to tell him not to be silly, but she respected his feelings and obediently turned the lamp off again. 'Better?' she asked huskily, his large frame just a silhouette now in the light that filtered through from the living room.

'Much better,' he agreed, moving towards her, and she sank down onto the side of the bed, trying to draw him with her.

But Liam had other ideas. Ignoring the stiffness in his hip, he knelt in front of her, burying his face in the hollow between her breasts. 'Do you know how much I've wanted this?' he asked thickly, his hands slipping beneath the blouse at her waist. And then, more impatiently, 'How the hell do you take this thing off?'

'Let me,' said Rosa shakily, crossing her arms and pulling the offending garment over her head. 'It's easy when you know how.'

'Don't I know it?' said Liam, shoving his own jacket to the floor. His sweater followed it, but when he realised that only his shirt separated all her unblemished loveliness from his disfigured torso he paused. Then, in a strangled voice, he added, 'Are you really sure about this?'

'As sure as I've ever been about anything in my life,' Rosa assured him in a breathless voice. Her fingers started on the buttons of his shirt. 'Can I?'

Liam's breath caught in his throat. 'If you want to.'

'I want to,' she whispered, and moments later he felt the cool draught of air across his heated skin.

She leaned towards him, her lips finding the pattern of lines left by his injuries and tracing each one with her tongue. There was no revulsion, no aversion. Just tender contact with his skin.

It was his cue to urge her back against the mattress, covering her with his body, loosening the clasp of her bra and freeing the incredible warmth of her breasts against his chest. He couldn't resist taking one swollen nipple into his mouth, and she gave a little moan as he did so. He rolled the tight bud against his tongue and suckled greedily. Dear God, why had he stayed away so long?

She shifted restlessly beneath him, her fingers tangling in his hair as she arched her body towards his. And, although Liam would have liked to prolong this, he knew he wasn't going to be able to. Already his erection was threatening to burst out of his pants.

It had to be almost twenty-five years since he'd been in such a state of arousal, he thought incredulously. Not since he was a teenager had he ever been in danger of losing control—not just of his body but of his mind, too. The blood was thundering through his veins in anticipation of what he was going to do to her. He actually came out in a sweat at the thought of burying his shaft in her hot sheath.

He pushed his hand down between them and found the button at the waistband of her trousers. It opened easily, and with a shuddering breath he slipped his hand inside. Encountering lacy silk, he frowned, remembering how nervous she'd seemed earlier. The idea that she might have dressed for some other man caused his blood pressure to rise even more.

But he refused to ruin the beauty of this moment by allowing his own jealousy to destroy the mood. Instead, his hands moved beneath the lace and cupped her mound.

'That feels so good,' he whispered, one finger penetrating the silky curls of hair to find the swollen nubbin trapped within her folds and rubbing gently. 'I knew it would.'

'For me, too,' said Rosa hoarsely, her hands tangling with his as she struggled to loosen his trousers. 'Please,' she added brokenly. 'I want you inside me when I come.'

Liam's breathing faltered. The image her words was creating caused him to quicken his efforts to free her from the rest of her clothes, and pretty soon her trousers and the lace thong joined her blouse on the floor.

'Now you,' Rosa urged huskily, and with only a momentary hesitation Liam loosened his pants and shoved them down his legs.

Now Rosa could slip her hands into the waistband of his boxers, and she took full advantage. Her tantalising fingers shaped his butt, squeezing his cheeks, pressing his erection into the parted curve of her legs.

'Take these off, too,' she ordered him unsteadily, and, with her help, the boxers also found their way to the floor.

But when she would have taken him into her hands he stopped her. 'Give me a break,' he groaned, his action as much a need to protect his self-restraint as a desire to hide his scarred flesh a little longer. 'I'm only human.'

'I'm so glad,' she said, her breath catching in her throat, and in spite of his efforts to prevent it she managed to wrap her soft fingers around him. If she noticed the hard ridge of skin that arrowed down into his groin she didn't mention it, her soft caresses almost driving him over the edge. 'Luther Killian can't possibly be as sexy as you.'

Liam swallowed convulsively. 'What do *you* know about Luther Killian?' he asked thickly.

'Oh, I bought a book of yours in Scotland, and I've finally managed to read it.'

'Finally?'

Although he was aching to possess her, he forced himself to enjoy the foreplay, and she trembled beneath him. 'Mmm,' she said unsteadily. 'I couldn't read it when—when I was on the island. It reminded me too much of you.

But when I'd finally decided I was never going to see you again I thought it was the closest to you I was going to get.'

'Ah.' Liam released the breath he'd hardly been aware he was holding. 'And now?'

'And now I just want to do it with you,' she told him in a shaky voice. 'Please.'

CHAPTER TWELVE

LIAM REALISED he must have slept when he opened his eyes to find himself alone in the bed.

He hadn't been conscious of Rosa getting up. He hadn't been conscious of anything, really, since the shuddering climax of their lovemaking. Which was why he felt so relaxed, he supposed, so sated with pleasure. For a few moments he was content to just lie there and relive every minute of it.

He felt weak, thinking about what had happened. He'd known Rosa was responsive, but she'd completely over-whelmed him. She been so hot, so downright sexy, that he'd abandoned every inhibition he'd ever had.

He'd even forgotten why he'd been so apprehensive of making love with her. And if she'd been aware of any faults in his appearance she hadn't shown it. She'd actually made him believe in himself again, believe that he'd found a woman who saw the man and not the flaws.

He recalled the moment when he'd felt his erection tight against her vagina. Pushing into her that first time, he'd been half out of his mind with pleasure. She'd assured him there was no need for him to wear a condom, and the sensation of skin against skin had been a potent stimulant.

He'd been aware of Rosa holding her breath as he'd possessed her. 'Are you all right?' he'd asked roughly, hoping she wasn't about to bail on him, and Rosa had expelled a little sigh.

'I was just thinking how big you are,' she'd confessed, a catch in her voice.

'And that's a problem?'

'Not to me,' she'd responded at once. 'Maybe to you.'

'Oh, baby!' Liam's voice had revealed an uneven thread of humour. 'That's no problem. You're so hot, I feel as if I'm burning up!'

'And that's good?'

'That's very good,' he'd assured her fervently. 'Just don't expect me to wait too long.'

But when he'd finally penetrated her fully, he'd found he'd wanted to prolong it. With her tight around him, and her breasts crushed against his chest, he'd wanted it to last and last. It had felt so good to be a part of her, cradled deep within her. He'd usually found the anticipation so much better than the realisation, and he hadn't wanted anything to spoil something so beautiful.

But then Rosa had wound a slim leg about his, and caressed his calf with the sole of her foot. It had been such a simple thing—a sensual abrasion, that was all—but it had almost blown his mind. Every movement she'd made had aroused him further, and the urge to fulfil all the fantasies he'd had about her had instantly focussed on the heavy shaft in its tender sheath.

He'd begun to move then, slowly at first, testing the slick muscles that had expanded around him. There'd been a wilful pleasure in pulling back from her, almost to the point of withdrawal, and then thrusting in again, feeling the cravings he had build and build.

He couldn't remember when the mindless excitement of what he'd been doing had taken over. He just knew he'd quickened his pace to try and calm the feverish beating of his heart.

And Rosa had responded, moving with him, so that he'd felt the gathering momentum of her orgasm almost before she'd been aware of it herself.

Of course the sounds she'd made and the ripples of her climax had totally stoned him. His own release had followed close behind, and what had begun as a gentle supplication had quickly accelerated into a glorious abandonment to sensuality.

His own orgasm had seemed to last for ever. Long after he'd been sure he must have drained himself into her, he'd still been shaking in her arms. He'd never had an experience like it. All the doubts he'd had coming here, the tension he'd felt when he'd seen Rosa again, had all melted away. He knew he'd done the right thing by taking the detour, and he was fairly sure she felt the same.

But where was she? Easing himself up on one elbow, Liam tried to see his watch. What time was it? It was still dark outside, so it obviously wasn't morning. But how long had he slept?

The sound of a man's raised voice jarred him out of any sense of complacency. It came from the living room, and he realised he'd been hearing the buzz of voices for some time. He reached for the lamp and turned it on, pulling the sheet over his lower limbs as he did so. Just after 9:00 p.m. he saw with a frown. What the hell was it? Had Rosa got up and turned the television on?

He thought about calling her, but that seemed too presumptuous. He decided to wait until she came back before asking what was going on. And he knew she would, sooner or later. What they'd shared was not going to go away.

And then the man used Rosa's name.

'For God's sake, Rosa,' he exclaimed, his voice raised as before. 'I thought we were going to talk about this.'

Liam didn't hear Rosa's answer. She spoke in a much lower tone, and he wondered if that was because she was considering him. Or was it just that she didn't want him to hear what she was saying? Or know that she had another visitor? Maybe the one she'd dressed up for, he thought, with an uncontrollable spurt of jealousy.

Thrusting the covers aside, he swung his legs to the floor. Then, rescuing his boxers from where he'd tossed them, he pulled them on over his ankles before standing up. Thankfully, although his leg still ached, the rest had restored some strength to his muscles. If he had to walk back to his car tonight, he reckoned he could just about do it.

By the time he'd put on his jeans and shirt, the voices were barely audible. He pulled his sweater over his head and shouldered into the leather jacket, thinking that if he had to meet Rosa's visitor, whoever he was, he was going to be prepared.

The lamp gave off little illumination, so he took a chance and opened the door of the room across the hall. As he'd hoped, it was a bathroom, and he turned on the light and quickly ran a comb thorough his unruly hair.

He was hungry, he thought, coming out of the bathroom again. Bloody hungry. He'd forgotten good sex could do that for you: first the senses, then the stomach. Perhaps they could send out for a pizza, he thought, his mouth already

watering at the prospect of melted mozzarella. Then—
well, then the possibilities were endless.

He was about to enter the living room when the man's
voice rose again.

'I don't give a tinker's cuss who this bloke is,' he
declared angrily. 'He doesn't have any rights where you're
concerned. For Pete's sake, Rosa, I'm your husband—'

'*Ex*-husband,' Liam thought she interjected, but the man
continued as if she hadn't spoken.

'Don't I deserve some consideration? I thought we'd
agreed to try and start again.'

Liam didn't hear Rosa's answer. Instead of going in
search of the voices, he was now standing motionless, his
shoulders pressed against the wall of the hall. So he'd been
right, he thought. She *had* been expecting another visitor.
Her ex-husband, no less. His jaw clamped savagely. What
kind of game was she playing? The poor guy sounded as
if she'd fed him the same line she'd fed Liam.

He wanted out of here! And fast. He felt as if he'd been
taken for a fool. What had she been doing? Using him to
make the other guy jealous? Well, she'd succeeded on two
counts. He was as sick as a parrot, too.

The voices seemed too far away to be in the living room.
And he didn't kid himself that Rosa had taken the argument
into the hall outside. He frowned. They had to be in the
kitchen—the kitchen where he'd kissed her earlier. His
stomach clenched, but he ignored it. If that was so, maybe
he could grab his coat and get out before either of them was
any the wiser.

He chanced a look into the room and saw he was right.
Someone—Rosa, probably—had picked his coat off the
floor and deposited it on a chair. The chair nearest the

door, he saw with some irony. Was it her way of indicating that he had already been on his way out?

The floor creaked as he crossed it, but Rosa and her husband—*ex-husband*, what a joke!—were too engrossed in their discussion to pay any attention. Then they were silent, but although Liam tensed nothing happened. God, he wondered sickly, was he kissing her? Even though he told himself he didn't care, he still wanted to go in there and shove his fist down the other man's throat.

But common sense deterred him. Besides, as the guy had said, what right did he have to interfere in Rosa's life? He meant nothing to her and, whatever he'd imagined, she could mean nothing to him. Not really. She'd done him a favour, actually. She'd shown him that not all women were like Kayla Stevens, and that was good.

He carried his coat instead of trying to put it on, leaving the door of the apartment unlocked because to close it completely would have made too much noise.

Then, treading carefully, he made his way downstairs and out of the building. He'd made it, he thought with some relief as he stepped onto the street. Then, pulling on his overcoat, he walked away without looking back.

'What was that?'

Rosa thought she'd heard something, and, pushing Colin aside, she went into the living room. But there was no one there. The room was empty, as before. She must have imagined it, she thought. Colin being here was making her as edgy as a cat.

'So where is he, this bloke you've shacked up with?' demanded Colin unpleasantly. 'Oh, I get it.' He viewed the towelling robe she'd hastily pulled on when he knocked at the door with a scornful eye. 'I got you out of bed, didn't I? So—what? Is he keeping out of my way because he's scared I might deck him?' He sneered as he strode past her. 'Let's see who's been screwing my wife, shall we?'

'Don't you dare!'

Rosa grabbed Colin's arm, trying to stop him from going into the hall that led to the bedroom, but he wasn't deterred. 'Wakey, wakey!' he called, pressing the switch and filling her bedroom with harsh light. Then he turned in some confusion. 'There's no one here.'

Rosa wished her face was less expressive. She'd have liked to say, *Who did you expect*? but the shock she'd got was more than equal to his.

And Colin knew her too well to be deceived. 'Well, what do you know?' he said mockingly. 'He's run out on you.' His lips twisted contemptuously. 'Didn't I tell you? I'm the only man you can rely on, Rosa.'

Rosa thought she would have laughed if she hadn't felt so heartsick. She thought she knew exactly why Liam had left, and it had nothing to do with whether he was reliable or not. He must have heard them talking, and, remembering what Colin had been saying, she wanted to scream in frustration. She'd told Liam she was divorced, that she'd been divorced for over three years, yet he must have heard Colin boasting about the fact that she was still his wife.

Of course she wasn't. But if Liam had heard all their conversation it would have put some doubt in his mind. Colin was so arrogant, so smug, so sure she'd agree to go back to him. But, although she was sorry his second marriage had proved as unsuccessful as his first, there was no way she ever wanted to be with Colin again.

'Just get out,' she said now, pointing towards the door.

And, although she'd thought he was going to argue, Colin had evidently decided he'd said enough for tonight.

'Hey, the door's unlocked,' he said. 'Obviously that's how he sneaked out without us hearing him. Who is he, Rosa? Don't I have a right to know who my competition is?'

'You have no rights where I'm concerned,' Rosa retorted coldly. 'And don't come here again. As far as I'm concerned, you dropped off the face of the earth three years ago.'

Colin's jaw sagged. 'You don't mean that, Rosa.'

'Trust me—I do,' she told him, pulling the outer door open. 'I hope I never see you again.'

Colin hesitated, and she briefly wondered what she'd do if he chose to ignore her. Scream her head off, she reflected. With a bit of luck her elderly neighbour would hear her and call the police. But in the event he went of his own accord, muttering that she'd regret this for the rest of her life.

Only that you came here, she thought bitterly as she slammed the door behind him. Then, collapsing onto the sofa, she felt the tears streaming down her face. She couldn't believe the evening that had begun so marvellously had ended so disastrously. And all because she'd agreed to speak to her ex-husband when he'd called her earlier in the day.

She'd even made a special effort with her appearance because Colin was coming, she thought bitterly. She'd had a shower and put on her best underwear, just to make herself feel good. She had no feelings for Colin, but that hadn't stopped her from wanting to look her best when he saw her. She'd wanted him to wish he'd never cheated on her, even if by doing so he'd probably—no, definitely—done her a favour.

And now Liam would think the worst of her. But when Colin had knocked at the door all she'd thought about was trying to stop him from waking Liam. She hadn't even intended to invite him in, but Colin had pushed past her anyway, evidently assuming she was glad to see him.

It hadn't been until she'd explained that there was someone new in her life that he'd got so abusive, lying about why he'd come here, trying to pretend that she'd agreed to start again.

It had all been just a dreadful mistake. And it was her fault. If she'd never agreed to see Colin she wouldn't be in this position now. But, dear God! She'd had no hope of ever seeing Liam again, let alone him coming to her apartment. To think he'd driven all this way just to believe she was no better than that woman he'd been engaged to.

Of course he didn't know she knew anything about his broken engagement. However, since coming home, Rosa had combed the internet for anything she could find about him.

There was pathetically little, in spite of his success. But then, he'd said that he shunned publicity. In one interview she'd read, he claimed he let his books speak for themselves. He also maintained that authors weren't necessarily interesting people just because they had the ability to tell a good tale.

There was little about the attack that had caused his injuries either. Rosa guessed Liam's attitude had forced the press to back off. Besides, the man who'd done it had killed himself after believing he'd killed his victim. There'd been no prolonged investigation, no infamous court case. Liam had spent several weeks secluded from the public in hospital, and then returned to his penthouse apartment with a security firm to guard his privacy until he'd recovered.

His girlfriend had abandoned him publicly after he'd left the hospital, but Rosa wondered if she'd really waited that long. According to the reports, she'd left him for a South American playboy who rode polo ponies for a living. She'd professed herself heartbroken for hurting Liam, but said she loved Raimondo. It had been love at first sight and there was nothing she could do to change it.

That had made the headlines. One of the many articles made much of the fact that beautiful model Kayla Stevens had soon been seen on the arm of her new lover, Raimondo Baja.

Miss Stevens used to be the girlfriend of hot new author Liam Jameson, who recently suffered a near-fatal attack from a crazed fan. Jameson, whose first book, Hunting the Vampire, has just been optioned by Morelli Studios for a slated seven-figure sum, wasn't available for comment. But his agent, Dan Arnold, says Mr Jameson wishes the couple every happiness for the future.

I bet he did, Rosa had thought cynically, when she'd read it, but now all she could think about was that she'd let him down again. What twisted truth had he thought he'd gained from Colin's lies about her? What had he heard that had convinced him she couldn't be trusted either?

Scrubbing the tears from her cheeks, Rosa got to her feet. She shouldn't sit here feeling sorry for herself. She should do something about it. But what could she do, short of getting dressed and going looking for him? And that would surely be a wasted effort. She had no idea where he might go—except as far away from her as possible, she appended bitterly.

She didn't know where he might spend the night. She didn't even have the castle's phone number. And there was no way she could desert her responsibilities and go looking for him. She was due in school again tomorrow, at eight-thirty sharp.

Leaving the living room, she went through to the bedroom, looking about the room that had been such a heavenly haven an hour ago and now looked as abandoned as she felt. She stood in the doorway, blinking back another bout of tears, and then went into the room and flung herself on the bed.

Burying her face in the pillow, she could still detect his scent, a mixture of some citrusy fragrance and the clean male scent of his body. And something else: the disturbing aroma of sex.

How was she going to get over this? She felt as if she'd been hollowed out inside so that she was totally bare, totally bereft.

She didn't need to pretend any more, she thought. She was in love with him. In love with Liam. And how futile was that?

And then a name crept into her mind. Dan, she recalled, pushing herself up from the pillows with a feeling of excitement. Dan Arnold. Yes, that was it. Dan Arnold. Liam's agent. Surely he would know Liam's phone number? And, although she didn't hold out any hope of him giving it to her, he might be prepared to give Liam a message from her.

Flinging back the covers, she thrust her feet to the floor and stood up, only to groan in pain as her toes encountered something hard and unyielding beneath the sheet. Wincing, she pulled the sheet aside, prepared to see one of the shoes she'd discarded earlier. But it wasn't a shoe. It was a mobile phone.

Feeling peeved, Rosa bent to pick up the offending article with impatient fingers. 'Damn thing,' she muttered to herself, taking a moment to massage her bruised toes. What the devil was her phone doing on the floor in here?

And then she realised it wasn't her phone at all. Goodness, she was so stupid! This had to be Liam's phone. *Liam's.* It must have fallen out of his pocket when he'd tossed his jacket on the floor. Evidently his lack of contact on the island didn't prevent him from carrying a cellphone on the mainland.

'Oh, my God,' she whispered, sinking down onto the side of the bed again. He probably used this phone to ring his agent and his publisher and anyone else he needed to get in touch with when he was travelling. In her hands, she probably held the means to solve her problem. Was it really going to be that easy?

The phone had been turned off, she saw, and now, taking a breath, she turned it on. Immediately a screensaver of the castle appeared, before clearing again to reveal the fact that Liam had three messages.

Three messages! Rosa wet her suddenly dry lips. Dared she access them? Dared she take the chance that one of them might be from Dan Arnold?

Yes!

Dialling the required number, she waited in anticipation for the first recorded message to be replayed. 'Liam?' she heard an unfamiliar woman's voice say. 'Where the hell are you? I thought you told me you'd be checking into the Moriarty at about half-past seven. It's past eight o'clock now, and I've been sitting in your suite for the past hour. Give me a ring when you get this, there's a sweetie. You know I worry about you.'

Rosa cancelled the call at that point. Now she was the one who felt stupid. She'd thought Liam had come to see *her*, when in fact she'd evidently just been an afterthought. He must have decided to call in on her on his way to London to meet this other woman. And whether she was his mother, his sister, or his girlfriend—she shuddered—she'd totally misunderstood his reasons for coming to Ripon.

Not caring if she broke it or not, Rosa flung the phone across the room and, getting off the bed, started stripping the covers from it. She wanted no trace of Liam Jameson left in this apartment, she told herself savagely.

Only when the bed was remade with clean sheets did she again give way to the scalding tears that had never been far away...

CHAPTER THIRTEEN

'WELL, I THINK you're crazy!'

Lucy Fielding turned from making her brother a cup of coffee in the state-of-the-art kitchen of the suite, and gave him an impatient look.

'You're entitled to your opinion, of course,' said Liam tightly, giving in to the temptation to lift his aching leg onto the sofa beside him. He glanced behind him. 'Isn't that coffee ready yet?'

Lucy pursed her lips, but she obediently poured a mug of dark Americano from the jug and carried it across to him. 'There you are.'

'Thanks.' Although Liam's system was already buzzing with the amount of caffeine he'd consumed in the last few hours, he made a play of taking a hungry mouthful from the mug Lucy had given him. 'Yeah, that's good.'

Lucy acknowledged his thanks with a careless shrug of her shoulders, and then came to sit on the opposite end of the sofa so that he was forced to face her. 'Not that I consider coffee an adequate substitute for breakfast,' she added reprovingly. 'But it's such a relief to see you I'm prepared to be generous.'

'Gee, thanks.' Liam looked at her from beneath his lashes. 'Sorry you had to wait so long.'

'So you should be.' Lucy shook her head. 'You know when you rang I was considering phoning the police and asking if there'd been an accident on the motorway.'

'Yeah, well, I explained about that, didn't I?' said Liam ruefully. He'd realised he'd lost his mobile phone just after he'd got onto the M1. 'I had to wait until I reached a service area before I could call.'

'Okay.' Lucy inclined her head. 'And I was so relieved to hear from you I'd have forgiven you anything then.'

'What, and you've changed your mind now?' suggested her brother mildly. 'Well, tough.'

'I didn't say that.' Lucy sighed. 'As Mike's away until Friday, I'd planned on spending the night in town.' She paused. 'So, tell me again: you say you took a detour to see some woman you met in August and her husband turned up—is that right?'

Liam's expression darkened. 'I don't want to talk about it.'

'I think you should.' Lucy regarded him closely. 'What's going on, Lee? There's more to this than what you've told me. How did you meet her, anyway? I thought you didn't take women to Kilfoil.'

'I don't.'

'So what was she doing there?'

Liam expelled a weary breath. 'Looking for her sister.'

'On the island? Or at the castle?'

'Both,' said Liam flatly, wishing he hadn't asked for the coffee now. It was too hot to swallow in one gulp, and politeness forbade him from just leaving it after Lucy had taken the trouble to make it. 'Forget it, Lucy, please.'

Lucy's lips tightened. 'I can't,' she told him shortly. 'You forget, I was around when Kayla walked out on you, and I don't like the idea that some other woman has been playing you for a fool.'

Liam groaned. 'Rosa's not like that,' he said wearily, tipping his head back against the cushions.

'So what *is* she like?'

'Tall, slim, red-haired.'

Lucy snorted. 'That's not what I meant and you know it, Lee. What's she like really? Is she like Kayla?'

'She's nothing like Kayla,' he said forcefully, looking at her again. 'I wouldn't insult her by using her name in the same breath as Kayla Stevens.'

'Kayla *Baja*,' Lucy corrected him drily. 'Who, by the way, is back in London. I've heard that she and Raimondo have split, and she's been telling anyone who'll listen to her that you're the only man she's ever loved.'

Liam gave her an incredulous look. 'You're kidding?'

Lucy shook her head. 'No, I'm serious. She cornered me in Harrods the other day and asked me if I'd seen you recently.' She smiled. 'Naturally I let her think we were seldom out of one another's pockets. I didn't think it was wise to tell her that we only see you a couple of times a year.'

Liam pulled a face. 'You know where I live.'

'But you're not exactly accessible, are you?' Lucy protested. 'And you hardly come down to London anymore.'

Liam sighed. 'I'm a writer, Lucy. I do work, you know.'

'I know.' Lucy hesitated. 'And Kayla?'

'Kayla can go—screw herself,' said Liam, moderating his language for his sister's sake. 'I don't care if I never see her again.'

And it was true, he thought incredulously. For so long

he'd avoided talking about Kayla, even thinking about Kayla, but suddenly he didn't care what anyone said. Whatever hold Kayla had had over him was gone. He could think of her now without either pain or regret. He shook his head at the feeling of freedom it gave him.

'I'm pleased to hear it,' remarked Lucy, her smile appearing. 'Obviously Rosa—what is it you said she was called? Channing? No, Chantry. Yeah, Rosa Chantry— obviously she must have something none of the others have had.'

Depression descended abruptly. 'Leave it, Lucy.'

'How can I leave it?' She stared at him frustratedly. 'Didn't she tell you she was married?'

'She's not married,' muttered Liam reluctantly. 'Or at least I don't think she is.'

'What?' Lucy blinked. 'But you said—'

However, Liam had had enough. Thrusting his half-empty mug of coffee onto the low table in front of him, he got heavily to his feet. 'I need a shower,' he said grimly, cutting her off with a sweeping movement of his hand across his throat. 'Then I want to speak to Dan before I go and see Aaron Pargeter. You're welcome to stay here, if you want to. But don't expect me to entertain you today.'

'So what's new?' said Lucy in a cool voice. 'But I might stay another night, if that's okay with you. You still owe me dinner.'

Liam regarded her with an expression that mingled affection with irritation. 'Okay,' he said, in an entirely different tone. 'Dinner tonight it is. So long as you promise not to tell me how to run my life.'

Lucy's face cleared. 'Bastard,' she said succinctly, and Liam was smiling when he left the room.

* * *

The next couple of days were bloody.

Rosa wasn't sleeping well, and although her mother had called a couple of times, asking her to go round for a meal, Rosa didn't think she could be civil to Sophie in her present frame of mind.

Her sister had abandoned her course at university about a month after the start of the autumn semester. It was too dull, too boring, she'd told Rosa and her mother. It wasn't what she'd expected, she said, and she was presently filling in at an advertising agency in Harrogate, who apparently considered her appearance more than compensation for her lack of experience.

Rosa had to admit the job suited her. Occupying the reception desk, she was the perfect image the agency wanted to promote. And, although Sophie would probably get bored with that, too, in time, for the moment she was content.

Nevertheless, that didn't make Rosa any more enthusiastic about spending an evening listening to her boast about how important her job was. Particularly as every time she saw Sophie she couldn't help thinking about Liam and what she'd lost. It had been bad enough before, but it was much worse now. She didn't even want to think about what had happened—or admit, if only to herself, that she'd known all along it couldn't last.

Wasn't that what she'd told him, for heaven's sake? Wasn't it she who'd promised him she expected no commitment from him? Maybe she was just kidding herself by thinking it was what he'd heard Colin say that had driven him away. Maybe all he'd wanted was a one-night-stand, a little diversion on his way to London.

She didn't know where the other woman came in, of course. All she could think was that she must be very tolerant if she didn't object to him indulging in a quickie on his way to meet her. Anyway, at least the woman had given her an address to send the phone to. Despite its being slightly chipped, she'd mailed the phone to Liam via the Moriarty Hotel the following day.

It didn't help that when she came out of school on Friday evening she found Colin Vincent waiting for her. He was standing beside her car, and judging by his pinched expression he'd been waiting in the cold for some time.

'What do you want?' Rosa asked, not in the mood to be charitable. She felt tired—drained, actually—and was looking forward to the weekend and a chance to catch up on her sleep.

'You're not very friendly,' said Colin resentfully, as she tossed the bags containing the work she would have to do at home onto the back seat. 'I thought you might have cooled off by now.'

'Cooled off?' Rosa stared at him.

'Calmed down, then,' amended Colin impatiently. 'Look, can we go somewhere to talk?'

Rosa gasped. 'We don't have anything to talk about, Colin,' she said. 'I thought I made my position perfectly clear. I don't want to see you again.'

Colin's jaw jutted. 'But you don't mean that.'

'Don't I?'

'No.' He was obviously searching for the right words. 'Look—I know who that bloke was, okay? The one who ran out on you. Sophie told me.'

'Sophie?' Rosa was stunned.

'Yeah.' Colin shifted a little uneasily. 'I mean, after you threw me out the other night I knew there had to be some explanation. So earlier on today I gave Sophie a ring.'

Rosa stared at him. 'You know where she works?'

'Oh, sure.' Colin grimaced. 'One of the guys at the garage told me. Terry Hadley. Do you remember him? He works in—'

'I don't give a damn where some *guy at the garage* works,' Rosa interrupted him angrily. 'But I would like to know how he knows Sophie.'

Colin looked down at his feet. 'Well, she's been seeing him, hasn't she?'

'*Seeing* him?'

'Going out with him, then,' muttered Colin tersely. 'For heaven's sake, Rosa, don't you know anything?'

'Obviously not.' Rosa shook her head. The last she'd heard, Sophie was still involved with Mark Campion. 'How long has this been going on?'

Colin looked sulky now. 'Does it matter? Since she got back from university, I suppose. She's big girl, Rosa. She doesn't need your permission.'

'No.'

Rosa's lips tightened, but she said nothing more, simply pulled open her door and slid into the driving seat.

'Hey!' Colin caught the door when she would have closed it. 'What about me?'

'What about you?'

'Come on, Rosa. When am I going to see you again?'

Rosa started the car. 'Never, I hope.'

'I don't believe you.' Colin refused to let go of the door. 'I mean, come on. This guy you met in Scotland—Liam Jameson—you don't seriously expect to see him again?'

'No.' It hurt, but Rosa had to be honest. With herself as much as him.

'There you are, then. Hell,' he snorted, 'the guy's a bloody millionaire! I dare say he could have any woman he wanted. You're attractive, Rosa, I know that, but you're not in the same league as the women he mixes with. Have you ever seen a picture of that model he was engaged to?' He rolled his eyes. 'She is one hot cookie!'

'Oh, go away, Colin,' said Rosa wearily, amazed that his words should upset her as much as they did. He was like a petulant child, she thought, and he was almost thirty-seven. 'I've told you. I don't want to see you again. What more do you want me to say?'

'Yeah, what more do you want her to say, Colin?' asked a low, harsh voice she'd never expected to hear again. 'Get lost, why don't you? While you still can.'

Rosa turned off the engine and sprang disbelievingly out of the car. But before she could speak, Colin muscled forward.

'Who the hell do you think you're talking to?' he demanded, his face turning an unpleasant shade of red. 'This is a private conversation. Why don't you get lost before I stick my fist in your face?'

'In your dreams,' said Liam mildly, his eyes moving briefly to Rosa before returning to the other man. 'On your way, Colin. I'm afraid I don't know your surname, but I guess I can live with that.'

Rosa was horrified. She knew only too well that Colin had an ugly temper. And, looking at Liam, leaning casually against the rear door of the small saloon, she could only think how vulnerable he was.

But that didn't stop her from drinking in the sight of him like a dying woman in the desert. He was wearing his long overcoat again, open now, to allow him to tuck his fingers under his arms. His feet were crossed at the ankle, and in spite of the anxiety she was feeling he looked the picture of complacency. Too complacent to be facing a man who was used to using his fists to get his way.

Colin seemed not to know how to take Liam. But his attitude had turned truculent and he moved aggressively towards the other man. 'Who do you think you are, talking to me like that?' he snarled. 'I'll go when I feel like it, and not before.'

'Your call,' said Liam carelessly, his green eyes moving back to Rosa with seeming indifference to any threat Colin posed. 'Hi,' he said, addressing her for the first time, and all Rosa's insides turned fluid. 'You look tired,' he added huskily. 'Has this joker been getting you down?'

Rosa's lips parted, but before she could speak Colin lunged forward and grabbed the lapels of the other man's coat. 'Who are you calling a joker?' he growled, pushing his face into Liam's, using every move, every gesture, to intimidate. 'Come on, talk to me, Mr Big-Time! You're not so mouthy now, are you?'

'Colin—'

'You think?' Rosa's cry of protest went unheard as Liam turned his gaze back to Colin's, with no trace of fear in the mocking smile he gave him. 'We're not all morons, you low-life. We don't all have to threaten violence to prove our masculinity.'

Rosa groaned. Liam was being deliberately provoking, and she knew exactly what her ex-husband would do.

'Why, you—'

Colin's arm drew back, but before he could deliver the punch he obviously intended, Liam's fist connected with his midriff. Rosa heard the sickening sound of bone against yielding flesh, and then Colin had to let go of Liam's coat to bend double, gasping for breath.

'You—you bastard,' he choked, when he could speak again, but Liam looked unperturbed.

'I've been called worse,' he remarked, straightening away from the car. 'Do you want to try again?'

'God, no!' Rosa cried, putting herself between them. 'This is a school, for heaven's sake. What kind of an example are you setting the kids?'

'The kids are long gone,' said Liam flatly, turning to her. 'Or are you saying you feel sorry for this—?'

He refrained from using the word that trembled on his tongue, but Rosa quickly shook her head. 'You know I'm not,' she exclaimed, her tongue running helplessly over her dry lips. 'But—but what are you doing here? I sent your phone to the hotel. Didn't you get it?'

'Screw the phone,' said Liam, putting his arm across her shoulders and pulling her towards him. 'Come here,' he muttered thickly, and, uncaring that Colin was staring at them now, with bitter, impotent eyes, he kissed her.

'For God's sake, Rosa,' Colin exclaimed angrily, but she hardly heard him.

'Get lost, Colin,' she whispered dreamily, when Liam lifted his head. 'Can't you see you're wasting your time here?'

Colin glared at her. 'You'll regret this, Rosa.'

'Oh, I hope not,' said Liam, walking her round the car and putting her into the passenger seat before taking his own seat behind the wheel. He looked up at the other man. 'Why don't you go and cry on Sophie's shoulder? She sounds just your—bag, hmm?'

Colin hadn't expected that, and he turned scandalised eyes in Rosa's direction 'Did you hear that?' he demanded, grabbing the door again. 'Rosa, did you hear what he called your sister?'

Rosa looked up at him. 'I think he was talking about you, Colin,' she said with a giggle as Liam gave an uncontrollable snort of laughter. 'Bye.'

Yet, despite what had happened, they were both oddly quiet as Liam drove the small car off the school's premises. It was as if Colin had provided a conduit between them, and now that he was gone neither of them could think of what to say.

Liam broke the silence. 'Which way?' he asked. They'd reached the main road, which was busy at this hour of the afternoon. 'I haven't got the first idea of how to get to your place from here.'

Rosa glanced at him. 'Don't you remember?' she asked tentatively, and Liam grimaced.

'If you mean the other night, I walked from the market square,' he told her, taking his chance and turning into the stream of traffic. 'So—this way, right?'

'Right,' she agreed, wishing she'd known he'd had no transport on Tuesday evening. Maybe if she'd got dressed straight away and gone after him, she could have—

Could have what? she wondered, arresting the thought almost as soon as it was formed. Just because he was here it didn't mean he hadn't lied to her in the past. He'd let her think he'd come all the way from Kilfoil to see her, when in fact he'd been on his way to London to see someone else. Another woman. How did she know he wasn't on his way to Scotland now, and had decided to call in for another quickie on the way back?

'What's wrong?'

Liam had sensed her sudden withdrawal, the moment when her mood had changed from being pleased to see him to one of wary distrust. In the excitement of seeing him again she'd obviously forgotten how they'd parted. What was she thinking at this moment? he wondered. That they'd been together before and he'd let her down?

'What are you doing here?' she asked at that moment, her gaze fixed on the lights of the cars ahead of them. 'And where's your car? Don't tell me you've left it in the market place again?'

'I didn't use a car,' Liam told her, trying to keep his mind on his driving. 'My pilot has a pal who owns a farm near Ripley. He dropped me off there, and his pal ferried me into town.'

Rosa couldn't help turning to stare at him then. 'Are we talking about your helicopter?' At Liam's nod, she went on, 'I thought you preferred your car.'

'I do, usually,' he conceded. 'But this way was easier and quicker. I've got to go back to London again tomorrow.'

Rosa swallowed her chagrin. 'Tomorrow,' she echoed blankly. And then, because she couldn't help herself, 'I don't know why you bothered coming here at all.'

Liam swore under his breath. This wasn't the sort of conversation he wanted to have when he was in control of an automobile. Dammit, it was a lethal weapon, and he had hoped they could get back to her place before starting a post mortem on his shortcomings. He knew he'd let her down. He'd let himself down. And he only had a limited number of hours to convince her he wouldn't do it again.

'You know why I came,' he said between his teeth. 'Haven't I proved it?'

'How?' Rosa was scornful. 'By punching Colin before he could punch you?'

'I won't dignify that with an answer,' he retorted, reaching another junction and glancing frustratedly up and down the busy road. 'Which way?' he asked again, and Rosa told him. 'Just save it, will you?' he added, as he took a chance and had a horn blown at him for his pains. He raised a finger in salute and put his foot on the accelerator. 'This is awfully bad for my image. I'm usually such a considerate driver.'

'Why do I find that hard to believe?' she asked provokingly, but Liam had got over his spurt of anger.

'Because you don't know me very well yet,' he said, taking one hand off the wheel to lay it on her thigh. And although she flinched away, he gripped the firm flesh above her knee with hard fingers. 'Don't worry,' he added huskily. 'You soon will.'

'Like the woman who was waiting for you at your hotel in London?' exclaimed Rosa painfully, and Liam was obliged to take his eyes off the road to give her a searing look.

'How do you—? Rosa, that was my sister,' he muttered incredulously. 'Surely you didn't think—?' He broke off again, forced to turn his attention back to the road. He gripped the wheel like a lifeline, and she saw his knuckles whiten in the light from the dash. 'Lucy is my sister,' he said again, harshly. 'Don't say another word until we get to your apartment.'

CHAPTER FOURTEEN

LIAM HAD TO PARK the car farther down Richmond Road, there being no vacant space in front of number 24. While he was getting out and locking the vehicle, Rosa hurried back to her gate.

She'd already opened the door and run up the stairs to her apartment before she heard Liam slogging up the stairs behind her. Obviously he was still having trouble with his leg, and it was an effort not to turn and offer him her help.

He wouldn't have wanted it, she assured herself, switching on the lights and turning up the thermostat on the wall. But all the time she was accomplishing these mundane tasks, the words *my sister* kept buzzing around in her head. Was that really who she'd heard? His sister? She wanted to believe it, she really did, but could she bear it if he was lying and hurt her again?

Liam entered the apartment with some relief, allowing the door to swing closed behind him and sagging back against it. Then, when he caught Rosa watching him from the kitchen doorway, he said, with an attempt at self-mockery, 'Getting old, hmm?'

Rosa pressed her lips together, but although she looked as if she didn't believe him, she didn't contradict him.

Instead, she slipped her leather coat off her shoulders and said stiffly, 'Why don't you sit down?'

'Yeah, why don't I?' he agreed, limping to the sofa and dropping down gratefully onto it. He looked up at her enquiringly, 'Why don't you join me?'

Rosa hesitated, but then she shook her head. 'Wouldn't you like a drink?' she asked, in that same unnatural voice. 'You must be cold.'

'Believe me, cold is something I'm not,' he assured her flatly. 'Come on, Rosa. Come and sit down. You know you want to.'

'Do I?'

For a moment her temper flared, and Liam's eyes darkened with sudden impatience. 'If the way you kissed me earlier is anything to go by, then I'd say yes,' he said harshly. 'Look, I know you're suspicious of me. Well, I don't blame you after the way I've behaved. But we're not going to resolve anything if you persist in behaving like an outraged virgin!'

Rosa was indignant. 'Is that supposed to make me want to forgive you?' she asked scornfully. 'Because I have to tell you, it's not working.'

'Oh, Rosa!' Liam sighed. 'Don't make me have to come after you.'

Still she didn't move. 'It's not my fault if your leg's painful,' she retorted unsympathetically, and Liam wanted to grab her and make her admit that she was just as glad to see him as he was to see her.

Instead, he said, 'It is, actually.'

Rosa gasped. 'I didn't ask you to drive from one end of the country to the other.'

'No.' Liam conceded the point. 'But that's not why I've had to check in to the clinic in London again.'

Rosa stared at him now. 'What?'

'I said—'

'I know what you said.' She took a couple of tentative steps towards the sofa. 'What clinic? What are you talking about?'

Liam sighed, closing his eyes for a moment. 'Do we have to talk about this now?'

'Yes.' Rosa nodded. 'Tell me.'

Liam opened his eyes again. 'Come and sit down, then.'

'Not until tell me what you mean. About it being my fault.'

'Oh, God!' Liam groaned. 'Well, I guess, strictly speaking, it was my own fault that I got caught in the storm.'

Rosa frowned. 'You mean, before I left the island?'

'Yeah.' Liam patted the seat beside him. 'Come on, Rosa. I promise I won't touch you if you don't want me to.'

Rosa stayed where she was. 'Tell me about the clinic first,' she said. 'What kind of clinic is it?'

Liam shrugged. 'The kind that deals with people who've been physically disabled in some way.' He paused, and when she still made no move to join him, he went on, 'When I was—attacked…' He paused again, and then added wearily, 'Do you know about that?'

'Only that some crazy guy tried to kill you.'

'Well, that about sums it up, actually.' Liam gave a short, mirthless laugh. 'This guy—his name was Craig Kennedy, by the way—he apparently confused me with one of my characters—'

'Luther Killian?' Rosa looked surprised.

'No. Not Killian. A rogue vampire called Jonas Wilder, who'd made a lot of money out of horror fiction.' He pulled a wry face. 'I guess you get the connection.'

'And he thought you were this Jonas Wilder?'

'In the flesh,' agreed Liam drily. 'The anti-Christ personified.' But, although he was trying to make light of it, Rosa could see the dark shadows that still lingered in his eyes when he spoke of it. 'Happily, he was less successful at achieving his ends than Luther.'

'Oh, Liam.' Rosa came towards him now, dropping down onto the sofa beside him and taking one of his hands in both of hers. 'You must have been terrified!'

Liam grimaced. 'I guess I was too shocked at the time to feel anything but disbelief. The medics said I must have put up a fight because of the defensive injuries I sustained. I remember him lashing out at me, screaming that he was going to rid the world of another monster.' He forced a smile. 'Ironically, he was using a steel blade. Any vampire freak could have told him that you need a wooden stake, driven through the heart, to destroy a vampire.'

Rosa caught her breath. 'That's not funny.'

'Hey, I know that.' Liam regarded her with rueful eyes. 'I'm no hero, Rosa. I had pretty horrific nightmares for— well, for months after it happened.'

'Oh, Liam!' She lifted his hand and pressed her lips to his knuckles, and he saw the tears glistening in her eyes. 'It must have been awful.'

Liam gave a concessionary nod, but he withdrew his hand from hers. 'It wasn't good,' he agreed. 'But I don't want your pity.'

'It's not pity,' she protested, staring at him. 'I just don't know what to say, that's all.'

Liam took a deep breath. 'You could say you're pleased to see me,' he remarked after a moment, and Rosa's shoulders rounded in defeat.

'You know I am,' she said huskily. 'But—but when I thought you'd just called here on your way to London to see another woman—'

'I was on my way to the clinic, actually.' Liam sighed. 'I didn't tell you because it's not something I'm particularly proud of.'

Rosa supposed she could understand that, although as far as she was concerned he had nothing to be ashamed of. 'And did you?' she asked instead. 'Check yourself into the clinic?'

'Yesterday,' he agreed. 'Then I checked myself out again this morning and flew up here. But I have to go back.'

'Oh!' Rosa nodded. 'That's what you meant when you said you had to go back to London tomorrow.'

'Yeah.' Liam considered her pale face. 'Do you believe me?'

'Of course.'

'There's no "of course" about it,' retorted Liam. 'A little while ago you were accusing me of going to London to see another woman.' He frowned. 'How did you get to speak to Lucy anyway? She never said she'd had a call from you.'

Rosa gasped. 'Does she know about me?'

'Oh, yes.'

'You told her?'

'She wheedled it out of me,' said Liam drily. 'My sister is nothing if not determined.'

'Gosh!' Rosa's cheeks turned pink.

'*Gosh?*' Liam gazed at her disbelievingly. 'My God, I've never heard anybody actually use that expression before. Do you say "goodness" and "oh, bother," too?'

Rosa stared at him for a moment, as if she didn't know

how to take him, and then she realised he was just teasing her. 'Oh, you!' she exclaimed, punching his arm but without any real desire to hurt him, and Liam caught her hand and pulled her against him.

'That's better,' he said, his voice thickening with satisfaction. Then his mouth found hers, and for a long time he didn't say anything at all.

His kiss was hot and hungry, showing her in so many ways that only her recalcitrance and his self-restraint had kept them apart this long. He seemed starved for her, his hand sliding into her hair, angling her face to make it easier for him to deepen and lengthen what had become a wholly carnal possession. The erotic slide of his tongue against hers caused her to tremble uncontrollably, and she fumbled her arms around his neck and clutched a handful of his hair.

'This was worth coming back for,' Liam groaned, shifting to accommodate the sudden bulge between his legs. He sucked on her lower lip, biting her and tasting her, drawing the tip of her tongue between his teeth. 'And I was afraid you'd never want to see me again.'

'You didn't really think that,' whispered Rosa, tugging his ears reprovingly. 'Or you wouldn't be here.'

'No.' He conceded the point, and she thought he never looked more attractive than when he was pretending to be chastened. 'Still, you can probably thank Lucy for part of that.'

'Lucy?' Rosa drew back to rest her forehead against his. 'Your sister?'

'For her sins.' He nodded. 'It was she who helped persuade me that I was behaving like an idiot.'

Rosa's eyes widened. 'How did she do that?'

'The way she usually does things,' said Liam wryly. 'She keeps on and on about something until you're compelled to tell her what she wants to know if only to shut her up.'

'And she wanted to know about me?'

Liam gave her a measured look. 'As if you didn't know.'

Rosa dimpled. 'Go on. I want to hear what she had to say.'

'Yeah, well—' Liam pulled back now, cradling her face between his palms. 'Before I tell you, perhaps you'd like to explain how you found out about Lucy?'

'Oh…' Rosa sighed. 'Can't you guess?'

'Humour me.'

'All right. All right.' She sighed again. 'If you insist on having your pound of flesh, I listened to the message she'd left on your phone.'

'Ah.' Liam's lips twitched. 'That wouldn't have anything to do with the fact that when I got the phone back it was chipped in several places?'

Rosa gave him a defiant look. 'You noticed?'

'Oh, yeah.' Liam's thumbs stroked across her cheekbones, a sensuous caress that caused a shiver of helpless anticipation to slide down her spine. 'Lucy pointed it out to me.'

'And I suppose you both had a good laugh about it?' said Rosa accusingly, but Liam shook his head.

'No.' His jade eyes darkened. 'It gave me the courage to come back here and find out if you were just bugged because I ran out on you or because of something else.'

Rosa shrugged. 'Like what?'

'Like—well, having listened to Lucy's message myself, I had to admit it could be—misconstrued.'

Rosa swallowed. 'So now you know why I thought you were going to meet another woman?'

'Yeah, I know.'

'And I suppose you think it was lucky that Colin was there this afternoon when you came to meet me.'

Liam gave her a strange look. 'I wouldn't put it quite like that.'

'No, but it saved you having to ask me if I was still seeing him,' Rosa declared tremulously. 'I mean, when you walked out of the apartment you obviously thought I'd been lying—'

'Don't!' Liam moved one hand to cover her mouth, preventing her from going on. 'Don't, baby,' he said again, his eyes full of compassion. 'I don't need you to tell me what a fool I've been. God, I've been regretting not giving you a chance to explain what was going on ever since I left.' He paused, removing his hand and briefly replacing it with his lips before continuing, 'But try and understand, if you can. I know my faults, better than anyone. I know I'll never win any beauty competitions. And I dare say you heard that the girl I was engaged to when I was attacked walked out on me when she discovered that, as well as looking like a monster, I might not be able to function as a man anymore.'

Rosa gasped. 'You *don't* look like a monster. And—and you can—you know—'

She broke off and Liam grinned. 'Oh, yeah,' he said humorously. 'You know I'm not impotent. But as for the rest—'

'Liam, you're the only one who sees your injuries as anything more than a few fading scars,' Rosa protested huskily. She lifted a finger and tapped his temple. 'They've gone from your body, but you're still keeping them in here.' She leaned towards him and kissed his forehead. 'You've got to let them go. They don't matter, believe me. Not to me. Not to any woman worth her salt.'

'Well, as you're the only woman I care about, I suppose I'll have to believe you,' he murmured, nuzzling her neck. 'But, if I'm honest, I'll admit I *was* glad to see your ex again.'

Rosa frowned. 'You were?'

'Yeah.' Liam's grin deepened. 'If you must know, I've been itching to smack that bastard ever since he came to the apartment. Still,' he added smugly, 'I think he got the message.'

Rosa felt a smile lurking at the corner of her own lips. 'He got the message,' she confirmed. 'And there was I, worried sick that he might hurt you.'

'Hey, after I was on my feet again, I attended a course on self-defence,' said Liam comfortingly. 'Hopefully, I'll never have to face another maniac with a knife, but, compared to Craig Kennedy, Colin was a piece of cake.'

'So I noticed.' Rosa slipped her arms around his neck again. 'Now, are you going to take off your coat?'

'I will if you will,' he replied teasingly, his fingers slipping beneath the hem of the sweater she'd worn to school. Then he groaned. 'I should have known it wasn't going to be that simple.'

'What do you mean?'

Liam shucked his overcoat and jacket off his shoulders. 'See—I'm just wearing a shirt.' He grimaced. 'I don't know how many layers you're wearing.'

'As it happens, it's cold in the classroom,' said Rosa indignantly. 'And I'm only wearing a vest under my blouse.'

'Only!' Liam was mocking. 'So—take them off.'

Rosa drew a shaky breath. 'Now?' She glanced towards the door. 'Don't you want to go into the bedroom?'

'Not particularly.' Liam's eyes were dark and undeniably sexy. 'I think we should christen the sofa instead.'

Rosa's breathing quickened. 'You shouldn't say things like that,' she exclaimed reprovingly. 'What if someone comes?'

Liam arched dark brows. 'Are you expecting anyone?'

'N-o.'

'All right.'

Rosa's tongue circled dry lips. She could do this, she told herself. Even though she'd never done a striptease for any man, least of all Colin. Her ex-husband had always behaved as if sex was something you did in bed and nowhere else, and she wondered now whether that had been his fault or hers.

Her fingers went to the hem of her sweater and, taking a deep breath, she hauled it over her head. Her hair was probably all over the place now, she thought, but, refusing to worry about it, she started on the buttons of her blouse.

However, she was all thumbs, and after watching her struggling for several tense seconds Liam brushed her hands aside and tackled the job himself.

But the buttons proved just as resistant to his efforts as they'd done to hers, and after a moment Liam gave up. Taking hold of the neckline, he simply tore it open. 'That's better.'

Rosa blinked at him. 'You didn't have to destroy it.'

'I'll buy you another,' he said carelessly. 'Something equally as unflattering, if that's what you want.'

Rosa bit her lip. 'You're too impatient.'

'I'm getting there,' he agreed mildly. He fingered the hem of her vest. 'Does this have buttons, too?'

'You know it doesn't.' Rosa was finding it increasingly difficult to breathe at all. Pulling the vest over her head, she cast it and the blouse aside. 'Satisfied?'

'By no means,' he murmured wryly. Then, flicking the

elasticated strap of her bra, he added. 'You didn't say anything about this.'

Rosa trembled. 'I'm sure you know how to take one of these off.'

'I'm sure I do, too, but I want you to do it.' His eyes caressed her. 'Please.'

Rosa shook her head, but her hands went obediently behind her back to release the catch. When the loosened straps tipped off her shoulders Liam completed the job by pulling them off her arms.

'Beautiful,' he said, just looking at her, and Rosa forgot all about being self-conscious in the sensual warmth of his eyes.

He put out his hands and gripped her bare midriff, but although her nipples were aching for him to touch them, he only allowed his thumbs to brush the undersides of her breasts.

His hands were faintly rough and unfamiliar, but their abrasion against her soft flesh caused a gnawing hunger down deep in her belly. She wanted him to touch her every-where, most particularly between her legs, and the waiting was becoming as intolerable to her as it had been to him.

With unsteady fingers she sought the buttons on his shirt, and he let her. Having more success with his larger buttons, she soon achieved her objective, and when she pushed the shirt off his shoulders he didn't try to stop her.

The only reaction she noticed was the sudden tenting of his pants as her fingers touched the hair that grew down the middle of his chest. And when he saw where she was looking he uttered a rueful groan.

'Yeah, yeah, now I'm impatient,' he said, giving in to the urge to lift her breasts with his hands. The swollen tips pushed provocatively against his palms and, unable to stop himself, he bent and took one into this mouth.

But it wasn't enough for either of them, and Liam's fingers fumbled with the button at the waist of her trousers.

'I'll do it,' she said breathlessly, and while she pushed her trousers and her panties down her legs, Liam did the same.

For the first time, Rosa had the opportunity to see the scar that began low on his stomach and arrowed down the inner part of his thigh.

He saw her looking, but he didn't try to cover himself. 'Ugly, isn't it?' he said roughly, half expecting to see revulsion in her face even now.

But all Rosa did was bend her head and bestow a line of kisses from the harsh gash that marked the top of the wound to the more sensitive place between his legs.

And by then Liam was breathing heavily. 'Enough,' he said unsteadily. 'I want to be inside you when I come, and unless you stop right now there are no guarantees.'

Rosa smiled. 'So what are you waiting for?' she asked, lying back on the sofa, one leg raised provocatively. She trailed a tempting hand down her body. 'I'm not going anywhere.'

EPILOGUE

SIX MONTHS LATER, Rosa stood at the bedroom window, gazing out at the view that never failed to enchant her. It was spring, and Kilfoil was just beginning to burgeon with colour. There were daffodils and tulips growing in the lee of the castle wall, and last night Sam had shown her the first shoots of the orchids that she'd discovered were his secret passion, growing in one of the hothouses he tended.

Standing here, watching the ocean that was today flecked with white foam, Rosa could hardly believe that she'd been married to Liam for over six weeks. Of course she'd been at Kilfoil since Christmas, except for the four weeks they'd spent in the Caribbean after they were married, but she felt as if she'd always lived here. Like Liam, she had no desire to live anywhere else. This was their home.

But it had been an unbelievable six months since he'd turned up at the school that afternoon. In the beginning, Rosa had been sure she must be dreaming. The fact that Liam loved her had seemed too good to be true.

Yet it wasn't.

Her family had been stunned when she'd first intro-

duced Liam to them. Her mother had been doubtful that
he could be serious about her elder daughter. 'Now, if it
had been Sophie,' she'd said, in her usual unthinking way,
'I wouldn't have been surprised.'

Rosa had weathered this, as she'd weathered all her
mother's unkind comments in the past, but Liam hadn't
liked to see her being hurt. 'The trouble with your mother,'
he'd said when they were alone, 'is that she doesn't realise
that although she's got two beautiful daughters, only one
of them's a real woman.'

Sophie herself had been surprisingly philosophical.
Although it was in her nature to flirt with every man she
met, she wasn't offended when Liam teased her about it.
She'd told Rosa that she thought Liam was a real dish, and
that she wished it *had* been him who'd taken her to London,
instead of that creep Jed Hastings.

The only real fly in the ointment had been Kayla
Stevens-Baja.

Liam had had to return to the Knightsbridge clinic, and
when she'd discovered he was in London, Kayla had
thrown herself on his mercy, begging him to forgive her and
telling him he was the only man she'd ever really loved.

Of course Kayla had made sure it made headlines, and
although Liam had been phoning Rosa every day, telling
her how much he missed her, she hadn't been able to help
worrying that the other woman might persuade him to go
back to her.

However, a couple of days after the headlines about
Kayla's visit to the clinic had appeared in the tabloids,
Liam had turned up in Ripon again—this time with a ring.

Their engagement had appeared in *The Times* the following day, and although Liam would have liked Rosa to

resign from her job and return to Scotland with him, he'd
agreed to wait until Christmas for her to join him.

And now...

She was drawing a tremulous breath when a drowsy
voice said, 'What are you doing?'

Turning, Rosa saw her husband was awake, too.
Propped up on his elbows, the warm quilt loose about his
lower limbs, Liam looked wonderfully tanned and
relaxed, and Rosa left the window to kneel beside him on
the bed.

'I was just admiring the view,' she said, aware that the
filmy nightgown left little to his imagination.

'Mmm.' Liam's smile was possessive. 'I know exactly
what you mean.' But he was looking at her, not towards the
windows, and she pushed him playfully back against the
pillows.

'You're impossible,' she said, straddling his supine body
so he couldn't get up again. 'But I'm just so happy to be
home I'll forgive you.'

Liam arched his dark brows. 'Didn't you enjoy our honeymoon?' he asked in a mock-wounded voice, and she
pulled a face at him.

'Our honeymoon was—heavenly,' she told him con-
tentedly. 'I loved the Caribbean. You know I did. But this
is where we live.'

Liam grinned up at her. 'You know, I didn't know real
redheads could go brown,' he murmured provocatively.
'But you've got a lovely peachy tan.'

Rosa caught her breath. 'Are you implying I'm not a real
redhead?'

'Oh, no.' Liam's eyes dropped lower. 'I know you are.
Who better?'

Rosa couldn't help herself. A faint colour touched her cheeks, and to divert him she said, 'At least I'm not the skinny creature I was when we first met.'

'No.' Liam agreed with her, his hands curving over her hips, making her intensely aware of his morning erection beneath her bottom. 'You're fattening up nicely. Mrs Wilson will be pleased.'

Rosa was horrified. 'I'm not fat, am I?' she protested, scrambling off the bed again and scurrying across to the adjoining dressing room with its long mirrored doors. 'Oh, God, I *am* getting fat!' she exclaimed, running anxious hands over her midriff. 'I've got quite a mound here.' She made a worried sound. 'I'll have to cut down on those chocolate puddings Mrs Wilson keeps tempting me with.'

Liam appeared behind her then. He was naked, and for a moment she was diverted by the muscular beauty of his body. The scars were still there, of course, but these days she hardly noticed them, and Liam himself was no longer self-conscious about being seen without clothes.

'Stop stressing,' he said, sliding his arms around her from behind and drawing her back against his still-aroused body. 'I love you just the way you are.'

Rosa shook her head. 'But I've never been fat,' she said, shivering at the sight of his hands moving over the offending curve of her stomach. He only had to touch her and she went up in flames.

'You don't think it could be something else, do you?' he suggested, his lips tracing the tender curve of her neck. He looked at her reflection in the mirror. 'I mean, you haven't been married to me before.'

Rosa caught her breath. 'What are you saying?'

'Well, we have been sleeping together for the past six

months,' he pointed out mildly. 'And, so far as I'm aware, we haven't taken any precautions.'

Rosa stared back at him. 'You think—I could be pregnant?'

Liam shrugged. 'I know you insisted that you couldn't have a baby,' he said softly, 'but I'm not convinced. My sisters have both been pregnant, and this looks awfully similar to me.'

Rosa expelled a shaken breath. Then, with tentative fingers, she explored the gentle mound below her ribcage. It did feel awfully firm to be just fat. Goodness, she thought, that was a possibility she'd never considered.

After being married to Colin for five years and never getting pregnant, she'd naturally assumed that she had been to blame.

She tried to think. How long was it since she'd had her period? She realised that she hadn't had that inconvenience for at least eight weeks. Since before she and Liam had got married, in fact. Oh, God! She trembled. Could it be true?

'You know,' went on Liam gently, 'it could have been Colin who couldn't father a child.'

Rosa turned her head to look into his eyes. 'You think?' she asked, gazing at him in wonderment, and Liam gave her a wry smile.

'Why not?' he asked smugly. 'He was no good at anything else, was he?'

A nervous giggle escaped her. 'And—if I am, how will you feel?'

'Hey, if you're happy, I'm happy,' he said huskily. 'I would have liked to have you all to myself for a little bit longer, but that's what grandparents are for, isn't it?'

'Do you think your parents will be pleased?'

Rosa had met Liam's mother and father, and his two sisters and their families, at the wedding, and she'd liked them a lot. But then, she'd thought, how could she not love the people who had made Liam the man he was?

'They'll be delighted,' he assured her firmly. 'I mean, I'm getting older all the time. The old biological clock is ticking.'

'I don't think you have anything to worry about,' said Rosa rather breathily, drawing back to admire his very prominent maleness. 'Come on, I'm getting cold here. And we have something to celebrate.'

Their son was born six and a half months later. Sean Liam Jameson was delivered—despite his father's anxiety—in the main bedroom at Kilfoil Castle, attended only by the local midwife.

Liam had made arrangements for Rosa to be airlifted by helicopter to the mainland hospital as soon as she went into labour. But unfortunately an autumn storm had stranded a group of fishermen aboard a fishing boat that was drifting without power in the North Sea. Rosa, despite a little anxiety of her own, had insisted that rescuing the fishermen was more important than taking her to the hospital. She was fit and strong and, according to the midwife, perfectly capable of delivering her child without either a doctor or a delivery suite.

And she had. The labour had been surprisingly easy, and short, and when the nurse put the baby into Liam's arms for the first time he looked absolutely stunned.

'He's so beautiful,' he said, handing her to his wife, and Rosa smiled.

'Just like his father,' she whispered, touching the baby's soft cheek, but Liam shook his head.

'You're the beautiful one,' he told her fiercely.

And, despite the fact that she was hot and tired, and soaked with sweat, Rosa knew he meant it...

A STORMY
SPANISH SUMMER

PENNY JORDAN

Penny Jordan is one of Mills & Boon's most popular authors. Sadly, Penny died from cancer on 31st December 2011, aged sixty-five. She leaves an outstanding legacy, having sold over a hundred million books around the world. She wrote a total of one hundred and eighty-seven novels for the Mills & Boon imprint, including the phenomenally successful *A Perfect Family*, *To Love*, *Honour & Betray*, *The Perfect Sinner* and *Power Play*, which hit the *Sunday Times* and *New York Times* bestseller lists. Loved for her distinctive voice, her success was in part because she continually broke boundaries and evolved her writing to keep up with readers' changing tastes. *Publishers Weekly* said about Jordan: 'Women everywhere will find pieces of themselves in Jordan's characters' and this perhaps explains her enduring appeal.

Although Penny was born in Preston, Lancashire, and spent her childhood there, she moved to Cheshire as a teenager and continued to live there for the rest of her year. Following the death of her husband she moved to the small traditional Cheshire market town on which she based her much-loved Crighton books.

Penny was a member and supporter of the Romantic Novelists' Association and the Romance Writers of America—two organisations dedicated to providing support for both published and yet-to-be published authors. Her significant contribution to women's fiction was recognised in 2011, when the Romantic Novelists' Association presented Penny with a Lifetime Achievement Award.

CHAPTER ONE

'FELICITY.'

There was no emotion in the voice of the tall, dark-haired, aristocratic Spaniard looking down at her from his six-feet-plus height. No welcome of any kind for her. But even without the disapproval and the almost rigid distaste she could see in his expression, Felicity knew that Vidal y Salvadores, Duque de Fuentualba, would never welcome her presence here on his home soil—*her* home soil in one sense, given that her late father was Spanish.

Spanish, and Vidal's adopted uncle.

It had taken every bit of courage she'd had and nights of sleeplessness for her to come here, but there was no way she was going to let Vidal know that. No quarter would be asked from him by her, because she knew that none would be given. She had had proof of that.

Panic fluttered in her stomach, rising swiftly inside her to set her heart thudding and her pulse racing. She must not think about that. Not now, when she needed all her strength. When she knew that that strength would dissolve like a mirage in the heat of the Andalusian sun if she allowed those dreadful, shameful memories to surface and those sickening images to form inside her head.

Fliss felt she had never longed more for the comforting and supportive love of her mother—or even the courage-inducing presence of her trio of girlfriends. But they, like her mother, were now absent from her life. They might be alive, not dead like her mother, but their careers had taken them to distant parts of the world. Only she had remained in their home town, and was now its Deputy Tourism Director—a responsible, demanding job.

A job that meant she could tell herself she was far too busy to have the time to build up a meaningful relationship with a man?

Thinking such thoughts was like biting down on a raw nerve in a tooth, the pain immediate and sharp. Better to think about why she had decided to use some of the leave entitlement she had built up through the long hours she worked in order to come here, when the reality was that her father's will could have been dealt with quite easily in her absence. That was certainly what Vidal would have wanted to happen.

Vidal.

If only she had the courage to fly free of her own past. If only she wasn't shackled to the past by a shame so bone deep that she could never escape from it. If only... There were so many if onlys in her life—most of them caused by Vidal.

In the heat of the concourse outside the busy Spanish airport into which she had just flown, filled with other people milling around them, he took a step towards her. Immediately she reacted, her body tensing in angry rejecting panic, her brain freezing so that she couldn't either speak or move.

It might have been seven years since she had last seen him, but she had recognised him immediately. Impossible for her not to do so when his features were cut so deep into her emotions. So deep and so poisonously that even now the wounds caused by those cuts had still not healed. That was nonsense, Fliss told herself. He had no power over her now—no power of any kind. And she was here to prove that to him.

'There was no need for you to meet me,' she told him, forcing herself to raise her head and look him in the eyes. Those eyes that had once looked at her in a way that had flayed the skin from her pride and her self-respect and left them raw and bleeding.

Her stomach churned again as she watched his far too handsome, arrogant, aristocratic male profile tighten into hauteur. His mouth curled in contemptuous disdain as he looked down at her, the late-afternoon Spanish sunlight shining on his thick dark hair. She was five feet seven, but she had to tilt her head back to meet his gaze, her own firing up from warm blue into heated violet as she met the look he was giving her.

She was hot and travel weary, and her body reacted to the unfamiliar heat as she resisted the need to lift the heavy weight of her thick, dark gold shoulder-length hair away from the back of her neck. She could already feel it starting to curl round her face in the humid heat, overcoming the effort she had made to straighten it into an immaculate elegance. Not that her appearance could ever compete with the true elegance of the smartly turned-out Spanish women around her. She favoured casual clothes, and was dressed in a pair of clean but well-washed and faded jeans, worn with a loose white cotton top. The jacket she had been wearing when she had boarded her flight in the UK was now stashed away in her roomy leather handbag.

Vidal frowned as his gaze was drawn inexorably to the windblown sensuality of her naturally honey-streaked hair, reminding him of the last time he had seen it. Her hair, like her body, had been spread against her bed, enjoying the amorous attentions of the boy who had been fondling her before Vidal and her mother had interrupted their illicit intimacy.

Angrily Vidal looked away from her. Her presence here was unwanted and unwelcome, her morals an affront to everything he believed in, but like the dark matter at the heart of a poisoned wound there was also that kernel of self-knowledge that raked his pride and refused to be locked away and forgotten.

To have looked into the wanton sensuality of her face, to have witnessed the manner in which she, at sixteen already an experienced tramp, had flaunted that sensuality mockingly in front of him, without a trace of shame, should have filled him with disgust and nothing but disgust. Only along with that disgust, like a sword plunged straight through his body, there had been that momentary pride-searing, lightning surge of desire. It had burned a brand of searing self-contempt through him, and the embers had never fully cooled.

She might be able to get under his skin, but he could never allow her back into his heart.

She shouldn't have come here, Fliss told herself. Not knowing that she would have to confront Vidal. Not knowing what he thought about her and why. But how could she not have come? How could she have denied herself this final opportunity to know something of the man who had fathered her?

Unlike her, Vidal looked impeccably cool in the heat, his suit that shade of neutral light beige that only continental men seemed to be able to wear with confidence, the blue shirt he was wearing beneath his jacket somehow emphasising the falcon gold of his eyes. A hunter's eyes, a predator's eyes, cold with cruelty and menace. She knew she would never forget those eyes. They haunted her nightmares, their gaze sliding over her like ice, their chilling contempt burning her skin and her pride.

She was not going to allow Vidal to see how she felt, though. She wasn't going to shrink away in fear beneath their incisive, lacerating focus, just as she wasn't going to be intimidated by him. Only to herself was she prepared to admit that it had been a shock to find him waiting for her at the airport. She had not expected that—even though she had written to the lawyers informing them of her plans—plans she knew he would not like or approve of, but which she had no intention of changing. A thrill of triumph laced with adrenalin shot through her at the thought of getting the better of him.

'You haven't changed, Vidal,' she told him, summoning her courage. 'You still obviously hate the thought of me being my father's daughter. But then you would do, wouldn't you? After all, it was in part thanks to you that my parents were forced apart, wasn't it? You were the one who betrayed them to your grandmother.'

'They would never have been allowed to marry.'

Fliss knew that that was true—her mother had said so herself, with more sadness in her voice than bitterness— but Fliss wasn't going to give up the opportunity to seize the moral high ground from Vidal so easily.

'They might have found a way, if they'd had more time.'

Vidal looked away from her. Inside his head was a memory he didn't want to have brought back to him: the sound of his own seven-year-old voice, naively telling his grandmother about the way in which he and his au pair had unexpectedly bumped into his adopted uncle when she had taken him on a visit to the Alhambra— not realising then that his uncle was supposed to have been in Madrid on family business, and certainly not realising the significance of that seemingly unexpected meeting.

His grandmother had realised what it meant, though. Felipe had been the son of her oldest friend, Maria Romero, an impoverished but aristocratic widow. When Maria had learned she had terminal cancer, and only a matter of months to live, she'd asked her friend to adopt twelve-year-old Felipe after her death and raise him as her own son. Both his grandmother and Maria had held the old-school belief that those of certain families—of certain blood and tradition—should always and only marry those who shared those things.

Guilt. It was a heavy burden to bear.

'They would never have been allowed to marry,' he repeated.

He was hateful, arrogant, with a pride as cold as ice and as hard as granite, Fliss thought angrily. Technically her mother might have died from heart failure, but who was to say that part of that failure had not been caused by a broken heart and destroyed dreams? Her mother had only been thirty-seven when she'd died, and Fliss eighteen, just about to go to university. Eighteen and a girl still—but now, at twenty-three, she was a woman.

Was that a hint of guilty colour she could see burning up the golden skin bequeathed to him by generations of high-born nobles of supposedly pure Castilian blood? She doubted it. This man wasn't capable of such feelings—of any kind of real feelings for other people. His blood didn't allow that. Blood which some whispered had once been mixed with that of a Moorish princess coveted by the proud Castilian who was her family's enemy and who had stolen her away from that family for his own pleasure, giving to the wife who shared his bloodline the boy child born of his forbidden relationship, and leaving his stolen concubine to die of grief at the loss of her child.

Fliss could well imagine that a family that had spawned a man like the one standing in front of her now could have committed such a terrible act. When her mother had first told her the tale of that long-ago Castilian *duque* she had immediately linked him in her own thoughts to the current *duque*. They shared the same cruel disregard for the feelings of others, the same arrogant belief that who they were gave them the right to ride roughshod over other people, to make judgements about them and then condemn them without ever allowing them to defend themselves. The right to deny a child access to her father, prevent her knowing and loving her father simply because they did not consider that child 'good enough' to be a part of their family.

Her father. Inside her head Fliss tasted the words, rolling them round her tongue, their flavour and intimacy both confusing and new. She'd spent so much of her life secretly wondering about her father, secretly imagining them meeting, secretly wanting to bring about that meeting. At home, in her smart flat in an elegant Georgian house which had been converted into apartments set in beautifully maintained gardens, complete with a tennis court and an indoor swimming pool and gym for the use of the residents, Fliss had a box in which she kept all the letters she had secretly written to her father but never sent. Letters she had kept hidden from her mother, not wanting to hurt her. Letters that had never been sent—all bar one of them.

Her great-grandmother might have been the one to originally part her parents, but it was Vidal who had prevented *her* from making contact with him. Vidal who had denied her the right to get to know her father because he had not thought her 'good enough' to be acknowledged as part of his family.

At least her father had attempted to make some kind of reparation for allowing her to be shut out of his life.

'Why have you come here, Felicity?'

The coldness in Vidal's voice stirred Fliss's pride.

'You know perfectly well why I am here. I'm here because of my father's will.'

As she spoke the words *my father*, Fliss felt her emotions pushing up under the control she always tried to impose on them. There had been so much pain, so much confusion, so much shame within her over the years, born of the rejection of her and her mother by her father's family. And for her it was Vidal who personified that rejection. Vidal who'd denied and hurt her—in many ways far more than her father himself had.

Vidal. Fliss forced down the emotions threatening to swamp her, afraid of what might happen to her once they did, of what she might have to confront within herself once their roaring tide subsided, leaving her vulnerabilities revealed.

The truth was that she wasn't here because of any material benefit that accrued to her from her father's will, but because of the emotional benefit—the emotional healing she longed for so much. There was no power on this earth, though, that would ever be able to force her to reveal that truth to Vidal.

'There was no need for you to come here because of Felipe's will, Felicity. The letter his lawyer sent to you made the terms of it perfectly clear. Your presence here is neither needed nor necessary.'

'Just like in your eyes neither my mother nor I were needed in my father's life—not needed and not necessary. Quite the opposite, in fact. How arrogant you are, Vidal, to feel you have the right to make such judgements. But then you are very good at making judgements that affect the lives of others, aren't you? You think you are so much better than other people, but you aren't, Vidal. Despite your rank, despite the arrogance and pride you lay claim to through your Castilian blood, in reality you are less worthy of them than the poorest beggar in the streets of Granada. You despise others because you think you are superior to them, but the reality is that *you* are the one who should be treated with contempt. You are incapable of compassion or understanding. You are incapable of real emotions, Vidal, incapable of knowing what it truly means to be human,' Fliss told him emotionally, hurling the words at him as feelings she had suppressed for too long overwhelmed her.

White to the lips, Vidal listened to her. That she of all people should dare to make such accusations against him infuriated him.

'You know nothing of what I am,' he told her savagely.

'On the contrary—I know a great deal about you and what you are,' Fliss corrected him. 'You are the Duque de Fuentualba, a position you were born to fill—*created* to fill, in fact, since your parents' marriage was arranged by both their families in order to preserve the purity of their bloodline. You own vast tracts of land, both here and in South America, you represent and uphold a feudal system that requires others to submit to your power, and you think that gives you the right to treat them with contempt and disdain. It was because of *you* and what you are that I never got the chance to know my father whilst he was alive.'

'And now you are here to seek revenge? Is that what you are trying to tell me?'

'I don't need to seek revenge,' Fliss told him, fiercely repudiating his accusation. 'You will by your very nature bring that revenge down on your own head—although I am sure you won't even recognise it for what it is. Your nature, your outlook on life, will deny you exactly what you denied my parents—a happy, loving, committed lifelong relationship, entered into for no other reason than the two people within it loved one another. My revenge will be in knowing that you will never know what real happiness is—because you are not genetically capable of knowing it. You will never hold a woman's love, and most pitiful of all you will not even realise what you are missing.'

His very silence was unnerving on its own, without the look he was giving her, Fliss recognised. But she was not her gentle, vulnerable mother, made fearful and insignificant by a too arrogant man.

'Has no one ever told you that it can be dangerous to offer such opinions?'

'Maybe I don't care about inciting danger when it comes to speaking the truth,' Fliss answered, giving a small shrug as she added, 'After all, what more harm could you possibly do to me than the harm you have already done?'

That was as close as she dared allow herself to get to letting the pain inside her show. To say more would be too dangerous. She couldn't say any more without risking letting him see the scars he had inflicted so deep into everything that she was that she would bear them for ever. They—*he*—had changed her life for ever. Had deprived her of her right to love and be loved—not just as a daughter, but as a woman. But now was not the time to think of the damage that had been done to her, both to her emotions and her sensuality. She would never give Vidal the satisfaction of knowing just what he had done to her.

Vidal fought against the threat to his self-control. 'Let me assure you of one thing,' he announced grimly, each word carefully measured. 'When it comes to my marriage, the woman who becomes my wife will not be someone—'

'Like me?' Fliss supplied tauntingly for him.

'No man, if he is honest, wants as his wife someone whose sexual morals are those of the gutter. It is in the nature of the male to be protective of his chosen mate's virtue, to want the intimacy he shares with that mate to be exclusive. A man can never know for sure that any child his mate carries is truly his, therefore he instinctively seeks a mate whom he believes he can trust to be sexually loyal to him. When I marry my wife will know that she will have my commitment to her for our lifetime, and I will expect the same commitment from her.'

He was angry. Fliss could see that. But instead of intimidating her his anger exhilarated her. Exhilarated her and excited her, driving her to push him even harder, and to go on pushing him until she had pushed him beyond the boundary of his self-control. A frisson of unfamiliar emotion shivered down her spine. Vidal was a man of strong passions who kept those passions tightly leashed.

The woman who could arouse them—and him—would have to be equally passionate, or risk being consumed in their fiery heat. In bed he would be…

Shocked, Fliss veered away from pursuing her own thoughts, her face starting to burn. What was happening to her? She felt as though she had been struck by a thunderbolt, the aftershock leaving her feeling sick and shaky. How could she have allowed herself to think like that about Vidal?

'You shouldn't have come here to Spain, Felicity.'

'You mean you didn't want me to come,' Fliss responded at Vidal's coldly delivered words. 'Well, I've got news for you, Vidal. I'm not sixteen any more, and you can't tell me what to do. Now, if you'll excuse me, I would like to go and check in to my hotel. There was no need for you to come here to the airport,' she told him, intent on dismissing him. 'We don't have anything to say to one another that can't be said tomorrow, at our meeting with my late father's attorney.'

She made to step past him, but as she did so his hand shot out, his long tanned fingers curling round her arm and restraining her. It seemed odd that such an elegant hand with such fastidiously well-cared-for nails could possess such feral male power, but it did, Fliss recognised as her flesh pulsed hotly beneath his hold. Her blood was beating with unfamiliar speed, as though responding to *his* command and not the command of her own body.

Her sharp, 'Let me go,' was met with a dark look.

'There is nothing I would like to do more, I assure you. But since my mother is expecting you to stay with us, and will be awaiting our arrival, I'm afraid that that is not possible.'

'Your mother?'

'Yes. She has come especially from her home in the mountains to our townhouse, here in the city, so that she can welcome you into the family.'

'Welcome me into the family?' Fliss shot him a derisory look. 'Do you think I *want* that after the way "the family" treated my mother—the au pair not good enough to marry my father? The way they refused to acknowledge my existence?'

Ignoring Fliss's angry outburst as though she hadn't spoken, Vidal continued coldly, 'You should have thought of the consequences of coming here before you decided to do so—but then you are not someone who thinks it important to think of the consequences of your behaviour, are you, Felicity? Neither the consequences nor their effect on others.'

Fliss couldn't bring herself to look at him. Of course he *would* throw that at her. Of course he would.

'I have no wish to meet your mother. My hotel booking—'

'Has been cancelled.'

No, she couldn't. She wouldn't. Panic hit her. Fliss opened her mouth to protest, but it was too late. She was already being propelled firmly towards the car park. A sudden movement of the crowd pushed her closer to Vidal's side, and her own flesh was immediately aware of the male strength and heat of his body as her thigh came into brief contact with his, hard with muscle beneath the expensive fabric of his clothes. She recoiled, her mouth dry, her heart thudding, as memories she couldn't bear to relive mocked her attempts to deny them.

They moved swiftly along in the full glare and heat of the high summer sun—which was surely why her body had started to burn so hotly that she could feel the beat of her own blood in her face.

'You should be wearing a hat,' Vidal rebuked her, his critical gaze raking her hot face. 'You are too pale-skinned to be exposed to the full heat of our sun.'

It wasn't the sun that was the cause of the heat burning her, Fliss knew. But thankfully only she knew that.

'I have a hat in my case,' she told him. 'But since I expected to go straight to my hotel from the airport by taxi, rather than being virtually kidnapped and forced to stand in the sun's full glare, I didn't think it necessary.'

'The only reason you were standing anywhere was because you chose to create an argument. My car is over here,' Vidal told her. His arrogance caused Fliss to grit her teeth. How typical it was of everything she knew about him that he made no attempt to apologise and instead tried to put *her* in the wrong. He had lifted his hand, as though to place it against the small of her back and no doubt propel her in the direction of the waiting vehicle, but her immediate reaction was to step hurriedly away from him. She could not bear him to touch her. To do so would be a form of self-betrayal she could not endure. And besides, he was too... Too what? Too male?

He had seen her hasty movement, of course, and now he was looking at her in a way that locked her stomach muscles against the biting contempt of that look.

'It's too late for you to put on the "shrinking virgin, fearful of a man's touch" act for me,' he warned her

She wasn't going to let him speak to her like that. She couldn't.

'I'm not acting,' she told him. 'And it wasn't fear. It was revulsion.'

'You lost the right to that kind of chaste reaction a long time ago, and we both know it,' Vidal taunted.

Anger and something else—something aching and sad and lost—tightened painfully in her chest.

Once—also a long time ago, or so it seemed now—she had been a young girl trembling on the brink of her first emotional and sensual crush on a real-life adult man, seeing in him everything her romantic heart craved, and sensing in him the potential to fulfil every innocent sensual fantasy her emerging sexuality had had aching inside her. A sensation, lightning swift and electrifying, raced down her spine, sensitising her flesh and raising the tiny hairs at the nape of her neck.

A new shudder gripped her body. Fresh panic seized her. It must be the heat that was doing this to her. It couldn't be Vidal himself. It could not, *must* not be Vidal who was responsible for the sudden unnerving and wholly unwanted tremor of physical sensation that had traced a line of shockingly sensual fire down her spine. It was some kind of physical aberration, that was all—an indirect manifestation of how much she loathed him. A shudder of that loathing, surely, and not a shiver of female longing for the touch of a man who epitomised everything that it meant to be a man who could master and command a woman's response whenever he chose to do so. After all, there was no way that she could ever want Vidal. No way at all.

The recognition that her pulse was racing and her heart hammering—with righteous anger, of course—had Fliss pausing to take a calming breath, her hostility towards Vidal momentarily forgotten as she breathed in the magical air of the city. It held her spellbound and entranced. Yes, she could smell petrol and diesel fumes, but more importantly she could also smell air heated by the sun, and infused with something of the historic scents of the East and its once all-powerful Moorish rulers: rich subtle perfumes, aromatic spices. If she closed her eyes Fliss was sure she would be able to hear the musical sound of running water—so beloved of the Moors—and see the rich shimmer of the fabrics that had travelled along the Silk Route to reach Granada.

The historic past of the city seemed to reach out and embrace her—a sigh of sweetly scented breath, a waft of richly erotic perfumes, the sensual touch of silk as fine as the lightest caress.

'This is my car.'

The shock of Vidal's voice intruding on her private thoughts jolted her back to reality, but not quickly enough for her to avoid the hard male hand against her back from which she had already fled. Its heat seemed to sear her skin through her clothes. So might a man such as this one impose his stamp of possession, his mark of ownership on a woman's flesh, imprinting her with that mark for all time. Inside her head an image formed—the image of a male hand caressing the curve of a naked female back. Deliberately and erotically that male hand moved downwards to cup the soft curve of the woman's bottom, turning her to him, his flesh dark against the moonlight paleness of hers, her breathing ragged whilst his deepened into the stalking deliberation of a hunter intent on securing its prey.

No! Her head and her heart were both pounding now as conflicting emotions seized her. She must concentrate on reality. Even knowing that, it still took her a supreme effort of will to do so.

The car he had indicated was very large, very highly polished and black—the kind of car she was used to seeing the rich and powerful being driven around in in London.

'So you aren't a supporter of green issues, then?' Fliss couldn't resist taunting Vidal as he held open the front passenger door of the car for her, taking her small case from her and putting it on the back seat.

The clunk of the door closing was the only response he gave her, before going round to the driver's door and getting into the car himself.

Did his silence mean that she had annoyed and angered him? Fliss hoped so. She *wanted* to get under his skin. She wanted to be a thorn in his side—a reminder to him of what he had done to her, and a reminder to herself.

He hadn't wanted her to come here. She knew that. He had wanted her to simply allow the lawyers to deal with everything. But she had been determined to come.

To spite Vidal? No! It was her heritage she sought, not retribution.

The essence of this country ran in her own blood, after all.

Granada—home to the last of the Moorish rulers of the Emirate of Granada and home to the Alhambra, the red fortress, a complex of such great beauty that her mother's face had shone with happiness when she had talked to Fliss about it—was part of her heritage.

'Did my father go there with you?' she had asked her mother.

She had only been seven or so at the time, but she had never referred to the man who had fathered her as 'Daddy'. Daddies were men who played with their children and who loved them—not strangers in a far-off country.

'Yes,' her mother had responded. 'I once took Vidal there, and your father joined us. We had the most lovely day. One day you and I will go there together, Fliss,' her mother had promised. But somehow that day had never come, so now she was here on her own.

Through the tinted windows of the car she could see the city up ahead of them, its ancient Moorish quarter of Albaicín climbing the hillside that faced the Alhambra. Close to it was the equally historical medieval Jewish quarter of the city, but Fliss wasn't in the least bit surprised, once they were in the city, to find Vidal turning into a street lined with imposing sixteenth-century buildings erected after the city's capture by the Catholic rulers Isabella and Ferdinand. Here on this street the tall Renaissance-style buildings spoke of wealth and privilege, their bulk blotting out the rays of the sun and casting heavy, authoritative shadows.

She might have been surprised to discover that Vidal drove his own car, but she was not surprised when he slowed the car down and then turned in towards a huge pair of imposing double-height studded wooden doors. This area of the city, with its air of arrogance and wealth, was perfectly suited to the man who matched its hauteur—and its visually perfect sculptured classical magnificence.

Fliss was relieved to be distracted from that particular thought by the sight of the sunny courtyard they had just entered, its lines perfectly symmetrical, and even the sound of the water splashing down into the ornate stone fountain in its centre somehow evenly timed.

The house—more a palace, surely, than merely a house—enclosed the courtyard on all four sides, with the main entrance facing the way they had come in. On the wall to their right a two-storey archway led into what had looked like formal gardens from the glimpse Fliss had seen before Vidal had brought the car to a halt alongside a flight of stone steps. The steps led up to a wooden studded door that matched the style of the doors they had just driven through. Around the middle floor of the three-storey building ran what looked like a sort of cloistered, semi-enclosed walkway, whilst the windows looking onto the courtyard were shuttered against the late-afternoon sunlight. On the stonework above the windows Fliss could see the emblem of Granada itself— the pomegranate—whilst above the main doorway were carved what she knew to be the family's arms, along with an inscription which translated as 'What we take we hold'.

It wasn't just the way her job had encouraged her to look at new areas with an eye to their tourism potential that caused her to note these things, Fliss admitted. She had made it her business as she grew up to read as much as she could about the history of Vidal's family—and of course that of her own father.

'Does it ever concern you that this house was built with money stolen from the high-ranking Muslim prince your ancestor murdered?' she challenged Vidal now, determined not to let the beauty and the magnificence of the building undermine her awareness of how the fortune that had bought it had been made.

'There is a saying—to the victor the spoils. My ancestor was one of many Castilians who won the battle against Boabdil—Muhammad XII—for Ferdinand and Isabella. The money to build this *palacio* was given to him by Isabella, and far from allowing the murder of anyone, the Alhambra Decree treaty gave religious freedome to the city's Muslims.'

'A treaty which was later broken,' Fliss reminded Vidal sharply. 'Just as your ancestor broke the promise he made to the Muslim princess he stole away from her family.'

'My advice to you is that you spend more time checking your supposed facts and rather less repeating them without having done so.'

Without allowing her time to retaliate, Vidal got out of the car, striding so quickly round to the passenger door that Fliss did not have time to open it. Ignoring

his outstretched hand, Fliss manoeuvred herself out of
the car, determined not to let herself be overwhelmed
by her surroundings and instead to think of her mother.
Had *she* felt intimidated by the arrogance and the disdain with which this building frowned down upon those
who did not belong to it but who were rash enough to
enter? Her mother had loved her time in Spain, despite
the unhappiness it had eventually brought her. She had
been hired by Vidal's parents as an au pair, to help Vidal
with his English during the school summer holidays, and
she had always made it plain to Fliss just how much she
had liked the little boy who had been her charge.

Was it perhaps here in this house that she had first
seen and fallen in love with Vidal's adopted uncle—
the man who had been her own father? Fliss wondered
now. Perhaps she had seen the handsome Spaniard for
the first time here in this very courtyard? Handsome,
maybe—but not strong enough to stand by her mother
and the love he had sworn he felt for her, Fliss reminded
herself starkly, lest she get carried away by the romantic
imagery created by her surroundings.

She knew that her mother had only visited the family's house here in Granada very briefly, as most of her
time in Spain had been spent at the *castillo* on the ducal
country estate, which had been Vidal's parents' main
home.

The thought of what her mother must have suffered caused a sensation inside Fliss's chest rather as
though iron-hard fingers had closed round her heart
and squeezed it—fingers as long and strong as those
of Vidal He had played his own part in her mother's

humiliation and suffering, Fliss thought bitterly, and she turned quickly away from him—only to give a startled gasp as her foot slipped on one of the cobbles, causing her to turn her ankle and lose her balance.

Immediately the bright sunlight that had been dazzling her was shut out as Vidal stepped towards her, his hands locking round her upper arms as he steadied her and held her upright. Her every instinct was to reject his hold on her, and show him how unwelcome it was. He moved fast, though, releasing her with a look of distaste, as though somehow touching her soiled him. Anger and humiliation burned inside her, but there was nothing she could do other than turn her back on him. She was trapped—and not just here in a place she did not want to be. She was also trapped by her own past and the role Vidal had played in it. Like the fortress walls with which the Moors had surrounded their cities and their homes, Vidal's contempt for her was a prison from which there was no escape.

Walking past him, Fliss stepped into the building, standing in a cool hallway with a magnificent carved and polished dark wood staircase, to take in the austere and sombre magnificence of her surroundings.

Portraits hung from the white painted walls—stern, uniformed or court-finery-dressed Spanish aristocrats, looking down at her from their heavily gilded frames. Not a single one of them was smiling, Fliss noticed. Rather, they were looking out at the world with expressions of arrogance and disdain. Just as Vidal, their descendant, looked out on the world now.

A door opened to admit a small, plump middle-aged

woman with snapping brown eyes that swiftly assessed her. Although she was simply dressed, and not what Fliss had been expecting in Vidal's mother, there was no mistaking her upright bearing and general demeanour of calm confidence.

She realised her assumption was wrong when Vidal announced, 'Let me introduce you to Rosa, who is in charge of the household here. She will show you to your room.'

The housekeeper advanced towards Fliss, her gaze still searching and assessing, and then, ignoring Fliss, she turned back to Vidal. Speaking in Spanish, she told him, 'Where her mother was a dove, this one has the look of a wild falcon not yet tamed to the lure.'

Fresh anger flashed in Fliss's own eyes.

'I speak Spanish,' she told them both. She was almost shaking with the force of her anger. 'And there is no lure that would ever tempt me down into the grasp of anyone in *this* household.'

She just had time to see the answering flash of hostility burn through the look Vidal gave her before she turned on her heel to head towards the stairs, leaving Rosa to come after her.

CHAPTER TWO

ON THE first floor landing Rosa broke the stiff silence between them by saying in a sharp voice, 'So you speak Spanish?'

'Why shouldn't I?' Fliss challenged her. 'No matter what Vidal might want to think, he does not have the power to prevent me from speaking the language that was, after all, my father's native tongue.'

She certainly wasn't going to admit to Rosa, or anyone else here, her early teenage dream of one day meeting her father, which had led to her secretly saving some of her paper-round money to pay for Spanish lessons she'd suspected her mother would not want her to have. Fliss had come to recognise well before she had reached her teens that her mother was almost fearful of Fliss doing anything to recognise the Spanish side of her inheritance. So, rather than risk upsetting her, Fliss had tried not to let her see how much she had longed to know more about not just her father but his country. Her mother had been a gentle person who had hated confrontations and arguments, and Fliss had loved her far too much to ever want to hurt her.

'Well, you certainly haven't got your spirit from either

of your parents,' Rosa told her forthrightly. 'Though I
would warn you against trying to cross swords with
Vidal.'

Fliss stopped walking, her foot on the first step of the
next set of stairs as she turned towards the housekeeper.
Her body had immediately tensed with rejection of the
thought that she should in any way allow Vidal to control any aspect of her life.

'Vidal has no authority over me,' she told the housekeeper vehemently. 'And he never will have.'

A movement in the hallway below her caught her attention. She looked back down the stairs and saw that
Vidal was still standing there. He must have heard her—
which was no doubt the reason for the grim look he
was giving her. He probably wished he *did* have some
authority over her. If he had he may have prevented
her from coming to Spain—just as years ago he had
prevented her from making contact with her father.

In her mind's eye she could see him now, standing
in her bedroom—the room that should have been her
private haven—holding the letter she had sent to her
father weeks earlier. A letter which he had intercepted.
A letter written from the depths of her sixteen-year-old
heart to a father she had longed to know.

Every one of the tenderly burgeoning sensual and
emotional feelings she had begun to feel for Vidal had
been crushed in that moment. Crushed and turned into
bitterness and anger.

'Fliss, darling, you must promise me that you will
not attempt to make contact with your father again,'
her mother had warned her with tears in her eyes, after

Vidal had returned to Spain and it had been just the two of them again.

Of course she had given her that promise. She had loved her mother too much to want to upset her—especially when...

No! She would not allow Vidal to drag her back there, to that searingly shameful place that was burned into her pride for life. Her mother had understood what had happened. She had known Fliss was not to blame.

Maturity had brought her the awareness that, since her father had always known where she was, he could quite easily have made contact with *her* if he'd wished to do so. The fact that he had never done it told its own story. She was not, after all, the only child to grow up not wanted by its father. With her mother's death she had told herself that it was time to move on. Time to celebrate and cherish the childhood and the loving mother she had had, and to forget the father who had rejected her.

She would never know now just what it was that had changed her father's mind. She would never know whether it had been guilt or regret for lost opportunities that had led him to mentioning her in his will. But she did know that this time she was not going to allow Vidal to dictate to her what she could and could not do.

In the hallway below, Vidal watched as Fliss turned on her heel and followed Rosa along the landing to the next flight of stairs. If there was one thing that Vidal prided himself about—one characteristic he had worked on and honed—it was mastery of his own emotions and reactions. But for some reason his gaze—normally so obedient to his command—was finding it necessary to linger on the slender silken length of Fliss's legs as she walked away from him.

At sixteen those legs had been coltishly slender. She had been a child turning into a woman, with pert small breasts that pushed against the thin tee shirts she'd always seemed to wear. She might have behaved towards him with a calculated mock innocence that had involved stolen blushing half-looks, and a wide-eyed pretended inability to lift her supposedly fascinated and awed gaze from the bare expanse of his torso when she had walked into the bathroom whilst he was shaving, but he had witnessed the coarse reality of what she was: promiscuous, and without morals or pride. By nature? Or because she had been deprived of a father?

The guilt he could never escape wrenched at his conscience. How many times over the years had he wished unsaid those innocent words that had led ultimately to the forced ending of the relationship between his uncle and his au pair? A simple mention to his grandmother that Felipe had joined them on an expedition to the Alhambra here in Granada had been their undoing—and his.

There had been no way that the Dowager Duchess would ever have allowed Felipe to marry anyone other than a woman of her choice. Nor would she ever have chosen a mere au pair as a bride for a man whose blood was as aristocratic as that of his adoptive family.

As a child of seven Vidal had not understood that, but he had quickly realised the consequences of his

innocent actions when he had been told that the gentle
English au pair of whom he had become so fond was
being dismissed and sent home. Neither Fliss's mother
nor Felipe had had natures strong enough to challenge
his grandmother's authority. Neither of them had known
when they were forced to part that there would be consequences to their love in the form of the child Fliss's
mother had conceived. A child whose name and very
existence his grandmother had ruled was never to be
mentioned—unless she herself did so, in order to remind
his uncle of the shame he had brought on his adoptive
family by lowering himself to conceive that child with
a mere au pair.

How justified his grandmother would have believed
her ruling to be had she lived long enough to know what
Felipe's daughter had become.

Vidal had felt for Felicity's mother when the two
of them had returned early from a visit to London to
discuss various private matters to find that not only was
Felicity having an illicit teenage party that had got badly
out of hand, but also that Felicity herself was upstairs
in her mother's bedroom with a drunken, ignorant lout
of a youth.

Vidal closed his eyes and then opened them again.
There were some memories he preferred not to revisit.
The realisation that he had inadvertently betrayed his
au pair's love affair. The night his mother had come into
his room to tell him that the plane his father had been
in had crashed in South America without any survivors.
The evening he had looked at Felicity sprawled on her
mother's bed, her gold and honey-streaked blonde hair

wrapped round the hand of the youth leaning over her, whilst she stared up at him with brazen disregard for what she had done.

Brazen disregard for *him*.

Vidal's chest lifted under the demanding pressure of his lungs for oxygen. He had been twenty-three—a man, not a boy—and appalled by the effect Felicity was having on him. Revolted by the desire he felt for her, tormented by both it and his own moral code—a code that said that a girl of sixteen was just that—a *girl*—and a man of twenty-three was also exactly that—a *man*. The seven-year age gap between them was a gap that separated childhood from adulthood, and represented a chasm that must not be violated. Just as a sixteen-year-old's innocence must not be violated.

Even now, seven years later, he could still taste the anger that had soured his heart and seared his soul. A bleak black burning anger that Felicity's presence here was re-igniting.

Vidal flexed the tense muscles of his shoulders. The sooner this whole business was over and done with and Felicity was on a plane on her way back to the UK the better.

When Felipe had been dying, and had told him how badly he felt about the past, Vidal had encouraged him to make reparation via his will to the child he had fathered and then been forced to abandon. He had done that for his uncle's sake, though—not for Felicity's.

Upstairs in the room Rosa had shown her into, before telling her that refreshments would be sent up for her and then leaving, Fliss studied her surroundings. The room was vast, with a high ceiling, and furnished with heavy and ornate dark wood furniture of a type that Fliss knew from her mother's descriptions was typical in expensive antique Spanish furniture. Beautifully polished, and without a speck of dust, the wood glowed warmly in the light pouring in through the room's tall French windows. Stepping up to them, Fliss saw that they opened out onto a small balcony, decorated with waist-high beautifully intricate metalwork, its design classically Arabic rather than European. Try as she might, Fliss could not spot the deliberate flaw that was always said to be made in such work, because only Allah himself could create perfection.

The balcony looked down on an equally classical Moorish courtyard garden, bisected by the straight lines of the rill of water that flowed through it from a fall spilling out of some concealed source at the far end of the courtyard. Either side of the narrow canal were covered walkways smothered in soft pink climbing roses, their scent rising up to the balcony. On the ground alongside them were white lilies. The pathways themselves were made from subtle blue and white tiles, whilst what looked like espaliered fruit trees lined the walls of the courtyard. In the four small square formal gardens on the opposite side of the rose walkways, white geraniums tumbled from Ali Baba–sized terracotta jars, whilst directly below the balcony, partly shaded from the sun by a sort of cloistered, semi-enclosed area, there was a patio complete with elegant garden furniture.

Fliss closed her eyes. She knew this garden so well.

Her mother had described it to her, sketched it for her, shown her photographs of it. She had told her that it was a garden originally designed for the exclusive use of the women of the Moorish family for whom the house had been built. It was obviously an act of deliberate cruelty on the part of Vidal to have given her this room, over-looking the garden he knew her mother had loved so much. Had he given her the room her mother had slept in? Fliss suspected that he hadn't. Her mother had told her that she and Vidal had occupied the top storey—the nursery quarters—when they had come to stay with Vidal's grandmother, who in those days had owned the house, even though Vidal had been seven years old at the time.

Fliss turned back into the room. Heavily embossed with a raised self-coloured pattern, a rich deep blue brocade fabric hung at the windows and covered the straight-backed chairs placed at either side of the room's marble fireplace. The cream bedspread was piped in the same blue, with tasselled blue brocade cushions orna-menting its immaculate cream width. The dark wooden floorboards shone, and the antique-looking blue-and-cream rug that covered most of the floor was so plush that Fliss felt she hardly dared walk on it.

It was all a far cry from her minimalist apartment back at home. But this decor just as much as the decor she had chosen for herself was a part of her genetic inheritance through her father. Had he not rejected her mother, had he not denied them both, she would have grown up familiar with this house and its history, taking it for granted. Just as Vidal himself did.

Vidal. How she loathed him. Her feelings towards him were far more bitter and filled with contempt than her feelings towards her father. Her father, after all, had had no voice. As her mother had explained to her, he had been forced to give them up and to turn his back on them. *He* had not opened her letter pleading to be given a chance to get to know him and then told her that she must never ever try to contact him again. Vidal had done that. *He* had never known her personally and looked at her with a gaze of cold contempt, then rejected her and walked away from her, as Vidal had done. *He* had never scorched her pride and burned a wound deep into her heart with his misjudgement of her. Vidal had.

It was here in this house that decisions had been made. They had impacted on her and on her parents in the most cruel way. It was from here that her mother had been dismissed. It was here that she had been told that the man she loved was promised in marriage to another—a girl chosen for him by his adoptive family, who was in her final year at an exclusive school that groomed highly born girls for their marriages. A girl, as her mother had told Fliss, Felipe had sworn to her he did not love and certainly did not want to marry.

It hadn't mattered what Felipe wanted, though. All his promises to Fliss's mother, all his protestations of love, had been as beads of light caused by the sun's rays touching the drops of water as they fell from a fountain. So beautiful and entrancing that they stopped the heart, but ephemeral and insubstantial when it came to reality.

There had only been time for the two of them to

snatch a final goodbye embrace and share the fevered illicit intimacy that had led to her own conception before they had been torn apart—her mother sent back to England and Felipe instructed to do his duty and propose to the girl who had been chosen for him.

'He swore to me that he loved me, but he loved his adoptive family too and he could not disobey them,' her mother had told her gently, when she had asked as a girl why he had not come after her.

Her poor mother. She had made the mistake of falling in love with a man who had not been strong enough to protect their love, and she had paid the price for that. Fliss would never let the same thing happen to her. She would never allow herself to fall in love and be vulnerable. After all, she had already had a taste of how that felt—even if her feelings for Vidal had merely been those of an inexperienced sixteen-year-old.

Shaking herself free of her painful thoughts, she looked at her small case. Her mother had told her about the traditional way of life of this aristocratic, autocratic Spanish family that Vidal now headed. Vidal had said that his mother had insisted she stay here. Did that mean she could expect to be formally received by her? Perhaps over dinner? She hadn't brought any formal clothes with her—just a few changes of underwear, a pair of tailored shorts, some fresh tops, and one very simple slip of a dress: a handful of non-crushable matt black jersey that she had fallen in love with on a trip to London.

She was just about to lift the dress from her case and shake it out when the door opened and Rosa came in, carrying a tray containing a glass of wine and a serving of tapas.

After thanking her, Fliss asked, 'What time is dinner served?'

'There will be no dinner. Vidal does not wish it. He is too busy,' Rosa answered haughtily in Spanish. 'A meal will be brought for you if you wish.'

Fliss could feel her face beginning to burn. Rosa's rudeness was unforgivable—but no doubt she was taking her cue from Vidal.

'I have no more wish to eat with Vidal than he does with me,' she told Rosa spiritedly. 'But since Vidal told me specifically that it was his mother's wish that I stay here, instead of in the hotel I had booked, I assumed I would be expected to have dinner with *her*.'

'The Duchess is not here,' Rosa informed her curtly, putting down the tray and turning grim-lipped to the door. She had disappeared through it before Fliss could ask her any more questions.

Vidal had lied to her about his mother's presence here in the house and about her wish to see her. Why? Why would he want to have her here beneath his own roof?

Just for a moment she wished she was back at home— and more than that she wished that her mother was still alive. Filled with the sadness of her emotions, Fliss sat down on the edge of the bed.

Her mother had given her the best childhood ever. A wonderfully generous bequest of an elderly relative Fliss herself had never even known had enabled her mother to buy them a lovely home in a quiet country village— large enough for Fliss's grandparents to move in with them—as well as providing an income which had meant her mother had been able to be at home with her. Her mother had talked openly to her about her father, referring to him with love in her voice and her eyes, and no resentment or bitterness. She had only clammed up when Fliss had begged her to bring her to Spain so that she could see the country for herself. She had refused to criticise Vidal when Fliss, with a seven-year-old's sharpness of mind, had worked out that *he* must have been the one to betray her parents.

'You mustn't blame Vidal, darling,' her mother had told her gently. 'It truly wasn't his fault. He was only a little boy—the same age as you are now. He was not to know what would happen.'

Her gentle, loving mother—always so ready to understand and forgive those who hurt her.

Initially Felicity—named for 'happiness', according to her mother—had accepted this defence of Vidal. But then he had come to visit them, and after initially behaving towards her with kindness he had started to treat her with disdain, putting as much distance between them as he could, and making it plain that he disliked her. How her vulnerable teenage heart had ached over that unkindness.

From the minute she had first seen him, stepping out of the expensive car he had driven from London to their house, Fliss had been smitten, developing a huge crush on him. She could vividly remember the day she had inadvertently walked into the bathroom when he had been shaving. Her besotted gaze had been glued to his naked torso. Of course that kind of intimacy had sent her febrile teenage longings surging out of control. Theirs had normally been a mostly female household, so the sight of any bare male chest would have had her studying it in secret curiosity, but when that bare chest belonged to Vidal…

She had felt almost sick with excitement and long-ing when she had finally managed to step back out of the bathroom, her imagination working overtime and conjuring up various scenarios in which she had not merely looked at it but even more breathtakingly excit-ingly been held close to it. It was all very well to mock her sixteen-year-old naivety now, but wasn't it the truth that she was still every bit as personally unfamiliar with the actual reality of sexual intimacy, bare skin to bare skin, now as she had been then?

Clumsily Fliss turned round, as though in flight from her own knowledge of herself. But the fact was that there was nowhere to run to from the reality of her virgin state. No matter how many defensive barricades she had built around herself, no matter how strong an aura of adult womanly confidence she had taught herself to manifest, and no matter how closely she guarded the secret of her past-its-sell-by-date virginity, she could not escape from the truth.

What was the matter with her? she challenged herself. She had lived with being sexually inactive for years. It had been her own decision to make and to keep. It was just one of those things. The pace of modern life, the need to establish her career, had somehow prevented her from meeting a man she wanted enough to let go of the past.

It would be pure self-indulgence for her to start feeling sorry for herself. By many people's standards Fliss knew that her childhood had been a privileged one. She still considered herself to be privileged now—and not just because she had had such a wonderful mother.

With her grandparents and her mother dead, the big house had seemed so empty—and yet at the same time filled with painful memories. At the height of the property market, before it crashed, Fliss had been approached by a builder who had offered her an unexpectedly large sum of money for the house and its land. After trying to work out what her mother would have wanted her to do she had gone ahead and sold the house to him, and bought herself the flat in the converted Georgian townhouse. Her work in the Tourism Department of the very pretty market town in which she lived kept her busy, and she had plenty of friends—although many of her schoolfriends were now pairing off and making 'nesting' plans, and her three closest friends from school and university, whilst single like her, now lived and worked overseas.

A brief rap on her bedroom door had her getting up off the bed and tensing as she waited for the door to open and Rosa to appear—no doubt radiating further disapproval.

However, it wasn't Rosa who stepped or rather strode into the room, but Vidal himself. He had changed from his business suit into a more casual shirt and a pair of chinos, and had also had a shower, to judge from the still-damp appearance of his slicked-back hair. Her heart turned over inside her chest cavity in slow painful

motion, her breath seizing in her lungs. Her awareness of
the intimacy of him being in her bedroom brought back
too many memories of the past for her to feel comfortable even before the door had closed and locked.

Once before Vidal had come into her bedroom…

No! She would not allow herself to be dragged into
the dark agony of that dreadful place where those memories were stored. It was the present she needed to focus
on—not the past. It was she who must challenge and
criticise Vidal—not the other way around.

Summoning her strength, she demanded, 'Why did
you tell me that your mother would be here when that
was a lie?'

The sudden surge of blood creeping up along his jaw
betrayed his real reaction to her challenge, even if he
was trying to deny it by giving her a coolly dismissive
look.

'My mother has been called away to visit a friend
who is unwell. I was not aware of her absence myself
until Rosa informed me of it.'

'Rosa had to tell you where your mother is? How typical of the kind of man you are that you need a servant
to tell you the whereabouts of your own mother.'

The hot, angry red blood surged over the sharp thrust
of his jawline like an unstoppable tide.

'For your information, Rosa is *not* a servant. And
as for my relationship with my mother—that is not a
subject I intend to discuss with you.'

'No, I'm sure you don't,' Fliss answered him grimly.
'After all, it is in no small part because of you that I
never got to have a relationship with my *father*. You

were the one who intercepted my private letter to him. And you were the one who came all the way to England to bully my mother into pleading with me not to try to contact him again.'

'Your mother believed it would not have been in your best interests for you to continue to write to Felipe.'

'Oh, so it was for *my* sake that you stopped me communicating with him, was it?' Fliss's voice was icy with sarcasm as the memory of all the anguish and humiliation Vidal had caused flooded past her defences. He was cruel and arrogant. Willing to destroy others without compunction so that he could have his own way. 'You had no right to stop me knowing my father, or denying me the right to at least see if he could love me. But then we know that love for another person isn't a concept someone like you understands, is it, Vidal?'

She could feel the aching burn of her emotions in the hot tears that threatened to flood her eyes. Tears! She would never—*must* never—ever cry in front of this man. She must never show him any weakness. *Never.*

'What could you possibly know about loving someone—about loving *anyone*?' Fliss hurled accusations at him in furious self-defence. She'd say and do anything to stop him guessing at the pain within her that his words had touched. 'You don't know what love is!'

She had no idea what she was really saying as the wild words tumbled from her lips. All she knew was that they sprang from an unending well of pain deep inside her.

'And you *do*? You who—' Furiously angry himself,

Vidal closed the distance between them, shaking his head in disgust as he stopped speaking.

But Fliss knew perfectly what he had been about to say, and the accusation he had been about to fling at her.

Now panic as well as pain had her well and truly in its grip

'Don't touch me,' she ordered, stepping back from him, her voice shaking with dread.

'You can stop the play-acting, Felicity.' Immediately Vidal's anger was replaced by a look of contempt. 'And we both know that it *is* play-acting, before you attempt to deny it and perjure yourself even further.'

Her panic levels were going through the roof, sky-high and out of control, defeating her as she struggled to bring some rationality to her reactions and her emotions.

The memories had come dangerously close, muddying the waters of what was present and what was past. Her heart was jumping around inside her ribcage and she was sixteen years old again, floundering helplessly at the confusion of feelings that were forbidden and frightening.

'I know what you're thinking,' she lashed out wildly, 'but you're wrong. I don't want you. I never wanted you.'

'Want me?'

The silence in the room was like the still centre at the eye of a storm. It was like knowing with all her senses that the danger was there and soon it would crash down on her and consume her. And there was nowhere she could run to escape it.

'Want me? Like this, you mean?' Vidal said softly.

'This' was being ruthlessly dragged into his arms and then being pinioned against him, trapped between him and the wall behind her, as he bound her to his body so intimately that she felt as though she could feel the bones and the hard male muscles that lay beneath the sleek flesh that padded them. Unlike her own, his heartbeat was steady—steady and determined. The heartbeat of a victor who had successfully captured his prey.

Was this how that long-ago Moorish princess had felt held in the vice-like grip of her captor?

Fliss's own heartbeat raced, her pulse flickering in a wild primeval dance that took away her ability to think or even feel rationally. Had she, that long-ago young woman, also felt the same searing, soaring, confusing of fear and triumph? Fear for her independence—fear of the wild clamouring that was beating through her. And had she felt triumph because she had been able to drive the man holding her beyond his own self-control? Because she had broken something in him? Even though the price of that victory would be him exerting his power over her in retaliation?

A mêlée of thoughts and feelings rioted inside her, turning her into a version of herself she barely recognised.

He shouldn't be doing this, Vidal knew, but somehow he couldn't stop himself. A thousand nights and more of dragging himself from forbidden dreams in which he held her like this overwhelmed his self-control. She wasn't sixteen any more; she wasn't forbidden by his own moral code—even if his pride burned and recoiled at the thought of still desiring her.

The girl with the wide-eyed gaze, filled with all the heady innocence of a sixteen-year-old in the grip of her first sexual desire for a man, had never existed anywhere other than in his imagination. All the nights he had lain sleepless and tormented the bed *she* had been lying in had been far from chaste.

As he bent his head towards hers he could feel the thud of her heartbeat and the soft warmth of her breasts pressed against his chest—those breasts from which he had ached so badly to peel the tee shirt covering them so that he could reveal their perfection to his gaze and touch, so that he could pluck on the tormenting thrust of her nipples with his fingertips, so that he could draw them into his mouth and caress them until her body arched with longing for his possession.

No! He must not do this.

Vidal made to release her, but Fliss shuddered violently against him, the small sound she made deep in her throat drowning out his denial.

Vidal was looking into her eyes, forcing her to look back at him. Close up, his eyes weren't one solid colour but several shades mingling together into topaz-gold. The unblinking intensity of his gaze was dizzying her, just as the heavy thud of his heart beating was commanding her own heart to match its rhythm.

In another heartbeat he would kiss her, and she would feel the cold, unforgiving dominance of those sharply cut lips. Her own parted—on a protest against what he was doing, not a sign of her docile acceptance of it, and certainly not in eager anticipation of it.

And yet…

And yet beneath her clothes, beneath her top and her plain, practical neutral-coloured bra, her breasts had begun to ache with a sensation that seemed to have spread down from where his hand was covering the pulse in her throat to the tightening peaks of her nipples. Fliss trembled in its grip, shockingly forced to admit to herself that what her body and that ache within it was signalling was *not* angry rejection. Instead a burgeoning female desire was running through her veins like heavy, melting liquid pleasure—a pleasure that lapped at her senses and undermined her self-control, replacing it with a growing sensual longing.

Vidal's breath grazed her skin, clean and slightly minty. Beneath the newly cleansed scent of his skin her senses picked up something else—something primitive and dangerous to a woman whose own sensuality had broken past the barriers of her self-control. The scent of alluring raw maleness, which called out to that sensuality and somehow had her moving closer to him, her lips parting just a little bit more.

Their gazes clung and fought hotly for supremacy, and then his mouth was on hers. The pressure of those male lips was sending her senses into overdrive, causing a heat explosion of pleasure to melt liquid desire into her lower body.

Fliss tried to fight what she was feeling. She made a helpless sound—she could feel it reverberating in her own throat—a sound of protest, Fliss was sure. Although her ears translated it more as a shockingly keening moan of need. A need that was instantly increased by the insistent grind of Vidal's body into her own, and a tightening of his hold on her whilst his tongue took possession of the intimate softness of her mouth, thrusting against her own tongue, taking her to a place of dark velvet sensuality and danger. Her whole body was on fire, pulsing with a reaction to him which seemed to have exploded inside her. Her eyes closed...

Vidal felt the force of his own angry desire surging through him, sweeping aside barriers within himself he had thought impenetrable. The more he tried to regain control, the more savage his reaction became. Anger and out-of-control male desire. Each of them was dangerous enough alone, but incite them both, as this woman he was holding now had done, and the alchemic reaction between them had the power to rip a man's self-respect to shreds—and with it his belief in himself.

Behind his own closed eyelids Vidal saw her as his body most wanted her: naked, eager to appease the male passion she had induced and unleashed, offering herself. Her white skin would be pearlescent with the dew of her own arousal, the dark pink crests of her breasts flowering into hard nubs of pleasure that sought the caress of his fingertips and his lips.

Outside in the garden below them the gathering dusk activated the system that brought on the garden lighting. Sudden illumination burst into life, causing Vidal to open his eyes and recognise what he was doing.

Cursing himself mentally, he released Fliss abruptly.

The shock of transition from a kiss so intimate that she felt it had seared her senses for ever to the reality of who exactly had been delivering that kiss had Fliss shuddering with self-revulsion. But before she could gather her scattered senses—before she could do anything, before she could tell Vidal what she thought of him—he was speaking to her. As though what he had done had never happened.

'What I came to tell you is that it will be an early start in the morning, since we have a ten-o'clock appointment with your father's lawyer. Rosa will send someone up with your breakfast, since my mother isn't expected back until tomorrow. I also have to tell you that any future attempt by you to…to *persuade* me to satisfy your promiscuously carnal desires will be as doomed to failure as this one.' His mouth twisted cynically and he gave her a coldly insulting look. 'Over-used goods have never held any appeal for me.'

Over-used goods.

Trembling with rage at his insult, Fliss lost her head. 'You were the one who started this, not me. And…and you're wrong about me. You always have been. What you saw—'

'What I saw was a sixteen-year-old tramp, lying on her mother's bed, allowing a young lout to paw her and boast that *he* intended to have her because the rest of his football team already had.'

'Get out!' Fliss demanded, her voice rising in anger. 'Get *out*!'

He strode away from her and through the bedroom door.

As soon as she could trust herself to move she half ran and half stumbled to the door, turning the key in the lock, tears of rage and shame spilling from her hot eyes.

CHAPTER THREE

IT WAS too late to try and hold back the memories
now. They were there with her in every raw and cruel
detail.

Fliss sank down into one of the chairs, her head in
her hands.

She had been shocked and hurt when Vidal had told
her that he'd intercepted her letter to her father. Such
a cruel action from someone she had put on a pedestal
had hurt very badly, coming on top of Vidal's exist-
ing coldness towards her. Rejection by her father and
his family—something she had always tried to pretend
didn't matter—had suddenly become very real and very
painful. She had seen the warmth with which Vidal
treated her mother, and that had made her own sense
of rejection worse. He wasn't after being cold to them
both—just to her.

When her mother had told her that Vidal was taking
her out to dinner as a thank-you for his stay, Fliss had
asked if she might have some schoolfriends round to celebrate the ending of the school year and their exams. Her
mother had agreed—on the strict understanding that she
was only to invite half a dozen of her classmates. This

had seemed fair to Fliss and so she had been horrified when their get-together was interrupted by the arrival of what had seemed like dozens of teenagers—many of whom already the worse for drink.

She had tried to persuade them to leave, but her efforts had been met by jeers and even more rowdy behaviour. One of the boys—Rory—had been the ringleader of a wild crowd from her school. A swaggering bully of a boy who'd played in the school football team. He had gone upstairs with the girl who had arrived with him—a stranger to Fliss—and she had followed them, horrified when they went into her mother's bedroom.

In the row that had followed the girl had left, and Rory, furious with Fliss, who had been 'spoiling his fun', had grabbed her and pulled her down onto the bed. His actions had turned Fliss's anger to fear. She had tried to pull free and fight him off, but he had laughed at her, pouring cider over her from the bottle he had brought up with him and then pushing her back against the bed.

That was when the door had opened and she had seen her mother and Vidal standing there. At first she had been relieved—but then she had seen the look on Vidal's face. So had Rory, because that had been when he had made that crude and completely untrue comment about the rest of the football team, followed by an equally untrue statement.

'She loves it. She can't get enough of it. Ask any of the lads. They all know how well she's up for it. A proper little nympho, she is.'

Fliss could still remember the feeling of shocked disbelief icing through her, making it impossible for her to speak or move; to defend herself or refute his boast. Instead she had simply lain there, numbed with horror, whilst Vidal had pulled Rory from the bed and marched him downstairs.

Her mother's shocked, 'Oh, Fliss...' had been ringing in her ears as she'd followed.

Later, of course, she had explained what had happened to her mother, and thankfully her mother had believed her, but by that time Vidal had been on his way back to Spain, and the pain she had felt on seeing the contempt and loathing in his eyes as he'd looked at her had turned her crush on him into revulsion and anger.

She had never gone back to school. She and the three girls who had become her closest friends had gone instead to a sixth-form college, thanks to the excellence of their exam results, and Fliss had made a private vow to herself that she would make her mother proud of her. She would never, ever allow another man to look at her as Vidal had done. She had never discussed with anyone just what his misjudgement of her that evening had done to her. It was her private shame. And now Vidal had resurrected that shame.

Downstairs in the library, with its high ceiling and Biblical frescoes, Vidal stood motionless and white-lipped, staring unseeingly into space, oblivious to the grandeur of his surroundings. The bookshelves were laden with leather-covered books, their titles painted on the spines in gold, and the scent of leather and paper pervaded the room.

Vidal knew himself to be a man of strong principle,

with deep passions and convictions about his ancestry and his duty to it, and to the people who depended on him. Never before had the strength of those passions boiled over into the fury that Felicity had aroused in him. Never before had he come so close to having his self-control consumed in such intense fires.

If he hadn't been stopped when those lights had come on...

He would have stopped anyway, he assured himself. But a critical inner voice demanded silkily, *Would you?* Or would he have continued to be consumed by his own out-of-control emotions until he had had Felicity spread naked on the bed beneath him, as he sought to satisfy the hunger within him he had thought extinguished?

Vidal closed his eyes and then opened them again. He had thought he'd put the past behind him, but Felicity had brought it back to life with a vengeance.

He needed this to be over. He needed to walk away from the past and draw a line under it. He needed to be rid of it—and for that to happen he needed to be rid of Felicity herself.

Vidal's mouth compressed. As soon as they had seen Felipe's lawyer, and arrangements had been made for Vidal to buy from Felicity the house her father had left her, he would remove her from his life—permanently.

Upstairs in the bathroom adjoining her bedroom, the door safely locked, Fliss stood motionless and dry-eyed beneath the beating lash of the powerful shower. She was beyond tears, beyond anger—except for the anger that burned inside her against herself—beyond anything other than the knowledge that she could stand beneath the fiercely drumming water for the rest of her life—but no amount of water would ever wash away the stain she herself had stamped—dyed—into her pride via what she had done when she had responded to Vidal's contemptuous kiss.

Stepping out of the shower, she reached for a towel. Perhaps she should not have come here, after all. But that was what Vidal had wanted, wasn't it? The letter he had sent as her father's executor, advising her of the fact that her father had left her his house, had said that there was no need. No need as far as *he* was concerned, but every need for her, Fliss reminded herself as she towelled her hair dry. Her body was concealed from her own gaze by the thick soft towel she had wrapped around herself, which covered her from her breasts down to her feet. She had no wish to look upon the flesh that had betrayed her. Or was she the one who had betrayed it? Had she had more experience, more lovers, the lifestyle and the men Vidal had accused her of giving herself to—if she had not deliberately refused to allow her sexuality and her sensuality to know the pleasures they were made for—she would surely have been better equipped to deal with what was happening to her now.

She couldn't possibly *really* have wanted Vidal. That was impossible.

Her heart started to beat jerkily, so that she had to put her hand over it in an attempt to calm it.

It *was* impossible, wasn't it? A woman would have to be bereft of all pride and self-protection to allow herself to feel any kind of desire for a man who had treated

her as Vidal had. It was the past that was doing this to
her—trapping her, refusing to let her move forward.
The past and the unhealed wounds Vidal had inflicted
on her there...

It was the sound of her bedroom door rattling that
brought Fliss out of the uneasy sleep she had eventually fallen into, after what had felt like hours of lying
awake with her body tense and her mind a whirlwind of
angry, passionate thoughts. At first the image conjured
up inside her head was one of Vidal, his long fingers
curled round the door handle. Immediately a surge of
sensation burned through her body, igniting an unfamiliar and unwanted sensual ache that shocked her into
reality—and shame.

The darkness of the night, with its sensually tempting whispers and torments, was over. It was morning
now. Light and sunshine flooded into the room through
the windows over which she had forgotten to close the
curtains the previous night.

The faint knocking she could still hear on the door
was far too hesitant to come from a man like Vidal.

Calling out that she would unlock the door, Fliss
got out of bed, glad that she had done so when she discovered a small, nervous-looking young maid standing
outside the door and pushing a trolley containing Fliss's
breakfast.

Thanking her, Fliss quickly checked her watch. It was
gone eight o'clock already, and her appointment with her
late father's lawyer was at ten. She had no idea where
the offices were, or how long it would take to get there.

She'd have preferred to go there alone, but of course with Vidal named as her late father's executor that was impossible.

With the maid gone, Fliss gulped down a few swallows of the deliciously fragrant coffee she had poured for her, and snatched small bites from one of the fresh warm rolls which she had broken open and spread with sharp orange conserve. Her mother had told her about this special orange conserve, beloved of the family, which was made with the oranges from their own groves. Just tasting it reminded her of her mother, and that in turn helped to calm her and steady her resolve.

Half an hour later she was showered and dressed in a clean tee shirt and her plain dark 'city' skirt, her hair brushed back off her face and confined in a clip in a way that unwittingly revealed the delicacy of her features and the slender length of her neck. Fliss automatically touched the small heart-shaped gold locket that hung from her neck on its narrow gold chain. It had been a gift from her father to her mother. Her mother had worn it always, and now Fliss wore it in her memory.

A swift curl of mascara and a slick of lipstick and she was ready. And just in time, she reflected as she heard another knock on her bedroom door—a rather more confident one this time. When she opened the bedroom door it was to find Rosa standing outside, her expression as wary and disapproving as it had been the previous evening.

'You are to go down to the library. I will show you the way,' she announced in Spanish, her button-shiny, sharp dark eyes assessing Fliss in a way that made Fliss feel her appearance had been found wanting when compared with the elegance no doubt adopted by the kind of women a man like Vidal preferred. Soignée, sophisticated, designer-clad women with that air of cool hauteur and reserve her mother had told her that highborn Spanish women wore like the all-covering muslin robes once worn by the Moors who had preceded them.

So what? She was here to speak with her father's lawyers, not to dress to impress a man who filled her with dislike and contempt, Fliss reminded herself.

No sound other than that made by their feet on the stairs broke the heavy silence of the house's dark interior as Rosa escorted her down to the library, opening the door for her and telling her briskly that she was to wait inside for Vidal.

Normally Fliss would have been unable to resist looking at the titles of the books filling the double-height shelves that ran round the whole room, but for some reason she felt too on edge to do anything other than wish that the coming meeting was safely over.

Safely over? Why should she feel unsafe and on edge? She already knew the contents of her father's will so far as they concerned her. He had left Fliss the house he himself had inherited from Vidal's grandmother, on the ducal estate in the Lecrin Valley, along with a small sum of money, whilst the agricultural land that surrounded it had been returned to the main estate.

Was she wrong to feel that there was a message for her in this bequest? Was it just her own longing that made her hope it was the loving touch of a father filled with regret for a relationship never allowed to exist? Was it foolish of her to yearn somehow to find something of what might have been? Some shadowy ghost of regret to warm her heart, waiting for her in the home her father had left her?

Fliss knew that if Vidal were to guess what she was thinking he would destroy her fragile hopes and leave her with nothing to soften the rejection of her childhood years. Which was why he must not know why she had come here, instead of staying in England as he instructed her to do. In the house where her father had lived she might finally find something to ease the pain she had grown up with. After all, her father must have intended *something* by leaving her his home. An act like that was in its own way an act of love, and she longed so much to have that love.

Not that she couldn't help wishing the house was somewhere other than so close to Vidal's family *castillo*.

As grand as this townhouse was, Fliss knew from her mother that it couldn't compare with the magnificence of the ducal *castillo*, in the idyllically beautiful Lecrin Valley to the south of Granada.

Set on the south-westerly slopes of the Sierra Nevada, and running down to the coast with its sub-tropical climate, the valley had been much loved by the Moors, who had spoken of the area as the Valley of Happiness. Her mother's voice had been soft with emotion when she had told Fliss that in spring the air was filled with the scent of the blossom from the orchards that surrounded the castle.

Olives, almonds, cherries, and wine from the vines

that covered many acres of its land were produced in abundance by the ducal estate, and the house owned by her father was, Fliss knew, called House of Almond Blossom because it was set amongst an orchard of those trees.

Was Vidal trying to undermine her in having her brought to this so openly male-orientated room and then left here alone, virtually imprisoned in its austere and unwelcoming maleness? she questioned, her thoughts returning to the present. Why couldn't Rosa have simply called her down when Vidal himself was ready to leave for the lawyer's office? Why had she been made to wait here, in this room that spoke so forcefully of male power and male arrogance?

As though her hostile thoughts had somehow conjured him up, the door swung open and Vidal stepped into the room—just as she was in angry, agitated mid-pace, her eyes flashing telltale signs of what she was feeling as she looked towards him.

He was dressed in a pair of narrow black chinos that hugged the litheness of his hips and stretched with the movement of his thighs, drawing her treacherous gaze to the obvious strength and power of the male muscles there. As though having already been accused and found guilty of treachery, and deciding that it now had nothing left to lose, her gaze moved boldly upwards, its awareness of him unhampered by the white shirt covering the physical reality of his torso.

Aghast, Fliss realised that her imagination had joined in the betrayal and was now supplying her with totally unwanted images of what lay beneath that shirt—right down to providing her with a mental picture of every single powerful muscle his flesh cloaked from the memories her senses had stored after her proximity to him last night.

Only when her gaze reached his throat was Fliss finally able to drag it back down to the shiny polished gleam of his shoes as it quailed at the thought of daring to rest on his mouth, or meet the gaze of those topaz-gold eyes.

She felt slightly breathless, and her senses were quivering—with distaste and dislike, Fliss insisted to herself. Not with awareness or—perish the thought—some horrible and unwanted surge of female desire.

Her heart started pounding far too heavily, the sound drumming inside her own head like a warning call. Her lips had started to burn. She desperately wanted to lick them—to cool them down, to impose the feel of her own tongue against them and wipe away the memory of Vidal's kiss. So much treachery from her own body. Where had it come from, and why? She tried to think of her father and remind herself of why she was here, dredging up the broken strands of her self-control from the whirlpool into which they had been sucked.

Taking a deep breath, she told Vidal, 'It's nearly ten o'clock. I seem to remember that last night you warned me against being late for our appointment with the lawyer—but apparently that same rule does not apply to you.'

He was frowning now, obviously disliking the fact that she had dared to question him. His voice was cool and sharp as he answered. 'As you say, it's nearly ten o'clock—but since Señor Gonzales has not yet arrived, so far as I am concerned I am ahead of time.'

'The lawyer is coming *here*?' Fliss demanded, ignoring his attack on her. Her face flamed like that of a child caught out in a social solecism, or a *faux pas*. Of *course* a man as aristocratic and as arrogant as Vidal would expect lawyers to attend him—not the other way round.

The loud pealing of a bell echoing through the marble-floored hallway beyond the half-open library door silenced any further comment Fliss might have tried to make.

No doubt feeling that he had triumphed over her, Vidal strode away from her. Fliss could hear him greeting and welcoming another man, whose voice she could also now hear.

'Coffee in the library, please, Rosa,' Fliss heard Vidal instructing the housekeeper as the two men approached the open doorway.

She had no real reason to feel apprehensive or even nervous, but she *did* feel both those emotions, Fliss admitted as Vidal waved the small dark-suited man who must be Señor Gonzales into the library ahead of him, and then introduced him to her.

The lawyer gave her an old-fashioned and formal half-bow, before extending his hand to shake hers.

'Señor Gonzales will go through the terms of your late father's will in so far as they relate to you. As was explained to you in the letter I sent, as your father's executor it is part of my role to carry out his wishes.'

As he led them over to the imposing dark wood desk

at one side of the room's marble fireplace, Fliss recognised that note in Vidal's voice that said there had
been no need for her to come to Spain to hear what had
already been reported to her via letter, but Fliss refused
to be undermined by it. The lawyer, polite though he
had been to her, was bound to be on Vidal's side, she
warned herself, and she would have to be on her guard
with both of them.

'My late father has left me his house. I know that,'
Fliss agreed once they were all seated round the desk.
She broke off from what she was saying when a maid
came in with the coffee, which had to be poured and
handed out to them with due formality before they were
alone again.

'Felipe wanted to make amends to you for the fact
that he had not been able to acknowledge you formally
and publicly whilst he was alive,' Señor Gonzales said
quietly.

Silently Fliss digested his words.

'Financially—'

'Financially I have no need of my father's inheritance,' Fliss interrupted him quickly.

She was *not* going to allow Vidal to think even worse
of her than he already did and suggest that it was the
financial aspect of her inheritance that had brought her
here. The truth was that she would far rather have had
a personal letter from her father proclaiming his love
for her than any amount of money.

'Thanks to the generosity of one of my English relatives my mother and I never suffered financially from
my father's rejection of us. My mother's great aunt did

not reject us. She thought enough of us to want to help us. She cared when others did not.'

Fliss felt proud to be able to point out to the two men that it was her mother's family who had stepped in and saved them from penury—who had cared enough about them to *want* to do that.

She could feel Vidal watching her, but she wasn't going to give him the satisfaction of looking back at him so that he could show her the contempt he felt for her.

'Are there any questions you wish to ask now about your late father's bequest to you before we continue?' the lawyer invited.

Fliss took a deep steadying breath. Here it was—the opportunity she so desperately wanted to ask the question that she so much wanted answering.

'There is something.' She had turned her body slightly in her chair, so that she was facing the lawyer and not Vidal, but she was still conscious of the fact that Vidal was focusing on her. 'I know that there was a family arrangement that my father would marry a girl who had been picked out for him as his future wife by his grandmother, but according to the letter you sent me he never married.'

'That is correct,' Señor Gonzales agreed.

'What happened? Why didn't he marry her?'

'Señor Gonzales is unable to provide you with the answer to that question.'

The harsh, incisive slice of Vidal's voice lacerated the small silence that had followed her question, causing Fliss to turn round and look at him.

'However, I can. Your father did not marry Isabella y Fontera because her family withdrew from the match. Though they made some other excuse, it was likely they got wind of the scandal surrounding him. His health had deteriorated, too, so no more matchmaking attempts were made. What were you hoping to hear? That he withdrew from it out of guilt and regret? I'm sorry to disappoint you. Felipe was not the sort of man to go against our grandmother.'

Fliss could feel her nails biting into her palms as she made small angry fists of rejection. The golden gaze pinned her own and held it, making it impossible for her to escape from Vidal's thorough scrutiny of her. The way he was looking at her made her feel as though he would take possession of her mind and control her very thoughts if she let him. But of course there was no way she was going to do that. Pity indeed the woman he eventually married—because she would be expected to surrender the whole of herself, mind and body, to his control.

Her heart jolted against her ribs. In absolute contempt for what he was, Fliss assured herself, and certainly not because any foolish part of her was tempted to wonder what it would be like to be possessed so completely by a man like Vidal.

'What happened in the past happened, and I'd suggest that you would be a lot happier if you allowed yourself to move on from it.'

Fliss dragged her thoughts back from the dangerous sensuality they had escaped to and made herself focus on the sharp timbre of Vidal's voice.

'If you questioned your mother as antagonistically as you have spoken here you must have caused her a great deal of pain by never allowing the matter to be forgotten.'

The callousness of his accusation almost took Fliss's breath away. She had to fight not to let him see how easily he had found where she was most vulnerable, and defended herself immediately. 'My mother did not *want* to forget my father. She wore this locket he gave her until the day she died. She never stopped loving him.'

The gold locket chain shimmered with the agitated movement of the pulse beating at the base of Fliss's throat. Vidal could remember how it had shimmered with an equal but very different intensity of emotion the day Felipe had fastened it around Fliss's mother's neck.

It had been here in Granada that Felipe had bought the necklace for her. He had found them when they were on their way to visit the Alhambra, announcing that some unexpected business had brought him there from the family estate. They had been walking past a jeweller's shop when he had caught up with them, and when Vidal had told Felipe that it was Annabel's birthday his uncle had insisted on going into the shop and buying the trinket for her.

Vidal shook his head, dragging his thoughts back to the present.

'The house is mine to do with as I wish, as I understand it,' Fliss said, and dared Vidal to contradict her.

'That is true,' the lawyer intervened. 'But since the

house was originally part of the ducal estate it makes sense for Vidal to buy it from you. After all, you can have no wish for the responsibility of such a property.'

'You want to buy the house from me?' she challenged Vidal, her gaze steady.

'Yes. Surely you must have expected that I would? As Señor Gonzales has just said, the house belonged originally to the estate. If you are concerned that I might try to cheat you out of its true value—and I am sure that you are, given your obvious hostility towards me—I can assure you that I am not, and that it will be independently and professionally valued.'

Turning her back on Vidal, Fliss told the lawyer quickly, 'I want to see the house before it is sold.' When he began to frown she said fiercely, 'My father lived there. It was his home. Surely it's only natural that I should want to go there and see it, so I can see where and how he lived?'

The lawyer seemed uncomfortable, looking past her towards Vidal, as though seeking his approval.

'The house belongs to *me*,' she reminded him. 'And if I want to go there no one can stop me.'

There was a small silence, and then Fliss heard Vidal exhale.

'I have some business to attend to at the *castillo*, Luis,' he told the lawyer, using his Christian name for the first time. 'I will escort Felicity there tomorrow, so that she can satisfy her curiosity.'

The lawyer was looking relieved and grateful, Fliss recognised, as Vidal stood up, signalling that their meeting was over and saying, 'We shall meet again in a few days' time to progress this matter.'

Fliss noted that the lawyer avoided meeting her gaze when he shook hands with her before going, and that he and Vidal left the library together, leaving her still inside it and alone.

Alone.

She *was* alone now. Completely alone, with no family of her own. No one to support her; no one to protect her.

To *protect* her? From what? From Vidal? Or from those feelings Vidal aroused in her that led her body into responses to his maleness that were shamefully treacherous given what she already knew about him?

Shakily Fliss pushed the unwanted question away. So she had let down her guard accidentally, and somehow that had caused her to become aware of Vidal as a man. It had been a mistake, that was all—something she could put right by making sure that it didn't happen again.

The copy of her father's will that Señor Gonzales had given her was still on the desk. Fliss picked it up, her attention drawn to her father's signature. How many times as a child she had whispered that name over and over again to herself, as though it was some kind of magic charm that would cause her father to become a part of her life. But her father had *not* been part of her life, and she would not find him in the house in which he had lived. How could she when he was dead? She had to go there, though. She had to see it.

Because Vidal did not want her to?

No! Not because of that. Because of her father—not because of Vidal.

Fliss felt as though her emotions were threatening to suffocate her. She could hardly breathe from the force of her own feelings. She had to get out of this house. She had to breathe some air that was not tainted by Vidal's presence.

The hallway was empty when she walked through it, heading for the stairs and intent on getting her handbag and her sunglasses. She would go out and see something of the city—cleanse her mind of the unwanted influence that Vidal seemed to be exerting over it.

Ten minutes later Vidal watched from the library window as Fliss left the house. If he had had his way her departure would have been for the airport and England—and permanent. He had enough to think about without having her around, reminding him of things he would preferred to have left shrouded in the shadows of the past.

He still hadn't come to terms with his own behaviour last night—or with his inability to impose his will on his body.

CHAPTER FOUR

SHE had spent virtually all day exploring the city. The city, but not the Alhambra—she wasn't ready for that yet. She felt too raw after this morning's run-in with Vidal—too vulnerable to visit the place where her father had first declared his love for her mother, where the boy had witnessed that exchange and then reported it to his grandmother.

A small tapas bar had provided her with lunch. She hadn't been very hungry, and in fact felt she had not done proper justice to the delicious delicacies that had been served up for her.

Now, with her exploration of the conservation site that was the old Moorish quarter of the city behind her, she was forced to admit that her body had probably had a surfeit of hard pavements and intense sunshine. It craved the cool shade promised by the courtyard garden her bedroom overlooked.

The same shy maid who had brought her break-fast opened the door for her when she pulled the bell. Thankfully there was no sign of Vidal, and the library door remained firmly closed. She asked the maid how best she could get into the courtyard, thanking her when she explained that a corridor accessed from the rear of the hallway had a set of doors that opened into it.

While she was out she'd taken the opportunity to go shopping and buy some clothes to supplement those she had brought with her. Now that she was staying with the Salvetore family, rather than the hotel she'd booked, she realised she would need some more. After trying on a variety of things she had settled on a loosely gathered cotton dress in her favourite shade of cream, because it felt so light and cool, adding a simple linen shift in pale blue, a pair of tan cut-offs and a couple of softly shaped tops—cool, practical, easy-to-wear clothes in which she would feel much more comfortable than jeans and her city skirt.

In her bedroom, after a quick shower, she put on the cream dress. Simply styled, it was tiered in pleats from a square neckline banded with crunchy cotton lace. Worn with the flip-flops she had brought with her, the dress felt pleasantly cool and airy.

Back downstairs, she quickly found the corridor the maid had described to her, and the doors from it that led into the cloistered walkway that she could now see ran the full width of the courtyard. As she came out of the darkness of the corridor into the brightness of the sunlight beyond, momentarily dazzled by the light, Fliss came to an abrupt and self-conscious halt. She realised that she hadn't got the courtyard to herself.

The woman she could see seated at an ornate wrought-iron table, drinking a cup of coffee, had to be Vidal's mother. They had the same eyes—although in Vidal's mother's case their gaze was warm and gentle rather than cold and filled with contempt.

'You are Annabel's daughter, of course,' the Duchess said, before Fliss could retreat, adding, 'You are very like her. But I think you have something of your father's blood as well. I can see it in your expression. Please—come and sit here beside me,' she invited, patting the empty chair next to her own.

Hesitantly Fliss made her way towards her.

Tall and slender, her dark hair streaked with grey and worn in the kind of elegant, formal style that suited Spanish women so well, Vidal's mother smiled at her and apologised. 'I'm sorry I wasn't able to be here to welcome you yesterday. Vidal will have explained that I have a dear friend who is not very well.'

A small shadow darkened her eyes, causing Fliss to enquire politely, 'I hope your friend is feeling better?'

'She is very brave. She has Parkinson's disease, but she makes light of it. We were at school together and have known one another all our lives. Vidal tells me that he is taking you tomorrow to see your father's house? I would have liked to go with you, but my friend's husband was called away unexpectedly on urgent business and I have promised to keep her company until he returns.'

'It's all right. I mean, I understand…' Fliss told her truthfully. She stopped talking when she realised that the Duchess was looking past her into the shadows of the house, her smile deepening as she exclaimed, 'Ah, Vidal, there you are! I was just saying to Fliss how sorry I am that I shan't be able to accompany you to the *castillo*.'

Vidal.

Why was that quiver of sensation racing down her spine? Why did she suddenly feel so aware of her own body and its reactions, its womanhood and its sensuality? She must stop reacting like this. She must ignore these unwanted feelings instead of focusing on them.

'I'm sure Felicity understands why, Mamá. How is Cecilia?'

Immediately she registered Vidal's voice. Fliss's heart went into a flurry of small frantic beats that made her feel more breathless than she liked. It was because she hated him so much, she assured herself. Because she hated him for betraying her mother.

'She is very weak and tired.' The Duchess was answering Vidal, then suggesting to him, 'Why don't you join us for a few minutes? I'll ring for a fresh pot of coffee. Fliss looks very like her mother in her pretty cool dress, don't you think?' she asked.

'I suspect that Felicity has a very different personality from her mother.'

'Yes, I have—and I'm glad. My mother's gentleness meant that she was treated very unkindly.'

Fliss saw the colour leave the Duchess's face and Vidal's mouth tighten. Her remark was not the kind a guest should make to her hostess, but she had not *asked* to stay here with her late father's family, Fliss defended herself, before turning on her heel and heading for the opposite end of the courtyard, wanting to put as much distance as she could between herself and Vidal.

The only reason she had chosen to escape further into the garden and not the house was that to get into the house she would have had to walk past him. Knowing how shamefully vulnerable her body was to him, that was something she had not been prepared to do. Now, hidden from view of the cloistered terrace by the shadows thrown by the rose-covered pergola at the bottom of the garden, Fliss lifted her hand to her heart to calm its angrily unsteady thudding.

The petals on the roses trembled as her sanctuary was penetrated. A tanned male hand brushed aside the branches, and pink petals swirled down onto the tiled pathway as Vidal stepped into the rose-cented bower formed by the pergola.

Without any preamble Vidal launched into his verbal attack, telling her coldly, 'You may be as antagonistic as you wish to me, but I will not have you hurting or upsetting my mother—especially at this time, when she has her friend's health on her mind. My mother has shown you nothing but courtesy.'

'That's true,' Fliss was forced to agree. 'However you're hardly the person to tell me how to behave, are you? After all, you obviously didn't have any qualms about intercepting my letter to my father, did you?' she accused him vehemently, her voice wobbling slightly over the final word.

Fliss was shaking inwardly and outwardly. Her one desire was to escape from Vidal's coldly critical presence before she made a complete fool of herself by telling him how unfairly he had misjudged her and how much that misjudgement had hurt her. How much it still hurt her.

Avoiding looking at him, she started to walk quickly

back down the pergola—until she was brought to an abrupt halt when she slipped on the petal-scattered path.

The sensation of strong hands reaching for her, strong arms supporting her, brought her an initial and auto-matic surge of gratitude—but as soon as her body reg-istered the fact that the hands and arms, like the body she was now being supported against, belonged to Vidal that gratitude was replaced by panic. Frantically Fliss struggled to free herself, thoroughly alarmed by the way her body was already reacting to the intimate contact between them.

For his part Vidal had no wish to hold on to her. Turning to watch her rush away from him, he had seen how the sunlight shining through her thin cotton dress revealed the female curves of her body, and immedi-ately—to his grim disbelief—his body had responded to that sight and to *her.* Now, having her twisting and turning in his arms, her breasts rising and falling with agitation, her breath touching his skin in a silken caress, the scent and the feel of her was calling to an instinct within him that wouldn't be denied. An instinct that demanded he taste the erotically tender pink flesh of her lips, that he find and possess the soft rounded curves of her breasts, that he hold the cradle of her lower body close to the now swollen sexuality of his own.

In an attempt to push Vidal off, Fliss reached out wildly with her hand. Her whole body selate f with shock when her fingertips encountered the satin warmth of his bare chest. Fliss looked down at where her hand was resting and saw that Vidal's shirt was now unfastened almost to the belt of his chinos. Had *she* done that? Had she ripped open those buttons when she had clung to him earlier and then struggled against his confining grip? Her hand was now resting palm flat on his golden skin, and the dark cross of fine hair that narrowed downwards over his impressive six-pack made Fliss feel as though nature herself had used that male body hair to mark him out as her own.

Was it the scent of the roses or the scent of Vidal's skin that was making her feel so weak? She was forced to sway closer to him, her body bending pliably and willingly to his without needing to be guided there by the pressure of his hand on the small of her back, heating her body through the fine fabric of her dress. The topaz gaze was fixed on her own. Then as she caught her breath it slid deliberately to her mouth, capturing the small frantic moan of longing assent that escaped from her lips.

The quiver that shook her body as though she found her desire for him beyond her ability to control, that soft sigh of acquiescence, that liquid look of longing she had given him—they might all be a deliberate ploy to entice him, Vidal told himself. But whilst his mind might deride his folly for responding to them his body had no such inhibitions. Anger against it and against the woman he was holding exploded through him in a savage burst of primeval male need.

Beneath the fierce onslaught of his kiss Fliss's already shaky defences gave way, her trembling lips opening to the demanding thrust of his tongue, her breast swelling into the cup of his hand. A heavy, aching sensation was rolling though her lower body and beginning an insistent pulsing beat that grew in tandem with the fiery burst of pleasure Vidal's probing fingers and thumb drew from the aroused tip of her breast.

Fliss had never thought of herself as a woman whose sensuality had the power to overwhelm her self-control. On the contrary, she had believed in her most private thoughts that she had an unfashionably low sex drive. But now, shockingly, Vidal was proving to her that that judgement of herself must have been wildly wrong. Her out-of-control and unwanted arousal, her need for the intimacy it was causing her to ache and long for, was sweeping through her like a forest fire, burning away any resistance that tried to stand in its way. Her desire to have Vidal touching the flesh of her breast had flamed into life well before Vidal had lifted its sensually en-gorged roundness free of her bra, so that her nipple was pushing eagerly against the tightly drawn fabric of her dress, its shape and even its dark rose colour easily visible beneath the thin fabric.

The sight of that enticement, that incitement to his own desire, had Vidal bending Fliss back in his arms and then lowering his head over her body, so that he could taste her nipple, so close in colour to the petals of the roses that were providing them with their privacy. Unable to stop herself, Fliss gave a soft, aching gasp of delirious pleasure. The sensation of his tongue stroking and caressing her so-sensitive flesh, one second soothing its need, the next tormenting with a flick of his tongue, was driving her to fresh heights of aching longing, and it stole away what was left of her self-control. Her spine arched, lifting her breast closer to Vidal's mouth.

The sheer wanton sensuality of the seeking movement of Fliss's body combined with the erotic feel of her hot, tight nipple against his tongue made Vidal forget what she was and where they were. At last—at last he had her in his arms, this woman whose memory so tormented him. His hold on her tightened as he drew her nipple deeper and harder into his mouth. Far from satisfying the volcanic ache of male need, that action only increased the savage torrent of desire rushing through him.

Bent back over Vidal's arm, clinging to his shoulders for support, Fliss could only shudder violently with previously unknown pleasure. A pleasure that was so intense it was almost more than she could bear. She wanted to tear her dress from her body and hold Vidal's mouth captive over her breast whilst he satisfied the growing tumultuous ache the fierce suckling movement of his mouth was creating—and at the same time she wanted to hide herself from him and what he was making her feel as fast as she could.

A cord of sensation like forked lightning zig-zagged inside her, running from her breast to the heart of her sexuality, making her want to plant her hand over that part of herself to both hide and calm its frantic hungry beat.

Scooping her up, Vidal pulled her tightly against him, so that she could feel his arousal, igniting another shaft of lightning within her as she responded to the sensual male message from his body.

Above her she could see the blue sky. She could smell the hot scent of their bodies mingling with the heady perfume of the roses. If he were to lay her down now and cover her flesh with his own—if he were to take her and possess her... Fliss felt her heart lift inside her chest and thud like a trapped bird. Wasn't this what she had wanted all those years ago when she had looked at Vidal and yearned for him?

Shock coursed through her, filling her with revulsion for her own behaviour, making her demand emotionally, 'Stop it—stop it! I don't want this.'

The frantic panic in her voice cut through Vidal's own arousal, filling him with an appalled sense of self-disgust. What on earth had possessed him? He knew what she was. He had seen and heard it for himself.

As soon as he had released her Vidal turned his back to her, sharply aware of his body's hard arousal—an unwanted and unwarranted arousal as far as he was concerned. How could he have let that happen?

Shaking, Fliss adjusted her clothing, the pink stain colouring her face and her chest not just caused by her embarrassment. Her nipples ached painfully—not only the one Vidal had been caressing but the other one as well. Even something as simple and as necessary as breathing was bringing an uncomfortable awareness of their heightened sensitivity. Her sex itself felt hot and swollen, pressing against the barrier of her briefs, its dampness shamefully evident to her. She couldn't understand what had happened to her—how she could have gone from bitter anger to intense desire in the space of a handful of seconds just because Vidal had touched her. How *could* she feel like this?

Fliss focused on Vidal's disappearing back as he returned to the house. She wasn't going to allow herself to trail in his wake, following him like an adoring puppy, like the girl she had been at sixteen. And besides, the reality was that she didn't feel up to facing anyone else at the moment. Right now she preferred the privacy of the rose-covered arbour and its wrought-iron bench, where she could sit down and recover her composure.

It was a good ten minutes before she felt able to start walking back to the house. Ten minutes was surely long enough to ensure that Vidal was nowhere in sight, even if it hadn't been long enough for her heart to entirely resume its regular heartbeat. She was beginning to feel very afraid that that was never going to happen, and that she would be cursed for ever to bear the scars of the pain he had caused her.

Engrossed in her own thoughts, Fliss had all but forgotten Vidal's mother until she reached the patio area and saw that the Duchess was still seated there. It was too late for her to retreat. The Duchess had seen her and was smiling at her, and besides...

Taking a deep breath, Fliss bravely stepped up to her, apologising with genuine remorse. 'I'm sorry if my comments upset or offended you. That wasn't my intention.'

An elegant long-fingered hand—a feminine version of her son's, surely?—clasped Fliss's arm gently.

'I suspect that I am the one who owes you an apology, Felicity. My son tends to be rather more protective of me than is always necessary. It comes in part because of the man he is, and from being head of such a traditional family, but also I think it comes because he was thrust into the role of head of the family at too young an age.' A shadow of remembered sadness touched her expression as she explained, 'My husband died when Vidal was seven.'

Fliss caught her breath in shock, unable to stop herself from creating inside her head an image of a seven-year-old boy learning that he had lost his father. Sympathy for Vidal? She must not weaken herself by going down *that* route!

'Then when Vidal was sixteen his grandmother died—which meant that he had to take on the responsibilities of his inheritance.' She paused to say quietly, 'I'm sorry. I'm boring you, I expect.'

Fliss shook her head. She might be trying to tell herself that she wasn't interested in hearing Vidal's loving mother's stories of her son's youth, but the truth was that in reality a part of her wanted her to beg the Duchess to tell her more. It was disturbingly easy for her to picture Vidal at sixteen—tall, dark-haired, still a boy, but already showing the physical signs of the man he would become.

A small charge of sensation touched her skin; Vidal's touch, like Vidal's mouth against her flesh, had burned away barriers she had thought set in concrete—values and judgements.

Somehow she managed to drag her attention back to Vidal's mother, who was still speaking, telling her gently, 'Vidal was very attached to your mother, you know. He thought a great deal of her.'

Fliss managed to nod her head, although she couldn't trust herself to say anything.

Her mother hadn't really talked much about Vidal's mother—other than to say that she hadn't been Vidal's grandmother's first choice of a bride for her son, and that it was the Duchess who had insisted on Vidal having a more rounded and diverse upbringing than his paternal grandmother had wanted.

Unwittingly confirming what Fliss's mother had told her, the Duchess continued, 'My mother-in-law did not approve one little bit when I persuaded my late husband to hire a young woman to help Vidal improve his English. She thought it very unsuitable, and would have preferred a male tutor, but I felt that my little boy already had enough male influence over his life.'

Such a fond and loving warmth infused the Duchess's face that Fliss knew she was mentally picturing the child that Vidal had been. Fliss could picture that child too. Her mother had taken a good many photographs whilst she had been in Spain, and Fliss had grown up knowing who the dark-haired boy featured in some of them was. She had one of them with her now, in her handbag, taken at the Alhambra. It showed her mother and her father with a much younger Vidal, smiling into the camera through a curtain of water from a fountain. In it her mother had her arm round Vidal's shoulders—a protective, caring arm, as though, young as she herself had been, she was very aware of her responsibility towards the boy she was holding.

'Vidal's grandmother was a very strict disciplinarian who did not approve of what she thought of as my indulgence of Vidal.' The Duchess paused. 'Your mother suffered greatly at the hands of our family. Poor Felipe was such a quiet, gentle person. He hated upsets of any kind, and was very much in thrall to his adoptive grandmother. Understandably so. She had brought him up, following the death of his mother, according to her own strict regime and what she thought his mother would have wanted for him. He hadn't inherited any money from his parents and so was financially dependent on my mother-in-law. Felipe pleaded with her to be allowed to do the honourable thing and marry your mother, but she flatly refused to allow it. She wouldn't even agree to advance enough money to him to enable him to make financial provision for the two of you. She could be very unforgiving. In her eyes both Felipe and your mother had broken the rules, and deserved to be punished for doing so. Felipe had no money of his own, no home to offer your mother, no means of earning a living. His job within the family was that of managing the family orchards.'

'And his grandmother wanted him to marry someone else,' Fliss pointed out.

'She did,' the Duchess agreed. 'My mother-in-law could be very harsh at times—cruelly harsh, I'm afraid. I confess that I could never warm to her, nor her to me. But Vidal's father, like Vidal himself, was a very strong and moral man. He was in South America on business when his mother found out about the relationship. It is my belief that had he been here he would have done his best to see to it that matters were handled differently. As it was, he never returned. His plane crashed and everyone on board was killed.'

Fliss drew in a sharp breath, unable to stop herself from sympathizing. 'How dreadful.'

'Yes, it was, for all of us, but especially for Vidal. He had to grow up very quickly after that.'

Quickly, and into a man who was as harsh and unforgiving as the grandmother who had no doubt taken a hand in his upbringing, Fliss thought bitterly.

It was hard for a child to grow up with the death of one of its parents, but even harder for one parent to be alive and a child be denied contact. She could remember her mother answering her own naive childhood questions as to why her parents were not together and married.

'Your father's family would never have allowed us to marry, Fliss. Someone like me could never be good enough for him. You see, darling, men like your father, from important aristocratic families, have to marry girls of their own sort.'

'You mean like princes marrying princesses?' Fliss remembered asking.

'Exactly like that,' her mother had agreed.

'I had no idea that things had gone as far as they had when Annabel was sent away,' the Duchess was saying now, looking rather grim.

'I was conceived by accident on the night she and Felipe parted. Neither of them had intended... My mother said my father had always behaved like a perfect gentlemen, but the news that she was being sent away led things to get out of control.' Fliss immediately defended her mother, feeling that she was being criticised. 'My mother didn't even realise at first that she was pregnant. Then when she did her parents insisted that she write to my father to tell him.'

She wasn't going to have the Duchess thinking badly of her mother, who had, after all, been an innocent and naive young girl of eighteen, desperately in love and heartbroken at the thought of being parted from the man she loved.

'That was when my mother received a letter back saying that she had no proof that I was Felipe's child, and that legal action would be taken against her if she ever tried to contact Felipe again.'

The Duchess sighed and shook her head. 'My mother-in-law insisted. In her eyes, even if your mother had previously been acceptable to her as a wife for Felipe, the fact that she had allowed him such intimacies...' The Duchess gave a small shrug 'In families such as ours there is something of the long-ago traditions of the Moors with regard to the women of the family and the sanctity of their purity. In Vidal's grandmother's day girls of good family never so much as left the family home without the escort of a *duenna* to guard their modesty. That is all changed now, but I'm afraid a little of what has been passed down in the blood lingers. There is a certain convention, a certain fastidiousness, a certain requirement within the family that its female members abide by a moral code and that—'

'That brides are virgins?' Fliss suggested.

The Duchess looked at her. 'I would put it more that

the men of the family are very protective of the virtue of their women. It has always been my belief that had Vidal's father returned safely to us here in Granada he would have insisted that your mother's innocence was honoured and your position within our family recognised. You are, after all, a member of this family, Felicity.'

The sight of the young maid coming out to ask if they wanted fresh coffee had Fliss shaking her head and excusing herself. It had been a long day. And tomorrow would be an even longer one now that she had insisted she wanted to see the house that had been her father's home, which he had now left her. A day in which she would be spending time in the company of the one man her instinct for self-preservation told her she should be spending as little time with as possible…

CHAPTER FIVE

'FELICITY, I KNOW that Vidal plans to leave immediately after breakfast tomorrow morning for the estate, so I won't keep you up any longer.'

The Duchess and Fliss were drinking their after-dinner coffee, sitting at a table on the vine-covered veranda outside the dining room.

Fliss had been very relieved indeed to discover that Vidal would not be joining them for dinner, as he already had an engagement with some friends.

It was true that she was feeling tired—drained, in fact, by the tension of the day—so she thanked the Duchess for her kind consideration and stood up, agreeing that she *was* ready for bed.

Having suspected that even though there would only be the two of them for dinner the Duchess would dress formally, Fliss was wearing her black dress, thankful that she had packed it. The jersey dress was an old favourite, and it looked good on her, she knew. She had bought it in a sale, and even then had baulked a little at the price, but the matt black fabric was cleverly cut and draped, and Fliss had quietened her conscience by saying that the dress was an investment piece that would earn its keep in terms of cost per wear.

She had washed and dried her hair before dinner, noticing that the sun had already lightened some of its strands.

It was not quite midnight—early, she knew, for the Spanish—but she had to smother a yawn as she made her way back to the main hallway and the stairs, through a succession of rooms all with imposing double doors that opened one into the other in the classical fashion, each one of them filled with heavy and no doubt extremely valuable antiques.

Upstairs in her bedroom Fliss noticed appreciatively that the bed had been turned down invitingly for her, and that it had been made up with fresh sheets at some stage. It would be pure luxury to sleep in such beautiful sheets—Egyptian cotton, with an obviously high thread count, and smelling ever so faintly of lavender.

Her mother had always loved good-quality bedlinen. Had she developed that appreciation of it whilst she was in Spain?

Fliss sighed as she removed her dress.

Tomorrow she would see her father's house—his home—the home he had left to her, finally acknowledging her. Under the safe privacy of the shower she let her eyes fill with emotional tears. She would have willingly traded a hundred houses for a few precious weeks with her father and really getting to know him, she admitted stepping out of the shower and reaching for a towel, drying her damp body.

Wrapping a fresh towel round herself, she went into

the bedroom to remove her sleep shorts and top from the drawer where she had placed them, hesitating when she looked towards the bed and imagined the cool smoothness of the luxurious sheets against her bare skin. Such a sensual pleasure—a small, private self-indulgence…

Smiling to herself, Fliss removed the towel and slid between the waiting sheets, breathing in blissfully as she did so. Their touch against her skin was even more heavenly than she had imagined, subtly easing the tension of the day from her body. She would sleep well tonight, and that sleep would equip her to face tomorrow—and Vidal.

Tiredly, Fliss switched off the bedroom lights.

In the silent garden below Fliss's closed bedroom windows, with only the stars to see him, Vidal frowned up at those windows. Right now, instead of standing here, dwelling with irritation on Fliss's behaviour and her insistence on seeing her father's house for herself, he should have been enjoying the charms of the elegant Italian divorcée who had obviously been invited to his friends' dinner party as a dining partner for him. She had made her enjoyment of his company plain enough, discreetly suggesting that they conclude the evening *à deux* at her hotel. She'd been dark-haired, very attractive, and a good conversationalist. There would have been a time when he would have had no hesitation in accepting her offer, but tonight…

But tonight what? Why was he here, his mind filled with the irritation that Fliss was causing him, instead of in bed with Mariella? The reality was that, much as he'd enjoyed the company of his old friends, excellent though the meal had been, he had found his thoughts preoccupied with Fliss. Because of the problems she was causing him—that was why. There was no other reason. Was there?

His body was already reminding him of that unwanted ache of angry and unexpected desire she had aroused in it. He could still smell the scent of her body, still remember the taste of her. The taste and the feel.

Determinedly he suppressed the unwanted clamour of his senses. What he had felt was a momentary lapse, he assured himself, caused by his body's memory of a girl it had once desired. Nothing more than that. It was an aberration which was best ignored instead of focused on and thus allowed to grow beyond its real importance. It meant nothing. It was his problem and his misfortune—a misfortune that could never be revealed to anyone else—if he had come to realise there was a flaw in his nature that cleaved to an idealistic belief in a once-in-a-lifetime love, a flame that no other love could match.

In his case that flame had had to be extinguished.

Vidal knew himself. He knew that for him the woman he loved must be a woman he could trust absolutely to be loyal to their love in every single way. Felicity could never be that woman. Her own history had already proved that.

The woman he *loved*? Just because as a young man he had been foolish enough to look at a sixteen-year-old girl and create inside himself a private image of that girl as a woman it did not mean anything other than that he

had been a fool. The innocence he had thought he had
seen in Felicity—the innocence he had fought against
his desire for her to protect—had been as non-existent as
the woman created by his imagination. That was what he
needed to remember—not the feelings she had aroused
in him. There was no point in looking backwards to
what might have been. The present and his future were
what they were.

Grimly Vidal turned away from the window to walk
back into the house.

'How long does it take to get to the *castillo*?'

Fliss's question was delivered through firmly controlled lips as she stared straight ahead through the
windscreen of an imposingly luxurious limousine. She
was seated in the passenger seat whilst Vidal pulled
away from the family townhouse and into the busy
morning traffic.

'About forty minutes—maybe fifty, depending on
the traffic.'

Vidal's response was equally terse, his attention outwardly focused on the road ahead of him. Although
inwardly he was far more aware of Fliss's presence in
the car next to him than he liked to admit.

She was wearing a light-coloured summer dress, and
as she had walked out to the car ahead of him he had
seen how the sunlight striking through it revealed the
long slender length of her legs and the curve of her
breasts. Now, despite the leather smell of the car's upholstery, he could still smell the fresh scent of Fliss's skin—
clean and yet subtly, erotically female—its delicacy

causing within him an automatic need to move closer to her and so catch the scent properly.

Inside his head an image formed of Fliss's body pressed close to his in paganly sensual offering. Cursing inwardly, Vidal fought to suppress his own body's sexual reaction to that image, dropping his hand from the steering wheel and driving one-handed so that his arm could shield the physical evidence of his arousal from Fliss. He was thankful that she was staring ahead and not looking at him. The reality of seeing her now, as the woman she was and not the girl who had refused to leave his memory, should surely have diminished that desire—not increased it.

The silence between them was dangerous, Vidal acknowledged. It was allowing thoughts to flourish that he did not want to have. Better to silence them with mundane conversation than to give them free rein.

Keeping his voice neutral and distant, he told Fliss, 'In addition to showing you your father's house, I have some estate business to attend to before we return to Granada.'

Fliss nodded her head and then, unable to hold back the question, she asked him quickly, 'Did...did my mother ever visit my father's house?'

'Alone, you mean? To spend time in private with your father?'

Fliss could hear what sounded like disapproval in Vidal's voice. The same disapproval no doubt felt by his grandmother.

'They were in love,' she pointed out, immediately

defensive of any criticism of her parents. 'It would only be natural if my father—'

'Had taken your mother to his house with the intention of bedding her, without any thought for her reputation?' Vidal shook his head. 'Felipe would never have done that. But then I suppose I shouldn't be surprised that *you* should think of it, given your own behaviour and sexual history.'

Fliss sucked in her breath, her lungs cramping tensely before she exhaled, furious shaky. 'You know nothing of the reality of either of those things.'

Vidal turned to look at her, disbelief hardening his expression. 'Are you seriously expecting me to listen to this? I know what I saw.'

'I was sixteen, and—'

'And a leopard doesn't change its spots.'

'No, it doesn't,' Fliss agreed furiously. 'You're the living proof of that.'

'Meaning what, exactly?' Vidal challenged.

'Meaning that I knew then what you thought of me, and why you judged me the way you did, and I know you still feel the same way now,' Fliss told him.

Vidal's hands tightened on the steering wheel. She had *known* how he had felt about her, despite all he had done to try and keep his feelings hidden from her—for her sake, not for his own? But of course she had, Vidal taunted himself. He had assessed her maturity and her readiness to know of his desire for her on her age, mistakenly believing her to be an innocent.

'Well, in that case,' he assured her curtly, 'no matter what you know, let me assure you that I do not intend to

allow those feelings to affect my duty and my responsibility to carry out my late uncle's wishes with regard
to your inheritance.'

'Good,' was the only response Fliss felt able to
muster.

So it was true. She had been right. He had disliked
her all those years ago and he still did now. She had
already known that, so why did his confirmation of it
make her feel so…so hurt and abandoned?

She had known how he felt about her when she came
here. Or had she secretly been hoping for a miracle to
happen? Had she been hoping for some kind of fairytale
magic to wipe away the anguish she carried inside her?
Leaving her free to… To what? To find a man with
whom she could truly and completely be a woman, free
to enjoy her sexuality without the stain of shame? Why
did she need Vidal's belief in her innocence to do that?
She knew the truth, after all, and that should be enough.
Should be. But it wasn't, was it? There was something
within her that could only be healed by… By what?
By the touch of Vidal's hand against that sore place in
reparation and acceptance of her as she really was?

It was her father she had come here to seek—not
Vidal's acceptance of his misjudgement of her.

She had travelled a long way from the idealistic
girl who had looked at Vidal and completely lost her
heart. She knew that he was not the heroic figure she
had created inside her head from her own adoration
of him. He had shown her that himself when he had
so misjudged her. There was no reason at all for her
senses to be so aware of him now, for merely being here

with him to make her ache with a dangerous resurgence of her teenage longing. But that was exactly what was happening.

Try as she might, she couldn't resist turning her head to look at him, imprinting his image on her senses.

The open neck of the shirt he was wearing revealed the straight line of his collarbone and the golden sleekness of his throat. If she looked properly at him no doubt she would be able to see where beneath his shirt his body hair lay. She could remember the pattern of it from that time she had walked into the bathroom.

Stop it, Fliss exhorted herself desperately. The anxiety she was causing herself was raising tiny beads of sweat along her hairline, whilst her pulse and her heartbeat had started to thud nervously, as though in fear. She *was* afraid, she admitted. She was afraid of her own imagination and of the wilful power of the deep-rooted core of sensuality within her. It seemed to have grown out of nowhere, and previously she would have strenuously denied that she even possessed it.

Perhaps it was being here in her father's country that was unleashing previously hidden aspects of her makeup and bringing to life unfamiliar passions. It was much easier to cling to that thought than to allow herself to fear that it was Vidal himself who was responsible for this unwanted and dangerous flowering of such a deeply sensual side of her nature. Just as he had been when she was sixteen.

Vidal checked his rearview mirror—not because he needed to do so, but because it would prevent him from glancing sideways at Fliss. Not that he needed to look at her to see her. Inside his head he had a perfectly visible image of her—although this image was one that, in defiance of his wishes, showed her eyes cloudy with arousal and her lips softly parted from his kiss. Such thoughts were not acceptable to him. And such desires…?

Grimly Vidal pressed his foot down on the car's accelerator. They were free of the city now, and the powerful car leapt forward.

As a pre-teenager, curious about her father and his homeland, but knowing that her mother found it painful to talk about him, Fliss had spent many hours in bookshops and the library, studying maps, descriptions and photographs of Granada and the Lecrin Valley. Later at university she had gone online to learn more, but no amount of that kind of exploration could come anywhere near the reality of the countryside they were now in.

She knew, of course, that the Lecrin Valley formed part of the natural Parque de Sierra Nevada, and that after the expulsion of the Moors from the area it had been left virtually untouched for many centuries, so that the countryside was dotted with a wealth of Moorish monuments, flour mills, and ancient castles in addition to the whitewashed Pablo villages that had once been home to the Moor population.

Orchards of orange and lemon trees, heavy now in the summer with ripening fruit, surrounded these small villages, with their narrow main streets and their small dusty squares, and the smell of the citrus fruit permeated the air inside the car despite its air-conditioning. Not that Fliss minded. In fact she loved the sharp, sun-warmed smell, and knew that it would be something she would carry with her once she had returned home.

'It must be so beautiful here in the spring, when the orchards are in blossom.' The words were out before she could stop them and remind herself that she had vowed this morning to remain as aloof from Vidal as she could.

'It is my mother's favourite time of year. She always spends the spring on our estate. The almond blossom is her favourite,' he responded, in a curt voice that showed Fliss how little he actually wanted to make any kind of contact with her at all, even though he had turned towards her as he spoke.

Pain flowered darkly inside her, like a bruise on wounded skin. Fliss's breath caught in her throat, in denial of what she was feeling, trapped there by the thudding sensation in her heart that merely looking at him brought her.

And she *was* looking at him, she recognised. Just like all those years ago in the bathroom, she was physically unable to remove her gaze from him. Why did this have to happen to her? Why could *this* man bring to life feelings within her that no other man had ever touched? Was there some part of her that wanted to be humiliated?

The flush burning her skin grew even hotter. She mustn't think about Vidal. She must think instead about her parents, and about the love they had shared. She had been created out of that love, and according to her mother that made her a very special child. A child of love. Was it any wonder, knowing that, that she had been so stricken with shock and horror by Rory's behaviour that she had not been able to find the words to deny his lie about her? At sixteen she had naively believed that sexual intimacy should be a beautiful act of mutual love. She had had no desire whatsoever to experiment with sex, put off by what to her had seemed the coarse and vulgar attitude displayed by boys of her own age. Instead she had dreamed of a passionate, tender, adoring lover with whom she would share all the mysteries and delights of sexual intimacy.

And then Vidal had come to see her mother. The child she had heard so much about transformed into a hero who fitted her private template for what a man should be so perfectly that he had stolen her heart before she had even realised what was happening to her. Vidal—so handsome that just looking at him made her breath catch in her throat. Vidal—who carried about him such a powerful aura of male sensuality that even she at sixteen had been aware of it. Vidal—who knew her father. Was it any wonder that he had held so many of the keys that could unlock her emotional defences? Not that he had needed to unlock them. She had thrown down her barriers for him herself.

Shocked by her own vulnerability, Fliss tried determinedly to concentrate again on the countryside beyond the car window. They had turned off the main road now, and were travelling along a narrow road that was climbing between two outcrops of rock. Beyond them, she could see as the car crested the top of the incline, lay a lush, wide and fertile valley filled with orchards, and on the lower slopes of the ring of hills that enclosed it rows of vines.

'The boundary to the estate begins here,' Vidal told her, as they started to descend into the valley, still in that formal tone which told her how little he wanted her company and how much he wished she wasn't here with him.

Well, she didn't care. She wasn't here because of him, after all. She was here because of her father. But much as she tried to take comfort from that knowledge, comfort eluded her, and her aching heart refused to be soothed.

'You can't see the *castillo* yet, but it is at the far end of the valley—built there so that it could command a strategic position.'

Fliss caught a glimpse of the silver ribbon of a river, wending its way below them on the valley floor. The valley was a small perfect paradise, she recognised, caught off-guard by the unexpected sharp pang of envy that touched her as she thought of how wonderful it must have been to grow up here, surrounded by so much natural beauty. In the distance she could see the high peaks of the Sierras, and she knew that beyond the Lecrin Valley lay a sub-tropical coastline of great beauty.

But the coast and what lay beyond this place were forgotten as the road twisted and turned and then, up ahead of them, she could see the *castillo*. She had not realised it would be so large, so imposing, and her breath caught on a betraying gasp of awe. Its architecture was a blend of a traditional Moorish style and something of the Renaissance, and sunlight shone on the narrow iron-grille-covered windows of its turreted corners.

This wasn't a home, Fliss thought apprehensively.

It was a fortress—a stronghold designed to reveal the might and the power of the man who held it and to warn others not to challenge that power.

They had to drive past formal gardens and an ornamental lake before reaching the front of the *castillo*, where Vidal brought the car to a halt.

An elderly manservant was waiting to greet them once they had stepped into the vast marble hallway, and a housekeeper who smiled far more warmly at her than Rosa was summoned to escort her to her room after Vidal announced that she might want an opportunity to 'freshen up' whilst he spoke with his estate manager.

'Since it's almost lunchtime, I suggest that we delay our visit to Felipe's house until after we have eaten.'

Vidal might be using the word *suggest*, but what he really meant, and wanted her to know, was that he was giving her an order, Fliss thought angrily, forced to nod her head and accept his dictat, even though she wanted to insist that she see her father's house immediately.

A couple of minutes later, following the housekeeper down a long, wide corridor on the second floor, Fliss reflected that both the vastness of the *castillo* and its architecture reminded her of a long-ago visit to Blenheim, the enormous palace given to the Duke of Marlborough by Queen Anne. Here at the *castillo*, the ceiling of the long gallery-style corridor was decorated with ornate plasterwork, and the crimson-papered walls were hung with huge gilt-framed portraits.

They had almost reached the end of the corridor when the housekeeper came to a halt and opened the double

doors in front of her, indicating that Fliss was to precede
her into the room beyond them.

If she had thought that her bedroom at the family
townhouse in Granada was large and elegant, then she
had obviously not realised what the words could actually
mean, Fliss recognised. She put down the overnight bag
she'd brought with her, lost for words in the middle of
what had to be the most opulent bedroom she had ever
seen.

Gilt swags and cherubs adorned the half-tester bed,
whilst above it on the ceiling nymphs and shepherds
rioted in discreet pastel-painted pastoral delight. Ornate
gilt plasterwork decorated the cream-painted walls,
framing insets of rich gold cherub-imprinted wallpaper,
and matching silk curtains hung at the windows and fell
from the bedhead.

All the furniture in the room was painted cream—
feminine and delicate—as well as highly decorated with
a good deal of gilt rococo work. On the bed was a gold
coverlet made out of the same fabric as the curtains, its
cherubs stitched and padded to stand out. Against one
wall, between two sets of tall glass doors that led out
onto narrow balconies, stood a desk with its own chair,
and in the corner was a low table on which she could
see a selection of glossy magazines. Fliss, who had a
little knowledge of antiques, suspected that the cream-
and-gold carpet was probably a priceless Savonnerie,
made especially for the room.

'Your bathroom and dressing room are through here,'
the housekeeper informed Fliss, indicating the recessed

double doors on either side of the bed. 'I shall send a maid up to escort you to lunch in ten minutes.'

Thanking her, Fliss waited until the door had closed behind her before investigating the bathroom and dressing room.

The bathroom was very traditional, with marble floors and walls and a huge roll-top bath alongside a modern shower enclosure. Every kind of product a visiting guest might require was laid out on the marble surround to the basin. A quantity of thick fluffy towels hung from a modern chrome heated towel rail, whilst an equally thick and fluffy white robe hung from a peg behind the door.

The dressing room was lined with mirror-fronted cupboards large enough to hold the entire wardrobes of several families, and even possessed a *chaise-longue*. So that the male partner of the woman sleeping in the bedroom could lounge there and watch as she paraded in expensive designer clothes for his pleasure and approval? Inside her head Fliss had a swift mental image of Vidal, dark-browed and dark-suited, leaning against the gold silk upholstery of the *chaise*, reaching out to touch her bare shoulder, his gaze fixed on her mouth, whilst she—

No. She must not allow such thoughts.

Quickly stepping back into the bedroom, Fliss went over to open doors to one of the balconies, intending to breath in some fresh air. But she came to a halt when she saw that the balcony looked down on an enclosed swimming-pool area large enough to have belonged to a five-star hotel. The intense brilliant blue of the sky was reflected in the still waters of the pool, and beyond the walled pool area she could see the orchards, stretching up into the foothills.

This valley was a small earthly paradise—a paradise complete with its own danger, its own Lucifer as far as she was concerned, in the shape of Vidal. And was she tempted by Vidal as Eve had been tempted by the serpent, in danger of risking all that mattered to her morally for the sake of the sensual caress of a man who represented everything she most despised?

CHAPTER SIX

SOMEONE was knocking on her bedroom door. Quickly removing her rolled-up Panama hat from her case and grabbing her handbag, Fliss went to open the door, somehow managing to disengage herself from her troublesome thoughts and produce a smile for the maid who was waiting outside it.

In the room to which the maid showed her a buffet lunch had been laid out on a heavily carved wooden sideboard. Three places were set at the immaculately polished mahogany table, and the reason for that was made apparent when Vidal walked into the room, accompanied by a good-looking dark-haired younger man, who gave Fliss a warm smile of open male appreciation as soon as he saw her.

Vidal introduced them. 'Felicity—Ramón Carrera. Ramón is Estate Manager here.' Ramón's warm smile faded to a very respectful inclination of his head when Vidal added, 'Felicity is Felipe's daughter,' before striding over to the buffet and telling them both, 'Come—let us eat.'

Going to pick up one of the plates on the table, Fliss grappled with the unexpectedness of Vidal introducing her openly as his adopted uncle's daughter—thus acknowledging her as a member of the family as easily as though there had never been any past secrecy or unwillingness to recognise her. Why had he done it? Because he had felt it necessary to explain her presence and hadn't wanted anyone on the estate to jump to the conclusion that just because he had brought her here it meant they were personally involved romantically? Of course, being the man he was, he wouldn't want anyone thinking that. He had made his dislike of her plain enough, after all.

As she ate her food, whilst the two men talked about estate matters, Fliss pondered on why the thought of Vidal pointing out that she was here because she was Felipe's daughter and *not* because of any personal emotional involvement with him had the power to make her feel such an intense stab of angry pain.

'You have not tried our wine yet,' she heard Ramón saying, 'It's a new Merlot we have just started producing here.'

Dutifully Fliss raised the glass of red wine to her lips and breathed in its heady bouquet, intrigued by the hint of what smelled like scented blossom mixed with the rich smell of the wine itself, before taking a cautious sip. She had been right to be cautious, Fliss recognised, as she felt the wine's full-bodied warmth spreading through her body.

'It's excellent,' she told Ramón truthfully,

'It is Vidal who deserves your praise, not me.' Ramón smiled. 'It was his idea to import some new vines from a vineyard in Chile in which he has a financial interest, to see if we could replicate the excellent wine they produce there.'

'What we have produced here is unique to this area.' Vidal joined in the conversation. 'Something of the smell of our orchards has been incorporated in the wine.'

'Yes, I noticed that,' Fliss agreed, taking another sip from her wine glass. The wine really was good. Its scent was making her want to bury her nose in the glass to breathe in more of it.

'Vidal said that he wanted to produce a Merlot that reminded him of riding through the orchards on a warm spring morning,' Ramón enthused. 'A lovers' wine that is full of promise and the joy of being alive. It has been very well received in the industry. I think, Vidal, that we should perhaps have named it for Señor Felipe's oh-so-beautiful daughter,' Ramón told Vidal, giving Fliss another admiring look.

Vidal felt as though someone had sliced straight into his gut as he watched Fliss smile warmly at Ramón. She had not mentioned there being a current man in her life, but even if there was, given what he knew about her, she was hardly likely to think it necessary to stop at one—especially when she was far away from him.

Abruptly he stood up, announcing brusquely, 'We should make a move, I think. You will report back to me about that problem with the irrigation system before tonight, please, Ramón. If we are going to have to get a senior engineer out I would prefer it to be tomorrow, whilst I am still here.'

'I'll go and find out what's happening,' Ramón confirmed, rising from his own chair and then coming to hold Fliss's chair for her with a courtly gesture as she too moved to stand up.

Excusing himself to go and get on with his work, Ramón left Fliss and Vidal to walk out into the early-afternoon sunshine together.

Since she had expected that her father's home would be within walking distance of the *castillo*, Fliss was surprised when Vidal placed his hand beneath her elbow to direct her back towards the car. She could feel first her arm and then her whole body burning with the heat caused by her proximity to him, causing her an immediate panic and a need to get away from him. It would be unbearable if he should guess the effect he had on her. Fliss could just imagine how much he would enjoy the humiliation that would bring her. But no amount of fear of that humiliation though was enough to stop her nipples from hardening to push determinedly against the covering of her bra and her dress. It was almost as though they wanted to shame her by flaunting their arousal and their willing availability in front of Vidal.

Angry with herself, she took refuge from her unwanted sensual vulnerability to him and her inability to control it by telling him scornfully, 'I suppose it's beyond your dignity as a duke to walk to the house?'

This drew a grim look from him as he told her coldly, 'Since it's a mile-and-a-half walk along the road, or a mile as the crow flies, I thought it would be easier to use the car. However, if you prefer to walk…' He looked down at Fliss's flimsy sandals as he spoke, causing her to recognise with a new surge of anger that he had won that particular run-in between them.

They had travelled quite a distance down the long drive, in a silence that bristled with mutual hostility, before Vidal announced in a peremptory tone that would have immediately got Fliss's back up even without the added insult of what he had to say, 'I must warn you against indulging in a flirtation with Ramón.'

'I was *not* flirting with him,' Fliss snapped in outrage.

'He made it plain that he found you attractive, and you allowed him to do so. Of course we both know how eager you are to accommodate the desires of any man who chooses to express them to you.'

'Trust you to throw that in my face.' Fliss tried to defend herself. 'You just couldn't wait to do so, could you? Well, for your information—'

'For *your* information,' Vidal interrupted her coldly, 'I will not have you indulging your promiscuous sexual appetite with Ramón.'

She must not let the pain of what he was saying touch her. If she did—if she let it into her heart—then it would surely destroy her. It proved how vulnerable she already was that she should actually feel herself aching to tell him that he was wrong, and demand that he listen to the truth. Vidal would never listen to the truth because he didn't want to hear it. He wanted to think the worst of her—just as he had wanted to prevent her from making contact with her father. To him she was someone who just wasn't good enough to be treated with compassion and understanding.

'You can't stop me taking a lover if I want to, Vidal.' It was the truth, after all.

Without looking at her, Vidal replied grimly, 'Ramón is married, with two young children. Unfortunately his marriage is going through a difficult time at the moment. Ramón is known to have an eye for pretty girls, and his wife is not at all happy about his behaviour. I have no wish to see their marriage fall apart and their children left without a father, and I promise you, Felicity, that I will do whatever it takes to make sure that does not happen.'

Vidal had turned off the main drive and onto a narrow, less well-maintained track, at the end of which, rising above the heavily laden orange and lemon trees, Fliss could see the top storey and attic windows of a red-roofed house. It gave her the perfect, much-needed excuse not to respond to Vidal's crushing comment, but instead to retreat into what she hoped was a dignified silence—whilst her heart thumped jerkily against her chest wall in a mixture of anger and chagrin.

In that silence Vidal drove them through what felt like a tunnel of spreading branches. Sunlight dappled through them to create an almost camouflage effect on the bark of the trees, and the crops in the close-mown grass below them. And then Fliss got her first proper glimpse of the house. Her breath caught in her throat, her heart flipping dizzily with emotion. If it was possible to fall in love with a house then she just had, she recognised.

Three storeys high, whitewashed, it filled her with delight. There was delicate detail in its iron-grille-surrounded balconies, and there were bright slashes of colour from the geraniums tumbling from pots outside the house and the bougainvillea blossom against the lower walls of the house. Oddly, there was something almost Queen Anne about the architectural style of the building, so that there was a familiarity about it—as though somehow it was welcoming her, Fliss thought emotionally as Vidal brought the car to a halt outside a pair of wooden double doors.

'It's beautiful.' The words were said before she could call them back.

'It was originally built for the captive mistress of one of my ancestors—an Englishwoman seized in a fight at sea between my ancestor's ship and an English vessel in the days when the countries were at war with one another.'

'It was a *prison*?' Fliss couldn't hold back her distaste.

''If you want to see if that way. But what I would say is that it was their love for one another that imprisoned them. My ancestor protected his mistress by housing her here away from the judgement of society, and she protected the heart he had given her by remaining true to him and accepting that his duty to his wife meant that they could never officially be together.'

After what Vidal had told her, Fliss had expected the house to wear an air of sadness and disillusionment, but instead the first impression she had when she stepped into the cool white-painted hallway with its tiled floor was that the house was holding itself still, as though in expectation of something—or someone. Her father?

The air smelled soft and warm, as though the house was regularly aired, but Fliss thought that beneath that scent she could still smell a hint of male cologne. An ache of unexpected longing and sadness swept through her, catching her off-guard, so that she had to blink away her betraying emotion. She had genuinely thought that she had wept all the tears she had to weep for the father she had never known many, many years ago.

'Did my…did my father live here alone?' she asked Vidal—more to break the silence between them than anything else.

'Apart from Ana, who was his housekeeper. She has now retired and gone to live in the village with her daughter. Come—I shall show you the house, and then once you have satisfied your curiosity I shall return you to the *castillo*.'

Fliss could sense that Vidal was holding both his impatience and his dislike of her on a very short rein.

'You didn't want me to come here, did you? Even though my father left the house to me?' she accused him.

'No, I didn't,' Vidal agreed. 'I didn't and don't see the point.'

'Just like you didn't see the point of me writing to him. In fact as far as you are concerned it would have been better if I had never been born, wouldn't it?'

Without waiting for Vidal's reply—what was the need, after all, when she already knew the answer to her own question?—Fliss moved further into the house.

Although it was far more simple in style and decoration than the *castillo*, it was still furnished with what Fliss suspected were valuable antiques.

'Which was my father's favourite room?' she demanded, after she had walked though a well-proportioned drawing room and explored the elegant, formal dining room on the opposite side of the hallway, as well as a smaller sitting room and a collection of passages, storerooms, and a small businesslike office situated at the back of the house.

For a minute she thought that Vidal wasn't going to answer her. His mouth had hardened, and he looked away from her as though impatient to be free of her company. She held her breath.

But then, just as she thought he was going to ignore her, he turned back to her and told her distantly, 'This one.' He opened the door into a small library. 'Felipe loved reading, and music. He…' Vidal paused, looking into the distance before he continued. 'He liked to spend his evenings in here, listening to music and reading his favourite books. The sun sets on this side of the house, and in the evening this room is particularly pleasant.'

The image Vidal was painting was one of a solitary, quiet man—a lonely man, perhaps—who had sat here in this room, contemplating what might have been if only things had been different.

'Did you…did you spent a lot of time with him?' Fliss could feel the words threatening to block her throat. Her hand went to it, tangling with the slender gold chain that had been her mother's, as though by touching it she could somehow ease away the pain she was now feeling.

'He was my uncle. He managed the family orchards.' Vidal gave a shrug which Fliss interpreted as dismissive and thus uncaring. 'Naturally we spent a good deal of time together.'

Vidal was turning away from her. Releasing her chain, Fliss looked back at the desk, her attention caught by the gleam of sunlight on the back of a small silver photograph frame. Driven by an impulse she couldn't control, she picked it up and turned it round. Her heart slammed into her ribs as she looked down at a photograph of her mother, holding a smiling baby Fliss knew to be herself.

Her hand shaking, she put the photograph down.

Vidal's mobile rang, and whilst he turned away to take the call Fliss studied the photograph again. Her mother looked so young. So proud of her baby. What had her father thought when he had seen the photograph? Had he been filled with regret—guilt—even perhaps longing to have the woman he loved and the child he had created with her there with him? She would never know now.

He had kept the photograph on his desk, which must mean that he had looked at it every day. Fliss tried to drive away the feeling of deep sadness permeating her, but still her questioning thoughts tormented her. Had he ever hoped that one day they would meet? He had never made any attempt to contact her.

Vidal had ended his call.

'We have to get back to the *castillo*,' he told her. 'Ramón has arranged for me to see the water engineer. A decision needs to be made with regard to the problem with our water supply. We can come back here in the morning if you wish to see upstairs.'

His voice suggested that he couldn't understand why she should want to, but Fliss had a more pressing question she wanted to ask.

'Did my father know about my mother's death?'

She could see the way Vidal's chest lifted as he breathed in.

'Yes, he did know,' he told her.

'How do you know he knew?'

She didn't need to see the way Vidal's mouth compressed or to hear his irritably exhaled breath to know that she was testing his patience. But she didn't care.

'I know because I was the one who had to break the news to him.'

'And he…*no one* thought that I might have needed to hear from him, my only living relative, my father…?'

All the pain she had felt at losing her mother at eighteen came rushing back over her.

'It was you—you who kept us apart,' she accused Vidal.

The look in Vidal's eyes silenced her, choking the breath from her lungs.

'Your father's health suffered a great deal when he was parted from your mother. His doctor felt that it was best that he lived a quiet life, without any kind of emotional pressure. For that reason, in my judgement—'

'In *your* judgement? Who were *you* to make judgements and decisions that involved me?' Fliss demanded bitterly.

'I was and am the head of this family. It is my duty to do what I think right for that family.'

'And preventing me from seeing my father, from knowing him, was what you thought "right", was it?'

'My family is also your family. When I make decisions concerning it I make them with due regard to all those who are part of it. Now, if you can manage to cease indulging in this welter of infantile emotionalism, I would like to get back to the *castillo*.'

'To see the engineer—because watering your crops is more important than considering the harm you have done and owning up to it.' Fliss gave a bitter laugh. 'Of course I should have realised that you are far too arrogant and cold-hearted to ever *think* of doing anything like that.'

Without waiting for him to reply, she headed for the door.

Fliss looked down at the food on her plate with a heavy heart, her hand going to her throat, where her mother's chain should have been. She could still feel the cold shaft of dismay she had felt when she had looked in her bedroom mirror and realised that it wasn't there.

At first she'd hoped that it had simply come loose and slipped down inside her top, but when several careful searches of the clothes she had removed and then the entire bedroom floor had not revealed the precious memento of her mother, she had been forced to recognise the truth. She had lost the chain and locket that had been such a treasured link not just with her mother but also her father—because he had given the jewellery to her mother in the first place.

Her distress went too deep for the relief of tears, and

so, dry-eyed and heavy-hearted, she had forced herself to change for dinner into her black dress—just as she was—trying desperately to force herself make polite conversation with Ramón's wife, Bianca.

The estate manager and his wife had been invited to join them for dinner—as a way of underlining the warning Vidal had given her earlier with regard to Ramón himself? Fliss wondered a little grimly. If so, there had been no need. Even without his wife she would not have felt inclined to encourage Ramón's lunchtime would-be flirtation with her. Charming though the estate manager was, his presence did not provoke any kind of desirous feeling within her, never mind create those feelings to the self-control-obliterating extent that Vidal's presence did.

Fliss's fork clattered down onto her plate as she fought to deny what she had just admitted to herself. By what cruel trick of nature could it have happened that she was so intensely and physically aware of and responsive to the one man above all others she should have been safe from finding in any way attractive?

Picking up her fork, she turned her attention to Bianca in an attempt to distract herself. Ramón's wife was an attractive, if rather remote-looking woman in her early thirties, with classically Spanish good looks. Given what Vidal had told her about Ramón, it was perhaps not surprising that Bianca's manner towards her should betray some reticence Fliss acknowledged, and she herself was hardly in the right mood to set about reassuring the other woman and drawing her out—although the good manners her grandparents and mother had insisted upon were urging her to do her best.

There were several times, though, when she wasn't able to prevent her hand from creeping up to her throat in search of the missing chain, and a shadow clouded her eyes when she was forced to accept its absence.

A white wine from the vineyard in Chile in which Vidal had a financial interest was served with their meal of fish, caught locally on the coast, and then a sweeter wine was poured by Vidal when the dessert arrived—an almond dish made from the estate's own almonds.

It was when he was filling her glass that he said unexpectedly to Fliss, 'You aren't wearing your chain.'

The fact that he had noticed it in the first place was enough to catch Fliss off-guard, even without the emotional pain of having to acknowledge its loss, but somehow she managed to control her reaction and admit huskily, 'No. I seem to have lost it.'

Was she imagining the way in which Vidal's gaze lingered on her throat before he moved on to fill first Ramón's and then his own glass? Her vulnerable flesh was certainly burning as though it had.

Desperate not to either think about her lost chain and locket or her contradictory reactions to Vidal, Fliss focused her attention again on Bianca, asking her about her children. She was rewarded with the first genuine smile the other woman had given her all evening, and Bianca launched into a catalogue of the wonderfulness of their two young sons.

Listening to her, Fliss couldn't help wondering what it must feel like to have a child and be a mother—to feel that sense of joy and fierce maternal pride she could see so clearly in Bianca's response. Bianca had produced a photograph of their sons. Dark-haired and dark-eyed, with warm olive skin, they looked like miniature images of their father.

Against her will, Fliss's gaze was drawn to Vidal, who was now deep in conversation with Ramón about the engineer's recommendations for fixing the problem with the water. Of course, she had no need to try to imagine what Vidal's sons would look like. After all, she had a photograph of Vidal himself as a boy. She had grown up with that image and it was surely imprinted within her for ever. His sons' mother would contribute to their gene pool, too, though, and she would be...

She would be everything that she herself was not, Fliss reminded herself, her hand trembling as she held her wine glass. Why on earth should she care who Vidal married, what his sons would look like, or even if he had any? Why, indeed? And equally, why did she have that curious ache of mixed longing and loss deep inside her body, right where her womb was?

CHAPTER SEVEN

THE evening was over, and Fliss was back in her bedroom. The bareness of her neck against the snowy backdrop of the towelling robe she had pulled on after her shower reminded her of what she had lost and filled her with fresh guilt.

Her mother had always worn, treasured, and guarded her locket. Fliss didn't have a single visual childhood memory in which she could *not* see it round her mother's neck, and now *she* had lost it through her own carelessness. Somehow in its own way that hurt as deeply and painfully as the loss of her mother herself, and brought back for her the confused and unhappy feelings she had had as a young child, questioning why she did not have a father. That chain and its locket had bound her parents together, and through that bonding it had bound them to her as well. It had been her only material connection that was shared by them both, and now it was gone. That precious link had been broken.

But she still had another link with her father, Fliss reminded herself. She still had the house that he had left her.

Only for now, she reminded herself. Vidal had made

it clear that he both expected and wanted her to sell it to him.

Fliss was just on the point of slipping out of the bathrobe and getting into bed when a knock on her door came. Hastily pulling the robe back onto her shoulders and clasping it closed in front of her, she went to answer the knock, assuming that it must be one of the maids.

Only it wasn't one of the maids. It was Vidal, and now he was inside the room and closing the door behind him.

'What do you want?' Would he hear the anxiety in her voice and guess that it came from an awareness of her own vulnerability to him? Fliss hoped not as she watched his mouth twist in cynical contempt.

'Not *you*, if that is what you are hoping for. A man— any man to satisfy the desire you probably hoped to extinguish with Ramón? Is that what you hoped I might be, Felicity?'

'No!' The denial was torn from her throat.

Make-up-free, her hair tousled and her feet bare, not to mention the fact that her body was equally bare beneath the enveloping robe, Fliss was acutely conscious of feeling at a disadvantage compared with Vidal, who was naturally still wearing the light wool suit and the pale blue shirt he had worn during dinner.

But it was her emotional vulnerability to him that disadvantaged her more, she told herself as Vidal dismissed her denial with a savage, '*Liar.* I know you, remember?'

'No, you don't. You don't know me at all. And if you've come here just to insult me—'

'Is it possible to insult a woman like you? I should have thought you were beyond that—a woman who gives herself to all and sundry in a tawdry mockery of what man-to-woman intimacy should really be.'

The words he spoke, each insult he made, felt like a knife wound to her heart and her pride.

'I've brought you this,' Vidal told her curtly, changing the subject, and opening his hand to reveal her chain and locket nestling in his palm

The sight of it robbed Fliss of the ability to speak. She had to blink and look again to make sure that she wasn't seeing things.

'My locket,' she said, and she shook her head in dis-belief as she switched her gaze to his face to demand disjointedly, 'How…? Where…?'

Vidal's shrug was dismissive, almost bored, Fliss felt, as he told her, 'I remembered that you were wearing it when we went into the house, so it seemed logical that you might have lost it there. After I had said goodnight to Bianca and Ramón, I drove over there. I recalled that you were playing with the chain when we were in Felipe's office, so I started my search there, and as luck would have it that was where I found it—on the floor next to the desk.'

'You did that for…?'

For me, she had been about to say, but she was glad that she'd paused before doing so when he told her flatly, 'I know how much it meant to your mother and how she cherished it.'

Vidal made himself cut across the hesitant vulner-ability he could hear in Fliss's voice. He didn't want to see her as vulnerable or deserving of compassion, because if he did—if he allowed that image of her into his head and his heart—it would mean… It would mean what?

It would mean *nothing*, Vidal assured himself grimly.

Fliss nodded. 'Yes. Yes, she did.' Of course he had not gone to look for it for *her*. Vidal would never do anything for her. 'I'm glad you found it,' was all she could allow herself to say, and she reached out to take it from him, her outstretched fingers curling back into her palm as she recoiled from actually touching him. Because she was afraid. Of what? Afraid of touching him, or afraid that once she did she wouldn't be able to stop?

He shouldn't have come here. He had known that. So why *had* he? Vidal derided himself. To test his self-control? To prove that he could walk through fire? To suffer the torment he was now suffering? He knew that beneath her robe Felicity was naked. He knew that given her sexual history, her sexual proclivities, he could reach for her and take her now, satiate himself in her, with her, until the need that gnawed unceasingly at him, that cried out to him, was silenced.

A tremor knifed through Fliss's body.

'Take it,' Vidal demanded, holding out his hand to her, the gold glistening in his palm.

For a moment they looked at one another, neither of them saying anything. Fliss's breathing and her balance were both slightly unsteady as her senses registered the sensual tension in the air between them. Vidal lifted his hand, and for a second Fliss thought that he was going to reach out and touch her. She moved back from him, forgetting that a low table was right behind her until she stepped back into it.

She heard Vidal curse as she stumbled, but even then she held up her hands to fend him off, prepared to fall rather than risk being touched by him. Only it was already too late. His hands were gripping her upper arms, and his face was hard with hostility and contempt as his gaze raked her face and then fell to the now open front of her robe.

One of them made a small sound. She wasn't sure if it was Vidal or herself. Her chest lifted abruptly, its movement driven by an urgent need to expand her lungs and take in more oxygen. Time seemed to hold its breath. She was certainly holding her own breath, Fliss knew, as they looked at one another in silence. Was she the first to break that eye contact, her gaze drawn helplessly down to Vidal's mouth, her own lips parting on a quivering gasp of longing? Fliss didn't know. She only knew that when she looked up into Vidal's eyes again they were smouldering with the sensual intent of a man who knew that the woman he was with wanted him.

'No.'

Her denial was a soft, agonised sound of despair, but Vidal ignored it. His gaze was obscured, so she couldn't see what was in his eyes as he looked down at her mouth. Fliss's heart was thundering with reckless, out-of-control thuds, driven by her heightened awareness of both him and her own longing. She watched as he lowered his head, his lips almost touching her own, his breath an unbearably tormenting caress against her mouth. Unable to stop watching, Fliss moved closer to him.

'Damn you!'

Fliss could hear the anger in Vidal's voice as he thrust her away from him. Her chain lay on the floor between them. Instinctively she moved forward to pick it up, and then froze in shock when Vidal took hold of her again.

'You just can't stop yourself, can you? *Any* man will do, won't he? Any man as long as he gives you this.'

He was kissing her, and she could feel his contempt. She could taste it. He wanted to humiliate her, to destroy her, and she wanted… She wanted to make him see that he was wrong about her. She wanted to punish him for misjudging her. She wanted to see his pride lying shredded in the wreckage of his misconceptions. And now she could do that. Now she could turn his anger-fuelled passion into her own salvation. The sacrifice of her belief that sexual intimacy should be something born out of mutual love would ultimately be Vidal's humiliation.

Maybe this had always been meant to happen? Maybe it was the only way she would ever be able to walk free of the emotional pain he had caused her? Maybe this was something she needed to experience to be able to finally destroy the foolish dreams she had once had?

Slowly and deliberately, as though her body was weighted and drugged, Fliss moved closer to Vidal, deliberately grinding her lower body into his in a motion she had seen actors using. She lifted her hand to the buttons on Vidal's shirt, concentrating on unfastening them as his tongue thrust fiercely against her own. A quiver of sensation ran through her but she ignored it. This wasn't about her own desire—at least not her own desire for Vidal—it was about her desire to be free of everything in her life that had been tied to him.

His shirt was unfastened now, and he was still kissing her. A hard, demanding kiss without any softening warmth or tender emotion. How long would it be before his anger cooled and he pushed her away again? She must not let that happen. Somehow she must keep feeding his anger until it became physical arousal and desire. And perhaps the best way to do that was to confirm his judgement of her.

Very carefully and deliberately she broke Vidal's kiss, and then equally deliberately she let the robe slide from her body. She stepped towards him and placed her lips against his, lifting her hands to his shoulders.

She heard Vidal groan, felt his hands clamping down on her waist, his mouth closing against hers.

A shiver of self-revulsion gripped her. What was she doing? She had gambled and lost in a mad moment of self-destruction, and now...

He couldn't let this happen. Vidal knew that. He would be damned for ever if he gave in to Felicity's allure. And tormented for ever if he did not. His body yearned and ached for her. For seven years he had had to live with the need she aroused in him. He looked down at her body and felt his own shudder violently as he fought against taking what she was offering. Of its own volition and against his will his hands lifted from her waist to her breasts, full and taut, the nipples already hard with sensual promise. They pressed against his palms.

'Oh!' Fliss gasped, caught off-guard by the shock of pleasure the sensation of Vidal's touch against her breasts had brought. She hadn't been expecting it and it widened her eyes and made her mouth soften. Desire? Her body trembled. Was it wrong to want him, or was it part of what must happen?

Vidal could see and feel Fliss's arousal. She wanted him! That knowledge severed the last strand of his self-control, plunging him into the millrace of his own longing for her.

He tried to dam the racing flood of his need. His heart was slamming into his chest wall. He knew what he should do, but it was impossible for him to stem the fierce tide of desire that possessed him. At some atavistic deep level his instinct said that Felicity was *his*—should always have been his, would be his.

Her lips clung to his, parting eagerly to the thrust of his tongue as he took and tasted the wild sweetness of her mouth.

Beneath the possessive pressure of Vidal's kiss, Fliss tensed on a soft moan of delight. There was no point in her trying to control the desire leaping to life inside her, racing from nerve-ending to nerve-ending. Why attempt the impossible? Why resist what was surely preordained by fate?

The seeking, all-conquering exploration of his tongue took her own into its fierce possession, sending a starburst of liquid arousal spilling through her whole body. And when Vidal withdrew his tongue from hers, to stroke the tip of it tormentingly against the now swollen fullness of her lips, Fliss clung to him, cast adrift in a wild inner sea of sensual intensity.

The reason they were here together like this no longer mattered. It had evaporated like morning mist beneath the heat of the sun, burned away by the power of their shared desire.

Now it was Fliss who captured Vidal's tongue, taking it deep within the warm wet intimacy of her mouth to caress it with her own. She was in Vidal's arms, and they were kissing as though the connection between them had sprung to life like an invisible force that bound them together.

She welcomed the possession of Vidal's hands against her naked breasts, straining towards him as though to offer him their arousal, her whole body shuddering wildly when he rolled her nipples between his thumb and forefinger in a caress of erotic delight that had her digging her nails into the hard muscles of his arms.

Vidal didn't need her to tell him what he was doing to her, or what she wanted. He seemed to understand her need instinctively, arousing it, matching it, feeding and sustaining it with his touch and the growing passion of his kisses.

She had no will apart from the will to submit to the pleasure Vidal was giving her, Fliss thought dizzily, lost in the erotic heat that enveloped her, enclosing her in its embrace, possessing her senses, her thoughts and her will-power just as Vidal was possessing her body. She wanted what was happening more than she had ever wanted anything in the whole of her life. It was what she had been born for, what she longed for. It was her fate and her destiny—a completion that had the power to make her whole.

Vidal's hands moulded and caressed her breasts as he kissed her again, the rhythm of his fingers caressing the eager hardness of her nipples and matching the equally rhythmic thrust of his tongue against her own, creating a swiftly growing crescendo of hungry longing that pulsed and ran through her body in a silent song of female arousal. As though her desire had been hot-wired to respond only to Vidal's touch, her body moved to the rhythm he was imposing on it, the lamplight giving her naked flesh a softly golden sheen highlighted by the arousal-induced flush that bathed her chest and throat.

A voice inside Vidal's head urged him to stop, telling him that it was his duty to deny himself the pleasure that was feeding his desire for her, but that desire was too savagely primitive for him to resist. He had felt it the very first minute he had set eyes on her and seen her in the flesh—hitting him, possessing him, compelling him in a way that every fibre of his logical brain wanted to resist and deny. But now—dangerously—it had overwhelmed that logic, and he was answering to something within him that he had previously not realised existed: a male urge to conquer, to possess, to own for himself the woman he was holding and caressing. A thousand years of history and male pride, of conquest and victory, was surging through him with all the power of a burst dam, destroying every obstacle in its way.

It was that age-old instinct and drive that belonged

to man's most potent needs that was compelling him now to smooth his hand over the quivering of Fliss's taut stomach and then to cup her hip as he pulled her into his own body so that her flesh could feel and know the desire it had aroused in his. On the wall, their conjoined shadows revealed the intimacy of their embrace, detailing the arch of Fliss's back as he bent her back over his arm, the aroused thrust of her nipple exposed to the lamplight, the meeting and joining of their lower bodies making them one.

Fliss was completely lost. The hard pulse of Vidal's erection felt against her bare flesh through his clothes filled her with a wanton, compulsive desire to feel his naked flesh against her own—to be able to reach out and touch him, to know him and to feel his life force.

She made no attempt to resist when Vidal picked her up and carried her over to the bed, placing her down on it. His gaze absorbed every detail of her naked body, lingering on her flesh as though he could not tear it away. A sensuality Fliss had not known she possessed caused her to move her body languidly beneath that gaze, a thrill of sweetly savage female pleasure speeding through her when she heard the stifled sound Vidal made before he joined her on the bed, holding her, shaping her, taking her mouth in an erotic kiss and keeping possession of it and her whilst he caressed her body.

The touch of his fingertips against her stomach sent jolting waves of dangerously intense delight surging through her—a delight fused with a female need to feel his touch against her even more intimately. Her body tensed, her breath locking in her lungs when Vidal's hand moved lower, covering her sex, infusing it with a heat that had her out-of-control desire for him flowering moistly in the sensitive flesh protected by the folded lips that she could feel swelling and opening beneath his hand.

Another minute—less than that, a mere handful of seconds—and he would discover her wet eagerness for his possession. And she *was* eager for it. She yearned for it, ached for it, hungered for it. In her imagination she could already feel his thrust within her, and her body was pulsing frantically under the stimulation of what she was thinking. She wanted him so much, so completely, so overwhelmingly, her desire for him was storming through her.

Vidal's own breathing was harsh and unsteady, his mouth against her skin passionately demanding. The brief grate of his teeth against her swollen nipple as he drew on it caused her body to convulse on the raw pleasure of that fierce caress. She wanted him so completely and totally that nothing else mattered.

Vidal slowly released Fliss's nipple, and then raised his head to look at her. In her eyes was all that Vidal needed to see to know that she wanted him. The look there matched the aroused anticipation of her naked body.

'Take off your clothes,' she told him huskily. 'I want to see all of you. I want to feel your skin against mine, your body against mine with nothing between us. I want you inside me, possessing me as a man should possess a woman. I want *you*, Vidal.'

Fliss listened to her own words, her own demands,

with a vague sense of shock—as though they had some-how come from someone else. But Vidal didn't seem to be shocked or even surprised by them. Instead he was doing what she had asked, his gaze never leaving her face, almost pinning her to the bed as he stripped off his clothes whilst his movements allowed the light to play greedily over the stunning reality of his male flesh.

Almost wonderingly Fliss reached up to trace the line of dark body hair that bisected his torso, only stopping when he trapped her hand flat against his belly as she reached his belly button. Without a word Fliss sat up, and proceeded to retrace the path taken by her fingertips with a line of soft kisses which gradually became more intense as her own desire gripped her.

Now both her hand and her head were held immobile in Vidal's grip, their quest short-circuited, their goal denied.

Above her downbent head she could hear Vidal talk-ing to her, his voice strained and muffled. 'I can't let you go on. Not now—not whilst my body craves the intimacy of yours so badly.'

'Yessss!' Fliss answered him fiercely. 'Yes, Vidal.'

When he released her and moved back from her, get-ting off the bed and reaching for the trousers he had discarded, Fliss started to reach out to him frantically, to protest—and then she stopped, her eyes widening when he removed his wallet and opened it.

It was just as well that he had taken measures to prepare himself should he have ended up in bed with Mariella, Vidal acknowledged grimly as he removed the protective sheath from its wrapper.

The interruption to their intimacy had given Fliss time to recognise what was happening—what she was doing. Away from the heat of the desire Vidal's caresses had aroused in her something about the brisk expediency of his preparations had broken the spell she had been under. The reality of what was happening was now in stark contrast to the fantasy she had been creating. This surely was the time to stop, to be practical and truthful and tell Vidal the truth. But how?

She took a deep breath, and her voice was unsteady as she told him huskily, 'There's no need for you to… to do that, because…'

Because I'm a virgin, she had intended to continue. But before she could do so Vidal interrupted.

'I might not be able to control the desire you arouse in me, Felicity,' he told her harshly. 'But I am not such a fool as to take the kind of risks with my sexual health that intimacy with you would involve without this protection. You may be the sort of woman who boasts that her pleasure is increased by the danger of unprotected intercourse, but I am not a man who wants to put either my own or my future sexual partners' health at risk by going down that road. Of course if you'd prefer not to go any further…'

A horrible feeling of sickening shame was filling her, and for a minute Fliss was tempted to tell him to leave. But then the anger she had felt earlier surged up inside her again, and with it her need for justice.

Her chin lifted, and her lashes were shielding her eyes from Vidal's scrutiny as she shrugged and said in what she hoped was a suitably deceptive breathy voice. 'Not go any further now, when you've…when I want you so much, Vidal?'

Had he been hoping that she would end it? That she would have the strength of will that he knew he did not? Vidal asked himself grimly, as his body reacted immediately and openly to her deliberate sensuality.

He could see the swollen pink softness of her mouth, her lips half parted, and her eyes were almost closed, as though she was already swooning with the pressure of her desire.

Anger and shame, Vidal felt them both—against himself and against Felicity as well. But they weren't strong enough to hold back the need that was driving him, taking him beyond logic and reason to a place where all that existed was his longing for this one woman.

He thrust into her slowly, needing to absorb every second of something so long denied, already knowing in that place deep within himself he had fought so hard to ignore that their bodies would match perfectly, and that hers would take and hold his in exactly the same unique way in which she already held his emotions in thrall.

He shouldn't be feeling like this. He knew what she was, after all, but it was as though something within him didn't want to recognise that reality—as though some weakness in himself refused to believe that reality and instead wanted what was happening between them to belong to them alone. His body registered and responded to what he was feeling. What he wanted… What he needed.

His earlier driven anger gave way to a longing to

shed the past and take them both to a place where they could start anew, with this burning ache of mutual need and desire untouched by what had gone before. He was losing sight of what was real, Vidal warned himself. The certainty of the contempt and anger that had informed his beliefs for so long, was fracturing under the pressure of what physical intimacy with Felicity was doing to him. Deep within himself Vidal could feel the growing ache of a yearning that he couldn't banish for things to be different, for *them* to be different, so that what was happening between them could be born of...

Had he forgotten the past? Did the past really matter? Wasn't it more important that she was here now in his arms, with him in the way that he had so longed for her to be? Where was his pride? Was he really admitting to himself that he loved her?

Vidal didn't know. He only knew that holding her like this now was sweeping away the barriers he had put up against her. His pride might say that he must not love her, but what about his heart? Denial, anger, longing, loss. Vidal felt them all—a torment of if onlys that overwhelmed him with a passionately regretful longing.

Somehow, instinctively, Fliss sensed the change within Vidal, and before she could resist it her own body was responding to it, welcoming it, wanting it, wanting *him* as the grimness of her earlier determination gave way to something far more elemental and irresistible. She wanted Vidal to feed that feeling, to caress and entice this quivering of a new and intense desire filling her. It was so much stronger than the anger-driven determination she had previously felt, Fliss thought shakily.

She was wholly unable to stop the sounds of her pleasure bubbling in her throat as her flesh responded to the building rhythmic thrust of Vidal's body within her own with increasing pleasure. That pleasure gripped her and flooded her, holding her captive, demanding her submission, making her forget why it was that their intimacy was happening.

Lost in the bitter sweetness of what might have been, Vidal tensed with disbelief when he felt the barrier within Fliss. His brain couldn't ignore the message being sent to it. In the space between one breath and the next, one thrust and the next, a confusion of thoughts exploded through his head. He looked down at Felicity, whose reactions were slower. Her flesh, softened and aching with desire, was reluctant to give up its pleasure. Resistance to the thought of being denied seized her as she realised that Vidal had stopped the delicious movement that had been giving her so much delight. In his expression she could see shock and the prospect of withdrawal. A withdrawal her body did not want.

'*No.*'

Her charged denial could have meant anything, but Fliss knew that Vidal understood it meant everything. She clung to him, urging him to complete the sensual possession he had begun, her gaze on his willing him to give her what she ached for so badly.

What was happening to her? Where was the anger she should be feeling? How had Vidal managed to steal it away from her and replace it with this aching sweetness

and this longing for Vidal that now possessed her? Fliss
didn't know. She wasn't capable of logical reasoned argument any more. Her feelings were too strong for that.
She only knew that everything she had always wanted
was here, with Vidal.

Vidal. His name and her own longing ached silently
within her, her body, her flesh, clinging to his in a mute
plea.

Vidal felt the quiver within Fliss that held him to
her. He should end this now. There were questions that
needed to be asked. Old history must be rewritten. But
they were here in this moment, in this place he had
wanted to take her for what felt like a lifetime. And she
wanted him.

Reality had no place here. This was a place of broken
dreams that could be mended, shattered hopes restored
and old pain banished.

His body made its own decision, and its possessive
movement within her caused Felicity to make a soft
purring sound deep in her throat. The way she was looking at him now was the way she had looked at him at
sixteen, in her innocent longing. Only now her gaze was
the gaze of a woman—her desire the desire of a woman.
He had ached for her for so long. *Loved* her for so long.
No! But it was too late for him to make that denial. His
body wasn't listening. It was gripped by a tide it was
impossible to stem.

He moved within her, carefully but surely, silenc-
ing the small sound she made as her flesh tightened in
what began as pain only to be transformed into pleasure,
until her body was free to respond to his possession as

it wanted to. As it had been created to do, Fliss thought hectically as the world and reality began to lose focus, and there was only Vidal to cling to between waves of pleasure spiked with a need that grew with each one.

Finally the need that drove her reached its culmination in a burst of pleasure so intense that she could hardly bear it, crying out to Vidal in a tangle of words mingled with tears of release as he held her and let his own body take its pleasure in the final dying spasms of hers.

CHAPTER EIGHT

VIDAL looked into the darkness, probing it, trying to find a way through it. The bedroom was warmly lit and everything was clear. Some things were painfully clear, etched in sharp detail inside his heart for ever. The darkness he needed to probe lay within himself, within his gross negligence in not knowing. In not having known. It broke his pride, and worse than that—after all, what right did he have to pride now? Instead he was filled not just with his own pain but far more importantly with Felicity's.

The shattering of his delusion showed him how unworthy of her the love he had fought so hard against admitting actually was. Somehow he should have *known*. He would never forgive himself for that failing, and he suspected neither would Felicity.

'Am I right in thinking that the…intimacy we have just shared was at least on your part aroused by a need to punish me? To prove to me that I was wrong about you?'

'I haven't spent the last seven years plotting to be seduced by you, if that's what you mean,' Fliss parried.

They were still in bed together and, much as she

would have liked to get up and protect herself by getting dressed again, she suspected that if she did Vidal would know immediately she was doing so because she felt vulnerable.

Vulnerable because her body felt almost giddily euphoric and delighted with itself, delighted with Vidal, and all too ready to explore the possibility of experiencing a repeat of the pleasure he had just given her. It was as though in place of her virginity Vidal had given her flesh a need that it believed only *he* could satisfy. And if that was true…

But, no—she must not start thinking like that. She must remember instead how she had felt before that pleasure. She must remember why it had been so important to her that Vidal confronted the reality of her virginity.

Vidal pressed her before she could say anything else. 'No more games, Felicity.' His voice was controlled and empty of emotion. 'You urged me to take your virginity not to pleasure me or even yourself but to punish me. Not as an act of intimacy, but as an act of retribution.'

Since his voice was so expressionless it was surely strange that she should feel as though he was holding within him a great weight of some hidden emotion. He was just trying to make her feel she was in the wrong, Fliss told herself. And he was doing it because he didn't want to admit that *he* was the one who had been wrong.

'You misjudged me and you kept on misjudging me,' she reminded him. 'You kept on throwing my supposed past in my face. I didn't deliberately set out to plan what happened, if that's what you think, but when the opportunity presented itself, yes—I did want it to happen.'

'You could have stopped when you recognised I had realised that you were a virgin.'

A quiver of apprehension flickered down her spine. Had he guessed that she had ended up wanting him so much that the original purpose of what she was doing had ceased to matter? That way lay fresh humiliation for her. She was twenty-three now, not sixteen, and the very idea of having secretly longed for him for all those years was not one she was prepared to entertain.

'Maybe I felt that if I did there would always be a question over the…the factual evidence, and that you might choose afterwards to believe that you had imagined my virginity.'

'Maybe?'

Fliss gave a small nervy shrug. 'What was the point in leaving things there? You've always disliked me, Vidal,' she continued before he could answer her. 'We both know that. I wanted to make sure that we both knew the truth.'

'So you remained a virgin on the off chance that the opportunity might arise for you to confront me with that truth?'

He was mocking her. Fliss was sure of it. She could feel her self-control slipping away from her.

'Have you any idea what it's like to be branded as you branded me? Not just by your words and your beliefs about me, but…but by the way in which they impacted on the way I felt about myself. I'm twenty-three. How do you think I felt about the thought of having to explain to a man I might fall in love with that I haven't had sex. He'd think I was a freak.'

'So it's my fault, is it, that you were still a virgin?'

'Yes. No. Look, I don't see the point in us discussing this. I just want to draw a line under it and move on. Like I've said, I know that you've never liked me, or the fact that I exist. You proved that when you wouldn't let me write to my father.'

'You wanted me.'

The words slipped so adroitly under her guard caused Fliss to exhale shakily in shock.

'No. I wanted justice.'

'You were aroused by me—by my touch, my possession.'

'No. I was aroused by the knowledge that you would be forced to admit you were wrong. Strong emotions can do that. After all, you don't even like me. But you… you…'

'Made love to you? Aroused you? Possessed you?'

He was too quick, his logic too sharp for her to combat right now, when all she could do was think about the delight of the pleasure he had given her. And long for a repeat of that pleasure? Desperately, Fliss struggled to find a way in which she could be as practical and unaffected by what had happened as Vidal obviously was. But the truth was that there wasn't one. The truth was that if he turned to her now and took her back in his arms…if he touched her as he had done before…

'I don't want to talk about it. I just want you to go.' No, she didn't. She wanted him to stay. She wanted him to stay and hold her and—and what? Love her? She wasn't sixteen any more, Fliss reminded herself.

Vidal closed his eyes. Why was he doing this? What was he hoping for? To force her to say she loved him in the same way that he had been forced to accept his misjudgement of her? Was that really the kind of man he was? A man whose pride demanded that she love him simply because he loved her? There was a sour taste in Vidal's mouth, a heavy weight on his heart. Hadn't he already damaged her enough?

Fliss heard Vidal exhale. Not in a sigh of regret, of course. That was impossible. She didn't trust herself to turn round and look at him when she felt him move away from her to leave the bed. She didn't watch him either as he dressed and thankfully, finally, left the room.

Her earlier euphoria had left her now. She felt drained and empty, hollowed out emotionally apart from the forlorn ache deep inside her heart. What she wanted more than anything else was to be held in Vidal's arms, to know that what they had shared was special. Was she really so much of a fool? Was that really what she had expected? That like in some fairy story her kiss would instantly transform everything and cause Vidal to fall passionately in love with her?

Passionately in love with her? That wasn't what she wanted at all. Was it?

Wasn't there hidden away inside her the kernel of her sixteen-year-old self, with all the dreams and romantic illusions—delusions—she had then possessed? And wasn't the truth that the intimacy they had shared had left her in great danger of that kernel splitting open, so that the seed inside it could grow into new life?

Fliss buried her face in her hands, her whole body shaking as she tried to tell herself that it was all right; she was safe and she did *not* love Vidal.

In his own room Vidal stood motionless and silent. He should really take a shower, but Felicity's scent still clung to his skin, and since that was all he would ever know of her now, apart from what was captured within his memory and his senses, he might as well indulge himself and cling to it for as long as he could. Like an adolescent overwhelmed by his first real love.

Or a man knowing his only love.

He couldn't hide from the truth any longer. He had never stopped loving Felicity.

This was the place to which his jealousy and passion had brought him. This barren place of self-loathing and regret—a true desert of the heart in which he would be for ever tormented by the mirage of what might have been. It gave him no comfort or satisfaction to know that Fliss had wanted him, or that her desire—the desire *he* had aroused in her—had ultimately overtaken whatever ideas of retribution and punishment she might claim, had kept her in his arms. He knew enough about the power of true desire to recognise it—in himself and in her. He could, had he had the stomach for it, have forced her to admit her desire for him—but what satisfaction would that have given him?

He had done her a terrible wrong in misjudging her, and there were no excuses he could plead in mitigation

of that wrong, no way back to change it. He would have
to live with that for the rest of his life. A second intolerable burden to add to the one he already carried, had
carried for the past seven years. The burden of loving
her without reason or logic and so completely that there
could never ever be room in his life for another woman.
There. He had admitted it now. He had loved her then
and he still loved her now—had never stopped loving
her, in fact, and never would.

It was the burden that Felicity herself carried, though,
that weighed most heavily on his conscience and on his
heart. Out of his pride and jealousy had come the belief
that by guarding her innocence until she was mature
enough to receive his courtship he could eventually win
the heart of the girl with whom he had fallen in love. As
that young man, that arrogant and selfish man, he had
not been able to bear the thought of another man taking
what he had wanted and denied himself. He had been
furious with Felicity for choosing another man above
him, and he had misjudged and punished her for that.

CHAPTER NINE

'I SHALL leave you here to complete your examination of the house. My meeting with the water engineer should not take too long. As soon as it's finished I shall come back for you, and then we can return to Granada.'

Fliss nodded her head. Her throat felt too raw with pent-up emotion as she stood with Vidal in the hallway to her father's house. She had barely slept, and disturbingly her body, as though totally divorced from the reality of the situation between them, had reacted to his proximity in the car this morning as though they were real lovers, aching to be close to him. Several times she had felt herself being drawn to move nearer to him, her senses craving the intimacy of just being close.

Was it always like this after having sex? Was there always this need for continued closeness? This desire to touch and be touched? To be held and to know that that other person shared your thoughts and feelings? Somehow Fliss did not think so—which meant...

'This morning I couldn't find my mother's locket.' She rushed into speech in an attempt to block from her thoughts memories of their intimacy, but simply referring to the initial cause of it was enough to have her whole body burning—and not just burning but aching as well.

'I have it. The catch is faulty. I shall get it repaired for you in Granada.'

'Thank you.'

'Before I leave you, there's something I must say.'

Fliss had never seen Vidal look more grimly stern, never heard his voice contain such harshness—not even on that dreadful evening when he had looked down at her with such cruel contempt as she lay trapped in Rory's hold.

Automatically she tensed, as though waiting for a blow to fall, so Vidal's next words came as an unexpected shock.

'I owe you an apology—and an explanation. I realise that there are no words that can undo what has been done. No amount of explanation or acknowledgement of blame on my part can give you back the years you have lost when you should have been free to…to enjoy your womanhood. All I can do is hope that whatever satisfaction you took from last night is sufficient to free you from the pain I inflicted on you in the past.'

Although Fliss had flinched over that word *satisfaction*, not really sure if he was trying to subtly taunt her by referring to the sexual delight he had given her, she managed not to betray herself in any other way.

'The accusation I made against you that evening was born of my…my pride and not your behaviour. You had looked at me with an innocent desire and…'

'And because of that you thought I was promiscuous?' Fliss finished for him. Her face was burning over his reference to her 'innocent desire', but much as she wanted to refute it she knew that she couldn't. That was definitely not a subject she wanted him to dwell on, so she told him fiercely, 'There's no need for you to say any more. I know what motivated you, Vidal. You disliked and disapproved of me even before you met me.'

'That's not true.'

'Yes, it is. You wanted to stop me from writing to my father, remember?'

'That was—'

'That was how you felt about me. I wasn't good enough to write to my father—just as my mother hadn't been good enough to marry him. Well, at least my father had second thoughts about our relationship, even if *you* still wish it didn't exist.'

For her sake maybe it was better to allow her to believe what she was saying, Vidal decided. It could not undo the harm that had been done, of course. Nothing could do that. But he could not and would not burden her with his love—a love she did not want. She desired him, though. Perhaps he was late in recognising that loving her meant putting her happiness first, but now that he *had* recognised that it would be shameful and wrong of him to use her first taste of adult desire as a means of trying to persuade her that she could grow to love him. He couldn't do that. Not even if it meant watching whilst she walked away from him.

The empty house, as though its silence had been disturbed by her arrival, had ultimately settled and sighed around her in the way old houses do, reminding her of the similar sighs and creaks she had experienced from her old family home when she had walked round it one last time before saying her final goodbye to it. Fliss had thought of her mother and her father as she'd walked from room to room, her sadness for them and for all that they had never had filling her emotions and her thoughts. Two gentle people who had simply not been strong enough to fight against those who had not wanted them to be together.

But she was the living proof that their love had once existed, she reminded herself as she stood in the doorway of the house's master bedroom. Not her father's bedroom. According to Vidal, her father had preferred to sleep in a smaller room, almost cell-like in its simplicity, further down the corridor. A room that in its starkness told her nothing about the man responsible for her existence.

Now, with her exploration of the house complete, she had nothing to do other than wait for Vidal to return. Nothing to do, that was, other than try not to think about the intimacy they had shared. As a sixteen-year-old she had spent many private hours in fevered imaginings of Vidal making love to her. Now that he had... Now that he had she wanted him to do it again—and again. She wanted the pleasure he had given her to be hers exclusively, wanted Vidal himself to be hers exclusively.

What had she done to herself? Fliss wondered bitterly. In proving to Vidal that he had misjudged her she had simply exchanged one emotional burden for another. Now she had no anger with which to conceal her real feelings for Vidal. Her *real* feelings? Could one fall in love for life at sixteen? Could one really know that the possession of one's first lover, was the only possession one would ever want? Her heart and her senses gave her their answer immediately and forcefully. She loved Vidal, and her anger against him for misjudging her was entangled with her pain because he did not love her back.

She loved Vidal.

From the window of the master bedroom she could see a car coming down the rutted driveway and heading for the house. Vidal's car. He had come to collect her, as he had told her he would, and soon they would be on their way back to Granada. Soon she would be on her way back to London and her own life there. A life without Vidal. Could she bear that? She would have to.

Fliss reached the hallway just as Vidal opened the front door. His, 'Have you seen everything you wanted to see?' elicited a nod of her head.

She didn't trust herself to actually speak to him—not right now, with her heart aching for him and for his love.

Later that day, driving away from the *castillo* and the estate, Fliss knew that from now on whenever she smelled the scent of citrus fruit she would think of the Lecrin Valley, of the touch of Vidal's hands on her skin, the passion of his kiss on her mouth, and the possession of her body by his. Bittersweet pleasure, indeed.

CHAPTER TEN

THE Granada townhouse contained an air of impatient bustle—due, Fliss knew, to the fact that its lord and master was about to fly to Chile for a business meeting with his business partner there later in the week.

'It's foolish, I know, but I can't help feeling a little anxious whenever I know that Vidal is about to fly to South America. It always reminds me of the death of his father, and makes me worry for Vidal's safety—although I can never say that to Vidal himself, of course. He would think me overprotective,' the Duchess confided to Fliss as they had their morning coffee together out on the courtyard terrace, two days after Fliss's return from the *castillo*. 'You will be returning to England soon, I expect,' she added, 'but you must keep in touch with us, Fliss. You are part of the family, after all.'

Part of the family? Vidal certainly didn't want her to be part of the family.

As though her thoughts had somehow conjured him up, Vidal himself walked out of the house and came over to join them, bending swiftly to kiss his mother's cheek and smile at her. His look for Fliss was notably cold and dismissive.

'I've arranged for you to see Señor Gonzales tomorrow morning, so that the paperwork with regard to the sale of your father's house to me can be set in motion,' he told her.

'I'm not going to sell it.'

The words were out of their own volition, spoken as though Fliss had no control over them, shocking her as much as they obviously infuriated Vidal. Until that moment it had never occurred to Fliss to even *think* of keeping her father's house, but now that she had told Vidal that she wasn't going to sell it, defying what she knew were his expectations, she suddenly realised how right it felt that she should keep it.

Almost as though they had physically reached out and touched her, she felt as though somehow she could sense her parents' approval and delight. They *wanted* her to keep the house. She felt that more surely than she had ever felt anything before in the whole of her life. In a rush of aching emotion Fliss knew that no matter how much Vidal tried to bend her to his will and make her sell the house to him she wouldn't—because quite simply she couldn't.

'The dower house is part of the ducal estate,' Vidal told her grimly. 'When it was given to Felipe—'

'When my father left it to me,' Fliss interrupted him, 'he did it because he wanted me to have it. If he had wanted it returned to the estate then that's what he would have done. It's mine, and I intend to keep it.'

'To spite me?' Vidal suggested coldly.

'No,' Fliss denied. 'I intend to keep the house for

myself...for...for my children. So that they at least can know something of their Spanish ancestry.'

What children? An inner voice mocked her. The only children she wanted were Vidal's children—children she would never be allowed to have. But her words seemed to have been enough to infuriate Vidal further. Fliss could see that.

His eyes burned molten gold with anger as he challenged her, 'And these children—you will bring them here to Spain, will you? With the man who has given them to you?'

'Yes!' Fliss told him, refusing to be intimidated. 'Why shouldn't I? My father left the house to me because he wanted me to have something of him to cherish. Of course I will want to share that with my own children.' Overwhelmed by what she was feeling, she accused him emotionally, 'You might have been able to stop me making contact with my father, but you couldn't prevent him from leaving his house to me—although no doubt you tried.'

Fliss couldn't say any more. She simply couldn't trust herself to speak. Shaking her head, she got up from the table and almost ran into the house in her desperation to escape from Vidal's presence before she broke down completely.

Only when she had reached the safety and privacy of her bedroom did she let her feelings get the better of her.

And then her bedroom door opened, and she froze with disbelief as Vidal strode in.

This time he hadn't bothered knocking. This time

he'd simply flung the door open and marched in, slamming the door behind him.

He was angry—furiously, savagely, passionately angry. Fliss could see it and something within her leapt to match those feelings—a wild, tempestuous intensity of emotion that had her facing him defiantly.

'I don't know what you want, Vidal—'

He didn't let her get any further. 'Don't you? Then let me show you.'

He had closed the distance between them before she knew it, reaching for her, with a man's passion, a man's need, she recognised dizzily.

'*This* is what I want, Felicity, and you want it too. So don't even bother trying to pretend that you don't. I felt it, saw it, *tasted* it in you, and it's still there now. Didn't it ever occur to you that in giving yourself to me you might have unleashed something that neither of us can control? Something for which we will both have to pay a price? No, of course it didn't. Just as it obviously never occurred to you that a man who is aroused to possessive jealousy at the sight of the sixteen-year-old girl he wants but has denied himself, out of the moral belief that she is too young, might just leap to the wrong judgement when he finds her in bed with someone else.'

What was he doing? He shouldn't be in here, saying things like this. He should be keeping as much distance between Felicity and himself as he could. It had been those words she had thrown at him about wanting to keep her father's house for her children that had done it—the anguish of the thought of her with another man's child, conceiving that child, bearing it, loving it as she loved the man who had given it to her, had been more than he could bear. The voice within him that was urging him to stop, to leave now whilst he still could, was being drowned out by the pain of his longing for her.

'I wasn't in bed with Rory,' was the only protest Fliss could manage to make, and even that was a whispered flurry of words whilst her mind, her body, her senses grappled with exactly what Vidal had just said to her.

Vidal wanted her, desired her? Had been jealous at the thought of her with someone else?

'I promised myself I wouldn't do this,' Vidal was saying angrily. 'I told myself that it demeans me as a man to use the sexual desire we feel for one another for such a purpose. But you leave me with no other choice.'

'I leave you with no other choice?'

She wasn't going to let herself think about what he had just said—about them sharing a sexual desire for one another—and she certainly wasn't going to think about the effervescent surge of joyous delight his words had given her. Instead she would focus on the practical and the logical, on the sheer arrogance of his belief that he could walk in here and expect... What exactly *did* he expect?

Her body had started to overheat, and her thoughts were spinning out of control, wild, sensual, erotic and very dangerous thoughts that wanted to send her into his arms, into his possession.

'Not when you throw in my face your plans for the future. A future that includes taking a lover who will give you his children. He may give you that, but first I shall give you *this*, and you will give me the passion you promised all those years ago. Don't bother trying to deny it. You have already shown that you want me.'

'Any woman worth her salt can fake an org…sexual pleasure,' Fliss corrected herself frantically.

'Anyone male or female can say the words and act out a fiction of sexual delight, but the human body does not lie. And your body wanted me. It welcomed me, it ached and yearned for me, and when the moment came it showed me that I had given it pleasure. As I shall do again now. And you will not stop me, because you will not wish to stop me, even though you might try to tell yourself that you do.'

Fliss made a small mewling sound in her throat, but it was too late to protest more strongly because Vidal was kissing her, fiercely and passionately, and she was kissing him back with equal hunger and need.

Vidal's hand cupped her breast, his fingers finding her already erect nipple.

This was the last thing she had expected—and yet the first thing she had wanted. She couldn't deny it. She still tried to, though, but the words didn't come. Her body, her senses, her emotions were already saying yes.

Vidal acknowledged how hard he had tried to fight the need for her that was sweeping over him right now, and how completely he had failed. He hadn't planned for this to happen. In fact he had done everything he could to avoid it happening. But right now he was no more able to control his need for her than she was able to conceal her response to him.

Pointless. Pointless to fight, pointless to flee, and even more pointless to allow herself to love him—and that was exactly what she was doing, Fliss recognised, as Vidal looked deep into her eyes and then kissed her slowly and lingeringly. The sensation of his mouth moving on hers with such deliberate and controlled sensuality was stealing her resistance from her. All she wanted to do was respond to him, give to him, be held and touched and possessed by him. The force of that need made her whole body tremble in his arms like a reed in the wind, needing his support to protect her from her own vulnerability.

Vidal moved back and pulled off his shirt, then cupped her face and kissed the side of her neck, sending hot shivers of pleasure running over her skin so that her control ran from her like sand taken by a ceaseless and unstoppable tide.

'Touch me,' he whispered against her ear, and that rough, broken note of urgency suggested that his whole desire was for her touch and he was on the point of breaking his self-control. Surely more a figment of her own imagination than true reality? But Vidal was lifting her hand and placing it against the warm flesh of his chest, holding it there as he implored her, 'Touch me, Fliss, as I've wanted you to touch me from the moment I saw you.'

Unable to stop herself, Fliss obeyed his whispered command. Wasn't this, after all, what she had ached and longed for herself? Now, as she stroked and explored her way over Vidal's torso, she could feel the surge of the blood beneath his skin rising up to meet the trembling excitement of her fingertips—just as she could feel the movement of his muscles as she grew bolder and explored further and lower, to the flat plane where his flesh disappeared beneath the edge of his chinos.

'*Yes.*' The heated urgency of the demand Vidal smothered against the rise of her breast came just when her hand reached the barrier of his trousers, and could only mean one thing. But still Fliss hesitated. To have come this far was dangerous. To go any further would be fatal, taking her to a state of being and emotion that once inhabited she knew she would never want to leave.

'So you still want to torment me, do you?' Vidal accused her. 'Then maybe I should do a little tormenting of my own.'

Before she could stop him he had swung her up into his arms and was carrying her into his own bedroom, minimalist and masculine in design and decor, even if the large bed on which he was placing her seemed to Fliss to be the most sensually dangerous place she had ever known. Or was that because Vidal was now undressing her and himself, between kisses she was sure were designed to arouse her to the point where she ached for him so much that she was willing to do anything to have the pleasure he was giving her? Each kiss, each touch was taking her deeper and deeper into a place of such intense need that nothing else existed, and her now naked body was trembling with the force of her longing.

'See how much you want me?' Vidal asked her.

Fliss couldn't deny it. She did want him. She wanted him, needed him, longed for him, loved him.

Her body shuddered in mute confirmation of that admission.

Vidal leaned forward and stroked her body from her hip to her breast with a fiercely demanding caress that ended with him bending his head to take her nipple between his lips, drawing the need up through her body until it was trembling and pulsing in response to him. His free hand was cupping her other breast, his knee urging her legs apart.

The desire that ripped into her was a volcano of molten heat. The satisfaction of feeling his naked erect flesh against her own sex, initially so pleasurable, quickly became another form of exquisite torture as she ached for even more intimacy, grinding her lower body against him whilst Vidal in turn lifted her against himself, opening her legs to wrap them around his body and hold him closer.

Fliss craved the sensation of him within her, the movement of his flesh inside and against her own. Just the thought of it made need surge through her in unbearable longing, but Vidal was pushing her away, removing himself from her, leaving her. Was this what he had meant about tormenting her?

Yearningly Fliss reached to him, but he shook his head.

'Not yet,' he told her softly. 'I want to touch all of you, to taste all of you, to know all of you first.'

He was stringing kisses along the back of her knee and then the inside of her leg, whilst his fingers stroked apart the willing swollen heat of the lips covering her sex. The pulse already beating there increased in intensity, driving her towards the goal her body now craved. The caress of Vidal's touch against the intimate wetness of her sex was both a pleasure and an incitement to want more, to want *him*. Fliss knew it as she curled her fingers round his wrist in a mute plea for what she really wanted.

Vidal denied her, bending his head and dipping his tongue into the moist arousal of her sex, lightly caressing the very heart of it, and then less lightly, whilst Fliss clung to what was left of her reason until she could cling to it no more, and then her cries for him to complete the pleasure he was giving her with the stroke of his flesh within her rose and fell against the fevered backdrop of their unsteady breathing and the inward clamour of their frantic heartbeats.

'Now! *Now*,' Fliss begged Vidal, all control and restraint lost as she was sucked into the maelstrom of desire Vidal had aroused within her. Her senses, already stimulated and aroused, absorbed the reality of his maleness as he stopped, poised over her, wantonly glorying in awareness of his need, of his erection taut and hard.

Fliss shivered in an agony of pleasure as she felt the strength of it pressing against the entrance to her own body. Her sex ached with longing, its muscles quivering in eager anticipation of the pleasure his possession of her promised. His first swift, urgent thrust made her cry out in a paroxysm of heart-stopping pleasure. Her body waited on the crest of that pleasure for more of what it craved.

Another thrust—deeper, harder—had her body tightening around him.

Her fiercely passionate 'yes' was breathed against
Vidal's mouth, her longing and arousal overwhelming
her completely.

'You want me,' he told her.

'Yes. Yes. I want you now, Vidal. I need you now.'
The hot, passionate words tumbled from her lips as she
clung to him, holding him within her, trembling with
pleasure and anticipation.

'Tell me again,' he urged as he stroked deeper inside
her. 'Tell me how much you want me.'

'So much—too much. More than there are words for,'
Fliss told him as she pressed frantic kisses against his
face.

Now he was moving within her, satisfying her need
and yet increasing it at the same time. Helplessly Fliss
clung to him as the tension within her grew, until it
possessed every bit of her, every pulse of her blood and
her heart, all that she was. And then all at once it was
there, a brief second of hanging in space, and then the
implosion, the fierce contraction of her body that took
her over the edge of arousal and into the eye of a storm.
Her orgasm was shot through with the pulse of Vidal's
release.

Lost in the wonder of their closeness, helpless and
vulnerable to all that she was feeling, Fliss clung to
Vidal, knowing that this wasn't desire alone that possessed her, this was *love*. And his feelings for her?

Against her ear she could feel the warmth of his
breath. Her voice trembled as she whispered softly,
'Vidal?'

Vidal's chest tightened. He could hear the emotion in

Felicity's voice. The way it had trembled when she had said his name had felt like a physical caress against his skin. That emotion, though, came from the satisfaction of desire. Nothing else.

He exhaled slowly. Taking another deep breath, he told her curtly, 'Now we are even. You used my desire for you to prove that I misjudged you. Now I have used yours for me to prove that you lied when you said you didn't want me.'

Fliss could hear Vidal speaking coldly as she lay there, still wrapped in the vulnerability of loving him so intimately and intensely, wholly unable to protect herself from the cruelty of what he was saying now.

CHAPTER ELEVEN

SHE couldn't lie here like this for ever, in the grip of a grief so intense that it went way beyond the release of any tears, Fliss told herself. She must have showered and dressed after Vidal had gone, she recognised, but she had no memory of having done so. All she could remember was his final words to her, his final cruelty. She had been crazy to think that what had happened between them just now could change anything. He hated her.

Someone was knocking on the bedroom door. Fliss stiffened, and then trembled. Had Vidal come back? Did he want to utter more cruel words? Her heart pounded with pain. There was a second knock on the door. She would have to answer it. She got to her feet and walked unsteadily towards the door, exhaling with what she told herself was relief when she opened it to find the Duchess standing outside in the corridor, her face creased with tension.

'Can I come in?' the Duchess asked. 'Only there's something I have to say to you—about Vidal and what you said earlier.'

Numbly Fliss realised that in the heat of the moment, when she had been arguing with Vidal earlier, she had

completely forgotten that his mother was also there—a
silent witness to the accusations Fliss had made against
her son. Unable to do anything else, she nodded her head
and held open the door, closing it once the Duchess was
in the room.

'I had to speak to you,' the Duchess told Fliss as
she sat in one of the chairs by the fire, obliging Fliss to
take the other or be left standing over her visitor. 'No
mother likes to hear her child being spoken of as you
spoke of Vidal earlier. You will learn that for yourself
one day. But it is not just for Vidal's sake that I want to
talk to you, Felicity. It is for your own as well. Bitterness
and resentment are destructive. They can eat away at a
person until there is nothing left but those destructive
emotions. I would hate to think of such damaging emotions destroying you—especially when those feelings
are not necessary.'

'I'm sorry if I hurt or offended you,' Fliss apologised. 'That wasn't my intention. But the way Vidal has
behaved—preventing me from making contact with my
father—'

'No, that is not true. It was not Vidal. On the contrary,
in fact. You owe Vidal so much, and it is thanks to him
that you have had— Oh!'

Guiltily the Duchess placed her hand over her mouth,
shaking her head.

'I only came up here to defend Vidal, not to… But
I've let my emotions run away with me. Please forget
what I said.'

Forget? How could she. '*What* is not true?' Fliss demanded, urgently. 'And what do I owe him? Please, tell me.'

'I can't say any more,' the Duchess answered, very obviously flustered and uncomfortable. 'I have said too much already.'

'You can't say something like that and then not explain,' Fliss protested, feeling equally emotional.

'I'm sorry,' the Duchess apologised. 'I shouldn't have come up here. Oh, I am so cross with myself. I'm sorry, Fliss. I really am.' She got up and walked towards the door, pausing there before opening it to repeat softly, 'I really am sorry.'

Fliss stared at the closed door. What had the Duchess meant? What was it she had started to say and then refused to tell her? It was, of course, only natural that a mother should defend her child, Fliss could understand that. But there had been much more than maternal protection in the Duchess's voice. There had been certainty, knowledge. A knowledge that *she* did not have. What kind of knowledge? Something to do with Fliss's father? Something to do with the fact that Fliss had never been allowed to contact him? Something she had a right to know. Something that only one person could tell her, if she had the courage to demand an answer.

Vidal himself. And *did* she have that courage?

The Duchess's slip made Fliss feel as though a secret door had suddenly appeared in a room she had thought she knew so well that it could not hide any secrets. It was an unnerving, uncomfortable experience. There was probably nothing for her to discover, no secrets for her to learn, no darkness for her to fear beyond that secret door.

But what if there was? What if…? What *could* there be? Vidal had told her himself that he had intercepted her letter to her father and that she was not to write to him again. The evidence had spoken for itself. Hadn't it?

She needed to talk to Vidal, Fliss recognised.

Vidal was in his own suite of rooms, working, Rosa informed Fliss in a tone that suggested he would not want to be interrupted, when Fliss asked her where he was.

Not giving herself time to change her mind, Fliss started to climb the stairs. All the way up her stomach was cramping and her knees were almost knocking. Her mouth was dry with apprehension.

As she walked along the corridor, part of her wanted her to turn round, her courage almost failing her. The door to Vidal's rooms was slightly ajar. Fliss knocked on it hesitantly and then waited, a cowardly relief filling her when there was no immediate reply.

Letting her hand fall to her side, she was just about to step back from the door when she heard Vidal call out briskly in Spanish from inside the room, in a voice that commanded obedience, for her to enter.

Feeling decidedly unsteady, Fliss turned the handle.

She might not have touched any alcohol, but she felt slightly light-headed—light-headed and, she recognised, rather dangerously emotional.

The first thing she realised as she stepped into the room and let the door swing shut behind her was that this room was decorated in a far more modern and pared-down fashion than the rest of the house, in shades of grey and off-white, and was furnished as a functional working office. The second was that Vidal was standing in the doorway between the room she was in and a shower room adjacent to it, with only a towel wrapped round his damp body, and he was looking at her in a way that told her that her presence was neither expected nor wanted.

Unable to say anything, but helpless with longing and love, and humiliatingly aware that she was in danger of betraying everything that he made her feel, Fliss forced herself to drag her gaze away.

Only now did it dawn on her that Vidal had instructed her to come in in Spanish because he had assumed she was one of the servants. He certainly wasn't at all pleased to see her. She could tell that from the grim expression on his face.

To her dismay he was actually turning away from her, about to walk off.

'No!' Fliss protested, darting forward and then coming to an abrupt halt when he turned round so quickly that only a couple of feet separated them. 'I want to talk to you. There's something I want to know.'

'Which is?

Why did you stop me communicating with my father? That was what Fliss had intended to ask him but for some reason she heard herself saying instead, 'Was it really you who stopped me from making contact with my father?'

The silence in the room was electric, the air almost humming with Vidal's tension, and Fliss knew immediately from his unmoving silence that her question had caught him off-guard.

'What makes you ask me that?'

Should she lie to him and say it was just curiosity? If she wanted to hear the truth from him then maybe she should start the ball rolling by offering him her own truth first. Fliss took a deep breath. 'Something your mother let slip, by accident, that made me think what I've always assumed to be fact might not be.'

'When the decision was taken it was done with your best interests in mind,' Vidal told her obliquely.

He was choosing his words carefully—too carefully, Fliss realised. Too carefully and in a way that suggested to her that he was concealing something—or protecting someone?

'Who took that decision?' she demanded, adding fiercely, 'I have a right to know, Vidal. I have a right to know who made that decision and why it was made. If you don't tell me I will go back and ask your mother and I shall keep on asking her until she tells me,' she threatened wildly.

'You will do no such thing.'

'Then *tell* me. Was it your grandmother? My father? It has to be one of them. There wasn't anyone else. The only other person involved was my mother...' Fliss had almost been speaking to herself, but the sudden movement of Vidal's head, the brief tensing of his jaw when she mentioned her mother, gave him away, made her stiffen and stare at him in disbelief. Her voice was a raw, emotional whisper as she demanded, 'My mother?

It was my *mother*? Tell me the truth, Vidal. I want to know the truth.'

'She believed she was doing the right thing for you,' Vidal told her, sidestepping her question.

'My *mother*! But you were the one who brought my letter back. You...' Fliss felt so weak with shock and disillusionment that she couldn't help saying tremulously, 'I don't understand.'

The admission was a small agonised whisper that made Vidal want to go to her and hold her protectively, but he fought the urge. He had sworn to himself that he must allow her to have her freedom, that he must not impose on her the burden of his love for her. It was hard, though, to see her so distressed and not be able to offer her the comfort he longed to give her.

Instead all he could do was say quietly, 'Let me try to explain.'

Fliss nodded her head, sinking down into the nearest chair. Her thoughts and her emotions were in total disarray, and yet totally focused on what her questions had revealed. But still there was something about the sight of Vidal wearing only that towel around his hips that touched her senses as though they were a raw wound, reminding her of all that she could never have.

'After my father's death, control of the family's affairs and finances passed back to my grandmother. I was a minor, and my grandmother was my trustee along with the family solicitor. My grandmother's treatment of your father, combined with her refusal to help your mother financially or recognise you, resulted in your father having what was in effect a minor breakdown.

Your father was a kind, loving man, Felicity, but sadly his mental health was damaged by my grandmother's determination to ensure he married well. He was a very gifted amateur historian, and as a young man he wanted to pursue a career in that field. My grandmother refused. She told him that it wasn't acceptable for him to take up any kind of paid occupation. As I said before, your father was a kind and gentle man, but my grandmother was a strong-willed woman who rode roughshod over everyone and thought she was doing the right thing. She bullied and cowed him from the moment she realised he wanted to choose his own path in life. She never allowed him to forget that she was trying to do what his birth mother would have wanted for him, and that caused so much guilt and confusion in him. That was why he gave up your mother so easily, and I believe it was also why he had a breakdown when he learned of your mother's pregnancy. He wanted to be with you both so much, but he could not stand up to my grandmother. He never recovered fully from that breakdown.'

Fliss could hear the sadness and the regret in Vidal's voice and recognised that he had cared a great deal about her father.

'I have never ceased to feel guilty that it was my thoughtless comment that provoked my grandmother into questioning Felipe and your mother about their relationship. And I never will.'

That Vidal should make such an admission caused Fliss's heart to ache for the pain she could tell he felt.

'You were a child,' she reminded him. 'My mother

told me that she felt your grandmother had her own suspicions about her and my father anyway.'

'Yes, she told me the same thing when I first visited her—after my grandmother's death. Her kindness was balm to my guilt.'

'When you first visited her?' Fliss questioned. 'When was that?'

She could see from Vidal's frown that he had said more than he'd intended. His voice was clipped, his words sparing, as though he was being forced to say more than he wished to say, when he told her, almost reluctantly, 'After my grandmother's death I visited your mother. As head of the family it was my duty to...to do so—to ensure that both you and she—'

'You came to England to see my mother?' Fliss interrupted him.

'Yes. I thought she might want to have news of your father. The manner in which they had been parted had not been...kind, and there was you to consider—their child. I wanted your mother to know that you and she would be made very welcome if she were to choose to bring you to Spain. I thought she might want your father to see you, and you to meet him.'

Vidal was trying to choose his words very carefully. Felicity had suffered so much pain already. He didn't want to inflict still more on her.

Fliss, though, had guessed what Vidal was trying to shield her from.

'My mother didn't want to go back to Spain? She didn't want me to meet my father?' she guessed.

Vidal immediately defended Fliss's mother. ''She

was thinking of you. I'd had to tell her about Felipe's breakdown, and she was concerned about the effect that might have on you.'

'There's more, isn't there? I want to know it all,' Fliss insisted.

For a minute she thought that Vidal would refuse. He turned away from her to look towards the window.

'I have a right to know.' Fliss persisted.

She heard Vidal sigh.

'Very well, then. But remember, Felicity, all your mother wanted to do was protect you.'

'Nothing you can tell me will change how I feel about my mother,' Fliss assured him truthfully. And nothing could change how she felt about Vidal either, she knew. He had misjudged her, and it seemed she had misjudged him, but her love for him remained as true now as it had been all those years ago.

Vidal turned back to look at her. Fliss held her breath. Could he somehow read in her eyes her love for him? Quickly she dropped her lashes to conceal her expression.

'Your mother told me that she did not want there to be any contact between you and the Spanish side of your family,' Vidal began. 'She asked me to give her my promise that there would not be. Initially she was afraid that it might lead to you being hurt. You were a young girl, with perhaps an idealised vision of your father that she recognised he could not match, and then later she was equally afraid that you might—out of daughterly love—sacrifice your own freedom to be with your father. I gave her the promise she asked for, so when your letter to your father arrived—'

'You kept it from my father. Yes, I can understand that now, Vidal. But why didn't you simply destroy it? Why did you bring it to England and…and taunt me with it?'

The pain in her voice cut into Vidal's heart.

'I thought it best to discuss the situation with your mother in person. I didn't intend to *taunt* you, as you put it, I merely wanted to ensure that you did not write to your father again.'

'You came all the way to England just to discuss that?'

Vidal made a small dismissive gesture with one hand, as though to sweep her question away, and immediately Fliss knew.

'You didn't just come for that, did you? There was something else.'

There was another pause whilst Vidal once again looked towards the window before turning back to tell her, 'As I said earlier, as head of the family I felt it my duty. Your mother had had a very difficult time, enduring the loss of the man she loved, and the totally unacceptable financial hardship she had to suffer before…'

'Before she inherited all that money,' Fliss said slowly. 'Money from an aunt who Mum had never once mentioned to me and who I never met. Money that Mum often said she was grateful to have because of all that it would do for me. Money to buy us a lovely house in the country that she said was especially for me. Money that meant Mum didn't have to work so that she could be there for me. Money to send me to a good school and then university.'

Her mind was frantically scrambling over small facts and clues that suddenly, when put together, created a potential truth that shocked her to the core.

'There was no wealthy aunt, was there?' she challenged Vidal in a small bleak voice. 'There was no aunt, no will, no inheritance. It was *you*. You paid for everything...'

'Felicity—'

'It's true, isn't it?' Fliss demanded. The blood had drained from her face, leaving shadows beneath the curve of her cheekbones. 'It's true,' she repeated insistently. 'You were the one who bought the house, who gave Mum an allowance, who paid for my education.'

'You and your mother had every right to what I provided for you. I was only redressing the wrong done to you by my grandmother. Your mother was reluctant to accept anything from me at first, but I told her then as I tell you now that it would only have added to the guilt the family was already carrying if you were not given something of what should have been yours.'

'I've been so wrong about you.' Fliss's throat was so raw with emotion she could hardly speak. 'I've misjudged you so badly.'

She was so agitated that she stood up to pace the small area in front of the chair, almost wringing her hands in her despair.

'No, Fliss. You simply misinterpreted the facts as you saw them. That is all. I am the one who has been guilty of misjudgement—and a far greater misjudgement than yours.'

'Please don't be kind to me,' Fliss begged. 'It just makes things worse.'

How much worse only she could be allowed to know. Now she could see Vidal as he really was, instead of coloured by her own erroneous beliefs. Now she could see how tall he stood, how honourable he was, and how truly empty her life would be without him in it.

'I want you to have my father's house,' she told Vidal. 'I don't want any money for it. It's right that it should return to being part of the estate. I'm going home, Vidal.' she added. 'As soon as it can be arranged.'

'Felicity—'

Vidal took a step towards her, causing Fliss to step back. If he touched her now she would fall apart. She just knew it.

'I can't stay here now.'

'You've had a shock. It isn't wise to make decisions in the heat of the moment.'

As he spoke Vidal was reaching out to her. Another second and he would be touching her. She couldn't let that happen. She didn't dare.

Fliss stepped back, forgetting that the chair was there, and would have fallen over it if Vidal hadn't grabbed hold of her.

She could hear the heavy thud of his heartbeat, smell the warm scent of his skin. He was only holding her arms, but the whole of her body was responding to being so close to him, yearning and aching for him.

Fliss moved to pull back from him, and then gasped

when instead of releasing her Vidal's hold on her tightened. She looked up at him, her eyes widening as he lowered his head towards her. His breath seared her lips. Sensual heat flooded her body.

'No,' Fliss protested, but her protest was lost beneath the passion of his kiss.

She wanted Vidal so much. She loved him so much. But Vidal did not love her.

'No!' Fliss cried out, pushing him away. 'Don't touch me. I can't bear it. I've got to leave, Vidal, I love you too much to stay—'

Horrified by what she had revealed, Fliss could only stare up at Vidal, who was standing as still as a statue, looking back at her.

'What did you say?' Vidal's voice was harsh.

He was angry with her, and no wonder, Fliss thought. She had embarrassed him and made a fool of herself.

'What did you say?' Vidal repeated.

In a panic, Fliss stepped back from him, shaking her head as she fibbed, 'I didn't say anything.'

Vidal had stepped back from her, but now he was closing the distance between them.

'Yes, you did.' His topaz gaze held hers. 'You said you loved me.'

Fliss had had enough. Her self-control was at breaking point and her heart felt as though it was already broken. What did her pride matter now, when she had already lost so much?

Lifting her head, she told Vidal, 'All right, yes, I *do* love you. The children I want to have—the children I want to know their Spanish heritage—are your children,

Vidal. Don't blame me if you don't want to know any of
this, if you don't want to hear. You made me tell you.'

'Not want to know? Not want to hear the words
I've been aching to hear since you were sixteen years
old?'

'What?' Now it was Fliss's turn to question him. 'You
don't mean that,' she protested.

'I mean it more than I've ever meant anything in
my life.' Vidal assured her. 'The truth is that I fell in
love with you when you were sixteen, but of course you
were too young for a man's love, and it would have been
dishonourable and very wrong of me to have spoken to
you of my feelings then. I told myself that I'd wait until
you were older, until you were mature enough for me
to court you properly as a woman.'

'Oh, Vidal,' Fliss breathed.

'It's true,' he assured her. 'That was why I misjudged
you. Because I was jealous. Jealous that someone else
had taken you from me. I did you a terrible wrong, Fliss.
I don't deserve your love.'

Fliss could see that he meant what he was saying,
and her heart ached for him.

'Yes, you do,' she insisted. 'And if I'd known then
how you really felt about me, I suspect I'd have done
everything I could to persuade you to change your
mind.'

'That is what I was afraid of,' Vidal admitted tenderly. 'It would have been the wrong thing to do for both
of us but especially for you.'

When Fliss started to protest, Vidal stopped her.

'You were too young. It would have been wrong. But

hearing that boy boasting in the way that he did sent me a little mad, I think. I told myself afterwards that the girl I loved didn't exist, that I'd created her inside my own imagination. I told myself I should be glad that you were not the innocent I had thought, because had you been my self-control might have betrayed me and I might, out of my love for you, have broken the trust your mother had in me.'

'So you stopped loving me?'

'I tried to tell myself I had, but the reality is that I ached and longed for you. Only my pride kept me away from you—especially when your mother died. You haunted my dreams and made it impossible for me to put any other woman in your place. I resigned myself to living without love, and then you walked back into my life. I knew that everything my pride had told me about the impossibility of loving you was a lie. I loved you no matter what. I realised that that first time we were in bed together—before I realised that I had misjudged you. I wanted to tell you how much I loved you, but I felt it would be wrong to burden you with my love. I wanted you to have the freedom to make your own choices, free of any burdens from the past.'

'You are my choice, Vidal. You are my love, and you always will be.'

'Are you really sure that I am what you want?' Vidal asked her with unfamiliar humility.

'Yes,' Fliss told him emotionally.

'I am your first lover.'

'The only lover I want,' she said fiercely. 'The only

lover I have ever wanted or will ever want.' Fliss knew
as she spoke that it was true.

'I hope you mean that,' Vidal told her thickly, 'because I am not generous enough to give you a second
opportunity to walk away from me.' When he saw the
way Fliss was looking at him Vidal warned her in a
voice rough with passion, 'Don't look at me like that.'

'Why not?' Fliss asked him mock innocently.

'Because if you do then I shall have to do this,' Vidal
told her, kissing her so passionately that Fliss felt as
though the desire he was arousing within her was melting her body right down to her bones.

'We've both fought so hard not to love one another,
but it was obviously a fight we were destined to lose,'
she told him breathlessly, once he had stopped kissing
her.

'And one in which losing I know I have won something far more precious—you, my darling,' Vidal responded, before kissing her again.

What a joy it was to know that she could respond to
him with all her heart and all her love, knowing that he
had given her his, Fliss thought as he kept on kissing
her while he carried her over to the bed.

'I love you,' Vidal told her as he placed her on it. 'I
love you and I will always love you. This is where our
love begins, Felicity. Our love and our future together—
if that is what you want?'

Wrapping her arms around him, Fliss whispered
against his lips, 'You are what I want, Vidal, and you
always will be.'

'I want you to marry me,' Vidal told her. 'Soon—as soon as it can be arranged.'

'Yes,' Fliss agreed. 'As soon as it can be arranged. But right now I want you to make love to me, Vidal.'

'Like this, do you mean?' he asked softly, as he started to undress her.

'Yes,' Fliss sighed happily. 'Exactly like that '

EPILOGUE

'HAPPY?'

Fliss raised her hand to touch Vidal's face, the wedding ring he had placed on her finger less than twenty-four hours earlier gleaming in the sunlight. Her sparkling eyes and the emotion that lit up her face gave Vidal his answer without the need for any words, but she still spoke, telling him emotionally, 'More happy that I ever believed possible.'

'Happier even than you dreamed of being at sixteen?' he teased her gently.

Fliss laughed. 'At sixteen I didn't dare dream of being married to you, Vidal.'

In several hours' time they would be boarding the private jet that would be taking them to the private tropical island where they were going to honeymoon, but right now the two of them were making a special pilgrimage, retracing together the steps taken all those years ago by her mother and her father, accompanied by young Vidal.

From the Alhambra they had strolled to the Generalife, the famous summer palace with its much-photographed water garden and its long canal and fountains bordered by beautifully tended flowerbeds. Sunlight danced on the jets of water thrown up by the fountains, and when Vidal stopped walking alongside one of them Fliss looked at him expectantly with love in her eyes.

'It was here that I saw your father take your mother's hand,' he told her softly, reaching out to take hold of Fliss's hand.

As she looked into the heart of the fountain it was almost possible for Fliss to imagine that she could see the shadowy images of those two young people.

'Our love will be deeper and stronger for knowing their story,' Vidal promised. 'Our happiness together is what they would both have wanted for us.'

'Yes,' Fliss agreed.

It might normally be forbidden, but Vidal had magically made it possible for officialdom to turn a blind eye so that there was no one to object when, very gently and carefully, Fliss opened her closed palm to allow the petals from some of the white roses from her wedding bouquet to fall into the water, where they floated gently.

'A release of the past and a welcome to the future,' Fliss told Vidal.

'*Our* future,' he responded, taking her into his arms. 'The only future I could ever want.'

BEHIND PALACE DOORS

JULES BENNETT

I'm dedicating this fairytale to my stiletto-wearing, tiara-worthy glitter sister, Kelly Willison, and her beautiful princess in training, Anna. You two are a bright, shimmering light in my life. The glow may be all the glitter, but I think it comes from your heart of gold. Love you both.

And also to my own little princesses, Grace and Madelyn. I love watching you grow into beautiful little girls. I can't wait to see you fall in love and live your own fairytale dream.

Award-winning author **Jules Bennett** is no stranger to romance—she met her husband when she was only fourteen. After dating through high school, the two married. He encouraged her to chase her dream of becoming an author. Jules has now published nearly thirty novels. She and her husband are living their own happily-ever-after while raising two girls. Jules loves to hear from readers through her website, www.julesbennett.com, her Facebook fan page or on Twitter.

Prologue

"Ever tried skinny-dipping?"

Victoria Dane gasped as Stefan Alexander, Prince of Galini Isle, stripped off his shirt.

"Umm…" She swallowed, watching as an impressive set of abs stared back at her. "No. No, I haven't."

He toed off his shoes.

"You're not going to…"

His soft chuckle caused goose bumps to spread over her body. Even at fifteen, she was totally aware of this handsome prince, who was technically a man, as he was three years older.

They'd quickly become friends since her mother was filming on his estate, and she assumed her girlish crush was normal. But was he really going to strip naked?

"I'm not doing it alone," he told her, hands on his hips.

Her eyes darted to his chest. "You got a tattoo?"

With a wicked grin, he nodded. "My first of many, I hope."

"What is it?" she asked, stepping closer to inspect.

Would it be rude to touch? Probably, so she slid her hands inside the pockets of her swim cover-up instead. Still, she imagined her fingertips sliding along the new ink.

"It's my family's crest," he told her. "I thought it appropriate to have that as my first. Besides, my father might not mind as much since it's symbolic."

The afternoon sun beat down on her, but Victoria knew the heat consuming her had nothing to do with the weather. She'd been on location with her mother for almost two months now, and she and Stefan had clicked from the moment they met. Of course, he probably saw her as a little sister and had no idea she was halfway in love with him.

The boys back home were nothing like this.

"Has your father seen it yet?" she asked, using the tattoo excuse to continue to stare at his chest.

"Nah. I've been careful to keep my shirt on around my dad since I got it two weeks ago. He'll throw a fit, but it's done, so what can he say now?"

Victoria moved toward the pool, dropped to the side and let her feet dangle in the cool water. "You're so relaxed about breaking rules and defying people. Aren't you worried you'll get in serious trouble one day?"

"Trouble?" He laughed as he sat down and joined her. "I'm not afraid of trouble. I'd rather be myself and live my life the way I want. I don't want to be ruled by what is considered to be the right thing. Who's to say what's right or wrong for me?"

She admired his take-charge attitude about life. He reminded her of her brother, Bronson.

"Don't you consider that lying?" she asked, still studying him. "I mean, you knew you were going to do it, so why not just tell your dad?"

Stefan glanced over to her, those bright blue eyes holding hers. "Lying by omission doesn't count in my book."

"Well, it does in mine. Maybe that's a cultural difference."

He scooped a hand in the water and playfully tossed it up onto her bare thighs. Shivers coursed through her.

"I think it's the difference between towing the line and living in the moment," he joked. "So how about that skinny-dipping?"

"I tow the line, remember? No skinny-dipping for me." Smiling at him, she placed a hand on his back and shoved him into the pool.

One

Every little girl envisioned a fairy-tale wedding. The long white train, the horse-drawn carriage, like the magical coach from Cinderella of course, and the proverbial tall, dark and handsome prince, chest adorned with medals and a bright blue sash that matched his eye color perfectly.

And while Victoria Dane wasn't living the fairy tale herself, she did have the glorious job of designing the royal wedding dress that would be seen by millions and worn by the next queen of Galini Isle.

Okay, so being the designer wasn't even a close second to becoming a queen.

"Victoria."

The familiar, soothing tone of her old friend's voice had Victoria turning from the breathtaking emerald ocean view. With a slight bow as was custom in this country, Victoria greeted the prince.

With his tight-fitting black T-shirt tucked into designer

jeans, most people would have a hard time believing Prince Stefan Alexander—owner of the most impressive set of blue eyes and some new ink peeking beneath the sleeve of his shirt on one impressive bicep—was the next in line to reign over this beautiful land.

Those muscles seemed to grow between each of their visits. Muscles he acquired from his passion of rock climbing. Yeah, that would make for a beautiful picture. A golden Greek god, shirtless and dangling high above the ground by his sheer strength....

There was one lucky bride waiting for her prince. Victoria would be lying if she didn't admit, even if only to herself, that at one time she'd envisioned herself as the one who would finally tame the great Prince Alexander, but his friendship had been invaluable and something she'd feared risking.

Strong arms that she had missed for the past few years pulled her into a warm, inviting embrace. Yes, this was the connection, the bond that phone calls and emails couldn't deliver.

"Prince Alexander," she said, returning his embrace.

"Don't 'Prince Alexander' me." His rich laughter enveloped her, making her feel even more excited to see him after so long. "And for God's sake, don't bow. Just because we haven't seen each other in a while doesn't mean I've become some royal snob."

"It's so great to see you, Stefan." She eased back and looked up into those striking blue eyes. "When you called to tell me you were getting married, I was shocked. She must be someone very special."

"The most important woman in my life," he said, lifting one of her hands to his lips.

Prince Charming had nothing on Stefan, and a slight surge of jealousy speared through Victoria at the fact another woman would be entering his life...and not just passing through like all the others.

He gestured toward the settee and matching chairs with bright orange plush cushions. "Let's have a seat and discuss my beautiful bride, shall we?"

Stefan dismissed his assistants with a silent nod. A man of his position and power didn't need to use words, but to Victoria he was still that rotten teen who'd tried to get her to go skinny-dipping in the royal pool...while a dinner party had been taking place in the grand ballroom.

"I've brought sketches of several dresses for you and your fiancée to review," she told him, laying her thin portfolio of designs on the tile tabletop and flipping it open. "I can also combine styles or come up with something completely different if nothing here catches her eye. They are all classic designs but different in their own way. Any would be flattering for the next queen."

"I've no doubt you'll make the perfect dress." He laid a hand over hers, a wide grin spreading across his devilishly handsome face. "It's so great to have you here, Victoria. I've missed you."

She returned his smile, unable to hide her excitement about not only seeing him again, but also the fact he'd finally found true love...something she'd started to have doubts about. And yes, she'd once wished his true love had been her, but their friendship was more important. As his best friend, she was thrilled that he was so happy and in love. She needed that reminder that not all men broke their promises of engagement.

"It's my pleasure to design for you, and it gives us both a reason to set aside our busy lives and get some face time," she told him, sliding her hair over her shoulder. "Phone calls just aren't the same."

"No, they're not," he agreed.

That sexy, sultry smile remained. Heavens, but the man was literally a tall, dark and handsome prince, and that cotton shirt stretched so perfectly over his broad shoulders and chiseled biceps. She wondered what the new tattoo was of, but if she knew Stefan, he'd find a reason to shed his shirt in no time.

Yeah, he'd changed over the years, and definitely in all the right places. Rock climbing does a body good.

"These are remarkable," he told her as he fingered through the drawings. "Did you do these yourself or do you have a team?"

A burst of pride ran through her. She may be one of the most sought-out designers, but each client earned her undivided attention and she loved hearing praise for her hard work…especially coming from such a good friend.

"I have a small team, but these are all my own. I was selfish when it came to your bride." She moved one thick sheet to the side, eager to display the rest of her designs. "I'm partial to this one. The clean lines, the cut of the neckline and the molding of the bodice. Classy, yet sexy."

Very similar to the one she'd designed for own wedding. Of course that had been six months, a slew of bad press and one shattered heartache ago when her up-and-coming actor/fiancé decided to publicly destroy Victoria. But working with Stefan and his fiancée would help her to remember that happily ever afters do exist.

When she'd met him as a teen on the set of one of her mother's films, she'd developed an instant crush. He'd been a very mature eighteen years old, compared to her fifteen, with golden skin and a smile she'd come to appreciate that held just a touch of cockiness.

She'd been smitten to say the least, but they'd soon developed a friendship that had lasted through the years. Fantasies had come and gone…and come again where she'd envisioned him proposing to her and professing his hidden, undying passion. But those were little girl dreams. Besides, Stefan always had a companion or two at all times.

"You would look beautiful in that gown."

Victoria shook off her crazy thoughts and jerked her attention to Stefan.

"Sorry. I realize your own engagement is still fairly recent, but—"

She straightened her shoulders and stepped back. "No, it's okay. But let's not talk about that. I'd much rather focus on your happiness."

He reached out, cupped her shoulders and gave a reassuring squeeze. "I'm still your friend. I know you didn't open up that much over the phone because of the timing being so close to the passing of my father, but you're here now and I'm offering you my shoulder if you need it."

Warmth spread through her. Other than her brothers, this was the one man she'd always been able to depend on. Even as they'd gotten older, their lives busier, she knew Stefan was always there for her.

"I may take you up on that," she told him with a smile. "But for now let's discuss you."

Because she needed to focus on their friendship and her work instead of her humiliation, her eyes drifted back over the designs. "A dress should make a woman feel beautiful and alluring. I wanted to capture that beauty with a hint of fairy tale thrown into the mix. When I don't know the client personally, it makes designing the dresses a bit harder, so that is why I chose to bring very different designs for her to look at. Do you know when your fiancée will arrive?"

Stefan leaned a hip onto the table and smiled. "Actually, she's already here. I have a proposition for you, Victoria."

Intrigued, Victoria rested one hand on the table and smiled. "And what is that, Your Highness?"

He chuckled. "Now you're mocking me."

"Not at all," she retorted with a grin, loving how they fell back into their easy banter as if no time had passed. "You just sounded so serious. What's your proposition?"

He took her hands in his, looking her in the eyes. "It has to do with my fiancée...sort of."

Oh, no. She recognized that look. It was the same naughty, conniving look he had when he'd wanted her to be his partner in crime in their early twenties...like the time when he'd asked her to pose as his girlfriend for a charity ball because he had a somewhat aggressive lady who wouldn't take no for an answer.

God. The sick feeling in her stomach deepened. The man was up to something no good.

"Stefan." She slid her hands from his warm, strong hold and rubbed them together. "Tell me there's a real fiancée and you're actually getting married."

"I am getting married and there is a fiancée." He threw her a wide, beautiful smile. "You."

Stefan waited for her response to his abrupt proposal. Damn, he'd meant to have a bit more finesse, but time was running out and he couldn't afford to tackle this wedding in the traditional sense. Nothing about this situation was traditional.

She placed her hands on either side of her temples as if to rub the stress headache away...he'd had a few of those moments himself recently. He'd never pictured himself as a one-woman man. And the thought always sent a shudder straight through him.

"I'm sorry to pull you into this," he told her. "I couldn't trust anyone else right now."

He prayed he chose the right words to make her understand. She was, after all, still recovering from an ugly public breakup, and she had always been such a good friend, no matter the distance between them. They'd shared countless phone calls in the middle of the night, during many of which she'd told him her dreams and he'd listened, hoping one day all those dreams would come true. And perhaps he could help that along.

"Why do you need me all of a sudden?"

"Galini Isle will go back to Greece if I don't marry and gain the title of king. My brother isn't an option because his wife is a divorcée and the damn laws are archaic. I couldn't live with myself if I didn't do everything in my power to keep this country in my family. I won't let my people down." He hated being forced into anything. "I want my title, but I do not want a wife. Unfortunately, I've looked for a loophole and there isn't one."

Victoria sank to the patio chair. "Again, why me?"

"I want a wife in name only. And I can't let my country revert to Greek rule. It's been in my family for generations. I refuse to be a failure to my family's name."

"This is crazy," she muttered, shaking her head.

Stefan stepped closer. "You've recently had scandal in your life. Why not show this fiancé who jilted you and the media who exploited your pain that you are stronger, you can rise above this and come out on top? What better way than to marry a prince?"

"You're serious?" she asked, looking back up at him. "How could we pull this off? I mean, we haven't been seen together in public for a couple years."

Stefan came over and took a seat directly beside her in the matching wrought-iron chair with plush cushions. "My people don't know who my bride is. I've made sure they only know there will be a wedding. I've been very secretive about this, which only adds to the mystery of the romance."

Romance. Yeah, that was the dead last thing on his mind right now. Couldn't he just have the crown? He was the prince, for crying out loud. Didn't that give him some clout? Why did he need a marriage to claim it?

"Once they see you, they'll know why I kept the engagement so quiet," he went on, knowing he was rambling, but he had to make her see this was the only way.

Damn, he hated vulnerability and being backed into a corner. Not only that, he hated putting Victoria in an awkward position.

Victoria laughed. "And here all this time I thought you were letting your romantic, protective side show."

"You are one of Hollywood's most famous single ladies—a bachelorette, I believe your country calls it—and I will simply explain I was protecting you from even more scandal and we wanted to express our love on our wedding day and not exploit it beforehand. Besides, there are all those articles and pictures from when we were in our teens and twenties. The media practically had us engaged at your twenty-first birthday party when I bought you a diamond necklace. The history is there, and the media will eat it up."

"Oh, Stefan." She sighed. "This is such a big decision. You can't expect me to give you an answer right now."

Leaning back against the chair, Stefan nodded. "I'm asking for only six months, Tori. After my coronation I'll have my title as king and the country will be secured with my family again."

"Then what?" she asked, her eyes searching his.

He shrugged, not really worried about anything beyond getting married and gaining his title. "After that it's up to you. You can stay married to me or you can end the relationship. The control is yours. Who knows, you may like being queen."

True, he may be a playboy, but he could think of multiple circumstances that would be worse than being married to the stunning Victoria Dane.

She stared out across the estate toward the ocean. Victoria's beauty was remarkable and surprisingly natural. She came from the land of perfection brought on by plastic surgeons, yet she looked more stunning than the fake, siliconed women he knew. And he was damn lucky she was in his life.

"This is the craziest thing I've ever heard." With a slight laugh she looked back to him. "You're taking something as serious as a royal wedding, a wedding that will create the new leaders for your country, and turning it into a…a lie. My God, Stefan, this is really putting the pressure on our friendship. Do you realize how risky this is? I can't lose you."

He sat forward, dead serious. "You could never lose me as a friend. If I thought that was the case I never would've asked you. Just think of this as a long, overdue reunion. I need someone I can trust not to back out at the last minute or use me for money in the end."

"Why did you wait so long to ask me?"

"Honestly I thought I could find a way around this." God knows he'd exhausted every avenue looking for one. "When I realized I couldn't, I knew I had only one option. You are the one person in my life I'd ever trust with something so personal, so serious."

She laughed. "I'd do anything for you, Stefan, you know that, but this is asking a lot. What about the people of your country? Won't they feel let down if we end the marriage? And how will this work out after your coronation? Will the country still remain yours?"

"No, my people won't feel let down," he assured her. "I will still be their leader. I will still keep control over my country. I just need the title to do so, which is where you fit in."

"You've really thought this through, haven't you?" She crossed her legs and shifted her body toward his. "You can't expect me to put my life on hold for six months. I'm a busy woman, Stefan."

He'd always admired her take-charge attitude and the way she matched him in this volley of wills. Not to mention the fact the woman was classy and beyond sexy.

Just as when he'd been in his late teens, Victoria Dane made his gut clench and still made him want her as more than a friend. But years ago he'd attempted to pursue her into something sexual. She hadn't taken him seriously, so to keep his ego intact, he played it off like he had indeed been joking. And the second time he'd been ready to take charge, she'd been in a relationship. But now she was free.

"I know you're busy, and I'm not trying to take your life away, but I do have something to offer you." He edged forward, taking her hand in his. "You'll get to show the world that you are stronger than the poor, humiliated woman they are making you out to be. The woman the media has portrayed as being overshadowed by her brothers and jilted by her fiancé. If you do this, not only will you design your wedding gown for this day, this could help you launch that bridal line you've been wanting. Make a play off the fairy tale of being a queen, if you like."

Her eyes darted back to the ocean. The sun was just starting to set, and Stefan knew as far as proposals went, this was probably the least romantic. But her apparent inner war with herself only told him that she was indeed considering his offer.

"I can practically see your mind working." He hoped she was leaning toward a yes decision. "This is a win-win for both of us, Victoria."

"Your way of thinking is not very Greek," she told him. "Aren't you all known for love?"

He laughed, squeezing her hand. "I think you know how passionate I can be about something I want."

She looked down at their joined hands. His dark, tanned skin next to her pinker complexion made for quite the contrast. But when she looked up into his eyes, he knew she wasn't going to deny him.

"You've always been determined," she whispered. "That's something I can understand. With my recent scandal and public embarrassment, I was adamant to get back on track, to take control of my life."

He waited, not wanting to interrupt as she guided her own words down the path toward everything he wanted.

"And what about the sleeping arrangements?" she asked, her wide eyes seeking his for answers.

Stefan laughed. "You know, you live in Hollywood where sin flows as freely as wine in my country, and you're blushing at the subject of us sharing a bed. I'm wounded."

Obviously this was something she hadn't expected, but he wasn't going to push. Yes, he'd desired her for years, but he wanted her to come to him. To realize that maybe something spectacular could happen between them behind the bedroom door.

He stroked his thumb over the soft skin on the back of her hand. "We'll have to share a room to keep up the pretense with the staff."

Her heart beat hard against her chest, and Victoria couldn't help the image that immediately popped into her head of the two of them entangled in satin sheets in a king-size bed. She knew that his dark skin was part of his heritage and not from lounging by the pool—which meant he would be lean and golden brown all over. There were rumors of hidden tattoos—some she'd seen, some she hadn't. The man simply exuded mysteriousness and sex. He'd been her best friend as a teen, and even though circumstances had gotten in the way of them seeing each other the past couple years, their phone calls and emails had kept that line of friendship open.

"I just don't know," she muttered aloud. "I'm scared of what this will do to us."

"We'll be stronger than ever," he assured her with a devastatingly handsome smile. "We've spent too many of the past years apart. Let's just focus on the fact we'll be together like old times. I need you, Tori."

Was she really about to risk more scandal and the bond she shared with Stefan? Yes, because he meant that much to her, and if the tables were turned, she knew he'd drop everything to help her. Besides, she was a member of the prestigious Hollywood Danes; it wasn't as if scandal hadn't been part of her life before.

For years she'd been in the spotlight as the sister of Hollywood's hottest producer and daughter of the Grand Dane—her mother's Hollywood-dubbed nickname. The threat of scandal followed her family everywhere.

Stefan's family had also had their share of scandal surrounding his mother's death years ago. His loyalty to his family—and his country—to maintain control of the crown was everything to him. And she completely under-stood family loyalty.

As she thought about it, Victoria was liking Stefan's proposal more and more. How could she not consider showing the world she could still come out on top—and with a sexy Greek prince, at that?

When Alex had put a ring on her finger, she'd been so determined to have a lasting, loving marriage like her mother, her brothers. Victoria didn't want pity, didn't want people looking at her as though she may fall apart if they brought up the broken engagement. Unfortunately, that's exactly what her family and friends were doing. But Stefan faced the topic head-on and didn't back down. He wasn't treating her like some wilted flower, but as a woman who was tougher than what most people thought.

Victoria was determined to come out stronger on the other side of this scandal. She was going to prove to everyone, including herself, that her iconic mother and hotshot brothers were not the only ones who could rise above anything life threw at them.

She looked down at her hand joined with Stefan's, knowing they could help each other…just like always. The arrangement was just on a larger scale than anything they'd ever confronted.

This proposition Stefan blindsided her with may truly be the answer to get everyone to stop throwing sympathy her way, to see that she was fine and had made her life her own. Not to mention she could use the publicity to help establish her bridal line, as he'd suggested. What better way to launch it than to design the royal wedding dress *and* wear it?

"You're thinking too hard," Stefan joked. "Go with your gut, Victoria. You know this is going to work. I won't let anything happen to you."

She looked into his vibrant eyes, confident he would do anything to keep her from facing heartache again. And that made his proposal even more appealing.

There was no denying the man was beyond sexy. He'd been dubbed the Greek Playboy Prince by all the media outlets for years. But Alex had been just as handsome, just as cocky…until he'd confessed he'd been using her for her family name to help further his acting career. Of course the truth had only come out after he'd impregnated another woman and had to call off the engagement.

Oh, how could she even sit here and compare the two men? Alex wasn't even worth her thoughts, and Stefan was everything to her.

Another look into his smiling eyes and Victoria nearly laughed. Stefan had been up-front and honest with her because that's the type of friend he was. What he was proposing was nothing like what Alex had done to her. Other than this marriage, what could she offer Stefan that he couldn't get himself? He certainly wasn't a rising actor like Alex had been. How could she deny him when she knew he was in a vulnerable state and he trusted only her?

"I'd expect you to be faithful, even if this is pretend," she told him.

"I assure you, you will have my undivided attention."

Swallowing the doubts and throwing caution to the wind, Victoria smiled. "Stefan, I'd be honored to marry you."

Two

Stefan had invited Victoria to stay in the palace so they could get some alone time to reconnect in ways that phone calls and emails couldn't provide. They had to attempt to make this seem like the real thing because the media would definitely pick up on any uncomfortableness between them if every touch, every lingering gaze didn't look authentic— like they were secret lovers.

Pretending to be infatuated by Victoria's beauty would be no hardship. Her flawless elegance had only flourished since the last time he'd seen her, and he was damned grateful she'd agreed to his insane proposal.

Parading her around the grounds with the royal photographer, snapping some pictures as they rode on horseback, cuddled beneath the trellis of flowing flowers and walked along the private, pristine beach, would help fuel this fire of his romance with the next queen of Galini Isle. Though he'd asked the photographer to keep Victoria's face out of the snapshots to add an aura of mystery. He'd always been proud and ready to show off the women on his arm. Victoria was the first one he'd protected from the camera. So once the photos started going out, they would hopefully create more talk of his upcoming wedding in four weeks.

Their brief time alone had already caused so many memories to resurface. She was still a tender heart where her family was concerned but lethal when it came to business. The beauty Victoria brought back into his life by being there in person was immeasurable. Holding her, laughing with her, staying up late last night talking again was amazing, and he vowed to never let so much time go between their visits again...if she ended up leaving at the end of the six months.

All thoughts of reconnecting were swept aside as Victoria entered the intimate dining area he'd had his assistants set up on the balcony off his master suite's second story. Stefan's breath caught, and he knew that spark of desire he'd always had for her would only spread and burn hotter now that they were spending so much intimate time alone.

Yes, he needed her to keep his country, but he wasn't a fool. No way would he let this prime opportunity pass him by to show her just how much he believed becoming friends with benefits was a great idea. He may not be ready for a "real" marriage, but he was past ready to have Victoria see him in a different way.

But he had to keep his thoughts and emotions to himself for now. The last thing she needed was him pushing anything more on her. Besides the fact she was saving him, she was coming out of a humiliating engagement to some prick who didn't know what a treasure he'd had.

When Stefan had initially learned of the breakup, he'd

immediately called, but in typical Victoria fashion, she'd assured him she was fine…hurt and angry, but she'd be okay.

And looking at her now, she was definitely more than okay.

Her long, strapless ice-blue chiffon gown was simple, yet so elegant and so beautifully molded to her slender curves, Stefan's palms itched to touch her. Years of friendship prevented him. Added to that, they'd never ventured into anything intimate. Either she'd been in a relationship or he'd been…preoccupied himself.

"You look beautiful, Victoria." He extended his hand toward her, pleased when she took it. "You'll be the perfect queen."

Her smile was genuine, but her eyes instantly darted to the waiting servant in the corner wearing a black tux. "I was hoping to have some time alone with you."

While he loved those words coming from her mouth, he knew she just wanted to talk. He squeezed her hand and gave a nod to his employee. Once they were alone, Victoria laughed.

"That's the second time you've nodded and someone has done what you wanted. You sure this prince-soon-to-be-king title isn't going to your head?"

Stefan shrugged, leading her to the table for two on the balcony. "They know what my needs are, so words are usually unnecessary. Besides, I'd much rather spend my evening with my stunning friend than boring staff. I have too many responsibilities with my title. I want to have the down time with you."

"Wow, I'm one rank above boring and responsibilities. You're such a charmer, it's no wonder you couldn't get another woman to marry you." She patted his arm and sighed. "I just hope my family understands my actions."

"We can't tell anyone that this is a paper marriage, Victoria." He turned her to face him, making her look him in the eye to know just how serious this situation was. "I cannot risk my title on the slip of a tongue."

He knew the strong bond she had with her family, knew she'd want to tell them, but he had to at least caution her as to the importance of this arrangement. Other than his personal assistant, Hector, and his brother, no one knew of this secret.

"I have to tell my mother," she insisted. "Trust me. She will know something is up and she will badger us both until she uncovers it if we don't confess now. Besides, she's always loved you."

"As a friend, yes," he agreed, then laughed. "I'm not sure she'll love me to play the son-in-law role."

She looked into his eyes, and a tilt of her perfect lips proved she knew he had a point. "Well, she does consider you a playboy, and she's not too keen on all your tats. But she does love you, Stefan. And she knows how much you mean to me."

He raised a brow. "What about your brothers?"

"I can't lie to them, either," she told him. "But you should know, of all families, mine understands the potential for scandal when secrets slip."

Because he could see the battle she waged with herself and because he knew she wouldn't back down on this, Stefan nodded. "If you promise this goes no further than your immediate family, I will agree to your terms. I trust them as much as I trust you."

"All right, Stefan," she told him, seeing his shoulders relax on his exhale. "My mother will be the silent observer until she sees if I'm just making a rash decision. But, I should warn you, my brothers will have some serious doubts. They will be all over you, especially after what happened with Alex."

Stefan intended to speak with both of her brothers privately. He had a business proposition for them that they may not want to pass up regarding a documentary to clear his parents' names in his mother's untimely death. Some thought his mother had committed suicide, while others were convinced his father had hired someone to have her killed. Both were pure nonsense, and he wanted to go into his reign with no blemishes on his family's name. But he would also reassure Tori's brothers that he would keep her from any more heartbreak or scandal.

"If I had a sister, I'd be very protective," he said with a smile. "I assure you, I can handle them. But we still have to make sure they know our relationship will have to look real, which means they'll have to rein in their behavior when we're out in the spotlight."

Stefan stepped closer, calling himself all kinds of a fool for torturing himself with her familiar floral aroma, her tall, lithe body close to his. But he couldn't help himself. He needed that intimacy, that closeness only Tori could provide. He told himself it was to get used to making this "relationship" seem real. In truth, he wanted to touch her, kiss her…undress her. Possibilities and images swirled around in his mind. Years he'd waited to have a chance with her, and here he was nervous as a virgin on a wedding night.

Na pari i eychi. Dammit. The last time he'd seen her in person two years ago he'd flown to L.A. to attend a benefit art show to raise money for a children's charity. His father was supposed to have gone but had fallen ill at the last minute, so Stefan had stepped in, all too eager to get to L.A. and try his hand at seducing Victoria.

But when he'd arrived at her home, she'd introduced him to some up-and-coming actor whom she'd just begun dating. Stefan had been totally blindsided with the sudden serious nature of the relationship. They talked on the phone, emailed or texted several times a week and no mention had been made of this other man.

Because she'd been beaming with happiness, Stefan had kept his lustful feelings to himself and tried to maintain a physical distance. But now she was here because that jerk, Alex, had humiliated her and crushed her heart.

Stefan had every intention of helping her heal. And now he knew there was no way he could hold his desire back. Eventually, he'd have to confess that he wanted her intimately, paper marriage be damned.

As if just realizing how close they'd gotten, Victoria looked up at him and licked her lips, making them moist and inviting. "I still think we have our work cut out for us. We've never been anything more than best friends."

It was just the opening he'd been waiting for. "Then we better start now making this believable."

In one move, Stefan had his arms snaked around her waist and his lips crushing hers, swallowing her gasp. He hadn't meant to push, really he hadn't, and the second their tastes and bodies collided, he knew this was a bad idea. Now he'd only want her more. But if his life depended on it, he couldn't pull away.

After the briefest of hesitations, she exploded in his arms, kissing him back with a passion he hadn't expected, but he would definitely embrace. For years he'd wondered, dreamed, and here she was kissing him as if she thought of him as a man and not just a friend. Obviously he wasn't the only one who'd imagined this moment.

And that aroused him even more and left him with the knowledge this was something that would have to be discussed sooner rather than later.

Needing more and taking it, he parted her lips with his tongue. Her fingers gripped his biceps as she leaned against him a bit more. And just like he'd imagined for years, she fit against him perfectly.

But before he could take more and allow his hands to roam freely over that killer body, Victoria stepped back, her hand immediately going to cover her lips.

"We can't…that was…"

Stefan closed the gap she'd just created, but not to pick up where she broke off. He intended to reassure her that what just happened was not a mistake. Hell no, it wasn't. An epiphany, yes, but no mistake.

"Interesting how flustered you are after one kiss," he told her with a smile, still tasting her on his lips. "We've kissed before, Tori."

With fingertips still on her lips, Victoria placed her other hand on his chest. "Our kisses were never anything like that."

Because he was a gentleman, at least where the ladies were concerned, he didn't mention the groaning she'd done when his lips had touched hers.

He wanted her to think about what happened… God knows he'd never forget. Her taste and the feel of her body were all burned into his long-term memory. But he needed to move slowly and stay on track.

"My top chef has prepared moussaka for us." He ushered her toward a chair and assisted her into it. "I remember how much you enjoyed Greek cuisine the last time you visited."

Victoria didn't even look at the meal; she merely gazed at him from across the intimate table complete with a small exotic bouquet of flowers and two tall white tapered candles.

"Are you going to pretend that kiss didn't make an impression on you?" she asked, arching a perfectly shaped brow.

Her bold statement had him smiling. Why lie? She knew him too well.

"I wasn't unaffected, Victoria." He held her gaze, needing her to see how serious he was. "Any man would be a fool not to be physically attracted to you. And I'd be a liar to say I hadn't thought of kissing you before."

"I'm not quite sure how to respond to that." She glanced down, then cleared her throat and met his gaze again. "I have to say, it's no wonder you have the reputation you do when you kiss like that. If you pull that stunt in public, the media will never think to question the engagement."

"They'll see nothing but *eros* when they look at us."

"What does that mean?" She laughed. "You always show off by throwing out Greek terms I don't know."

"Passionate, erotic love." Yet again, he held her gaze. "Cameras don't lie, and I know that's what they'll see. I will have no problem making the relationship look real."

Victoria shook her head. "I'm afraid your cockiness and ego may overshadow me in any picture, but I've found that ego charming over the years—must be from growing up with a very alpha brother. Your pride stems from confidence, which is always a redeeming quality in a man. But I know there's a soft side beneath that tough-guy persona. Besides, I've been around onlookers and cameras since I was born, so I actually don't notice them much anymore."

But they notice you.

"I'm glad to hear the media doesn't bother you because we'll have to pose for several formal pictures once we're married," he told her, taking the silver dome lids off the dishes. "Though something you may not be as used to is servants. As queen, you'll have your own assistants who will do anything and everything—from dressing you, to preparing your meals and escorting you anywhere you need to go."

Victoria's perfectly manicured hand stilled on her wine-glass. "I don't need someone to dress me—that's literally my job. And an escort? Is that really necessary? I can't stay here after the marriage until the title is official, Stefan. I have a life, a job to get to. If we need to put up a united front, you'll just have to come to the States and be with me there."

"For how long?" he asked. "With no one reigning as king, I am technically the…stand-in, if you will."

Victoria jerked in surprise. "You're acting as king now? I didn't know this."

He nodded. "Nothing is official until the coronation, but it's law that when the king dies, the oldest son will step in immediately. If something were to happen to me or if I did not marry, the country would go back to Greece. So this is all temporary until I fulfill my duties."

"So do you have to stay here the entire time?" she asked. "Are we going to spend our marriage apart?"

Stefan laughed. "Not at all. We will actually need to make several appearances together both here and in L.A. once we're married to ensure the public believes this is the real deal. What's your schedule like? We will come up with something."

His cell rang, interrupting their conversation. He pulled it from his pocket, glanced at the screen and hit ignore before sliding it back in his pocket…but not before Victoria saw the name of the caller. Hannah.

"Am I going to have to compete for your attention from your harem?" she asked with a laugh, even though inside she was dead serious.

"You will never have to compete for my attention, Tori." His eyes locked on to hers. "You're the only woman in my life right now. Let's get back to your schedule."

She wanted to believe him, so she did. He'd never lied

to her before, and she knew if Stefan told her not to worry, then she shouldn't. But no matter what his actions were, he couldn't force the other women to stop calling him. Surely once they were married the calls would stop. She hoped.

God, she was so skeptical. Damn Alex for making her that way. To doubt Stefan and his loyalty was laughable. He was going to great lengths to keep his country in his family. That act itself spoke volumes of what the word loyalty meant. So, no, she didn't think Stefan would do anything to betray her trust. He was the polar opposite of Alex.

"My workload is crazy." She ran her upcoming schedule through her head. "I'm swamped, but to be fair I'd say we should at least split the time between my home and yours."

"That shouldn't be a problem. I love your family and I love L.A." He moved around the table, unrolled her napkin and placed it in her lap, waiting until her eyes sought his. "But the first two weeks of our marriage, we are to remain in the palace. It's a tradition since the first king of Galini Isle. The country refers to it as the honeymoon phase."

Those expressive blue eyes widened. "I thought a honeymoon was when the couple went off to some undisclosed location to have privacy."

He tried to block the image of having her all to himself for two weeks. The instant erotic thoughts had him shifting back to his seat before he did something really embarrassing.

"This country prides itself on rituals. The *ethos,* or practice, is not to be dismissed."

Victoria stared at him from across the table. He could tell she was getting nervous, so he wanted to take her mind off what was to come.

"Tell me about what you're working on now, other than your own wedding dress," he added with a smile he knew would put her at ease.

In an instant her face softened, the corners of her mouth tilted up into a genuine smile and, yeah, he felt that straight to the gut. How would she look smiling up at him, hair spread across his pillow as he slid into her?

Damn. Now more than ever, he wanted her in his bed.

But he wouldn't pressure her. He'd wait until she was ready to come to him. And he had a feeling from that scorching kiss she'd be more than willing sooner rather than later.

Victoria was different than most women he dated, bedded. She was genuine. Rare in this world to find a woman this sexy and beautiful who didn't flaunt her body or use it to work her way through her goals. He'd always admired how she created a name for herself without riding on the coattails of her iconic family name.

"My brothers are working together on a film depicting our mother's life through the years. And I have to say they've gotten along so well since they put their differences aside and focused on our mother and this movie." She laughed, tossing her golden hair over one shoulder. "They're getting along so well, they even spend off hours together with their families. The kids at least provide a buffer and something else they have in common."

Stefan still couldn't wrap his mind around the fact Victoria's mother, the Grand Dane of Hollywood, gave up a child for adoption nearly forty years ago and the baby turned out to be Anthony Price, the long-time heated rival of Victoria's legitimate brother, Bronson Dane. Talk about confusing.

"I'm sure discovering Anthony was your half brother was quite a shock. I apologize for not being there more for you, but with my dad battling cancer then…"

"You were needed more here, Stefan." Victoria sipped her wine then picked up her fork. "I admit I was shocked, but my brothers took it the hardest. Mom gave Anthony up for adoption when she was starting in her career because she wanted him to have a good life and she wasn't ready for motherhood."

"That's a mature decision."

Victoria's eyes darted to his, and that sweet smile widened. "I knew you'd understand. You were always so open-minded. So many have called her decision selfish."

He shook his head, reaching for his own wineglass. "Selfish would've been keeping the baby, knowing she would put her career first."

She looked as if she wanted to say more, but she cut a piece of her meat and slid the fork between her perfectly painted pale pink lips. And like any man infatuated with a woman—or any man who had breath in his lungs—he agonizingly watched until the fork disappeared and she groaned with delight as her eyelids fluttered. Just when he thought his arousal couldn't get any stronger...

"This is still so amazing," she told him. "You have no idea how grateful I am that you remembered my favorite food."

He knew every single detail about her—her favorite color, the movies she'd seen countless times and even the old diary she kept all of her private thoughts in. He knew more about her than any other woman, which was why they had such a strong bond. He didn't mind listening to her talk about her life. Most other women talked about their lives in an attempt to impress him. Victoria impressed him simply by being there for him, making him smile and expecting nothing from him in return.

"So tell me about this film." He wanted to know more, wanted to support her. "What's your part?"

He also wanted to keep her relaxed, keep her talking all night—since that was his only option for now. Just like during their multiple phone conversations over the years, that sultry voice washed over him, making him wish for things he couldn't have right now. But at the end of this, who knew? Maybe they'd remain married. That would put quite a spin on the whole friends-with-benefits scenario.

He'd never had this type of arrangement before—even that would've been more of a commitment than he'd been willing to give. But for Victoria…hell yes, he'd be interested.

"I've never worked with my family before and never designed costumes for a movie, but I made an exception," she said with a glowing smile. "There's no way I could let another designer do this, not when it's so close to my heart."

"Sounds like you're going to be a busy woman," he told her, cutting into his tender meat.

"The designs are done since filming started a few months ago. But I'm needed on set in case of a malfunction or a last-minute wardrobe switch." She shrugged and sipped her wine. "My team back in L.A. is handling everything right now. My assistant may have to take on a bit more until our wedding is over, though. God, that sounds so strange to say."

He lay his fork down, reached across the table and took her hand. "Thank you for what you're doing for me, for my country. I'll never be able to express my gratitude."

"You've been my best friend since I had braces," she joked. "We may live far apart, but other than my family, you're the closest person in my life." She tightened her grip on his hand and tilted her head with a soft grin. "Besides, you've handed me a dream job designing the gown, and I get to play queen for a few months. Seriously, I'm getting the better end of the bargain."

Stefan laughed. "I wasn't sure you'd agree so easily. I should've known you'd stand by me."

"I admit I have reservations about lying to the public,

to my friends and employees." She shifted in her seat, breaking hold of their hands. "But I'm honored to stand by you. It's not often we find someone in our life we can truly depend on."

He hated the loss of her hands in his and the hurt in her tone. "I was afraid you'd be vulnerable since the breakup, afraid you'd shut this idea down before I could explain my reasons."

"Maybe I am still vulnerable." She chewed her lip, eyes darting down before coming back up to meet his. "But I won't let my heart get in the way of my life again, and I know I'm safe with you."

"Absolutely, Victoria." He'd die before he let her get hurt. "You know how much I care for you."

He admired Victoria for standing tall, not cowering behind her family when it would be so easy to do so after having her world ripped out from under her. He knew firsthand how hard life was to live in the public eye. The media was ruthless, and if the story wasn't there, they made one up and damn the consequences. Reputations could be damaged and ruined with just a small dose of ink from the written word and could take years to restore…if restoration was even possible.

Because of accusations thrown at his family after the death of his mother, he more than anyone knew how fast a reputation could be ruined.

The rest of the meal moved quickly through some laughter and easy conversation, but Stefan couldn't get his mind off that scorching kiss. He wanted his hands on her again, whether to torture himself or just have a brief moment of instant gratification, he didn't know. But he knew how to rectify the situation.

"Dance with me," he told her when she'd placed her napkin beside her now-empty plate.

"Right now?" She glanced around the spacious, moon-lit balcony. "There's no music."

He came to his feet, moved into the master suite and within seconds had the surround sound filtering out into the night. When he came back through the open double doors, he extended his hand.

"Dance with me," he repeated, pleased when her hand slid into his. "We should practice before the official royal wedding dance after the ceremony. It's been years since we danced together."

She came to her feet, and he took no time in pulling her body against his. Wrapping his arm around her waist, Stefan was more than eager to have her invade his personal space.

"No wonder you're the Playboy Prince," she murmured, her breath tickling his cheek. "You're very good at this. I can't imagine how you'd be pouring on the charm if I weren't an old childhood friend."

He eased his head back but kept their bodies flush and swaying to the soft, soothing beat. "I promised to keep this simple, to give you all control in the end. I never go against my word."

She smiled. "I'm sure you wouldn't, but I also know your reputation. And I was on the receiving end of that kiss."

"You weren't just on the receiving end...you were an active participant."

Victoria's breath caught. "That's a...pretty accurate statement, but we've been friends too long for us to let lust cloud our judgment. Sleeping together would not be wise, Stefan."

He leaned in close to her ear and whispered, "Who says?"

Her hand tightened in his as she turned to look him in the eye, their lips barely a breath apart. "I don't know if we're getting swept up into this idea of pretending or this physical pull is stemming from seeing each other after such a long time apart, but I can't risk losing your friendship just because of this sudden attraction."

"I don't know how sudden this is, at least on my end." He kissed her lips slightly and eased back. "I can't deny my desire for you, but I do promise not to do anything you don't want."

"I'm going to hold you to that," she told him. "I know this situation will be hard for you."

He laughed at her choice of wording. "You have no idea."

Three

Sliding a hand down the fitted satin bodice, Victoria stared at her reflection in the floor-to-ceiling mirror. The gown was perfect, and she was so thankful she'd made a handful of wedding dresses in her downtime just to keep on hand for when she decided to branch out and start a bridal line.

No one had seen any of the finished designs, but she'd told her mother where they were and to ship them all. Victoria had taken a couple apart and pieced them the way she wanted. Her mother had only grumbled and complained a little when she learned Victoria wouldn't be returning to L.A. before the wedding.

And that conversation was a whole different issue.

Of all the times she'd fantasized about her wedding day, both as a child and an adult, she'd never envisioned marrying Stefan under these extremely strange circumstances.

Yes, she'd pictured a few times how it would be if

they'd taken their friendship to another level. She wasn't too proud to admit that she'd fantasized his kisses a time or two…and that was *before* he'd taken her into his arms and captured her mouth, showing her exactly what she'd been missing all these years. How could she delete that arousing sensation from her memory? How could she get his taste from her lips?

And why would she want to erase such pleasure?

Because he was a playboy, and even though she believed him when he said he'd be faithful, that didn't stop his previous lovers from calling him.

So here she stood, confused, intrigued and ready to take a giant life-altering step toward marriage while two of Stefan's royal assistants adjusted the veil around her hair. Another assistant stood in front, touching up her blush and powder for at least the third time in an hour. Couldn't have the soon-to-be queen of Galini Isle looking peaked.

God, she sincerely hoped she didn't have to do this for every appearance as queen. Thankfully Stefan had assured her she wasn't required to do too much. Even though she was from an iconic Hollywood family, she didn't crave the limelight.

"Ladies, could I have a moment alone with my daughter?"

Victoria adjusted her gaze in the mirror to her mother, who stood just inside the arched doorway to one of the many suites in the royal palace.

Obviously comfortable with taking orders, the middle-aged ladies scurried away at Olivia's request. Once the door was closed, Olivia moved in behind Victoria and smiled.

"Are you sure this is what you want to do?"

Stamping down any doubts that rose deep within her, Victoria returned her mother's questioning smile. "I'm sure, Mom. Stefan needs me, and perhaps at this point in my life, I need him. He's my best friend."

"But in the past few years you've scarcely seen each other."

Victoria shrugged. "Distance doesn't matter. Not with us. You know we talk nearly every day, and it's nice to know I am the one he trusts. We have a bond, Mom. A bond stronger than most marriages, actually. This is just another chapter in our friendship. I was engaged for romantic love once. This time I'm doing it for another kind of love."

"That's what worries me, my darling." Olivia pulled the veil over Victoria's face, then placed her hands on her shoulders, giving a gentle squeeze. "As a mother I worry your heart will get mixed up in this. He's a wonderful man to you…as a friend. I worry that in the end Stefan will come out getting everything he wants and you will have just another heartache."

She'd hadn't told her mother she and Stefan had shared numerous scorching kisses. Opening up about that certainly wouldn't alleviate any worries. Best to keep some things private…especially until she could figure them out herself. Arousal and confusion combined made for a very shaky ground.

"I'm not worried at all," she assured her mother, knowing it wasn't completely a lie. "He's given me an open end to this marriage. I may love being queen or I may want to return to my life in L.A. once all this is over. We'll put in a few appearances once we're married and this will all seem legitimate. Neither of us will be hurt. We're both too strong to let this arrangement destroy us."

"You're fooling yourself if you think this will be that simple." Olivia tilted her head, quirking a brow. "I've seen Stefan's charm, Victoria. I've witnessed how he's looked at you since I arrived here. I've also taken notice how he's looked at you over the years. He's got an infatuation that I believe is beyond a friendship. There's no way the two of you can play house and not get tangled up in each other. He's one very attractive man. Lust clouds even the best of judgments."

Intrigued, Victoria wondered just what her mother saw over the years from Stefan. Lust? Desire? This past month had brought to light a deeper side to their relationship. Beyond the steamy kisses, Stefan had been attentive to each and every one of her needs. He'd had her favorite foods prepared, would bring her a freshly picked flower from the gardens as she was working, insisted on breaks to walk along the beach so she could relax. He'd been the prefect Prince Charming…all because he knew her better than she knew herself in some ways.

Victoria shook off the questions regarding just how deep Stefan's emotions were and the fact he'd made it perfectly clear he'd had thoughts of her as more than a friend.

"Mother, his appeal and his charm are nothing new to me. And no matter how you think he looks at me, I assure you we are only marrying for the sake of the country and to help launch my bridal line."

Though she knew from his promising kisses and honest words that was false. But since she was still reeling from that fact herself, that was another tidbit she'd keep inside. She had enough "what-ifs" swirling around in her mind without adding her mother's into the mix.

"Well, he'd be a fool not to think of you as more," Olivia retorted. "And since he's asked you to marry him, he's no fool. I've always wondered if the two of you would end up together. I can honestly say this is not how I'd envisioned it."

Nerves swirled around Victoria's stomach. As if having the title of princess weren't crazy and nerve wracking enough, she'd be sharing a bedroom with Stefan for months. There was no way to deny they had chemistry and no way she could lie to herself and say she hadn't replayed those kisses over and over.

Victoria turned away from the mirror, taking her mother's hands. "I'm going into this with my eyes wide open, Mom. With Alex I was blindsided, but Stefan isn't using me. He asked for my help at a time when there was no one else he could trust. And there's nothing that can damage my heart here because my heart isn't getting involved. Stefan won't hurt me."

Olivia looked as if she wanted to say something more, but Victoria squeezed her hands, unable to discuss this delicate topic any further with her mother. "Trust me."

With misty eyes full of worry, Olivia's gaze roamed over Victoria before she stepped back and sighed. "The last time I was at this castle I was playing a queen myself." She laughed. "I didn't even compare to how beautiful you look. Must be the difference between acting and real life. I can't believe how long ago that was."

Tears clogged her throat as Victoria hugged her mother, not caring about the crinkling of the silk fabrics.

"You were stunning in that film, Mom. Besides, I'm acting, too, aren't I? Playing queen for Stefan so his country will remain under his family's control. Ironic, isn't it? I always swore I'd never go into acting."

Olivia eased back, placing her hands over Victoria's bare shoulders. "You'll be queen for real, my darling. What happens inside the bedroom may not be real, but your title will be. Have you thought of that?"

As if she could think of little else.

Okay, well that was a lie. She'd thought immensely about the fact her fiancé/best friend had her stomach in knots. On one hand she was thrilled to be helping him obtain his goal as he helped with hers. She found herself admiring him for his determination to take what was rightfully his. Most other times she didn't think of him as a prince or king at all…and now, well, she thought of him as a man. A very sexy, very powerful man. Not powerful in the sense that he'd rule a country, but powerful in the sense that he'd dominate a room the moment he entered. He'd control any conversation, and he'd most certainly take charge in the bedroom.

And that path was precisely where her mind did not need to travel. She was letting her thoughts run rampant because of a few heated kisses. Very hot, very scorching, very toes-curling-in-her-stilettos kisses. Just because she'd once wondered "what-if," didn't mean that anything could stem from this arranged marriage. One day at a time is how she would have to approach this. She couldn't afford to let lust steal the greatest friendship she'd ever had.

But she knew her emotions were teetering on a precipice and it would take just a small nudge for Stefan to push her over the edge and right into his bed.

"Stefan and I have discussed everything, Mom." Victoria offered a comforting smile, hoping she wasn't lying to her mother. "I'm pretty sure we have this under control. He's assured me that he won't let me get in over my head. I'm basically an accessory for him at this point."

Accessory. She hated that term, but what else could a wife to one of the world's most powerful, sexy men be called? He didn't need her to do any public speaking or head up any charities, not in the short time they planned to be married, so the demeaning name, unfortunately, fit.

"I had to keep your brothers out of here, you know." Olivia stepped back, smoothing a hand down her raw silk, pale blue floor-length gown. "They insisted on making sure you were okay, so I had to assure them I'd check and report back."

Victoria laughed, turning to face the mirror and glance

at her reflection once more. "You can tell my self-imposed bodyguards that I am not having cold feet and I'm perfectly fine. They should be worrying about their wives standing up beside me in front of millions of people watching on TV. I swear, last I saw of Mia and Charlotte, they were so nervous I thought they were going to pass out."

"I'm going to see them now," Olivia said. "They will be fine, so I just want you to concentrate and worry about you. This is your day, no matter what the circumstances."

Olivia's hands cupped Victoria's shoulders as she laid her cheek against hers to look at their reflection in the mirror. "You're beautiful, Victoria. Stefan may change his mind about you having control in the end. He may not want to let you go once his title is secure."

"The Playboy Prince?" Victoria joked, using his nickname. "He'll let me go so he can shuffle back into the crowd of swooning women and place me back on that friend shelf."

Their kisses replayed once again in her mind. Could they go back to being just friends? Would she want them to? They hadn't even lived together for their allotted six months and already she had fantasized about taking those kisses further. How could she not? They were definite stepping stones to more promising, erotic things.

God, in heaven. What had she gotten herself into? She swore she wouldn't put her heart on the line again, but how could she not when Stefan needed her? Maybe she needed him, too. More than she ever realized.

Hundreds of guests filed through the grounds at Alexander Palace on the edge of the emerald ocean. Cameras were positioned at every angle to capture each moment as guests entered the Grand Ballroom. The world watched as the next king and queen of Galini Isle were about to wed in what the media had dubbed the most romantic wedding of the century. Obviously the mysterious bride angle had paid off.

Many of the headlines leading up to the nuptials had been amusing. Stefan's personal favorite: Playboy Prince Finally Settles Down.

The media could mock him all they wanted. He'd show them just how serious he was about this wedding…even if the idea of being wed scared the hell out of him.

He focused his eyes to the end of the aisle and his chest constricted, breath left his lungs.

Stefan couldn't think. At this moment, he couldn't even recall the exact reason he'd asked Victoria to marry him, but he was most thankful he had.

She floated—yes, floated—down the aisle like a glorious angel coming to rescue him, wearing an original-design gown that dipped just enough in the front to have his imagination running into overdrive, while still looking classy. Two strands of pearls draped over each of her toned biceps, hinting that they'd once been straps that a lover had slid off her slender shoulders. And damn if he didn't want to be that lover.

The dress cut perfectly into the curve of her waist and fell straight to the ground. A shimmery veil shielded her face, and Stefan couldn't wait to lift it, to kiss his bride and get another taste of the flavor he'd come to crave from her lips.

Stefan knew his best friend was a walking fantasy that every man would give his last dying breath for. Well, except for that bastard she'd been engaged to. Stefan straightened his shoulders and smiled. He hoped the jerk was watching his TV and regretting letting such an amazingly talented, beautiful woman out of his life.

Victoria's gaze met his, and Stefan's heart clenched as

a wide smile spread across her face from behind the iridescent veil.

"You've chosen a beautiful queen, Stefan. Victoria is perfect."

Stefan merely nodded at his brother's whispered compliment. Mikos Alexander stood as best man, and Stefan knew his brother breathed a sigh of relief when he'd discovered the country would remain under the Alexander name. Stefan had worried when his brother had married a divorcée, thus preventing him from claiming the throne, but Victoria was a perfect fit.

Never in his life would he forget how she'd stepped up to save him, selflessly and radiantly. Stefan moved forward, taking Victoria's hands in his.

She squeezed them before turning to the priest. In a blur their vows were said and the gold heirloom rings exchanged. As Stefan lifted her veil, Victoria chewed on her bottom lip as if nerves were getting the best of her.

"You may kiss your bride."

Stefan wasted no time in capturing Victoria's lips. Though he couldn't claim her mouth the way he wanted to, considering there were television cameras on them and millions of people watching to see how the Playboy Prince would act, he was still just as affected by that one, tender kiss as he had been when they'd been alone on his balcony and shared their first passionate encounter. He'd taken every opportunity since then to steal more…each one always sweeter than the last and leaving him wanting.

Easing her soft lips from his, Victoria's gaze landed on his. "Good thing we've been practicing," she whispered with a slight grin.

He smiled and placed a quick peck on her lips once more before taking her hand and turning to the crowd.

"I present to you Prince and Princess Alexander," the priest exclaimed. "Galini Isle's next king and queen."

Applause broke out and Stefan glanced toward Victoria's family seated in the front row. Her brothers were smiling, but a hint of caution clouded their eyes, and her mother, the grand Hollywood icon, had unshed tears and a smile on her face…a face full of worry.

Stefan couldn't feel any guilt right now. How could he? He was going to be king and Victoria was going to stand by his side. Finally he could explore his feelings further because while he knew he wanted to be with her in more than just a friendly way, he also wasn't sure just how much of a commitment he could offer after the six months if she decided to remain in their marriage. He did, after all, get his reputation for a reason.

Right now, though, he had to concentrate on his title and gaining his country's confidence by eliminating the black mark over his family's name. That was his first order of business. But seducing Victoria would certainly be a welcome distraction, even if a challenge, and one he couldn't turn down. Especially now that he'd had more than a few tastes.

As he and his new bride made their way back up the aisle, Stefan beamed knowing he'd just married the most beautiful, intelligent, sexy woman. And for the next six months, and maybe even more if she chose to stay, Victoria was not only his best friend, she was his wife…and possibly lover.

Arousal shot through him. He wasn't known as the Playboy Prince for nothing. Seduction had always been his partner in crime.

Victoria had never smiled so much in all her thirty-two years combined as she had tonight. Between the professional royal photo shoot with Stefan's brother and wife and Victoria's family and then of the two of them alone, then the grand parade after the ceremony where they were shown off through the entire seaside town, she'd almost convinced herself this was real.

Now they were at the reception back inside the grand ballroom of the palace, and Stefan held her in his arms as they danced their first dance as Prince and Princess Alexander.

The spacious room with high, stained-glass ceilings had been transformed from the ceremony and set up to host the reception in the hours they'd been gone for the traditional wedding parade.

A dance floor had appeared surrounded by elegant white silk draped between tall, thick columns. White silk also adorned each table, as did slender crystal vases with a spray of white flowers and clear glass beads in each.

Thousands of twinkling lights created a magical, fairy-tale theme. Ice sculptures and champagne fountains were in abundance. The ballroom had shifted into something from a dream and something fit for royalty.

And while so much beauty surrounded her, she couldn't think of anything else but the man in her arms. Her doubts, her confusion, it all slid into the very back of her mind as the slow, classical ballad played and she swayed against him.

His warmth, his familiar masculine scent and the powerful hold he had on her all made her want to put her head on his shoulder and relish the moment. So she did. He'd held her numerous times over the years. But she knew in her heart this time was different.

With a sigh, she closed her eyes, letting him lead in their dance, and rested her head just for a moment on one broad, muscular shoulder. The man was the proverbial good time, but right now she wanted to just lean on him, to draw from his strength and courage.

Her cheek rested against his smooth, silky sash. Victoria had known he'd wear his best royal dress for the ceremony, but her Prince Charming had truly been a sight to see, waiting at the end of the white-petal-covered aisle. It wasn't often in their years together she saw him in person dressed as a prince. Normally they were just hanging out in casual clothes. But with his tailored black suit with shiny gold double-breasted buttons, glossy black shoes, and a wide, blue sash crossing from shoulder to opposite hip, he exuded bad-boy prince. She knew beneath all the impressive gold buttons and fringe-capped shoulders lay a great deal of body art molding over and around his chiseled arms, chest and back. Sexy didn't even begin to describe her man.

Medals, which stemmed from charity work to his family's crest and various other ranks, also adorned one side of his jacket. The blue from his sash matched his eyes perfectly, and he couldn't look more fit for a royal role than if he were the star in one of her brothers' films.

The designer in her should've made notes on how well the lines were cut in his suit, but the woman in her was too busy admiring the view. Hey, he may be her best friend, but he was still one magnificently built man and she'd be a fool not to notice. But she'd been noticing more and more in the past month leading up to their nuptials. Was she getting caught up in the wedding, or was she beginning to see him as more of a man? He'd always been charming, but recently he'd become…irresistible. And her desire for him was starting to consume her.

The glamorous ceremony was something she'd remember for the rest of her life. With celebrities, other royalty and every media outlet on hand to snap thousands of pictures, the scene was something out of a modern-day fairy tale.

"You made a beautiful bride, Victoria," he murmured. "I'm one lucky prince."

She raised her head, looked him in the eyes and smiled. "Oh, I'm pretty lucky, too. I'm living every little girl's dream by marrying royalty and living in a palace."

"Only for two weeks," he reminded her. "After our honeymoon phase, we'll travel to L.A. I'm anxious to see you at work and visit with your family. It's grown considerably since I was there last."

"I'm anxious to get back, too, but I don't mind playing hooky. Not when I'm living a fantasy life."

"Speaking of fantasy," he murmured, raking his eyes down to where her cleavage nestled against his tux. "Have I told you how amazing you look today?"

"You're letting your reputation take over," she joked, though nerves danced in her belly at the hunger in his eyes. "My eyes are up here."

"Oh, I know where your eyes are." He smiled, meeting her gaze. "But I'm enjoying the entire view of my beautiful bride."

He wanted her and he wasn't hinting anymore, which only made her even more intrigued.

Obviously the ball was in her court. Game on.

"And my reputation has nothing to do with what I'm feeling right now." He pulled her body closer to his as he spun her in a wide circle around the perimeter of the dance floor. "Trust me, I'm the envy of every man around the world. I nearly swallowed my tongue when you came down the aisle."

"As a designer, I take that as a compliment." She laughed. "As a woman, I'm thrilled to know I have that effect on someone."

He shifted slightly against her, a wicked smile on his face. "Oh, I'm not unaffected."

Mercy. No, he wasn't. How had this dance gotten so far out of control? And why did she care? How could she avoid the fact Stefan was so open with his feelings? Should she even attempt to hide that she'd been thinking of him in a new light, as well? Those "what-if" thoughts from years ago were now more realistic and...obtainable.

Did she dare try to move to the next level with Stefan? The idea made her nervous and excited and, most of all, curious. All of her giddy emotions overshadowed the fear and doubts.

Their wedding night was fast approaching. Only hours until the reception drew to a close and they would be alone. Perfect timing?

Well played, Fate. Well played.

"You're blushing again," he told her, stealing a quick kiss. "I know everyone is watching us and the cameras are still rolling, but that kiss was purely selfish. I'm finding it hard to keep my hands off you, Victoria."

"Stefan." Her heart beat against his chest. "I'm not sure...I mean, yes, I'm finding myself more drawn to you than just as a friend, but won't taking another step here make this arrangement more complicated?"

"We won't know unless we try," he told her, nipping at her lips again. "I'd hate to let an opportunity pass me by. What if sleeping together is the best decision we ever made?"

"Is that where we're headed?" she asked, already knowing what he'd say.

Unfortunately, she kept hearing her mother's warning about getting her heart entangled in this man. Fortunately her heart had already been trampled and crushed, so there was no more to break. And she knew Stefan would never hurt her.

"How much longer are we staying?" she asked as the orchestra slowed the song down toward the end.

He smiled. "Anxious to get me all alone?"

Considering they'd known each other for so long and he knew her better than most people, he had a love for his family that rivaled her own and his loyalty to his country made her heart melt, she may have a little trouble avoiding his charms.

Oh, the hell with it. Why dance around this attraction? Six months of torture would be pure…well, torture. People did friends with benefits all the time, right? Granted she never had, but Stefan was special and he so obviously wanted her, which was good because she couldn't deny it any longer.

"Maybe I am," she told him with a grin, knowing she was playing with fire.

As the song ended, he pulled her close, close enough she could feel just how turned on he was, and whispered in her ear, "I've been waiting for you to say that. What do you say we go start on our honeymoon?"

And with that thrilling promise, he tugged on her hand and they slipped through the crowd and out the double doors.

Four

As he led her through the long, marble hallways, Victoria didn't care about the doubts and fears swirling around in her head, nor did she care about the fact she'd just left hundreds of guests in the main ballroom.

What she did care about was how much farther they had to go until they reached their destination because she wanted Stefan, and the realization of just how much she wanted him both thrilled and scared her. This sexual tension had been brewing before she'd come to Galini Isle a month ago—there had to have been an underlying current or she wouldn't have been so eager to have his mouth on hers when they'd shared their first kiss…or the several scorchers that followed.

But she couldn't think about anything from their past now or she'd remember that this man was her best friend… and he was about to become her lover. Something about taking their relationship to a level of intimacy aroused her even more. She could analyze later all the reasons this wasn't a wise move…but right now she didn't care. She. Wanted. Him.

When Stefan pulled her through a set of heavy double doors, she blinked into the darkness, trying to get her bearings, and wondered if they'd just entered his master suite.

His room was on this floor, but she'd thought it was farther down the wing. She'd been in his suite a few times, but for purely innocent reasons…as opposed to now, when the reason was a bit more naughty.

She remembered his king-size bed with navy silk sheets. The bed had always sat in the middle of his suite, dominating the room.

A man like Stefan with his bad-boy behavior wouldn't have something as boring as a bed in a corner. He'd want that bed and all the action taking place there to be center stage.

Stefan eased the door shut and with a swift click, slid the lock into place. He immediately set the lights to a soft glow.

Good, that would help her nerves if she didn't have to have spotlights on her. While Stefan had seen her in swimsuits, he'd never seen her fully naked—not for lack of his playful trying at times, but she'd always written off his silly remarks as jokes. Had there been genuine want behind his words?

Victoria turned around, amazed at the room spread out before her, and she laughed. This was his idea of a romantic wedding night? Stefan never failed to amaze and surprise her.

"If someone starts looking for us, they'd check my wing first," Stefan told her. He slid off his jacket, flinging it to the side without taking his eyes off her as he stalked— yes, stalked—right toward her. "They'd never think to look in the theater."

How many women had he snuck into this room or any other room in this magnificent palace, for that matter? She knew the media really exploited his bachelor status and the fact that he enjoyed women, but she also knew most of their accounts were accurate. Stefan never made any apologies for the man he was, and that's perhaps why people loved him so much. He was honest to a fault and sinfully charming.

Past women didn't matter to her. He was her husband now, and what he did before this moment was ridiculous for her to even entertain. She wasn't a virgin, and they weren't committing themselves to anything permanent. They were adults, best friends, and they were acting on these newfound sexual feelings. So why analyze it to death when there was one hot, sexy, aroused prince standing before her looking like he wanted to devour her? No woman would be stupid enough to turn that invitation down... especially from her own husband.

Wedding night or not, this would be one experience she'd never forget. She needed the awkwardness and doubts to get out of her mind because she wanted to concentrate on the here and now.

"You look beautiful." He closed the gap between them, running a fingertip along her exposed collarbone. Shivers coursed through her at his provocative, simple touch. "The way this dress molds to your body makes me wonder if you could possibly fit anything between this satin and your skin."

Her eyes roamed over his bronzed face and his heavy-lidded eyes as his finger continued to tickle its way back and forth across her collarbone, teasing her, tempting her. If one finger had that much of an impact on her senses, who knew what a full-bodied touch would do.

"I'm a designer," she told him, reaching up to slide one

button at a time through the hole of his dress shirt. "It's my job to make things fit and create an illusion of perfection."

His hands glided down her arms, slid to her hips and tugged her until she was pelvis to pelvis with him. Chills raced over her body, the promise of what was to come making her shiver.

"I'd say fitting won't be a problem, and there's no illusion." His gaze dropped to her lips, to her breasts pressed against his chest and back up to her face. "There's plenty of perfection without the tricks you may practice as a designer. I've known you for years, Tori, and there's nothing imperfect about you."

The attack on her mouth was fierce and oh so welcoming. The man knew what he wanted, and the fact that he wanted her made her feel alive again for the first time in months. Maybe that made her shallow, but she needed to feel beautiful, sexy and, yes, even needed.

Stefan may be her best friend, but right now she wasn't having thoughts of friendship. Desire shot through her as she pressed her body against his.

How many times had she kissed him, hugged him? How could she have taken for granted such a hard body?

Victoria eased back, continuing her work on his shirt. Stefan slid her hands away and pulled it over his head, ignoring the last few buttons that weren't undone.

That chest. She'd seen it many times before, but she hadn't seen this fresh ink and his finely sculpted body in some time. Victoria glided her hands up over his chiseled abs and outlined the new tattoo over one of his pecs.

"How come every time I see you, you have new ink?" she murmured, tracing the detailed dragon.

"I like the art," he said simply. "Let's discuss tattoos later. How the hell do I get you out of this thing on your head and this dress without hurting one of us?"

Victoria laughed, thankful he'd lightened the mood. This is what she needed. The playful side of Stefan. The side that always made her smile. Of course, she had a feeling he'd be showing her another side that would make her smile even more in a minute.

She reached up, sliding several pins from her hair and placing them on the counter along the wall. After removing the diamond tiaralike headband and veil, she laid it out along the counter, as well.

She realized she was taking her time. In part she wanted this moment to last. But she also couldn't help being a little afraid of where this epic step would take them.

"I wish I'd designed a dress that could just peel off," she told him, reaching behind her. "But I'm afraid there's a zipper, and you're going to have to get it."

She turned, giving him her back but throwing him a glance over her shoulder. "Sorry I wasn't thinking ahead."

"Oh, this is my pleasure," he told her with a crooked smile and a wink.

When his fingers came up to her back and slid to the zipper, she couldn't suppress the shiver that raced through her. Arousal quickly overrode her awkwardness and doubts that threatened to creep in.

As the material parted in the back, Victoria shimmied her arms slightly so the dress fell down the front of her, leaving her standing in a strapless bustier that lifted her meager chest into something voluptuous and enticing…at least she hoped that's how he saw her.

Stefan didn't know which god deserved credit for making Victoria realize that the two of them sleeping together wasn't a mistake, but he'd graciously drop to his knees and thank him.

"Oh," he whispered when she turned around. "Had I

known you looked that good, I would've insisted you go without the dress during the ceremony."

Just as he'd hoped, Victoria laughed. That rich, seductive sound washed over him. As much as his body wanted hers, he also wanted her to be comfortable. He couldn't allow any uneasiness to settle between them.

"This royal wedding would've been talked about until the end of time," she joked. "Besides, since I'm the designer, I would've looked rather strange coming down the aisle without a gown."

"Strange?" he asked, tracing the top of the silk material that covered her tan breasts. "No. Sexy as hell and the fantasy of every man? Absolutely."

Victoria bit her lip but held his gaze.

"Don't," he told her. "Don't think. Don't worry. Just… feel."

She shivered beneath his touch, and Stefan wished she knew the effect she had on him was just as potent. He had shivers racing through his body just thinking of what they were about to do. God, he'd waited so long to make love to her and here they were.

Of course, all those times he'd envisioned them sleeping together, he never once pictured her in a wedding dress beforehand.

She inhaled, causing her chest to press deeper into his touch. The rustling of the dress had him pulling back just enough so she could step out of it.

"One of us still has too many clothes on." She smiled, picking up her dress, and, with great care, she laid it over the back of one of the oversized leather theater chairs. "Normally you're so eager to show off your body. Are you getting stage fright, Prince Alexander?"

A naughty smile spread across her face. She was literally a sinful sight before him, but he'd never been known for being a choir boy.

"Oh, I'm not afraid of anything." He wasted no time in stripping down to his black boxer briefs. "I was merely admiring the view of my sexy new wife."

When Victoria's eyes raked down his body, pausing at his throbbing erection, then back up to meet his eyes, she bit her lip. Nerves were getting to her and he refused to let her overthink this.

"You were starting to relax. Come on, Tori." He reached out, sliding his hands up her bare arms and stepping into her. "You've seen me in swimming trunks skimpier than this."

Her eyes locked on to his, her hands coming up to rest on his chest. "True, but this is so much different. I just don't want this to change us...you know, afterward."

He kissed her lips, gently, slowly. Kissed his way along her jawline, down the long, slender column of her throat, pleased when she tilted her head back and groaned. He'd dreamed of this moment for so long. Longer than he liked to admit, even to himself. He'd never allowed any woman to have such control over his mind or his fantasies.

"Nothing will change," he assured her between kisses. "Unless it's better. And I'm positive in the next few minutes, things between us will get a whole lot better."

Victoria's arms circled around his neck as her head turned, her mouth colliding with his.

And that's when the dam burst. His, hers. Did it matter? He'd wanted her for years, and whether she'd wanted him that long or she'd just decided it in the past few weeks they'd been together he didn't know, but he did know he was going to have her. Now. Here.

Stefan encircled her waist with his hands, slid them on down to the slight flare of her hips and slowly walked her to the bar in the back of the room. When he hoisted her up onto to the counter, she laughed.

"In a hurry?" she mocked with a teasing grin.

"I've waited for this for a long time," he told her, staring at her moist, swollen lips. "I always swore if we ever came to this moment I'd take my time. But right now I can't wait another minute."

Her smiled weakened as she held his gaze. "I think I've been waiting for this for a long time, too. I just never realized..."

Stefan didn't want a confession, not now. He didn't want her to explore her feelings...or, God forbid, try to uncover his. He just wanted Victoria.

He stepped between her gloriously spread legs, slid his palms up her smooth, bare thighs and thumbed along the edge of her white silk panties.

When she hooked her thumbs through the thin straps and shifted from side to side to ease them off, he gratefully helped her slide them down her long, toned legs.

She reached around behind the bustier.

"Leave it," he ordered. "I like how you look right now."

With tousled hair, bare skin from the waist down and that white silk bustier molded to her curves and pushing her breasts up...yeah, he liked her just the way she was. All sexy and rumpled and ready for him.

"I want to feel your skin on mine," she told him, still working on the back of her lingerie.

How could he argue with her defense? No man with air in his lungs would turn down bare breasts.

"Then let me help," he offered.

He eased his hands around and, one by one, each hook-and-eye closure popped open. Thankfully it was cut low, so there weren't very many. When the garment was fully open, he stepped back.

Victoria held on to the front of the material still covering her breasts. "You're sure?" she asked.

Without a word, he brushed her hands aside, took the bustier and threw it over his shoulder. And finally, she was completely and utterly naked. And completely and utterly his.

He palmed one breast in each hand as he captured her lips once more. Arching her back, Victoria leaned into his touch, his kiss, and let out a soft, low groan.

Her arms came around his shoulders, her fingertips toying with the ends of his hair on the nape of his neck. She shifted, scooting to the edge of the counter, and wrapping her legs around his waist. Stefan let go of her breasts long enough to shuck his boxers and kick them to the side. With her legs around him, he palmed her backside and lifted her off the bar until she was settled right above him.

His eyes searched hers as he walked a few steps to the nearest wall, where he rested her back. He stayed still, waiting for any hint of a signal that she was uncomfortable or not ready to go through with this.

Stopping would kill him, but even with his hormones in overdrive he'd stop if she said the word. But when he looked in her eyes, all he saw was desire. Heavy lids, half-covered vibrant blue eyes…eyes that were focused on his lips.

At the same time he sealed his mouth to hers, he slid her down to take him fully. The flood of emotions within him was indescribable. Her body all around his, the soft feel of her skin, the fresh, floral aroma and her tiny little gasps had him nearly embarrassing himself and drawing their first encounter to an abrupt, climactic halt.

He moved within her, slowly, then, when her hips rocked faster, he increased the pace.

She tore her lips from his. "Please."

If she liked things fast and sweaty, they could very well kill each other before the six months were up because she was speaking his language.

Victoria gripped his shoulders, flung her head back and closed her eyes. That long column of her neck begged to be licked, savored. He nibbled his way up, then back down and nestled his face between her breasts.

"Stefan...."

Yeah, he knew. She was close, which was a relief because so was he. He normally prided himself on his stamina, but one touch from Victoria and he was ready to explode. He didn't take the time or the energy to think that this had never happened before. There was something about his Tori....

Her legs tightened around his waist as her whole body stiffened. He grabbed her face, forced her to look at him and for the briefest of seconds, when their eyes met, he felt a twinge of something he didn't recognize. But he certainly wasn't taking the time to figure it out, not when he had a sexy, wild woman bucking in his arms, finding her release.

Capturing her lips while she came undone around him was all he wanted. His tongue slid in and out, mimicking their bodies. His own release built and before he knew it he, too, let go. He gave in to Victoria's sweet body, allowing her to take him—her welcoming arms enveloping him and her soft words calming him.

Never had he experienced anything like this before. But he knew that the next several months with his best friend-turned-wife would be nothing if not life-altering.

And that epiphany scared the hell out of him.

Victoria sat in the oversize cozy leather chair in the palace theater waiting for the movie to start and eating from a tub of popcorn. Only moments ago the man beside her rocked her world in a way she hadn't known possible, and now he pretended as if their giant step beyond friendship were perfectly normal.

After they'd nearly killed each other in a bout of heated, frenzied sex, she'd thrown on his tux shirt instead of her gown. He'd slipped back into his pants, leaving his gloriously tanned and tattooed chest bare. He nearly had a whole sleeve of tats on one sculpted arm. The swirls slid over his shoulder and stretched from his back over his pecs. And Victoria wanted to trace every line, every detail with her fingertip, then follow with her tongue.

God, he'd turned her into a sex fiend. Knowing Stefan, that had been his goal all along.

Who knew he had such…skills. Well, given the amount of women the paparazzi put him with over the years, she should've known, but she'd not thought of his hidden talents before. Shame that.

But she'd be thinking of them now. She had a feeling they would be in the forefront of her mind for quite some time. Would she ever get used to seeing, touching her best friend in such a way?

"So do we talk about this or just watch the movie?" she asked, reaching into the giant tub of popcorn he'd prepared.

He propped his feet upon the footrest of his own oversized leather chair and threw her a smile. "I knew you wouldn't be able to just relax and watch the movie."

Relax? After what had just happened? Her body was still trembling and her orgasm had stopped twenty minutes ago. Yeah, definite skills. But even through the climax-induced haze, she had to know what he was thinking. She didn't care if that was too girly and mushy for him, she couldn't just pretend this moment hadn't changed her life.

"Do you feel different?" she asked, turning in her chair to face him.

A wicked grin spread across his handsome, devilish face. "Oh, yeah."

With a playful swat on his arm, she laughed. "Stefan, be serious. We're married and we just had sex."

"Just sex?" he asked, quirking one black brow.

Images of how they must've looked slammed into her. His golden, toned body plastering hers against the wall as she arched into his touch. Her glorious Greek prince staking his claim, dominating her.

"Okay, so it was amazing sex," she admitted as tingles continued to spread through her. "This isn't going to be weird now, is it? Because I really can't handle weird."

"The way you were groaning earlier and the way you're smiling now, I'd say you feel anything but weird."

Victoria rolled her eyes. "You're begging for compliments, aren't you? I already said it was great sex. I just don't want this to get uncomfortable between us."

He reached out, grabbed her hand and squeezed. "I care for you just as much as I always have," he assured her, all joking gone from his face. "You're still my best friend, but I've discovered that my best friend has a kick-ass body that I can't wait to take my time in savoring and getting to know better."

Chills and excitement coursed through her at his promise. If he was this confident, than why was she letting fear spread through her? Why borrow trouble when she'd just had the most incredible sexual experience of her life?

"I think this marriage is going to be one of the wisest decisions we ever made," she told him.

As the movie started on the screen, Stefan held on to her hand, occasionally stroking his thumb across her skin. The man had a tender side, and he wasn't afraid to express himself. They'd held hands before, but holding them after being so intimate took on a whole new meaning.

If the next six months of their marriage were anything like tonight, she'd certainly think twice about walking away. She may just be queen of Galini Isle forever.

"You picked my favorite movie," she told him as the title popped up on the screen. "You had this whole night planned, didn't you?"

He shrugged and grinned. "I actually had the movie planned because I thought you'd want to get back some sense of normalcy after the circus today. The sex was just a major added bonus."

"Oh, you have such pretty words," she mocked with a heavy sigh. "Watch it, Stefan, I may not find it in my heart to leave you after six months."

And while she was joking on the outside, inside her heart she feared she may have gotten in deeper than even she thought she would go.

Five

Victoria stood over the mahogany desk and sighed as she stared down at the scattered dress designs and random doodles. She'd started fresh sketches the day after her wedding and now, over a week later, she still wasn't happy with the results.

Nothing compared to her own lavish gown...of which many replicas were already being made by designers who only wished they would have had the initial idea.

And while that dress was her absolute favorite, Victoria didn't want to re-create it for resale. That unique design was hers, whether the marriage was real or not. She wanted to keep the gown special, but she would do others that were similar for future clients. And she knew she couldn't stop other designers from trying to mimic her gown, but they still wouldn't be the same. Hers was literally one of a kind.

Her thoughts circled back around to the "real" marriage.

She didn't know why she always put quotations around the word in her head. Her marriage to Stefan was as real as anyone else's marriage. In fact, she'd bet her entire year's salary that theirs was better than the majority of those living in Hollywood because she sincerely loved Stefan and would do anything for him…obviously a point she'd proven.

Not only did they share that bond and connection of their friendship, but the sexual chemistry was beyond amazing. Didn't married couples complain that after they said "I do" the light burned out on the passion? Yeah, there was no dimming the desire in the bedroom here.

After their initial lovemaking in the theater—and their movie night—Stefan had brought her into his master suite where they'd playfully undressed each other once again and enjoyed the benefits of the sunken garden tub in his master bath.

If this was how the whole friends-with-benefits thing worked, no wonder so many people jumped on board. Six months of Stefan attending to her intimate needs hadn't been part of the initial bargain, but it had become a surprising extra.

Unfortunately, her emotions were a jumbled mess. She had been stunned at what an attentive, passionate lover Stefan was, but when she started really thinking about their intimacy, she couldn't help but feel they'd passed the point of no return. After this six months, if she chose to leave, could they actually go back to just being friends?

Victoria turned her focus back to the pencil sketches staring up at her. Before her wedding she would've loved these designs, but now that she was technically a princess— still an odd term to grasp when referring to herself—she wished for all of her future brides to feel the same on their special day.

She wanted to launch her Fairy-tale Collection with magnificent gowns that women would love just as much as the one she wore, and if she was going to start this, she needed to stop coming up with garbage.

Raking her hands through her hair, she groaned.

"Bad time?"

She spun in the direction of the door to find Stefan entering their bedroom. In the past she'd always appreciated his fine build, but now that she'd seen, tasted and touched every delicious inch, she had a whole new admiration for her sexy husband...a weird sensation to associate with Stefan, but surprisingly a very welcome one.

Would it be too taboo for the prince to walk around naked? A shame, really, to cover such a magnificent creature.

If one didn't know he was a prince, they'd never guess from his attire. Though he did look mighty fine in his black T-shirt stretched over his broad shoulders and faded, designer jeans, it was the baseball cap pulled low to shield his face that captured her attention. Not often had she seen him in a hat, but he wore it well. And while he may look very American with his ensemble, he was every bit the Greek god she knew him to be.

"Perfect timing, actually." She turned away from her ghastly drawings and leaned back on the desk. "What's up?"

Those long legs ate up the space between them, and he rested a hip beside hers on the desk. "Well, I'm in the honeymoon phase and my wife is working. The tradition in my country is that these two weeks are for the husband and wife to get to know each other."

Wife. She didn't know if she'd ever get used to that term coming from Stefan's lips...especially when referring to her.

Victoria laughed. "I'm pretty sure we know each other quite well."

He reached around, fingering through her designs. "Still drawing random sketches?" he asked.

"Yeah. It's always easier to concentrate when I'm doodling and just let my mind relax."

He lifted a torn piece of scratch paper. "This looks like my family crest, but...are those initials?"

Victoria nodded. "I intertwined our initials together. Silly, isn't it?"

"Amazing how you're so extremely talented and still hard on yourself."

He took her hands in his and flashed a wicked smile. "Let's get out of here. Go down to the beach or have a picnic. Want to go for a ride on my new bike?"

"Is that a double entendre?" she asked, smiling. "How about we take a ride on the bike to the beach for a picnic?"

"And you'll lay off work the rest of the day?" he asked.

She watched him, those taut muscles beneath his shirt, the way the hat shielded those cobalt-colored eyes. As his best friend she hadn't been able to deny him anything, so as his wife and lover she definitely couldn't say no.

"Just today," she promised. "I really do need to get this line started, and these designs are crap right now."

Stefan pulled her up as he stood. "All the more reason you need a break. I know how you get when you're frustrated. Nothing will make you happy until you take a breather, refocus and come back to it. Besides, you're not sleeping well and I know it's because of work."

She jerked back. "How do you know I'm not sleeping well?"

"Because you normally snore like a train," he laughed. "All you've been doing lately is tossing and turning."

"I do not snore," she told him with a tilt of her chin. "You're lying."

He hugged her closer and nuzzled her neck. "Maybe I'm not wearing you out enough before bed."

The familiar masculine aroma that she always associated with him enveloped her. Amazing how their time apart didn't hinder his knowledge of how she worked. They may not see each other in person as often as she would've liked, but he still knew every layer to her. Even more so now since they'd slept together.

"If you want to ride my bike, in any form of the term, let me offer myself to your services."

Victoria laughed, smacking his shoulder. "I'm so glad you're willing to sacrifice yourself for my work."

With a loud smack, he kissed her on the lips. "Anything for my new bride."

"Let me change and I'll meet you in the kitchen."

His hand snaked up her shirt, his thumb skimming the edge of her lacy bra. "Do you need help changing?"

His touch affected her in ways she'd never known before, and she had to assume the chills and instant erotic pleasure that came from his fingertips stemmed from their playful, yet intense lovemaking.

"What I need is for you to get that picnic lunch prepared so we can go," she told him, swatting his hand away and taking a step back.

He shoved his hands in his jean pockets and smiled... Oh, the things that smile did to her insides, touching places she had thought dead since her exploited and humiliating breakup months ago.

She had known Stefan would be there to help her through the tough time, she just never imagined it would be with their clothes off.

Every time she thought of how fast, how thrilling their

new relationship was, nerves settled low in her belly. She was already getting too comfortable and she hadn't even put a dent in this six-month period.

Even though he'd given her control in the end, she couldn't help but wonder if he'd tire of her, physically, by then and if he'd be eager to get back to his old, playboy ways.

"I already had my chef prepare the food," he told her. "How soon can you be ready?"

"I'm just going to throw on some jeans and a tank."

Stefan rolled his eyes. "You are a fashion designer. You never 'throw on' anything. You'll go to the closet and think about it, try something on, discard it and start over."

Offended that he'd hit the nail on the head, she folded her arms over her chest. "For your information, I know exactly what I'm going to wear."

He quirked a brow and tilted his head. "Really? Then I'll just wait."

In her mind she went through everything she'd brought from the States. She hadn't had all of her things shipped since they were returning to L.A. after the two-week honeymoon period was over, so her options were limited.

"You're just waiting to see me naked," she joked, heading to her walk-in closet.

"An added perk," he agreed. "But I want to see you get ready as fast as you claim you can. This will be a first."

Victoria eyed her selection. If they were riding a bike, she would need pants, so she grabbed her favorite pair of designer jeans. Her eyes roamed up to the top rack of clothes where she'd hung her shirts. A little sleeveless emerald-green wrap shirt caught her eye—perfect. Sexy, cool and comfortable. She glanced to the shoe rack at the end of the closet and grabbed her gold strappy sandals. Not bike material, but perfect for the picnic and beach.

"Voilà," she announced, holding her items up in the air as she came from the closet, then stopped.

The man was lying across the bed wearing nothing but tattoos and a grin. He'd taken off his hat, too, leaving his hair messy and those cobalt eyes, beneath heavy lids, staring across the room at her.

"You don't fight fair," she told him, trying to remain in place and not attack her husband like some overeager teenager.

"Fighting wasn't on my mind at all." He laced his hands behind his head, forcing his muscles to flex beautifully beneath his tats. "Looks like you still need to undress."

Check and mate. And by the smirk on his face, he knew he had her. He'd played this scene perfectly.

How could she turn down such a blatant invitation? Even with their short time frame looming in her mind, she couldn't deny herself giving and receiving his pleasure.

She tossed her items to the floor, not caring where they landed. In a slow, what she hoped was sexy, striptease, she loosened the ties on her shirt and flung it off to the side, as well.

"Since I'm being rushed, I may need some help," she told him, sliding her thumbs into her jeans and sending them to puddle at her feet. She stepped out and smiled when his eyes roamed over her body...twice. "You want the job?"

"Sure, I'll help by getting you out of these."

He came to stand, all six-foot-plus glorious inches of him. He was beautifully tanned, magnificent and, for now, he was hers.

"Being with you like this should be awkward." She reached out, tracing his family's crest he had tattooed over his heart. "But it's not. I'm amazed how comfortable I've been being intimate with you."

"You're not going to want to leave me at the end of this six months," he joked, sliding the strap of her bra down one arm.

She reached around, unhooking the unwanted garment, and smiled. "Maybe not. We may just like being married to each other. This is the best relationship I've ever been in."

"You're just saying that to get me into bed," he told her, his hands coming up to cup her breasts.

"Yes, because it is so hard to get you naked and horny." She laughed.

The corners of his mouth kicked up at the same time he scooped her up and tossed her onto the bed. She bounced once before he was on her, pinning her hands above her head.

"I don't know why, but that smart mouth of yours has always been one of the things I love most about you."

She knew he loved her the way best friends loved each other, but when he said it like that, especially now that they were practically naked, the words sounded a bit more intimate and almost…awkward. She so did not want awkwardness to enter into this marriage or friendship. She enjoyed this friends-with-benefits arrangement they had. Her heart couldn't handle any more.

"You're thinking," he murmured, looking down. "None of that here. Work and everything else stays out of this bed."

She smiled, knowing he was the proverbial "fun guy," but he also knew when to be serious and when to work. The media had just caught him mostly in those "fun guy" moments.

But she knew the man beneath the playboy persona.

"Not thinking right now is perfect," she told him, looping her arms around his neck. "Marrying you was good for my creative mind."

He laughed. "Let me show you how creative I can be."

Six

Stefan's cell went off again. And again, he ignored it.

"Whoever is calling you must want you pretty bad," Victoria told him. "Why don't you just answer it?"

Because he wanted to ignore the fact that certain people did not believe this marriage was real and that he was officially off the market.

"Could be important," she went on as she slid her dainty feet back into her sandals and strapped them around her ankles.

After an intense bout of sex, a ride on his bike and a picnic at the beach, the last thing he wanted was an interruption to the day—especially by answering phone calls from past lovers. He had his best friend-turned-wife with him, and he was happier than he'd been in a long time. All of his goals were within his reach, and he didn't want anything to dampen his mood.

He'd promised Tori he'd be faithful, and he wasn't going

back on his word. Never before had he promised to be exclusive, something he made sure his lovers knew up front, but with Tori warming his bed, he didn't mind at all. He kept waiting for that feeling of being trapped to overtake him, but so far he'd not felt anything but complete and utter happiness.

"They'll leave a message," he told her, not really caring if they did or not.

Victoria leaned her hands back in the sand, shook her head and allowed her hair to fall past her shoulders and cascade down her back. As her gaze settled on the emerald waters before them, he smiled. It wasn't every man who could say he married his best friend…a hot, sexy, centerfold-material friend. Damn, he'd lucked out. An openended marriage was absolutely the way to go. Once the crown was his in a few months, he'd seriously have everything: title of king and Victoria in his bed with no major commitment to marriage.

And hopefully he could also convince her brothers to work with him on a documentary to clear his father's name.

"I'm not jealous, you know," she said, her eyes still on the orange horizon as the sun set.

He eased closer to her, drawing his knees up and resting his arms on them. "Jealous of what?"

"The women calling you. I'm sure that's why your phone vibrates and rings every half hour."

Stefan laughed. Victoria had never been one to mince words or back away from any uncomfortable topic. She was also very confident, like most American women were. He found that quality extremely sexy. What had that jerk Alex been thinking? Stefan only hoped they didn't run into the guy once they were back in L.A. Or if they did, he hoped the media wasn't around. The last thing he needed was a picture of him popping the other guy in his pretty-boy face.

"Go ahead and laugh," she went on. "But I know that's your entourage calling."

"And how do you know this?" He chuckled again, now at her description.

"Because if it had been your brother, one of your staff or anyone else important, you would've answered it."

He shook his head. "Possibly."

With a wide, sinful smile, she turned to face him. "So you admit your harem has been calling?"

"Maybe, but with the way you can't keep your hands off my body, I don't have time for others."

Victoria's laugh washed over him. "Your ego is even bigger than your bank accounts. I think we both know who initiated the sex this afternoon."

"You were the one who insisted on changing clothes. In a man's mind, that's code for 'I'm getting naked and you should join me.'"

"Oh, please." She rolled her eyes, still smiling. "If a woman says 'I'm going to the grocery store,' a man thinks that's a code for 'let's get naked.'"

Stefan didn't want to feel guilty about the women calling him. He couldn't help it. The fact he was married wasn't exactly a secret; it had been televised for the entire world to see. But a few of the women from his past knew him too well and had convinced themselves this marriage was a lie.

"Are you just a little jealous?" he asked, throwing her another smile.

Part of him wanted her to be, but the other part of him hoped she kept their relationship light and carefree.

Yes, he'd wanted Victoria on an intimate level for years, but now he had her where he wanted her. He didn't need emotions or anything too deep to creep into this new relationship they had discovered.

"I'm not jealous." She looked him dead in the eye, no smile, no glimmer of amusement. "But I won't be the other woman or played to look like a fool ever again."

Stefan turned, grabbed her by the shoulders and met her eyes. "There's no way in hell I'd ever treat you that way, Tori. And I'm not that jerk you were engaged to. Remember that."

He'd be damned if he'd let that bastard play the third wheel in their relationship, no matter their carefree set-up.

On a sigh, her head drooped. "I'm sorry. I don't have trust issues with you, Stefan. My mind just instantly ventured in the wrong direction."

"Hey." He placed a finger beneath her chin and lifted her face to meet his once again. "This marriage may not be a traditional one, but I say from here on out we keep your ex and my past out of it. Deal?"

"Deal."

The quick snapping of an automatic camera had him jerking his attention around.

He spotted a man crouched in the lush plants surrounding what was supposed to be the private beach to his family's palace.

Stefan jumped to his feet and took off after the unwanted intruder. "Stop," he yelled.

Hot sand squished beneath his feet, making him slide with each step. By the time he'd gotten to the area where the man had been in hiding, the guy was gone.

What the hell had the intruder overheard?

Stefan pulled his cell from his pocket and punched a button. "There's a man on the grounds," Stefan said before his security guard could utter a word. "If you find him first, take his camera. Then call the cops. I'm looking near the beach. Take the front of the palace."

Knowing Victoria would be fine for a few minutes, Stefan moved through the foliage in the direction the trespasser took off. No way in hell was he letting someone invade his privacy, and on his own secluded beach, as well.

Even though he knew without a doubt that Victoria didn't think anything of flashing bulbs and media circuses, he wanted their marriage, their life to be private. The bond they shared was so special, and even though the paparazzi had them practically married as teens, he didn't want their engagement or wedding tarnished. What transpired between him and Victoria was nobody's business.

But he had to find the guy and find out exactly what he'd overheard and take that damn camera. He couldn't afford for this secret to get out before the coronation. This country was his, damn it, and he'd do anything to keep it.

Besides, he wanted Tori all to himself…he was selfish like that. He wouldn't share her with the public any more than necessary.

More than anything, though, he wanted to shield her, protect her from any more pain. Because he cared for her more than any other woman in his life, he wanted to be the one to ride to her rescue and keep her life worry-free and happy.

Stefan spotted footprints in the sand and followed them up the embankment toward the tiny village. Sweat trickled down his back, but the heat was nothing compared to the anger in knowing someone had infiltrated his home. What the hell had his guards been doing? A discussion he'd be taking up later with the head of his security.

Stefan stopped when he spotted the man crouched down on the sidewalk, holding his camera, and from what Stefan could see, the man was looking through his shots. Probably checking to see if he needed to come back for more.

Without a sound, Stefan moved in from behind and wrapped an arm around the guy's neck, hauling him up to his feet.

"Drop the camera," Stefan growled in his ear.

Immediately the camera clattered to ground. With his free hand, Stefan pulled his cell from his pocket and dialed security to come collect the trash.

"You made a mistake in trespassing," Stefan told him, tightening his grip. "I don't take kindly to people invading my wife's privacy."

"I'm sorry," the man choked out. "Please."

"Whatever you *think* you overheard, forget it. If I even suspect you've gone to the media with lies, there won't be a place you can hide that I won't find you." Stefan loosened his hold but kept the guy in a lock until backup arrived. "I better never catch you on my property or even looking in my family's direction again or a smashed camera will be the least of your worries."

The heavy pounding of footsteps had Stefan shouting for the guards. "Over here," he yelled.

Once the guards had the trespasser secure, Stefan stepped around to get a good look at the man's face so he could remember it. Then he crouched down, picked up the broken camera and pulled the memory card out, sliding it into his pocket.

"Take him to the front while you wait for the cops," Stefan ordered his guards.

Tamping down his anger and wiping the sweat off his forehead, Stefan made his way back to Victoria. Her long, golden hair danced around in the ocean breeze, her face tilted up while she watched the water as if her privacy hadn't just been invaded.

"We secured the guy. Cops are on their way, and I personally confiscated the memory card." Stefan took a seat beside her. "Sorry about that."

With a shrug, Victoria turned to face him. "I'm used to it. Privacy really means nothing to me. I wouldn't know what to do with complete seclusion."

Stefan knew with her family she came into this world in the spotlight, but something about her statement struck him. She wasn't asking for privacy; no doubt she thought that was something she could never have. But why couldn't he provide her a little escape?

"What did he overhear?" she asked.

"I didn't give him the chance to say, but I made it very clear he's not to repeat anything or he will be found and dealt with."

Tori gasped. "You threatened him?"

"What did you want me to do? Ask him over for tea?"

On a sigh, Victoria shook her head. "I don't know. I just hope he didn't hear us. Pictures are one thing…"

Stefan wouldn't let some overeager cameraman ruin his future, or Victoria's. No matter the cost. He also wouldn't let the bastard ruin his day with his wife, either.

"Remember when we first met and we were trying to hide from all the cameras and crew for the film your mother was in?"

A genuine, beautiful smile spread across her face. "That was fun. We were purposely avoiding anybody so we could do whatever we wanted."

Stefan pictured the time in his mind, so clear and vivid. "I believe that's when I introduced you to alcohol."

On a groan, Victoria closed her eyes. "Don't remind me. I was so set on impressing you, I didn't want you to know I hadn't drank before."

"The look on your face after your first sip of whiskey kind of gave you away," he told her.

"You probably thought I was such a loser." She laughed, lying back on the blanket and looking up at the clear, blue sky.

"A loser? Nah. I thought you were innocent, and that's the kind of girl I was interested in."

And he had been…well, as much as a teenage boy could be interested in a girl. She'd been California fresh with all that silky blond hair and tanned skin. He'd instantly had a crush but had to play it cool.

So he did what any good boy would do. He'd plied her with alcohol and tried to talk her into skinny-dipping.

"You mean the kind of girl you were interested in corrupting?" she asked with a low laugh that made him pause to enjoy such sweetness.

There was just something about her that always made him smile. Their friendship never had any speed bumps, and for years he'd found himself wondering what something more with her would be like.

Of course, marriage to anyone never entered his mind, but so far being married to Tori really had its perks. She was playful in bed, and he appreciated the fact she wasn't getting too involved on a more heartfelt level.

"Maybe a little corrupting," he agreed. "I never did get you to go skinny-dipping."

Victoria shook her head. "That's something I've never done. It just sounds so…cold."

His eyes roamed over her body. She'd forgone the jeans and shirt and had ended up donning a beautiful pale blue strapless romper, and he wanted to slide his fingers between her breasts, loosen the knot and see the material puddle to the ground.

"Trust me." His eyes came back up to meet hers. "When I get you naked in the water, you'll be anything but cold."

Her breath hitched as she bit her lip and dropped her eyes to his mouth. Hell yeah. She was sexy personified, and she was all his for the next six months. After that… well, that ball was in her court. Going back to dating, and bedding, other women surprisingly wasn't a priority, not with Tori matching him both in bed and out.

Stefan slid one hand through her hair, his other hand cupping the side of her face. With the utmost care and tenderness, he tilted her head and secured his lips to hers. With gentle persuasion he coaxed her lips apart, pleased when she accommodated him. Her soft moan as she eased into his body aroused him more than all their frenzied kisses. Those fast-paced kisses were stepping stones to sex. This gentle, passionate kiss was a stepping stone to…what?

He told himself he was just enjoying the moment and not getting deeper intimately with her. Stefan didn't want to go down that path. But he did want to keep savoring his wife. He wanted to slowly strip her and see her body in the sunlight on the beach as he…

His cell phone chimed, breaking the moment. With a muttered curse, he eased back from those tender, swollen lips.

After jerking the phone from his pocket he answered, "Yes?"

"The police are here," the guard told him. "Would you like to come and talk to them or do you want me to take care of it?"

Stefan stared at Victoria. The moment of reminiscing had turned intense…something he hadn't counted on. Sex was one thing, but that flutter in his chest was not welcome.

Na pari i eychi. The woman was almost too perfect for

him. He couldn't afford to let himself get all emotional about their arrangement. He was a man—one known for his physical relationships. He had to remember that here.

"I'll be right there," he said before disconnecting the call.

Stefan came to his feet, put his hands on his hips and looked down at Victoria. "Police arrived. I'm going to go talk with them."

Still staring into his eyes, as if searching for answers about what had just happened, Victoria nodded and remained silent.

What *had* just happened? He didn't even know himself, but it was far too much. Besides, he couldn't focus on that right now.

"I can send someone to pick up our picnic later," he told her. "Are you staying here or coming back with me?"

"I think I'll stay here."

He studied her, trying to read if she was uncomfortable or just confused like he was. Was she feeling something beyond their friendship and sexual desire?

"Then I'll send someone down to make sure you're all right by yourself."

Victoria smiled. "I don't need a sitter, Stefan. I'll be fine. Go on and talk to the police. But you have the man's memory card, so don't be in a rush to press charges."

That was his Victoria. Always wanting the good in life to override the bad. She was a special woman and for now she was not just his best friend, she was his wife. He refused to delve deeper than that.

Victoria slid into her red silk nightgown and smoothed her hair back over her shoulder. The phone calls Stefan had been receiving shouldn't still be in the forefront of her mind, but they were, and she hated the fact she let the jealousy settle there for so long.

Stefan wasn't Alex. Stefan was the most loyal friend she'd ever had and no way would she compare the two men because Alex didn't even deserve the time of her thoughts.

What did deserve her thoughts were those blasted designs. Something just wasn't clicking. She'd never encountered this before, where all of the drawings weren't up to her own standards of perfection. Granted, they may be okay for some designers, but Victoria prided herself on flawless, shockingly stunning designs before she let anyone see them, and she wasn't going to change her ways with this new bridal collection.

She wanted her team back in L.A. to gasp with awe when they saw what she'd come up with. Unfortunately, if she took these current drawings to the table, her associates would only gasp in fright.

On the bright side, her random drawings of various forms of the Alexander family crest were quite impressive, if she did say so herself. Too bad that wasn't her main focus.

Soon-to-be brides around the world were waiting with high expectations to see what Victoria Alexander, Princess and almost Queen of Galini Isle, would come up with for the launching of her new line.

Maybe if she added a touch more lace. Lace said romance, but too much could scream tacky. Perhaps longer trains like so many girls dreamed of. Grown women still kept that little girl fairy tale in their mind. Their wedding day was supposed to be magical, and it all started with the dress because it set the tone.

Warm, strong hands cupped her shoulders and Victoria jumped.

"Easy."

She turned in Stefan's arms and smiled. "I didn't hear you come in."

His eyes dipped down to the V in her nightgown and a wicked grin spread across his lips. "Why cover up? Inside this room there should be a no-clothes rule."

Victoria rolled her eyes. "I barely get them on before you take them off."

"Exactly," he agreed, squeezing her almost-bare shoulders. "It's a waste of time. So tell me what had your mind so preoccupied?"

Reaching up, Victoria grabbed his forearms and held on. Sometimes it was just nice to have his strength, his shoulder to lean on. He never judged her and always listened with the compassion that only a best friend could.

"I've just hit a rough spot with the designs." Fear gripped her at the thought of being stuck in a rut, at the idea that she may be tapped out at the moment in her career she needed her creativity most. "This has never happened."

"You're stressing yourself," Stefan told her. "Take another day off to think about it. For that matter, take the rest of our time here off. Maybe once we get back to L.A., when you're in your element, the ideas will flow."

She hoped, but she couldn't count on what-ifs to get her through her career. Idly sitting by while waiting for something spectacular to jump in her mind wasn't how she worked. But taking a few days off couldn't hurt. It's not like the designs could get worse.

Offering a smile, she nodded. "You're right. I probably just need to get home."

Stefan slid her straps down her arms, the feather-soft touch of his fingertips she'd so quickly grown used to sending shivers all over her body. And her body never failed to respond to him since they'd first made love in the theater.

Made love? Yes, she felt confident using that phrase—

though she doubted Stefan would be. She loved him as her best friend, and the special relationship they had was unique. Granted this marriage may not be like many others, but at least they had a strong bond that was lacking in so many other couples.

"Now, since we have through the end of the week to enjoy this honeymoon phase," Stefan said, backing her toward the four-poster bed, "what do you say we continue making use of this alone time?"

And who could argue with a sexy Greek prince?

Seven

Stefan knew he wouldn't get out of Galini Isle without his entourage following him. While he was used to the guards being underfoot, now that he was king—or very soon to be—they took the role even more seriously.

Victoria didn't seem to mind the extras at her impressive Hollywood Hills home. Then again, her mind hadn't been on much else other than her designs. She'd drawn on the flight, she'd stayed up all hours of the night back in Greece, and she was still struggling.

Stefan hated to see her being so hard on herself. They'd been back in L.A. for only a few hours and she was already downtown at her office speaking with some of her staff.

The woman was a workaholic, but he admired her more than nearly anyone he knew. He also had a little surprise for her, hopefully to help get her creativity flowing in the direction she needed.

"Sir."

Stefan turned from the view of the city and faced the open living area to see his assistant, Hector, standing in the arched doorway.

"Yes?"

The man, who had been assistant to his father before his death, stepped forward.

"If you have a moment, Sir, we need to go over your schedule of events while we are in the States."

Stefan nodded. "Has something changed, Hector? I know Victoria and I are scheduled for the homeless shelter and a library appearance to help with funding."

"Yes, sir, but Her Highness's alma mater called and wanted to know if you both could put in an appearance. They were hoping to have a special dinner to honor the two of you. It won't be for a couple of weeks if you agree, because we'd need time to set up security."

Stefan sighed. "Let me ask her, but I don't think it will be a problem," he told Hector. "I can let you know by this evening. I don't want to disrupt her while she's at work."

Hector bowed. "Of course, sir. I will check for a spot on the schedule that will accommodate both of you should she agree."

When Hector quieted but remained standing and staring, Stefan smiled. "Is there something else?"

Hector's lips barely lifted into a grin, but he merely nodded. "You know I don't like to put my nose into anyone's business, but—"

Stefan chuckled. "It's your job to do so, yet you apologize for it every time you interfere. There's always a valid reason, so let's hear what it is."

Stefan gestured to the wraparound sofa and took a seat. "Something is on your mind because you've waited until Victoria left to come to me."

The elderly man sat, not fully relaxing because he remained on the edge of the cushions. "With Victoria gone, perhaps this would be a perfect time to call one of her brothers."

Stefan shrugged. "I will. But, I'd like to see them in person. They don't normally do documentaries, so I need to present all the facts before they can make a decision."

"Have you told Victoria about your idea yet?" Hector asked.

Shaking his head, Stefan replied, "No. She's so busy with work, and this really doesn't involve her."

Hector came to his feet. "Everything in your life now involves her. I wouldn't keep this to yourself too much longer, Your Majesty."

As was custom, Hector bowed before leaving the room.

His loyal assistant was under the illusion the marriage with Victoria was genuine, so of course he thought this idea involved her. Stefan would tell Victoria if her brothers agreed to the film. But right now she was busy and she'd already done so much by taking on this marriage and title. He wasn't going to pile more on her plate. He had to speak to Bronson and Anthony first, and he didn't want Victoria to feel as if she were obligated to help or caught in the middle.

Would they even go for something like this? Stefan didn't know Anthony very well, but he knew Bronson well enough to ask if he would entertain the idea.

A documentary with the Dane and Price names behind it would no doubt kill any suspicion that the film wasn't thoroughly researched and executed. That reputation of the filmmakers would certainly carry a lot of clout in clearing up the speculation of his father's involvement in his mother's untimely death.

Just because his father had admitted an extramarital affair, that didn't mean he'd planned an accident to remove his own wife from the picture so he could be with his mistress. Nor did it mean his mother had taken her own life. The curvy roads were slick, the brakes needed changing—a fact that had come out later from the police report—and his mother had insisted on not using a driver that day. The series of events led up to a tragedy, but Stefan refused to blame his father.

Oh, he'd blamed him at the time. Yelled and cursed at him for not loving his mother enough and for going around having an affair, but once Stefan saw the grief, the anguish that his father had gone through, even up to his own death, Stefan realized that his father was only human. His father may have strayed from the marriage once, but the man had been completely in love with his wife.

Stefan came to his feet again and moved to the floor-to-ceiling window, where he admired a view of the city in the distance. Somewhere in the crazy overpopulated town was his wife, his best friend. He wanted her opinion, but she had so much on her plate already and he hated to bother her with his own issues. Wasn't she already going above and beyond by helping him secure the crown and keep his country independent? He didn't want to make her feel like she needed to step in and persuade her brothers to agree to the film. Besides, as of this point, taking the blemish off his father's reputation didn't concern her.

Right now he wanted her to concentrate on her designs, on letting her creativity flow and her natural spirit shine through. She'd already done enough for him, and he wasn't going to ask for another favor for a really long time…unless he asked her to don a certain type of lingerie, and that didn't count as a favor when the enjoyment was mutual.

Raking a hand through his hair, Stefan recalled that Victoria's mother was planning a dinner party tomorrow. If the right time presented itself, he'd approach Bronson, but this wasn't something he'd announce at the table. He really did want to keep this quiet until he knew for sure this was a project Bronson and Anthony were willing to take on.

As the next king of Galini Isle, Stefan felt it was not only his duty as the son of a man wrongfully accused, but he also knew telling the truth was the right thing to do to keep his family's name and honor one of integrity.

And he hoped like hell that intruder on his property had taken the threat seriously, otherwise he'd have a whole new mess on his hands. He already had enough to deal with without worrying if his country was secure. So far this marriage was getting him closer and closer to his title. He couldn't lose it now.

As he glanced around the spacious, brightly decorated living room, he couldn't help but wonder what would happen at the end of the six-month period. Would Victoria stay with him? He had to admit, being married to his best friend was much better than he ever would've dreamed. And once they put in a few royal appearances now that their honeymoon phase was over and they were in L.A., Tori would get an even better sampling of what being royalty truly meant. Perhaps she wouldn't like all the hype and responsibilities.

He moved to a built-in bookcase and gazed over the snapshots of Victoria with her family and friends through the years. There were even a couple shots of the two of them together. In one they were laughing, Victoria's hand on his chest. The captured scene ran through his mind and he recalled that day so vividly. He'd come to visit her—it was actually one of the times he'd been about to tell her he wanted to explore a physical relationship. They'd been at a restaurant opening for a mega-movie star who had started a chain, and the media was swarming, waiting to get pictures of all the rich and famous.

He'd pulled her aside and asked her if they could skip the event. When she'd told him it was rude, he told her he'd rather be having a root canal without painkiller and she'd started laughing. Someone in the press had snapped the picture, and it had ended up in several media outlets with speculation that the two of them were more than friends.

But now fate had handed him this opportunity, and he didn't intend to screw it up. While he may not have married Victoria for love, he did respect her, and she was a perfect match for him. After all, she'd grown up in the spotlight as well, and they knew going in that their privacy was limited.

Besides, Victoria had her own life goals and issues to keep her occupied. Which was why he'd keep this documentary idea to himself until he found out if anything more would come of it.

He hoped the opportunity would arise tomorrow night to discuss possibilities with Bronson so he could finally bury his parents in his heart with the respect they both deserved.

Frustrated didn't even come close to describing the emotions swirling inside her.

Victoria let herself into her Hollywood Hills home and smiled at Stefan's permanent bodyguard/assistant positioned by the door. That would take some getting used to, but she was technically on her way to being a queen, so just one more thing she'd have to deal with…eventually. Right now she'd put it on the back burner because she didn't have the time or the energy to even think about her royal crown or any of the duties expected of her.

Her wedding gown designs were improving but still not to the point where she was ready to start whipping out her needle and thread.

Her team had bounced around ideas all day, and by the time four o'clock rolled around, Victoria was ready to strangle herself with a bolt of satin.

She bypassed the living area and headed straight up the wide, curved marble staircase that led to the second-story bedrooms. She assumed Stefan was around somewhere because his guard was at his post.

When she went into her walk-in closet, she slid off her Ferragamo pumps and sank her toes into the plush carpet. After unzipping her sheath dress, she folded it onto the shelf, where she had a pile that needed to go to the cleaners. Obviously something she'd forgotten to have done before her whirlwind proposal, marriage and step up the royal ladder.

Did royalty even worry about such mundane things as dry cleaning? Of course, people may think a member of the prestigious Dane family didn't, either.

Bracing her hands on the shoe island in her closet, Victoria bowed her head and sighed. She'd never felt out of control, never felt so overwhelmed that she wanted to burst into tears, but she was definitely there now.

How had her life become so out of control? How had all of her decisions, goals and dreams slipped away and turned into something else she didn't even recognize? She'd never had a problem designing before. But now that she was married and struggling with her rapidly growing emotions, she just couldn't concentrate.

Between work and Stefan, she was a mess of jumbled-up nerves.

Tears pricked her eyes, her throat burned and she shook her head. No. Tears solved nothing and feeling sorry for herself wouldn't help put life back on track where she was comfortable.

"Well, this is nice to see." Stefan entered the closet,

eyes roaming over her matching lace bra and panty set she was left standing in. But when his gaze landed back on her face, all joking and sexual looks vanished. "What's wrong? Are you okay?"

He closed the gap between them, taking her in his arms and holding her against his chest. And wasn't that just like him? Always ready to comfort, always ready to rescue the distressed damsel?

Victoria sniffed. "I'm just being overly dramatic today. Chalk it up to being female."

"Well, honey, you've been female the whole time I've known you, and it takes a lot to bring a strong woman like you to tears." He eased back, swiped at her damp cheeks and stared into her eyes with the compassion she'd always known from him. "Want to talk about it? Is it work?"

She had to be honest. He was her husband, after all, so they should share everything. And in some ways he knew her better than she knew herself, so he would most likely know if she was holding something back.

"I think everything just hit me," she told him. "Work, marriage. It's all moving so fast, I don't feel like I'm in control anymore."

He kissed her forehead. "You're in control, Tori. You just always put this pressure on yourself to excel and be the best, which is great, but sometimes you need to give yourself a break."

She studied his face, that handsome face that so many women dreamed about, and smiled. "Is that what you would do? Take a break?"

He shrugged. "Probably not, but I don't like to see you upset."

"You don't get upset?"

"Upset? No. I do get angry, which fuels me to work harder."

Her smile spread wider and she tilted her head.

"I get it," he said, laughing. "Those were angry tears?"

"Frustrated tears," she corrected. "But at this point, same thing."

He leaned forward, kissed her gently and stepped back. "Why don't you throw on some clothes and meet me downstairs."

Comfortable with her body, Victoria placed her hands on her hips. "Now I know the honeymoon's over." She laughed. "I'm standing here nearly naked and you're telling me to throw on clothes."

Heat instantly filled his eyes as he raked his gaze over her. "Oh, believe me, I'm having a very hard time being noble here, but sex isn't what you need right now. Just get dressed and come downstairs. Or wear that, but my guard will see more of you than I'm willing to share."

Stefan turned and left, leaving her staring after him.

Some married women didn't have a tenth of the connection she had with Stefan. And even though they married under less than traditional circumstances, she knew she had a good thing going…if she could just keep her emotions in check.

She threw on a pair of white shorts and a flowy green top. After sliding into a pair of gold sandals, she made her way downstairs. She didn't see the guard by the door, but she knew he wasn't far. Thankfully he did try to stay out of sight and give them privacy.

Victoria saw Stefan through the patio doors. She crossed the living room and walked out the open set of French doors to the warmth of the evening SoCal sunshine.

Stefan sat on one of the plush outdoor sofas she'd recently added and Victoria took a seat next to him.

"What's that?" She pointed to the small folder he held

on his lap. "Did you draw some secret, magical designs you're willing to share with me?"

He laid the folder on her legs. "Open it."

Intrigued, she pulled back the cover flap and gasped. "Stefan…" Page after page, she shuffled through designs and even some of the crazy doodling she'd done as a teen. "Where did you get these?"

"I kept them."

She eyed the papers, yellowing around the edges, and looked at him. "But…why?"

With a shrug, he turned to face her. "When you came to visit, you were always doodling and talking about being a designer. Sometimes I'd keep the papers you left laying around. I knew you'd make a name for yourself because you've always been so determined. You had such *pathos,* a passion, for designing." He laughed. "Even then you would sketch random images to help you think clearer."

Emotions clogged her throat and, dammit, for the second time today she was going to cry. Even all those years ago he'd had faith in her.

"These are, well…terrible." She laughed through watery tears.

He put a hand over hers, taking his other hand to cup her chin and hold his gaze. "They may be terrible to you, but they were your dream, Victoria. Look at them. Look close. You may see something ugly, but I see a promise that a young girl made to herself."

Oh, God. How did the man always know what to say?

"You're right," she whispered. "I just can't believe you kept them."

His hand dropped from her face. "Maybe I wanted to keep them so that when you became famous I could sell them."

A laugh burst from her. "You're so rich, you never would've thought to sell these."

His eyes settled on hers, and the heat she saw staring back at her had the smile dying on her lips.

"Maybe I saw the talent," he told her. "Maybe the crush I had on you prompted me to keep them."

Victoria's heart clenched. "Stefan, you didn't have feelings for me then."

"I did," he confessed. "I may have been young and foolish, but I did care more for you then than any other girl I knew."

Victoria couldn't handle this. Couldn't think what that revelation could've meant for the course of their relationship had he told her his feelings at the time.

"I'd hate to think if we dated seriously as teens or in our twenties we would've lost each other as friends. Besides that, you would've disappointed all those ladies," she joked. "Good thing you grew out of it, huh?"

Something she didn't recognize, or didn't want to recognize, flitted through his eyes. "Yeah, good thing."

As Victoria looked down at her designs, she remembered dreaming as she'd been drawing them. Dreaming of her wedding day, of her groom waiting at the end of the aisle.

And in all her dreaming, that man had been a prince. A prince who knew her inside and out, who cared for her as a friend and lover, who would do anything to make her happy.

Victoria could no longer deny that she was teetering on the edge of falling in love with her husband, and that out-of-control emotion scared her to death.

Eight

Stefan sat back and watched the chaos—otherwise known as dinner with his in-laws—which was becoming a little too hearth and homey to him between the newlyweds and the babies.

Bronson and his wife, Mia, took turns holding and feeding their little Bella, whom he believed Victoria told him was almost a year old now.

Victoria's other brother, Anthony, was holding histwo-month-old baby girl as Charlotte fed the eighteen-month-old Lily in her high chair.

And through all the cries, spit-ups and diaper changes, the Grand Dane of Hollywood, Olivia Dane, sat at the head of the long, elegantly accessorized table and smiled. Either the woman didn't realize that in a year or so her immaculate Beverly Hills home would be a giant playground or she was so in love with her family she didn't care that her fine china could end up in millions of shards on her marble floor.

"Bella, no, honey."

Stefan glanced to the other end of the table where Bella was throwing some orange, liquid concoction onto the floor. Why did all baby food look like already recycled dinner in a jar?

"Oh, don't worry about it." Olivia waved a hand. "Marie can clean it up when she clears the table later."

"No, I'll get it." Mia came to her feet and whipped out a bunch of wipes from who knows where. Obviously moms had a knack for always being ready for anything.

"I think Carly needs a diaper change," Charlotte said as she came to her feet, holding her baby to her chest. "I'll be right back."

Anthony stood, taking the infant. "Let me. Go ahead and finish eating."

Victoria laughed. "I love seeing my big strong brothers taking care of baby poop and puke."

Stefan dropped his fork to his plate with a clatter. "And that's the end of my dinner."

Patting his leg, Victoria laughed. "Oh, toughen up, Prince. Your day will come."

A shudder coursed through him at the thought of children being written into the archaic laws of his land. To be honest, he was surprised they weren't, but at the same time he was thankful.

And just as quickly as that shudder spread through him, another took over as he glanced to Victoria's smiling face. An image of her swollen with his child did something unrecognizable to his belly, his heart. He didn't want to examine the unwanted emotions any further because if she were ever swollen with a baby, it more than likely wouldn't be his.

She was on birth control. Besides, they hadn't even discussed kids. They hadn't discussed beyond the six months, other than to joke, much less anything permanent or long term.

"You okay?" Victoria asked in a low whisper. "You're staring with a weird look on your face."

He shook off the thoughts and returned her warm smile. "Fine. I admit I'm not used to babies, so all of this is new to me."

"We weren't, either," she admitted, placing her cloth napkin onto the table. "But we adjusted quickly, and I couldn't imagine our lives without all these little cuties."

He studied her face once again, wondering if she did indeed have babies in her dream for life. Had he put that aspiration on hold when he'd selfishly asked her to be his wife? Hell, he hadn't even asked, he'd basically begged…a moment he wasn't very proud of, but nonetheless he'd had no choice. Once she'd mentioned wanting a family someday, but was that still a desire? And if so, where would that leave them and their marriage?

Discussing her fantasies of a family would have to wait. For one thing he didn't think the topic was appropriate conversation at the dinner table with her family, and he had to speak with Anthony or Bronson, hopefully both, about his documentary idea.

Unfortunately, the right time had not presented itself.

Olivia scooted her chair back, the heavy wood sliding over the dark marble floor. "If everyone is done eating, we can go into the living room where the kids can play on the floor."

Stefan came to his feet and pulled Victoria's chair out for her.

"You married a prince and he pulls out your chair," Mia said, then turned to Bronson. "Are you taking notes?"

Bronson laughed, and glanced at Stefan. "Give a guy a break, would ya? You're making me look bad."

Victoria wrapped an arm around Stefan's waist and squeezed. "Can't help it if my man is always a gentleman, Bron. Looks like you need to step up your game."

Stefan didn't miss the way Bronson studied how Victoria was holding on to him, and he didn't miss the way the look of surprise resonated when Victoria said "my man."

Just where were they headed? And why the hell was it important for him to know? He was a man for crying out loud. The sex was amazing, she wasn't demanding of his time and she hadn't asked him for anything. Why was he suddenly analyzing everything like a damn woman?

Anthony came back in as they were all moving from the room. "She's all ready to go," he announced, handing Carly back to Charlotte.

Olivia went to get Lily from her high chair when Bronson spoke up.

"You ladies go on ahead," he said. "I'd like to talk with Anthony and Stefan."

Okay, so now the moment of opportunity had presented itself, but Stefan had a feeling this wasn't going to be the time to bring up his favor, not with the look Bronson was giving him.

Because he tended to be spiteful, Stefan leaned down and gave Victoria a kiss—and not a simple see-ya-later peck.

What he and Victoria decided to do with their marriage was nobody else's business, and he would fight for their privacy no matter who he went up against.

"Fine with me," Olivia said. "I'm just glad you're all not talking about the film."

"We just haven't gotten to it, yet," Anthony piped up.

"We will. Don't worry. We're only a few months into the shoot, still plenty to discuss."

"Yes, I'm aware of the time frame." Olivia rolled her eyes and adjusted a wiggly Lily in her arms. "I should've known better than to think we'd get through the night without shop talk."

"Play nice with the other boys," Victoria said with a wink.

Obviously she missed the way Bronson was throwing daggers. "Always," Stefan promised.

Once the ladies and babies were gone, Bronson crossed his arms over his chest. "What the hell kind of game are you playing with my sister?"

"No game." Relaxed, Stefan rested a hand on the back of his chair. "And before you get all big brother on me, let me tell you that I will not share how Victoria and I treat this marriage. It's none of your concern."

Anthony cleared his throat. "Excuse me, but did I miss something in the two minutes it took to change a diaper?"

"Stefan seemed to be on more than friendly terms with Victoria," Bronson supplied. "I'm just trying to make sure he's not playing a game with her. She's been hurt before."

"Bronson." Anthony sighed. "Simmer down. Stefan and Victoria are grown adults. If they want to…whatever, then that's their business."

Bronson cursed. "Did either of you pay attention when that jerk broke her heart? Did you hear her crying? See the way her self-esteem lowered? I won't watch someone I love go through that again."

Guilt tore at Stefan that Victoria had gone through all of that and he hadn't been able to help her more. But with his father's illness and death, there was just no way to be in two places at once.

Just the thought of her crying over some jerk who wasn't

worth her tears made his gut clench. She deserved all the happiness and love life could give.

"Listen," Stefan said. "We know what we're doing. Yes, we've grown closer than just friends, but that's our business. I won't explain our actions to you or anyone else."

Anthony chuckled. "Guess that settles that discussion."

Refusing to back down, Stefan continued to stare at Bronson. No, he hadn't heard the cries from Victoria because she'd always been so strong on the phone, but he knew she'd been hurt. A woman like Victoria who loved with her whole heart and was loyal to a fault couldn't come out of a relationship like that and not be scarred.

And he was no better than Alex. Wasn't he using her as well to gain a title? The only difference was he'd told her up front.

"I won't let her get hurt again," Bronson said. "I hate to sound all big and bad, but I had to tell you where I stand."

Stefan nodded. "Duly noted."

"If you two are done kissing and making up, can we get back to our family night?" Anthony asked.

Stefan knew an opening when he saw one. "Actually, I'd like to run something by you two since I have you here together."

Bronson gestured toward the doors. "Let's go out on the patio then."

Bronson led the way out the glass double doors and onto the stone patio surrounded by lush plants and flowers and a trickling waterfall.

Stefan took a seat in one of the iron chairs and waited for Victoria's brothers to get comfortable on the outdoor sofa across from him.

"What's up?" Bronson asked.

"I know you're both aware that my mother passed away when I was younger and there was speculation that she ei-

ther committed suicide or my father may have had something to do with the accident."

When both men nodded, Stefan went on. "I have wanted
to clear my family's name because my father never would
go public before. He just wanted the rumors to die down,
and he feared if he kept bringing it up people would assume he was covering his own tracks. Well, now that he's
gone, I want to shed some light on the situation and prove
that he had nothing to do with her accident, nor did she,
and they did indeed love each other very much."

Anthony eased forward in his seat. "What do you have
in mind?"

"I know that you two don't normally take on projects
like this, but I was hoping we could discuss working on a
documentary." Stefan wanted to hold his breath and wait
for a response, but at the same time, he wanted to keep
talking to convince them. "I have proof my father had
nothing to do with the accident and that my mother wasn't
depressed or suicidal. There's not a doubt in my mind that
while, yes, he had an affair, he was not trying to get rid
of my mother. The affair had been years before the accident, and when she died, I saw him go through pure hell.
I just want to clear his reputation and go into my title with
a clean slate for the Alexander name."

"You sound certain that this was an accident," Bronson said. "I'd be willing to discuss this further. I may not
typically do documentaries, but that doesn't mean I'm not
open to the possibility."

"I agree," Anthony said. "Could we set up a time to talk
about this in greater detail? I mean, we'd have to look at
the police reports and interview credible witnesses who
are willing to come forward."

"I can provide you with anything you need." A spear
of relief spread through Stefan. "Victoria and I are going

to be here for another few months, so whenever you two are free, let me know. We have a few engagements coming up, but our schedule in the States is still pretty light. I can work around your shooting times."

As Victoria's brothers discussed their upcoming schedules, Stefan couldn't help but be overly thrilled. He had no idea they would be so open to the idea and respond so quickly. Though they hadn't agreed to anything, they hadn't shot down the idea.

Moving forward with this project and his coronation, Stefan knew that if everything fell in the right place, his life would be just as he'd pictured it. Clean family reputation and his country secured in the Alexander name.

What more could he want?

Nine

"So what did my brothers talk to you about?"

Victoria's fingertip circled the top of her wineglass as she eased forward in her seat. Stefan had taken her to her office, then afterward she wanted to show him a new restaurant that had opened. They were just having drinks and a dessert, but sometimes it was nice to get out of the house and enjoy society like a normal person—or as normal as one could be between her iconic family and her royal status.

With the outdoor seating and sunset in the distance, the ambiance screamed romance...even if a bodyguard was seated a few tables away trying to blend in.

Yeah, this was now her "normal" life.

Stefan shrugged. "Nothing much."

Victoria glared at him across the intimate table. "You're lying."

His eyes came up to meet hers as he reached across and

took her hand from her glass. He kissed her fingertips one at a time, and she relished the familiar shivers that crept over her body at his simple, yet passionate actions. But she wasn't letting the question go.

"Stefan?"

Lacing his hand through hers, he smiled. "Yes?"

"You've never been a good liar, and all this charm isn't working on me."

He quirked a dark brow. "Oh, yeah? I guarantee your heart rate is up, and I know you want to kiss me because you're watching my lips."

Busted.

"I'm watching your lips because I'm waiting for the truth to emerge from them." No way would she admit that he could do so little and turn her on. "Did Bronson get too protective?"

"We simply had a misunderstanding, and now we don't," Stefan said. "Men don't stay upset like women. He just wanted to discuss something, and it's over."

Victoria would make a special trip to Bronson's house. No way was she going to be sheltered or coddled by her brother.

"What was Anthony there for? Peacemaker?"

Stefan smiled. "He is quite a bit more laid back, yes?"

"He wasn't when Charlotte left him," Victoria replied. "I'd never seen a man so relentless on keeping his family together. He would've walked through hell for her."

"I'd do the same for you."

Victoria jerked at his automatic, non-hesitant response. Surely he wasn't developing feelings for her...not like she had for him. God, if he ever found out she'd fallen in love with him their friendship would be strained. Right now, with the playful sex and always hanging out, they had a good thing. No way would she put this relationship in jeopardy by revealing her true feelings.

"Stefan…"

"I realize their marriage is quite different from ours," he told her, stroking the back of her hand with his thumb. "But you're the one woman in my life that I would sacrifice anything for."

This was the point in a conversation where some women would think this was a major confession of love…Victoria was not one of those women. She knew Stefan better than any other woman did. He was a charmer, a playboy, but most of all, he did love her. In the way all best friends love each other.

But the romantic in her, the smidgen of a sparkle that hadn't been diminished by Alex, sighed and smiled internally at the idea that her husband would sacrifice anything for her.

"I'm ready to head home," he said, giving her a look that she knew had nothing to do with friendship and everything to do with lust. "Why don't you finish that drink."

"Forget the drink," she told him with a slight grin. "I have wine at home."

She grabbed her bag off the back of the iron chair and stood at the same time he was there to help her from her seat. When she turned, their lips were a breath apart and Stefan sealed them together briefly but firmly, loaded with promise.

"We need to leave before I really give the media something to print," he murmured against her mouth.

She swayed slightly and his warm, strong hand came around and settled firmly against her bare back where her summer dress dipped low. The heat from his touch did nothing to help her wave of dizziness brought on by pure desire.

She'd never had even a fraction of this passion with Alex. Mercy, she was in trouble.

"I've got you, Victoria. Always."

The heat in his eyes made her wish this were more than a marriage of convenience or a businesslike arrangement. But she was too afraid to explore that deeper level of emotion until she could see just where they stood at the end of the six months.

With a smile, she nodded. "I'm ready."

He led her from the cozy outdoor restaurant to the car that was waiting for them at the curb. Victoria's driver had been replaced with one of Stefan's guards, and the man instantly appeared, opened the door and let them into the backseat. As she slid across, her dress rode up high on her thigh. Stefan came in beside her and placed a hand over hers before she could pull the material down.

"Leave it," he said, hitting the button to put up the soundproof one-way window divider. "I have the best idea."

Oh, Lord.

As the guard brought the engine to life and pulled from the curb, Stefan turned on the intercom to tell the man to take his time heading back to Hollywood Hills.

An hour in the backseat of the limo with a man as seductive and sensual as Stefan? Victoria's body hummed and tightened in anticipation.

When he clicked the button off, he turned, sliding his other hand up her thigh and pushing both sides of the dress to her hips.

"Convenient you wore a dress," he murmured, staring down at her bare legs and the peek of yellow satin panties that were exposed. "Hate to waste this opportunity."

As his hands squeezed her thighs, his lips captured hers. The wine they'd drank tasted so good on his tongue, intoxicating her to the point she didn't care they were in the back of her car getting ready to have what she hoped was hot, wild sex.

When her hands came up around his neck, he eased back.

"Scoot down in the seat," he whispered. "I want this to be all about you."

And there was no woman in her right mind who would turn down an invitation like that.

Victoria did as he asked as he eased her legs farther apart. In his strong grasp, she felt the tug on her panties until she heard the material give way and tear.

"You owe me a pair of panties," she joked.

As he settled onto the floor between her legs, he gazed up at her beneath heavy lids. Bright eyes pierced hers as he said, "I prefer you without them."

With his wide shoulders holding her thighs apart, Victoria wondered if they were really doing this. Were they actually going to get intimate in the back of a car? And not only that, but this was far more personal than sex. Was Stefan taking their relationship to the next level? Obviously yes, but was he even aware of how personal this act was?

She didn't care and couldn't think anymore the second his finger slid over her, parting her a second before his mouth fixed on her.

Instinct had her sliding down even more. The way he made love to her with his mouth had her gripping his shoulders, the edge of the seat, the door handle, anything to keep from screaming at the overwhelming sensations rocketing through her.

In no time, her body quivered, bursts of pure bliss shooting through her. Stefan stayed with her until the last of her tremors ceased.

Reality hit her as he literally crawled back up her body.

Those talented hands slid over her curves, and he took a seat next to her, lifting her up to settle on his lap. As he nestled her into the crook of his arm, she tucked her face against his warm neck.

"You're not seriously going to try to hide the fact you're completely turned on, are you?" she asked.

His soft chuckle vibrated against his hard chest. "Kind of hard to hide it, but I wanted this to be about you. We can continue at home if you'd like."

Victoria lifted her head, wondering if Stefan realized how this moment, even though it was in the back of a car, had changed the course of their relationship. Did he get this intimate with all of his women? She closed her eyes briefly, trying to block out the instant mental images. If she had anything to say about it, he'd not be with any other woman ever again. He'd put the ball in her court at the end of the six months, and she was seriously considering staying, making him see just how this marriage could and should work for all the right reasons—which had absolutely nothing to do with his title.

But if she stayed, could she be a loyal, devoted queen and still design? She couldn't give up her own goals to cater to his, but she wanted this marriage to work. There had to be a way.

Stefan stared down at Victoria. Holy hell. What had just happened? He'd meant to be giving, passionate, but something changed...something he couldn't put his finger on. The way she looked at him with her face flushed and her lids heavy made him want to rip off both their clothes and satisfy her once again before finally relieving himself of this constant state of arousal he seemed to have around her lately.

"I want to make you happy, Stefan," she told him, stroking her fingertip down his cheek and along his jawline.

Yeah, something definitely changed. She wasn't smiling, wasn't playful. Her words, her actions were from the heart.

Was she sinking more into this marriage than she should? Granted, he'd always wondered how they'd be together, but if she was falling for him, could he ever give her that deeper, loving, marital bond in return? He honestly didn't think he had it in him.

God, he didn't want to hurt her. Right now all he wanted was to enjoy the way they were living together. Why couldn't that be enough?

"You've made me happy by helping me, Victoria."

"You know I could never tell you no," she replied, flashing him a sexy grin. "Besides, I'm getting what I want, too."

Friends and business. That's what this had to be...no matter what flutter he thought he felt in his chest earlier. The emotion had to be ignored. Victoria was too important to him to risk their bond on something as questionable as love.

As the driver wound his way up the Hollywood Hills, Victoria sat nestled against his side. He loved the familiar lavender scent that always surrounded her and the sexy way she would sigh as she crossed her legs and curved her body more into his. And now that he knew she wore nothing beneath that dress, well, *sexy* was a vast understatement.

He would let her show him her appreciation when they returned home. For now he needed to come to grips with the fact that he didn't want to get too involved in this marriage on a foundation he couldn't control, but when he'd taken their lovemaking to another level only moments ago, he'd done just that.

And he had no one to blame but himself.

Ten

Victoria's smile never faltered, and they'd been serving meals to homeless veterans for the past two hours. Her beauty radiated throughout the entire gymnasium of the old school where the Vets chatted and tried to capture a piece of her time.

He didn't blame them. Victoria was so easy to talk to, so easy to be around—the crowd would've never known that minutes before they'd come in she was nervous about fulfilling her first royal duty. He'd told her to be herself because she was a natural.

As she put the group at ease with her thankfulness for their services and the occasional gentle hug, Stefan continued to refill plates and cups. He let her use her charm on the room, and all the while the cameras were eating this up and proving to the world that she was the perfect woman for this position.

"Sir." Hector came up behind him and whispered, "The

cameraman would like you to stay closer to Victoria so he can capture your charity work together. That was the point of the visit."

Stefan glanced around the room of men and women who had given their all for their country…something Stefan could relate to. Guilt weighed heavily on his shoulders.

"I'm not here for a photo op, Hector." Stefan turned to face his assistant and lowered his voice. "I'm here to assist these people and show them that my wife and I care about them. I don't give a damn about the photographer. If he wants a good shot and story, tell him to take pictures of all these people who have been forgotten."

Hector folded his hands in front of him. "Sir, the whole reason for coming was to showcase your role as your country's leader and so the world could see you and Victoria as a united front."

Stefan sighed. "We are a united front, Hector. Tell the photographer he can nab a picture of us when we're done. We'll pose for one then. Until that point, we are here to help, not for some show for the world so they just *think* we are helping."

Hector nodded with a slight bow and walked off. When Stefan turned back with the pitcher of tea, an elderly man wearing a navy hat with his ship's name embroidered across the top was looking at him with tears in his eyes.

"Thank you," the man said.

Stefan looked down at the elderly man, who had scarred hands and a weathered face. "Nothing to thank me for, sir. I'm the one who needs to thank you."

The man used the edge of the table and the back of his chair to come to his feet. Stefan stepped back to give him room.

"I've never met royalty before, sir," the man said. "It is an honor to have you and your beautiful wife here. And for you two to be so caring…well, it just touches an old guy like me to know there are still people who give a damn."

Stefan held out his hand, waited for the man to shake it. "What's your name?"

"Lieutenant Raymond Waits," he replied, straightening his shoulders.

"I will personally see to it that this shelter is funded for as long as possible." Stefan would make it happen no matter what. "I will also make sure my wife and I schedule a stop here twice a year when we are in the States."

The handshake quickly turned to an embrace as Raymond put his free arm around Stefan. He hadn't meant to get on a soapbox, but dammit, he understood loyalty to a country, and these vets deserved respect and love.

"Now, I better get back to refilling drinks or you'll be my only friend here," Stefan said when the vet pulled back, trying to look away as if embarrassed by the tears in his eyes.

Raymond nodded, taking his seat. As Stefan moved on, he glanced up to see Victoria watching him from across the room, and he didn't miss the moisture that had gathered in her own eyes. Obviously she'd seen the emotional moment.

Stefan smiled and winked at her, trying to lighten the mood because the last thing he wanted was for her to believe he was some sort of hero. He was just doing what was right.

By the time they needed to leave to get across town to the library for a fund-raiser, Stefan had already discussed the funding with Hector, who was putting a plan into motion. Now this is what being powerful was all about. Why have such control if you couldn't use it for the greater good?

They posed for just a few pictures with some of the soldiers and promised to return. Stefan hated that a piece of his heart was left with this group of remarkable men and women. He wanted to rule his country while keeping his emotions in check, not tear up when he came across charity cases.

Victoria swiped tears away as they headed to their waiting car. Once settled inside, he pulled her against his side and sighed.

"You okay?" he asked.

"You're amazing." She sniffed. "I don't care if the media portrays you as a bad boy, Stefan. I know the truth, and you've just revealed it to a room full of thankful vets."

He didn't want to be commended for doing what was right and good. "I wish I could do more," he said honestly. "But we'll do what we can where we can."

Tori reached up, cupping his cheek, and shifted to face him. "You're one amazing king, Stefan."

She touched her lips to his, briefly, tenderly. But he didn't want gentle, he wanted hard, fast. Now. He wanted to feel her beneath him, feel her come undone around him.

His hand slid up her bare thigh and her breath caught.

"Didn't we just do this the other day?" she asked, smiling against his mouth.

"Glad I could make an impression," he murmured. "But I plan on torturing you until we get to the library. It is across town, you know. I may even continue for the ride home afterward."

She slid a hand up over his denim-clad leg and cupped him. "Torture can be a two-way street, you know."

"I'm counting on it."

As his mouth captured hers again, his hand snaked up beneath her dress. When his fingertip traveled along the edge of her lacy panties, her legs parted. Yeah, he wanted what she was offering, but foreplay was so much fun, and he wanted to relish these next few moments of driving her wild. He'd always considered himself a giving lover, but with Victoria he wanted to focus on her and her pleasure. Everything about touching her, kissing her was so much more arousing than seeking a fast release.

Her palm slid up and down over the zipper of his jeans…a zipper that was becoming increasingly painful.

He tore his lips from hers. "Tori, you're way too good at this game."

When she put both hands on his shoulders and slid to the floor between his legs, he swallowed hard. "Way too good," he repeated.

And thankfully he'd put the divider up between them and the driver because she was reciprocating the favor he'd given her a few days ago.

How was he ever going to get over all of this if she chose to leave?

Victoria couldn't stop smiling. Finally, she'd managed to take control, shut Stefan up and make him lose his mind all at once. Yeah, she was pretty proud of herself.

The ride to the library and then home was quite memorable…for both of them.

As they walked up the brick steps toward her front door, a car pulling into the circular drive had her turning back to see who the visitor was.

Her heart stopped, her body tensing at the unwelcome guest.

No. This couldn't be happening. What was he doing here?

"Victoria?" Stefan touched her arm. "Who is it?"

Before she could answer, the car came to a stop and Alex unfolded himself from the two-door red sports car.

"I'll talk to him," Stefan told her, jaw clenching. "You can go inside."

Victoria held up a hand and shook her head. "No, you go on in."

"Like hell," she heard him mutter as she descended the steps to see what her ex could possibly want.

Victoria didn't want to play the alpha male drama game so she ignored Stefan's remark. All she cared about now was why Alex had showed up here like he still had a right to.

"Victoria," he greeted her as she came to the base of the steps. "You look beautiful as always."

Crossing her arms over her chest, she thanked God that seeing him did absolutely nothing for her.

"What are you doing here, Alex?"

His eyes darted over her shoulder, then back. "Can we talk privately?"

"You're kidding, right?" Stefan asked from behind her.

Victoria turned, gave him the silent "shut up" look, and turned back to Alex. "Whatever you want to say, say it so Stefan and I can go inside."

For the first time in his life Alex looked uncomfortable. Once again his eyes darted from Stefan to Victoria, and she knew he wasn't going to say anything as long as Stefan was around. This bulldog stare down could go on all night, and she had other plans, which involved her husband getting naked and staying that way for a long time. She wasn't going to let her ex who destroyed her ruin her evening or her life.

Victoria spun back around and walked up a few steps to Stefan before whispering, "Give me five minutes. He's harmless and he won't talk if you're glaring at him like my bodyguard."

"He hurt you, Victoria. He has no right being here."

Funny how Stefan wasn't being territorial. He was upset because Alex had broken her. God, her heart melted even more. Did he have any idea how romantic, how sexy that was?

Stefan eyed her and she was positive he was going to argue, but he leaned forward, kissed her slightly and said, "He can't touch you now."

Stefan turned and walked up the steps into the house, leaving Victoria even more stunned. But she couldn't think right now about all the amazing ways Stefan was showing her love. He may not even know it yet, but he was falling for her.

It ticked her off that her ex stood behind her. She was supposed to be seducing her husband, showing him just how good they were together. Instead she was dealing with the one man who'd used her, cut her down in public and tossed her aside as if she were useless.

Shoulders back, head held high, she faced him once again and met him at the bottom of the steps. Stefan was right; Alex couldn't hurt her again. She refused to let him have an ounce of control in her life anymore. She took pride in the fact she was stronger now, thanks to Stefan.

"You have five minutes," she told him, resuming her stance and crossing her arms.

"I made a mistake." He took a step toward her, reached out to touch her shoulder, and Victoria jerked back. "Please, Tori."

"You've got to be kidding me. First of all, I'm married."

Alex shoved his hand back in his pocket. "You don't love him like you did me."

Victoria smiled. "You're absolutely right. What I feel for Stefan is completely different. I would do anything at all for him. I've never felt so appreciated and treasured as I do with him."

"Is that the money and title talking?"

Before her mind could process what she was doing she found her open palm connecting with the side of his face.

"I will not defend myself to anyone, especially you," she told him, rubbing her thumb over her stinging hand. "Now get out of my sight before I let Stefan come back out and settle this in a very old-fashioned, clichéd way."

She didn't need to tell Alex what that was. Any man would know.

He rubbed the side of his cheek. "I didn't come to argue with you. I wanted to know if your marriage was for real, and I just couldn't imagine you fell in love with someone that fast and married. I mean, you always told me you two were only friends."

"We *were* always friends. Now I realize that Stefan was the only man for me. And this marriage is more real than anything you and I ever shared."

She didn't wait for him to respond. Victoria pivoted on her heel and marched up the steps, running smack into a hard, familiar chest, instantly enveloped by a scent she'd come to associate with her husband.

Strong hands wrapped around her biceps and pulled her flush with his body.

"It's okay," Stefan whispered. "I've got you."

He walked her into the house and she realized tears were streaming down her cheeks. Had he heard everything? Fear and worry took the place of the anger she'd felt only moments ago. She didn't want him to know how she felt yet. She couldn't chance ruining their relationship.

Any and every feeling she had for Stefan totally over-shadowed anything she'd ever had for Alex.

"We need complete privacy," Stefan murmured.

"Yes, Your Highness," one of the guards stationed inside the door replied.

Stefan swept Victoria up into his arms and she settled

her face against his neck. Alex's presence had awakened something in her, something she thought she'd never feel again. Love. But not love for her ex. No, she was utterly and completely in love with the man who carried her, the man who knew when to let silence express his care for her, the man who showed his tender, compassionate side at the shelter only an hour ago. The man who'd taken such joy in pleasuring her, in the bedroom and out.

Her husband. She knew she'd fallen for him, but this moment solidified the fact she was completely in love. And perhaps she'd been in love with her best friend since they met. On some level she knew that to be true. But now she knew without a doubt that she loved him wholeheartedly and without any reservations.

He'd given her the control over the end of their marriage and, to be honest, she wanted to make this relationship permanent. And not just permanent because they were friends and they got along in bed, but permanent because she knew Prince Stefan Alexander was her soul mate.

And Fate had given her the chance to see just how a marriage, a love life should be. Now she just had to show Stefan.

Eleven

He was the only man for her?

Dear God, what a bombshell. When the hell had she decided that? If she were having any notions of love...he couldn't even fathom where that would put them.

Stefan kicked the bedroom door closed, crossed the spacious room and gently laid Victoria on the chaise chair in front of the balcony doors. Sunshine streamed in through the windows, bathing their bedroom in bright rays.

"I'll get you some water," he told her, his voice rough.

"No." Victoria wiped her damp cheeks and sat up straighter. "I'm fine. Sorry for the tears. I was caught off guard."

Stefan stared down at Victoria, surprised that he was jealous over the ex, who was obviously out of her life for good, she was shedding tears over.

"I'm sorry it upset you to see him," he told her, easing

down on the edge of the chaise beside her hip. "I'll advise my staff to keep him away if he returns."

Victoria smiled. "I appreciate that, but I doubt he'll come back. He hates having his pride hurt, and my refusal to accept his lame apology and rush back into his arms really damaged his ego."

Her silky, golden blond hair lay over one shoulder, and his fingers itched to mess it up, to see it fanned out on her white, satin sheets as he made love to her again. She was always a stunning woman, but since they'd become intimate, her beauty had taken on a whole new level of sensuality.

But he couldn't pick up where they'd left off in the car, not when she was so upset and certainly not with the revelation he'd just heard.

"I wish you wouldn't cry," he told her, trying not to think about what he'd overheard. "That's one thing I cannot stand."

"My emotions are harder to hide than yours," she explained. "I can't just close them off, Stefan. I have feelings and sometimes they come out when I don't want them to."

He rubbed his hands over his thighs in an attempt to keep from reaching out to her. Treading lightly during these next few minutes was a must.

"I'm okay," she assured him, wiping her cheeks and pasting on a smile. "Really. Don't let Alex ruin our day."

Alex hadn't ruined the day, but her verbal epiphany had sure as hell put an unexpected spin on where they stood with this marriage—and its open ending once the six months were over.

He hated to bring up what was such a humiliating time in her life, but since Alex showed up, that had to be playing through her mind. What type of bastard would purposely have pictures taken with his new girlfriend, a pregnant one at that, while still engaged to another woman?

He was quite convinced Victoria's ex wasn't a man, but the lowest form of life for treating her the way he had. Stefan felt he deserved a shiny gold medal to add to the collection on his royal coat because he hadn't busted the guy in the face.

She turned her head, looking out the double glass doors that led to her balcony. As he watched her profile, he saw her eyes fill up again.

Well, hell. Now what had happened? This was precisely why he never got too involved with women. He just plain didn't understand the emotional roller coasters they seemed to always be on.

"I just had a bit of an epiphany, and it hit me harder than I expected."

A tight band formed around his chest and squeezed. Did that mean she truly felt what she'd told Alex about their marriage? Was she going to discuss it now? He sure as hell wasn't going to bring it up. Yeah, he was being a coward, but there was a first time for everything.

"Since you're so quiet, I'm assuming the mood is gone."

He nodded and sighed. No way could they become intimate right now, not with her emotions so high.

"I think we need to take a breather for today."

Hurt flashed in her eyes before her defiant chin lifted. "You've never been known for running away."

"I'm not running." He was sprinting. "You need some time to think." Some time to come to grips with her emotions that scared the living hell out of him.

Before she could guilt him more with her expressive blue eyes, he came to his feet, walked out into the hall, closed the door and leaned back against it. His chest ached, like someone was squeezing the breath from his lungs.

They'd only been married over a month. How in the world would they make it to the six-month mark with their feelings so at odds? Something about seeing her ex made Victoria realize her emotions were deeper than he'd thought. He only hoped she was just shocked by seeing Alex and once she truly thought about what she'd said, how she was feeling and where they needed to go from here, she'd see that maybe what she thought was romantic love was just a deeper level of friendship.

He rested his head against the solid wood door and closed his eyes. Sleeping together had changed things, but he'd had no idea Victoria would fall for him.

Stefan didn't have a clue about how to proceed from here, but he did know that if Victoria cared for him the way she thought she did, he was going to have one hell of a problem on his hands. And it had nothing to do with the crown or the documentary.

Love wasn't something he had ever experienced outside his family or his country. He certainly wouldn't try it out on the one person who meant the most to him. He couldn't risk losing Victoria's friendship by mucking it up with an emotion so questionable.

Love had no room in this marriage.

"So based on the information you sent us, we completely agree that this story shouldn't be kept silent."

Relief speared through Stefan at Bronson's statement. He'd called Victoria's brothers to see if they had time to meet last minute, but Bronson was the only one available. Anthony had to stay home with the kids because the baby was napping and Charlotte was out.

He'd had to leave the house. He couldn't face Victoria right now, not with her emotions so raw, so...gut wrenching. They needed a break and he needed to focus because sex and tears could cloud his vision.

He'd cut off his arm before he intentionally hurt her, but if she had feelings that deep for him, he wasn't sure how he could avoid damaging her already battered heart.

"Stefan?"

He focused back on Bronson, who had switched television shows for his sweet little girl, Bella. She was now enthralled in another program with crazy characters singing and dancing across the screen, making silly faces to get the toddler audience to laugh.

"Sorry," Stefan said. "Does Anthony feel the same way?"

"Absolutely." Bronson sat down on the leather sofa and stretched an arm across the back of the cushions. "We both believe that this story, if told the right way, would have the impact you want to make. Your father was simply the victim of bad timing, from the affair, to the public argument, to the death of your mother."

"So you'll take on this project?" Stefan asked, hopeful.

"If you trust Anthony and me to do the documentary justice, we'd be happy to. But, keep in mind we've never done this type of film before."

Stefan knew the two perfectionists wouldn't let him, or his country, down. Stefan wanted his people to see his family in the way he did, to see that his father was not a murderer, but a man who was grieving, a man who'd lost his wife after such a public scandal and had instantly gotten a less-than-stellar reputation.

With the beginning of his reign, Stefan wanted to wipe the slate clean and remove the dark stain from his family's name.

"You have no idea what this means to me," Stefan said. "I owe you."

Bronson eased forward in his seat across from Stefan and nodded. "You can pay me back by telling me why my sister called here in tears and my wife is currently on the phone with her."

Na pari i eychi. He should've known that this meeting wouldn't be simple.

"Victoria had a very emotional day." And wasn't that a vast understatement. "Whatever she wants to share with Mia, or you, is up to her."

Bronson sighed. "I probably don't need to tell you that Victoria is in this marriage deeper than you think."

Stefan swallowed the lump of guilt and fear that crept up. "No."

"And I'm the last person to give advice on how to go about keeping a woman happy, but try not to hurt her."

Could be too late for that.

"Can you at least tell me what happened today that got her upset?"

"Alex came by."

Which wasn't a lie, but it was a combination of Alex's appearance and her revelation that had her so distressed. Was she upset because she didn't want to love him? Or was she upset because she knew in her heart that he couldn't love her that way in return?

"What the hell did that bastard want?" Bronson all but roared.

Stefan shook his head. "I let Victoria talk to him alone, but she claimed he wanted to apologize. He didn't believe our marriage was real and thought she would take him back. I didn't hear what all was said, but I did see her give him an impressive slap."

Bronson chuckled. "She's only been that angry twice: once when we were kids and I tried to put her Barbie dolls' heads in the garbage disposal and once when I was being an ass to Mia. Victoria loves with her whole heart, and once it gets bruised, she's like a bear. You don't want to cross her."

Well, damn. Victoria hadn't come right out and said she loved him, but the implication was there. God, he couldn't do love, had never wanted to. So how the hell had he allowed this to happen? He'd told Tori going in that this wasn't about love, that the marriage was only about his country.

Why had she done this to herself and how had he not seen this coming?

Twelve

"Guess I had my first emotional breakdown."

Victoria sat on the simple white bench across from the guest bath where Stefan had showered after his early morning run. They hadn't spoken since her crying jag last night. He'd never come to bed and she assumed he'd slept in the spare room, but she couldn't go on with all this tension inside her body or her home.

"I guess so," he replied.

Stefan leaned against the door frame, all tanned and gloriously misty from the shower. One crisp white towel sat low on his hips, and he'd draped another around his neck. Muscles covered with beautiful tattooed artwork stared back at her, mocking her. No matter her heart's emotions, her body wanted him and instantly responded.

"I'm sorry about yesterday," she told him, bringing her eyes back up to his face. "Seeing Alex threw me off."

Stefan's dark brows drew together. "Why be sorry?"

Victoria resisted the urge to look down at the floor. Instead she tilted her chin, held his gaze and shook her head. "Because I made you uncomfortable."

The muscle in his jaw clenched, and she knew he was still uncomfortable. Was it just Alex's presence and her emotional breakdown that had made him ill at ease, or was it more? Had he heard what she'd said about their relationship?

The implications of her outburst to Alex were something Stefan was not ready for. She wasn't even sure she was ready herself, but she could no longer control her feelings toward her husband. Her heart clenched as if trying to protect itself from the inevitable hurt that would surely consume her once they discussed what her emotions meant to their marriage.

Stefan walked toward her, squatted down between her legs and took her hands in his. "I just have a lot more to deal with than I first thought. I can't take on more than protecting my country and gaining my title."

"I know, and I didn't mean to add to your worry."

His gaze traveled down and settled into the V of her silk nightgown before coming back up to meet hers. Shivers raced through her. So she hadn't completely scared him off.

But he let go of her hands, and that giant step back from intimacy spoke volumes. He was pulling away. Maybe the hurt would slither its evil way in sooner than she'd thought.

A chill crept over her.

Seduction had been on her mind when she'd dressed for bed last night, but he'd never come in, and now, catching him fresh from his shower, it seemed her efforts were moot. He was obviously having no part of her plan.

Was this how the rest of their marriage would play out? They'd dance around each other all because Stefan was afraid to confront her emotions—or his, for that matter?

She didn't believe for one second that he wasn't feeling more for her. She did believe, however, that he was going to fight that feeling for as long as she'd allow it.

"Come back to bed with me," she told him.

His eyes remained locked on hers. "I have some work to go over with Hector."

The steel wall had been erected in a matter of seconds, and he was making no attempt to let her in. But in his defense, he'd told her up front this could be nothing more and like a damn fool she'd been on board with the preposterous plan.

Stefan came to his feet, the subtle movement sending his fresh masculine scent wafting around her, enveloping her, and she knew that's as close as she'd come to being surrounded by her husband right now...and maybe for a while.

"Maybe I'll see you for lunch. I have a lot to do so don't wait on me."

And with that, he headed down the hall.

Victoria wasn't naive. She knew if Stefan could've gotten that title and crown any other way besides marriage, he would've jumped at that opportunity without question. But he couldn't get around it and he *did* need her. No, he was not the marrying type, but he was the type who thrived on loyalty, honesty and integrity...all a good base for marriage and love.

Since she couldn't actually say the words without him pulling back even more—if that were possible—all she could do was show him her love, show him they were meant to be.

With his upcoming coronation and responsibilities on his mind, he'd never complained, never even spoken of worries. He'd been right here with her, trying to help her get her line started, trying to get her to open her mind and really create some spectacular pieces.

Of course when he wasn't being loyal and helpful, he was being sexy and impossible to resist. How could she not love a man like that? And how could he not see that he loved her?

Stefan had been gone all day, but he was due to return home soon. Victoria had requested Hector remain in the front of the house and only to come around back in a dire emergency.

With a deep breath, she set her plan in motion by dipping her bare foot into the pool and gliding it along. Yeah, that would be refreshing once she submerged her entire body...nude.

Okay, so maybe there was a little bit of a reckless side to her, but Stefan brought it out. No way would she ever have thought to get into her infinity pool overlooking the L.A. skyline while wearing nothing but a suntan and a hair clip.

And no way in hell would she ever have done something like this for Alex.

Looking back she could admit that she'd been in love with Stefan for years, but it took the intimacy, the devotion, to finally open her eyes to her true Prince Charming. But she'd never really thought of him as a prince. To her he was her best friend, her confidant, now her lover and husband.

This afternoon they'd ended up sharing a strained lunch and he'd informed her he'd be busy the rest of the day—but at least he'd come for lunch. He had gone into her spare office to check emails and talk with Hector about the coronation. She let him do his thing because that whole royalty territory wasn't her forte. But she was going to have to get more comfortable with it because she intended to stick out this marriage, title and all. And while she was afraid of what being a queen truly meant, she wasn't afraid to sacrifice herself for the man she loved.

While she'd never played the meek and mild woman before, doing so with the title of queen wasn't even an option. She loved being able to assist with charities and use her name and title to help others. And when Stefan had taken charge with the Veterans' Homeless Shelter, her heart had melted. That's the type of work she wanted to get behind. That's the part of being royalty she could completely embrace.

Victoria slid out of her short silk robe and let it puddle next to the steps. The thick candles she'd lit all around the pool added just that extra bit of romance. When Stefan stepped out onto her patio, she wanted him to take in the scene: discarded red silk robe, flickering candlelight and his wife naked in the water.

She may be uncomfortable with this, but she was a Dane and everything was about setting the stage to pack a punch with the audience. And there was only one audience member she cared about.

Now all she had to do was float lazily on her back, wait and fantasize about how spectacular this night would be. Hopefully Stefan would see the way she stepped outside her comfort zone for him, and if he did, surely he'd realize that her love knew no limits.

And perhaps he could step out of his comfort zone, too.

Stefan raked his hands through his hair. His coronation was scheduled to take place in a few months and he was trying to get a start for this documentary so he could at least assure his people that a new era was going to begin, starting with the truth, to remove the black mark hovering over his father's name.

His investigators had found several people who were

willing to speak on camera if a film was produced. Hector had been working behind the scenes, as well, jotting down key things he remembered from that time…after all, the man had also been the assistant to Stefan's father and knew more than most.

But right now his mind was still plagued by the awkwardness with Victoria. He knew she'd picked up on the distance he'd put between them, but he needed the time to process everything. And he still hadn't come to a damn conclusion.

He made his way up to their room, where he fully expected her to be, so he was surprised to see a note resting on her pillow.

Meet me at the pool.

Intrigued, he tossed the note aside and headed back downstairs. When he stepped through the double glass doors, he stopped, taking in the ambiance all at once.

"I'm dreaming. No way is the prim and proper Victoria Dane skinny-dipping out in the open."

She moved through the darkened water like she had all the confidence in the world. "You've been trying since we met to get me here. I thought I'd put you out of your misery."

Arousal shot through him even harder as she flipped, floating on her back with those breasts poking out of the water. His palms itched to touch them. He'd been without her for two days. Way too damn long.

He pulled his T-shirt over his head and tossed it aside. After toeing off his shoes, he unfastened his pants and slid his boxer briefs down, then kicked them aside, as well. There was only so much willpower a man could have.

For a moment he simply stared. Finding a naked woman in a pool was every man's fantasy, but he wasn't stupid.

He knew how her mind worked. She was trying to draw him back into her web and she was spinning it beautifully.

"Are you going to stand there all night?" she asked. "I'm pretty lonely in here."

Like he needed another invitation.

Stefan didn't even bother with the steps. He dove right in, making sure he reached his hands out toward her body. As he came up, he glided his palms over every wet, luscious curve.

"You feel amazing," he muttered when his face was next to hers. "It takes a lot to surprise me, Tori. I honestly never dreamed you would've given into this skinny-dipping thing."

A naughty smile spread across her lips. "Well, when you first asked me, you just wanted to see me naked. Then it just became a game to see if I'd cave. But you've been working so hard, I thought you deserved a reward."

He nipped her chin, her jaw, all the while keeping his arms wrapped around her waist. "Reward, huh? I think I'll reward you for making a part of my fantasy come true."

Her gaze locked on his as her brows drew together. "A part? What am I missing?"

"I wanted you in the palace pool. On my turf."

Victoria rolled her eyes. "No way. Do you know how many staff members you have? There's never a moment of privacy there. At least here I only had to tell Hector to stay out front since the other guard is off for the night."

Stefan smiled. "I'm not complaining."

Resting a delicate hand on his bare chest, Victoria smiled. "I just want to enjoy our time together. However long it may be."

Something flipped in Stefan's heart—something he didn't want to explore or identify.

His arms tightened around her waist. Her vibrant blue

eyes, sparkling from the candlelight and full moon, studied his face. She bit her bottom lip as her gaze darted down.

"What is it?" he asked, tipping her chin up so she would look at him again.

"What will happen after the coronation?"

A sliver of fear slid through him. Was she thinking of staying at the end of the six months? Surprisingly, he wanted her to, but he didn't want her love…not in the way he feared she was heading.

Damn it. He was a selfish bastard. He couldn't have it both ways. He either had to let her go after the coronation or step up and face her feelings. He wasn't crazy about either of his options.

How could he love someone forever? He'd never thought that far ahead when it came to a relationship. Living in the moment was more his speed. What if he tried loving her and a year into the "real" marriage he decided he wasn't cut out for it? She'd be even more hurt. And Victoria deserved better than that.

Why did he have to choose? Hadn't he laid out a foolproof, simple plan before they married?

"I don't want to put a damper on this party," she told him. "Forget I asked. Just tell me what you want right now."

Everything she was willing to give.

She deserves better than what you're willing to give. She's sacrificed everything for you. Her heart is yours if you'll take it. If not, she'll get tired and leave, you selfish jerk.

Her wet body molded against his and her hips rocked against him as her arms encircled his neck. He wasn't going to explore further than right now. He didn't want to keep seeing that hurt seep into her eyes.

For now he would be a self-centered bastard and take

what she offered. In the end, when she realized she couldn't change him and needed more, she would walk away. And he would get what he deserved. But until that day, he'd enjoy every moment of being married to his best friend.

Victoria was just too damn sexy and tempting to turn away. And he knew by taking what she was offering, he was damning their friendship because he had a feeling she'd be leaving soon.

Thirteen

The shrill ringing of the phone jarred Victoria from an amazing dream. The second ring had her slapping a hand over the cell that sat next to her bed only to realize the ring wasn't coming from her cell, but from Stefan's.

If this was another woman…

Surely not. Those calls seemed to have either died down, or Stefan was doing a good job of intervening before she knew.

She glanced over, noting the man was completely out—if his heavy breathing meant anything. And he claimed *she* snored? Reaching across him, she grabbed his cell and answered it.

"Hello?"

"Victoria?"

"Yes." Not recognizing the woman's voice, she moved away from the bed and toward the balcony doors. "Who is this?"

The lady on the other end sniffed. Was she crying?

"This…this is Karina. Mikos's wife. He's been in a rock-climbing accident." Karina wept, and static came through the phone before she continued. "I need Stefan to come home."

Panic gripping her, Victoria looked back to her husband, knowing when she woke him she'd have to tell him news that could possibly change his life forever. This could not be happening.

"Of course," Victoria agreed. "We'll be there as soon as we can."

"Please hurry. The doctors aren't hopeful," Karina cried. "His injuries are substantial. He's in surgery now."

A sickening pit in her stomach threatened to rise in her throat. What would Stefan do if he lost his brother? He'd just lost his father. Fate couldn't be this cruel. Besides, Stefan and his brother were expert rock climbers. What could've gone wrong?

"As soon as my pilot is ready we'll be on the plane," she assured Karina. "Please keep us updated and try to be strong."

Her sister-in-law said a watery thank-you and hung up. Victoria stepped onto the balcony to call her pilot. Even at five o'clock in the morning, he wouldn't mind. He'd been a loyal employee to her family for years, and last-minute things occasionally arose.

Once she had the pilot readying the plane, she took a deep breath and bolstered up her courage to wake Stefan and tell him the news. She needed to stay strong and positive and be there for him no matter what.

When she sank down on the edge of his side of the bed, he roused and his lids fluttered. He flashed that sweet smile she'd grown to love waking up to, and she tried to return the gesture, but her eyes filled with tears.

So much for being strong.

"What happened? I thought I heard the phone ring." He glanced at the clock on the nightstand then back to her as if realizing early morning calls were almost never good news. "Victoria?"

"Your brother was in an accident. We need to get back home."

Stefan jerked up in bed. "What kind of accident? Who called?"

"Karina called and Mikos is in surgery. He was in a rock-climbing accident. That's all I know."

Stefan closed his eyes, shaking his head. "I need to call your pilot."

She laid a hand on his arm, waiting for him to open his eyes and look at her. "Already done. Now get dressed and let's go."

"Wait." He grabbed her hand as she started to rise from the bed. "You don't need to go."

Hurt threatened to seep in. "You don't want me to?"

"Yes, I want you to, but you're so busy here designing your bridal collection, and your brothers may need you on the set."

She'd drop everything without even thinking for the man she loved. Didn't he realize that?

"Do you think I'd choose any of that over family?" she asked.

He studied her face, then nodded. "No, I know what's most important to you." He lifted her hand to his lips and kissed her knuckles. "Thank you for making my family yours."

"We're a team, Stefan." She came to her feet. "Now let's get changed and I'll throw some things into a suitcase."

They worked in a rushed silence to get out the door and to the airport. By the time they boarded the plane, along with the guards, she could tell Stefan was a ball of nerves. He hadn't spoken, hadn't even really glanced her way. He was lost in thought and she had no doubt he was not only feeling helpless, he was reminded of the fact that his mother was gone and his father had just passed away eight months ago.

"It will be okay," she assured him, placing her hand over his during the takeoff. "Once we arrive and you can see him, you'll feel better."

Stefan merely nodded and Victoria knew he wasn't in a chatty, lift-your-spirits type of mood, but she wanted to stay positive for him and wanted him to know she was there.

"I know you're trying to help," he told her, squeezing her hand. "But you being here is really all I need right now."

Victoria swallowed her fear. "I wouldn't be anywhere else."

Stefan held on to Victoria's hand as they made their way down the hospital corridor. The gleaming white floors and antiseptic smell did nothing to ease his mind. He wanted to see his brother. Wanted to see that he was going to be okay and know what the hell had happened. He and Mikos had practically been raised climbing those rocks in Kalymnos. They climbed the hardest, most dangerous rocks for fun, and people had always tried to warn them they were risking too much.

He couldn't lose his last family member. He refused to believe fate would be that cruel to him.

As he approached the nurses' desk to ask where his brother's room was, Karina came rushing toward him, throwing her arms around his waist and holding tight.

"Oh, thank God you're here," she sobbed into his chest

before lifting her tear-stained face to look up at him. "He's out of surgery and so far he's holding his own."

Stefan held on to his sister-in-law's slender shoulders. "What's the prognosis?"

"Better than when he first arrived," she told him, tears pooling in her red-rimmed eyes. "They didn't think he'd make it through surgery. But since he has, they are monitoring him. He has…"

She dropped her head to her chest, sobbing once again. Stefan pulled her close, and as much as he wanted to know what the hell they were up against, he also knew the most important thing—his brother was alive. Karina had been here for hours all alone, and right now she needed someone to comfort her.

"I'll go see what the doctor says," Victoria whispered behind him.

He nodded and led Karina over to the sofa. "Would you like some water?"

Easing back from him, she shook her head and toyed with the tissue she had clutched in her hand. "No."

"Have you eaten?"

Again she shook her head.

"Victoria would be happy to get you something, or you can go and we will stay here," he offered.

"I can't leave," she told him. "I can't even think of eating. I just want someone to tell me for certain that Mikos will be fine. That he'll be able to walk again, talk again and not be a vegetable."

That meant his brother obviously had a brain trauma.

Stefan took her hands in his. "Does he have swelling in his brain?"

Karina nodded. "They drilled holes to alleviate some of the pressure, but all we can do is wait. They put him in a drug-induced coma."

Stefan closed his eyes. How many times had they been rock climbing in Kalymnos? Countless. It's what they did. Anything to be reckless and adventurous.

"He'll be fine," Stefan said, squeezing her hands. "He's tough, and there's no way he won't fight to come back to you."

Karina sniffed. "I'm pregnant."

Stefan sat up straight in his seat. "Excuse me?"

"I just confirmed with the doctor while Mikos was out climbing. I was going to tell him when he got home. What if…"

Again she collapsed against him and sobbed.

Dear Lord, a baby? Stefan couldn't imagine his brother not pulling through, but even if he did, what would they all be faced with?

His baby brother was just as strong and determined as he was. So there was no way, even if he woke up and couldn't walk, that his brother wouldn't move heaven and earth to get back on his feet…especially with a baby on the way.

Victoria rounded the corner and took a seat across from them. "The nurse said the doctor would be out shortly to talk to us. He's actually in Mikos's room right now evaluating him again."

"Thank you," Stefan told her.

"Can I get you guys anything?" she offered. "I saw a lounge down the hall. Coffee, water?"

Both he and Karina declined and Victoria nodded as she eased back in her seat. In no time the doctor came down the hall.

Stefan stood and extended his hand. "I'm Stefan Alexander. How's my brother?"

The doctor shook his hand. "I know who you are, Prince Alexander. I'm happy to tell you that your brother made it through the surgery better than any of my colleagues or I thought he would. We will be keeping a close watch on him, but even in his drug-induced coma, he's responding to us being in the room."

Hearing such positive news had Stefan expelling a breath he'd been holding for quite some time.

"So where do we go from here?" he asked.

"Well, I think it's good that you're all here. He needs strength and support from his loved ones to encourage him. I can let you visit, but only one at a time and not for very long."

Stefan nodded. "I understand. When do you believe he'll wake up?"

"That really depends on the swelling, when we will back off the meds, and how his vitals are when we try to bring him back from the coma. This could be a long process, but right now all we can do is pray and hope he'll fight the rest of the way."

Stefan had no doubt his brother would do just that. "Thank you, Doctor."

"Go see him," Stefan urged Karina. "Tell him your news and give him something to fight for."

Karina smiled. "You think I should tell him before he wakes up?"

"Absolutely." He leaned in, kissed her damp cheek. "Go on. We'll be here."

She all but ran down the hall, and Stefan sank to the sofa. Scared, helpless, yet optimistic, he really had no idea how to feel or what to do next. He just wanted his vibrant brother to be up on his feet and celebrating the good news of the baby.

"She's pregnant, isn't she?" Victoria asked, sitting beside him.

"Yes."

"Bless her heart. I can't imagine how scared she must be." She rested her delicate hand, the one that held his diamond ring and wedding band, on his leg. "What can I do for you?"

Stefan wrapped an arm around her, pulling her against his side. "Be here. Don't leave me."

She tilted her head to look up into his eyes. "Stefan, even if we weren't married I would've dropped everything to be with you."

And he knew in his heart she meant that. Which made her invaluable and precious. He'd always known she was the best thing in his life, but now he knew he couldn't get through another trying time without her. Yet if he couldn't commit to loving her the way she deserved, what did that possibly mean for their future?

Fourteen

"Can you tell us about your brother, Prince Stefan?"

"Is he going to pull through?"

"Was this an accident or a suicide attempt?"

That last question from the slam of paparazzi stopped Stefan cold outside the hospital as he and Victoria were trying to make their way to his car waiting at the curb.

"Excuse me!" Victoria shouted with her hands up. "But my brother-in-law is in there fighting for his life. We request that you respect our family's privacy. There will be a formal announcement on his prognosis later, but for now you can put on record that this was in no way a suicide attempt. We would appreciate if you would get facts straight before going to print."

Victoria looped her arm through his as she led the way, plowing past the flashbulbs and reporters screaming questions. Thank God she was experienced in handling the media circus. Being one of the famous Hollywood Danes, she was no stranger to the chaos.

She held tight to his arm as she pushed through the crowd and slid into the awaiting car. Before another question could be shouted their way, his driver slammed the door to the busybodies.

"They've never known the meaning of the word privacy," Victoria muttered. "I'm sorry."

"You're apologizing after that?" he asked, turning to look at her. "I can't thank you enough for handling that mess."

"That suicide comment was uncalled for."

He shifted, staring straight ahead. "Yes, it was. But you handled it beautifully."

"I hope it was okay that I mentioned a formal announcement later. I just assumed…"

Stefan glanced over to her as she closed her eyes and rested her head against the back of the seat. She was exhausted. Only yesterday she'd put in nearly twelve hours designing, then they'd made love until well after midnight and had woken up at five in the morning to fly to Greece. He was tired, but she was exhausted. He'd had his adrenaline to keep him pumping forward, but he had no clue what she was running on.

"That was fine. The media will spin a story or make up one if the truth isn't juicy enough. Letting them know there was more to come will pacify them for a bit," Stefan told her. "Once Mikos comes to and can speak for himself, this will be easier to handle."

Eyes closed, head still back, she gave a slight nod. "Yes, it will. Just tell me how I can help."

Stefan smiled. Even when she was dragging and on her last leg, she was still putting herself out there for him and his family. She was the strongest woman he knew and perfect to be reigning as queen…if she stayed.

No, he couldn't think about that right now.

"The best thing you can do is rest," he told her, wrapping his arm around her and pulling her down to his side. "Once we get back to the palace we'll both try to get some sleep."

And then he planned on staying at the hospital until his brother showed a vast improvement. He needed to give Karina some time to eat, to sleep, but once the doctor had assured them all that Mikos wouldn't be waking or likely showing much change for the next day or so, they'd all promised to go home, rest, shower and refuel and return the following morning.

Stefan glanced at his watch. He was so confused on time. Between not getting enough sleep before arriving and the time difference, he didn't know what time he thought it should be. But his body knew it was time for sleep.

By the time they reached the palace, Victoria had a soft, steady snore going. He smiled. He'd tried telling her once when they were teens that she snored when she'd stayed for a movie and had fallen asleep. Like any young lady, she refused to believe that she could do something so rude… or normal. So he'd let the moment go, until they'd fallen asleep once while on an evening picnic. They'd stayed out late and lain beneath the stars talking when she had drifted off and started snoring. She occasionally joked that maybe she did snore, but it wasn't loud like he claimed.

And every night for the past three months, he'd been lulled to sleep by those soft purrs, as she liked to call them. She may think it was a catlike purr, but it was more like a tiger growl.

When the driver opened the door, Stefan carefully slid her into his lap and eased from the car to carry her inside.

The palace wasn't a small place and his room was at the end of the long corridor, but that didn't matter, not when he held such precious cargo.

He wasn't about to wake her to make her do the zombie walk of exhaustion up to the room. Besides, she didn't weigh much, not when he was used to pulling his own body weight up while rock climbing.

Would he ever be able to climb again? If his brother didn't make it, he honestly didn't know. But he couldn't think like that. He wasn't scared to tackle the rocks again, but he didn't want to do it alone when he'd done it for so long with his brother.

Victoria was being strong through this process; he needed to mimic her actions in order to get Karina through this tough time.

The weight of Victoria in his arms felt so…right. He didn't know how he would've gotten through this initial shock of his brother's accident without her. She may have not done much, but being by his side, refusing to leave the hospital until he did and then handling the paparazzi like that only gave further evidence that she did love him.

But did she truly love him as deeply as she thought she did? Part of him wanted that to be true, but the friend side wanted her to be mistaken. He could admit his feelings for her had deepened since their wedding, but…love? No. He couldn't—wouldn't—go that far.

For years he'd wanted to explore their friendship to see what could come of it, but he never thought love or marriage would be a step in their lives.

Maybe fate didn't want them together since the timing was always off. Or maybe fate knew just when to throw them together for maximum support and impact. Between his father's death, her scandalous breakup and now his brother's accident, he knew they needed each other now more than ever.

Not to mention the upcoming coronation. Yes, they were always there to offer support and for consoling, but that's what friends did, right? All of that did not allude to love.

Stefan entered his suite, closing the high double doors behind him, and crossed to the bed, where he laid her down.

He stood over her, looking at all that pale blond hair spread across his navy, satin sheets. She was such a beauty, such an angel to have come into his life to save him over and over again.

How could he truly ever repay her?

Love had never been on his bucket list, had never been a priority. Love was something his brother had found, Victoria's brothers had found. Love wasn't something for a man who enjoyed women as much as he did or who didn't plan on marrying and settling down.

Yet here he was married to the most precious woman in his life. And, if he were being honest with himself, he'd admit that being married to Victoria was amazing. But they'd not really been married long and they'd been jet-setting back and forth. They hadn't lived in a realistic wedded atmosphere—or as realistic as it could get with being thrown into the proverbial spotlight as royalty.

As he slid off his own shoes and stripped down to his boxers, he slid in beside her and held her against his chest.

How would he manage if she stayed? Could he give her the marriage she deserved? She'd been engaged before—she obviously believed in happily ever afters—so why had she settled knowing he couldn't offer her a bond any deeper than their friendship and sex?

There were no easy answers, and Stefan had a sickening feeling he was going to hurt her before this was over.

* * *

Victoria had been working via phone and email with her staff back in L.A. Between a few mishaps on the set of her brothers' film that her assistant had to take care of and a glitch in the Italian silk she'd ordered not arriving on time, Victoria was ready to pull her hair out.

Added to all of the work tension, she was worried for Stefan. His brother was showing remarkable progress, but Stefan was so dead set on staying at the hospital to give his sister-in-law breaks whenever she needed them. Like any loving, dedicated woman, Karina wasn't leaving Mikos's side. Victoria envied their love.

On a sigh, Victoria sent off another email to her assistant to remind her to check on the dates for the bridal expo she hoped to be ready for…if that blasted silk would arrive.

As she was looking at possible backup outlets for material, her cell rang. Grabbing it from the oversized white desk in her suite, she answered.

"Hello."

"Tori," Bronson said. "So glad I caught you."

Her stomach sank. "There's another problem with a piece of the wardrobe?"

His rich laughter resounded through the earpiece. "Not at all. Your assistant did an amazing job coming to our rescue the other day. She deserves a raise."

And she was going to give her one, for all that poor girl would probably have to take on in Victoria's absence.

"So if it's not the wardrobe, what are you calling about?" she asked.

"I've been trying to reach Stefan, but it keeps going to voice mail. Are you with him by any chance?"

"No. And he keeps his phone off while he's at the hospital."

"How's his brother doing?" Bronson asked.

Victoria sank back into her cushy chair and dug her toes into the plush white carpet. "The doctors are astonished at the progress Mikos is making only two weeks after a near-death experience."

"That's great. You guys must really feel relieved."

"Stefan is still like a mother hen," Victoria told him. "He spends his days and evenings there. I think he'll feel better once Mikos is released and a nurse is with him at home."

"I hate to bother him," Bronson said, "but when he gets a chance could you have him call me?"

Victoria drew her brows together. "Something wrong?"

"Not at all," he assured her. "I just wanted to discuss that documentary we are going to be working on."

Victoria sat up straight. "Documentary?"

"Yeah, the one on his mother's death? Anthony and I are thrilled he came to us and trusted us to take on such a project."

Stefan went to her brothers for a film? And didn't say anything to her? A sliver of betrayal and dèjà vu spread through her. Had she been used again for her family name?

"Anyway, just tell him no rush," Bronson went on, no idea of the instant turmoil flooding through her. "He can call me when he gets a chance."

Victoria hung up, laced her fingers together and settled her elbows on the desk. Her forehead rested against her hands and she refused to let her past relationship make her have doubts and fears about this one.

Stefan was not Alex. Alex had used her to gain an upper hand in Hollywood. To be part of the Danes, to be on camera whenever possible and to gain access to her famous brothers.

Alex had never loved her the way she had him—or

thought she had—he'd only been with her to see how far
he could get with his goal of becoming famous.

A ball of dread filled her stomach.

Was Stefan using her? He'd technically used her to gain
his title, but she knew about that and was happy to help.
But was he using her as a way to get to her brothers? To
make sure that he was in the family and make it that much
harder for Bronson and Anthony to turn him down?

And what was this documentary about his mother's
death? She had no idea he was even thinking such a thing.
Oh, she'd known about the scandalous way the media had
portrayed the accident, but Victoria had never believed the
late King Alexander had anything to do with his wife's
death. The media just wanted to make it a Princess Grace
type of story and glamorize something that was so tragic.

So why hadn't he told her? And what else had he been
hiding?

Had he lied about other things—like all those calls from
other women? Had he not answered them because she'd
been sitting right there?

Oh, God, she was going to be sick.

Before her humiliation with Alex she never would've en-
tertained such terrible thoughts about Stefan and wouldn't
be analyzing this situation so hard, but she'd been burned
so badly, she was still scarred.

On a groan, she dropped her arms, headed to the desk
and tried to come up with some plausible explanation for
all of this. But she couldn't defend him. He'd taken her
already battered heart and pressed harder on the bruise.

Victoria had to confront him, and she knew if he told her
he had indeed used her, lied to her, she would not be able
to stay married to a man who had humiliated her like that.

She'd thought Stefan was different. How could she have
made the same mistake twice?

Fifteen

When stress overcame Victoria, she did what she knew best. She designed.

She grabbed a notepad and pencil from the drawer of Stefan's desk in the master suite and took it to the balcony overlooking the Mediterranean Sea. The tranquility, the peacefulness of the crystal-blue water ebbing and flowing to the shore should've calmed her nerves.

Unfortunately when you were lied to, even by omission, nothing could relieve the hurt and betrayal. Not even the beauty of the country she was legally the next queen over.

But the deception wouldn't have been so bad, so crippling if it hadn't come from her best friend...the one person outside her family she depended on, cared for. Loved.

Victoria dropped to a cushy white chaise and began sweeping her pencil across the paper. Soon a dress formed, but not just any dress. Her wedding dress. The dress she'd taken vows in, promising to love, honor and cherish her husband. The dress she'd designed for a princess.

Letting the pad fall to her lap, Victoria closed her eyes and leaned back against the chair. Why did life have to be so complicated, so…corrupt? Didn't anyone tell the full truth anymore? Was she naive in taking people at their word?

But she hadn't just taken anyone at their word; she'd taken Stefan at his. The rock of stability who had always been there for her. How dare he do that to her emotions, her heart? He of all people knew how she'd been battered and bruised. Why hadn't he come to her with the idea of the documentary? Why go to her brothers behind her back?

Another crippling ache spread through her, and she had no idea where to put these emotions. Did she cry, throw something, pack her bags and leave?

"There you are."

At the sound of Stefan's voice, Victoria turned her head. With a smile on his handsome face, he strode through the open patio doors. And she knew how to handle this situation. Right now she couldn't look at him as her best friend, couldn't see him as the man whom she'd confided in for years. No, she had to see him as was—a man who'd lied to her.

"Sketching another gown?" he asked, leaning down to her notepad. "That's the dress you wore for our wedding. Why are you drawing it again?"

Laying the pad aside, she came to her feet, ready to take the blow of the truth…if he revealed it.

"Just remembering the day I married my best friend," she told him, watching his eyes. "The day we promised to be faithful and honor each other. And even though I had my doubts and worries, I knew you'd never hurt me because we have something special."

He tipped his head to the side. "Everything all right, Tori?"

A sad smile spread across her face. "Not really. You see, I married you because you needed me and I wanted to get over the pain and humiliation of my last relationship. You promised to provide me with that support and stability. You promised to never hurt me, and I assumed that meant honesty, as well. Obviously I was wrong."

He reached for her, touching her arm, and she didn't step back. Because even though he'd damaged something inside, she still craved his touch. But she wasn't begging for his love. Never again would she put her heart on the line for such foolishness. And damn him for destroying that dream.

"What happened?" he asked, concern lacing his voice.

As tears threatened to clog her throat, she tamped down the pain, knowing she needed to be strong or she'd crumble at his feet and never stop crying. The inevitable emotional breakdown could and would be done in private.

"I learned the truth," she told him. "I discovered that no matter what your heart says, not even your best friend is trustworthy."

"Victoria, what the hell are you talking about?" he demanded. "I've never lied to you."

Moisture pooled in her eyes, making his face blurry. She couldn't lose it, not here, not when he'd try to console her and break her down.

"Bronson called." She stared into his eyes, wanting to see the moment he realized that she knew the truth. "He's ready to move forward with your documentary. And since you've used me for the title and your film, I guess that's my cue to exit stage left."

His eyes widened, and he took both her arms in his strong hands. "Victoria—"

"No. There's no excuse as to why you couldn't have told me. Not one. So don't even try. I'm done being hurt. I'm done being lied to. My God, if you lied about this, what else have you kept from me?"

She jerked away from his grasp, tilting her chin. "I will be leaving as soon as my jet is ready. Since your brother is doing better, you don't need me here. Actually, you shouldn't need me at all anymore. You're getting your crown in a few short months, but after the coronation I'll be divorcing you."

Sharp, piercing pain speared through her. She never imagined she'd be divorcing the one man she loved with her whole heart. Every shattered, broken piece of it.

As she moved by him, she stopped, looking into his eyes. His face was only a breath away.

"If you'd let me—"

Shaking her head, she stepped back. "I just want to hear one thing from you. Did you know you were going to ask my brothers to help you before or after we married?"

Stefan swallowed and held her gaze. "Before."

And the last of Victoria's hope died.

Head held high, shoulders back, Victoria walked inside, through their master suite where they'd made love countless times and out the door. She didn't break down until she was safely locked inside the guest bath down the hall.

Her iconic actress mother would be so proud of her departing performance.

Stefan's world was completely and utterly empty. Two days ago Victoria had gotten on her jet and left Galini Isle. Two days ago she'd stood before him, hurt swimming in her eyes, and accused him of betraying her trust, and in the next moment she was gone.

She'd known exactly how to bring him to his knees

and cause the most guilt. He hadn't been fully truthful with her and now he was being damned for it. Nothing less than he deserved.

Stefan slammed his empty glass back down on the bar in his study. Scotch wouldn't take the pain away, and to be honest, he deserved any heartbreak he had because he'd brought every bit of it on himself. He'd known she'd been lied to before. Why the hell hadn't he discussed his plans with her?

He hadn't called Bronson back. Who knew what Victoria had told her brothers when she returned home. For all Stefan knew, this project was over before it got started.

But right now he didn't give a damn about his project.

What he did care about was the fact that he'd damaged something, someone so beautiful. He didn't know if they could get past this trauma, not just for the marriage, but the friendship.

He had to get her back. He couldn't lose their friendship. Victoria was the single most important woman in his life, and living without her was incomprehensible.

Stefan gripped his glass, resting his other hand on the bar and hanging his head down between his shoulders. Hindsight was just as cruel as fate, in his opinion. He'd known he was using her, had known that he needed to in order to gain what he wanted. But fate had dangled all those opportunities in front of his face and he'd taken chances he never should've taken—the marriage, the documentary…the sex. Because all of those chances didn't just involve his life, they affected Victoria's.

He hurled the Scotch tumbler across the room, not feeling any better when the crackling of glass and shards splintering to the floor resounded in the room.

Seconds later his guard burst through the door. "Your Highness, are you all right?"

Stefan shook his head. No, he was not all right.

"Glass broke," he said. "I'll clean it."

With that, the guard backed out again, leaving Stefan alone once more. But alone wasn't good. Alone meant he had only his thoughts to keep him company, and it was those haunting thoughts that had that invisible band around his chest tightening.

Memories of Victoria washed over him—on their wedding day gliding down the aisle, swimming in the ocean, beneath him in bed, gazing up at him like he was her world.

If they were just friends, then this revelation about the movie wouldn't have hurt her so badly. He'd lost her as his wife…he refused to lose his best friend, too.

Victoria was still in her office. Her employees had left long ago, but she stood in the middle of her spacious sewing room in front of the three-way mirror trying her hardest to pin the dress without sticking herself…again. The design was finally coming along, and she wanted to get it finished tonight.

Working through a broken heart was the only way she would get past this. She had to throw all her emotions into her work because if she went home, if she had to stop and even think for a moment about her personal life, she'd crumble and may never recover.

A knot formed in her stomach. She hated regrets, and hated even more that those regrets circled around Stefan. Fury filled her, pain consumed her. But at the end of the day she only had herself to blame for falling in love with him. She should've known better. Hadn't she seen over the years how he was with women? Hadn't she witnessed firsthand how he'd discarded them when they got too close?

And Victoria had fallen into his trap, fallen for those

charms and assumed that bond they'd formed as teens would get them through anything. But even the strongest bonds could be broken with enough force.

On a sigh, she shoved a pin through the silk gathered at her waist and glanced up into the mirror. A scream caught in her throat at the sight of the man standing behind her.

"Need a hand?" Stefan asked.

She whirled around. "How did you get in here?"

"Door was unlocked."

She'd been so wrapped up in her anger, her hurt and work to check it after her last employee left.

"I've called you for days. You never answered or returned my calls."

Victoria crossed her arms over her chest, as if that could protect her from allowing any more hurt to seep in.

"I went by your house first," he told her, still remaining in the doorway as if he were afraid to come closer. Smart man. "I should've known you'd be here working."

"And as you can see, I'm busy."

She lifted the heavy skirt of her silk gown and turned back to the mirror. Reaching for another pin from the large cushion on the table beside her, she tugged at the bustline. If that didn't get pinned, she'd be spilling out, and she refused to ever let Stefan have the privilege of seeing her naked again.

"I flew all this way to talk to you, Tori. Don't shut me out."

With care, she slid the pin in, annoyed at her shaky hands. "I didn't shut you out. You did that when you chose to keep the film to yourself and use me for my brothers."

"*Na pari i eychi*, Victoria." He moved farther into the room, his eyes locking onto hers in the mirror. "You won't even listen to me? I've been up front with you about everything else other than the film, but you've already lumped me into that same jerk category as Alex and assumed the worst."

"So what if I have?" she asked him. "You took my trust and loyalty for granted. You knew going in you wanted to use my brothers for this documentary. Why not just tell me?"

Resting his hands on his denim-clad hips, he shook his head. "I knew you had enough going on in your life. This film really didn't involve you."

She was wrong. The hurt could slice deeper. She'd always heard that the people you love most could also hurt you the most. Too bad she had to experience the anguish and despair to understand the saying.

"I see." She swallowed, turning back around to face him. From up on the large pedestal where she stood, she was now eye to eye with him. "I've been your best friend, then wife and lover, but you didn't think this involved me. That pretty much says it all, doesn't it? I obviously wasn't as much a part of your life as I thought because I assumed we shared everything. My mistake and one I certainly won't make again."

"Tori, I can't change what I did, but I can't let you go, either. I need you."

"Ah, yes. The beloved crown and country," she all but mocked.

"Don't," he told her. "Don't let your anger get in the way of doing what is right."

She nearly laughed at that. *Doing what is right?* Fine, then, since she prided herself on honesty, she'd do what was right and tell him how she felt.

"I fell in love with you," she blurted out. Her eyes locked on his. "Crazy, isn't it? And I don't mean love in the way a friend loves another. I love you in the way a woman loves a man, a wife loves a husband. You don't know how I wish I could turn these emotions off."

When he remained silent, Victoria kept going, ignoring the dark circles beneath his heavy-lidded baby blues.

"I thought you loved me," she said, not caring that she was bearing her soul. This situation couldn't get any more humiliating, anyway. "I was naive enough to think that all your actions were signs that you were taking our relationship deeper, but you don't love me. If you did, I wouldn't be hurting like this right now. You only flew here because you care about yourself, not me."

Moisture filled Stefan's eyes, but Victoria refused to believe he was affected by her declaration.

"But I'm willing to give you a chance to speak for yourself. Do you love me? Is that why you're here?" she asked, searching his eyes. "Honestly?"

"As much as I ever did," he told her. "You're my best friend."

She lowered her lids over the burn, a lone tear streaking down her cheek. "Do you love me as more than a friend, Stefan?" she asked, opening her eyes.

"If I could love anyone, Tori, it would be you."

"So the answer is no."

Silence enveloped them, and she couldn't stand another minute in his sight. And since he was making no move to leave, and this was her turf, she'd have to be the one to walk away.

"You're the last man I will ever let humiliate me," she told him, damning her cracking voice. "And you're the last man I'll ever love."

He reached up and swiped away a tear with the pad of his thumb. "Can you at least work with me for the coronation?"

"I will stay married to you until then, but I cannot live

with you. This marriage will be in name only from here on out."

She stepped off the platform and started to move by him.

"But you'll you be at the coronation?" he asked.

She stopped in her tracks, her shoulders stiffened, but she did not turn around. "I would never go back on my word to a friend. I'll be there."

Countless times he'd lied. He'd lied his way through his teen years, lied when he knew the truth would only get him into trouble, but he couldn't mislead Victoria when she'd asked him if he loved her. Not even when he knew the truth would break her even more.

She'd accused him of humiliating her, which made him no better than the bastard who'd publicly destroyed her. The end result was the same. Victoria trusted and loved with her whole heart and had ended up hurt.

Stefan rested his hands against the marble rail on the edge of his master suite's balcony. Over and over during the past three months, he'd replayed his time with Victoria, looking for those moments he'd missed, trying to see exactly where he went wrong.

He knew she loved him as a friend. Friend love was something he could handle. But this deeper love he'd been afraid of coming from her was just something he couldn't grasp. He'd never loved a woman other than his mother. In his world love meant commitment and loyalty—two things he reserved for his country.

Victoria's declaration of love had speared a knife through his heart sharper and deeper than anything. Victoria Dane, the woman who'd captured his attention as a teen and quickly turned into his best friend, the woman who saved him time and time again with her selfless ways and her kind heart, and the woman who would've graciously helped him work on clearing his family's reputation, had walked out of his life. And there was no one to blame but himself.

He missed hearing her voice, missed knowing her smile would be waiting for him at the end of the day. Missed her body lying next to his. He missed everything from her friendship to their intimacy.

Every time he walked into their closet he saw her standing there in her silky lingerie trying to decide what to wear. When he lay in bed at night, his hand reached to her side as if she'd magically appear. And when he'd tried to take a stroll on the beach, he recalled the day he'd kissed her by the ocean, when he felt that something was turning in their relationship. He'd known then something was different, but he hadn't wanted to identify it.

He was going to go mad if he didn't concentrate on something else. Unfortunately, no matter what he did, all thoughts circled back to Victoria.

Stefan shoved off the rail and marched to his room. Maybe if he tried to rid their room of reminders, that would help. After all, he was still hanging on to her doodles and sketches. He yanked open the drawer on his desk and pulled out the random drawings from Victoria's late-night dress designs.

Something slid beneath his hand as he picked up the sketches. An SD card. And not just any SD card, but the one he'd taken from the intruder that day at the beach.

Obviously he felt the need to torture himself further because he found himself popping it into the computer. In actuality, he wanted to look at Victoria when she was happier, before he'd filled her life with anguish.

He rested his palms on the desk, waiting for the images to load. In no time several small pictures appeared on the screen, and Stefan sank into his office chair. He clicked on the first one, maximizing the image.

Click after click he saw the same thing over and over: Victoria smiling at him, hope and love swimming in her eyes, her hair dancing around in the ocean breeze and the sunset in the distance.

But the last image was different. The final picture was like a knife through his already damaged heart.

Victoria sat with her back to the camera, her face to the ocean as he looked at her. There was no smile on his lips, but it was the expression in his eyes. The image smacked him in the face. No man looked at a woman with such adoration, such passion, like nothing else mattered in the world, if he didn't love her. How could he not have realized that all this time, everything he'd felt, every twinge in his chest, had been love? All those times she'd smiled at him and he felt a flutter and each moment he wanted to just hold her near…damn, how could he have missed what was right in front of him?

Stefan fell against the back of his seat as the picture stared him in the face, mocking everything he'd had in his grasp and had let go.

The ache he'd felt for days intensified to a level he never knew existed. Pain consumed him, and he knew he had to take action or face a lifetime of loneliness because no woman could or would ever replace his Tori.

There was no way he would give her up without a fight. No way in hell. If he had to recruit her brothers, her mother, even God himself, Stefan had to win her back.

He would make her see that she *did* mean everything to him. She was his best friend, and he seriously didn't think he could get through life without her.

With his mind working in overtime, he started plotting how he would get his wife back.

Sixteen

Against her family's wishes and best attempts to talk her out of it, Victoria wasn't about to miss the coronation. Stefan may not have gone about their relationship the right way, but he did deserve to be king.

After all, his country was the one thing in life he actually loved. At one time she would've given anything to hear him say those words about her, too.

No matter the months that had passed, the pain was just as fresh, just as raw. Even though her bridal line had launched with great success, she couldn't enjoy the overwhelming attention and adoration her designs were getting.

Victoria smoothed a hand down the royal-blue gown she'd designed for the coronation. She'd wanted to match Stefan's bright sash that stretched from his shoulder to his hip. Though why she tried so hard was beyond her.

No, she had to be honest, at least with herself. She wanted him to shine. Wanted them to put up a united front for the public. If anyone knew about pretenses, it was her. Having come from the prestigious Dane family, she was all too aware of what could happen if the right image wasn't portrayed, and this was Stefan's final step into the role of king.

As she glanced in the mirror, she couldn't help but have a sense of déjà vu. This was the exact room she stood in six months ago when she'd married. Only this time she'd traveled alone. Her mother wasn't supportive and her brothers weren't too happy, either. Her sisters-in-law, well, they totally understood the stupid things women did for love.

And yes, after all she'd been through, she loved the man. Dammit, she couldn't help herself. Stupid female hormones. She wanted to hate him for the pain he'd caused, wanted to despise him for making her fall in love. But she only had herself to blame. How long had she known him? How many times had she seen a broken heart lying at his feet?

She smoothed her hair back and glanced from side to side to make sure her chignon was in place. A soft knock at her door had her cringing.

Showtime.

"My lady," one of the guards called through the door. "I'm ready to escort you down to the ballroom."

The ballroom would be transformed into a vibrant display of royal-blue silk draped over every stationary item. The bold color symbolized the country, and the crest would be hung from banners surrounding the room. After all, this was a celebration of the next reign.

Too bad she didn't feel like celebrating. She hadn't seen Stefan since he'd walked out of her office three months ago. She'd seen pictures of him via the internet rock climbing and surfing, always alone. All the tabloids were speculating a separation between them. Both she and Stefan had issued press releases stating they were each busy working on various projects, but they were very much still married and looking forward to the coronation ceremony.

Which wasn't a total lie. She was looking forward to it because after this day was over, she could divorce him and move on with her battered heart. But she still hadn't gotten the nerve to contact her attorney. She just couldn't. The thought of closing the door on their relationship brought on a whole new layer of pain she just wasn't ready to deal with. Because she knew there was no way in hell they could go back to being just friends.

Victoria crossed the room, her full silk skirt swishing against her legs. She opened the door with a smile on her face and looped her hand around the arm of the guard. Time to get her last duty as royalty over with.

"You look stunning, Your Highness."

She swallowed the lump of guilt over the pretense. "Thank you. I'm a bit nervous."

His soft chuckle sounded through the marble hallway. "Nothing to be nervous about. All you have to do is smile and take the crown."

The crown, the one that symbolized leadership and loyalty. And in a few short months, she'd give it up because she couldn't remain queen of this country. She couldn't stay with Stefan, no matter how she loved him or how much he claimed to care for her. Wasn't there a song about sometimes love not being enough?

Victoria descended the steps, ready to get this day over with. A day most women in her shoes would want to savor, relish, remember. Unfortunately, Victoria was too busy trying to erect a steel wall around her heart for when she saw her husband again.

* * *

Stefan stood outside the grand ballroom and watched as one of the palace guards escorted Victoria toward him. Her beauty had been in his dreams every night. That flawless elegance from her golden hair to her sweet smile to her delicate frame.

And every night he'd lain in bed alone, wishing he could have her by his side, wishing he could hear those very unladylike snores coming from the other side of the bed.

He knew he had it bad when he missed Victoria's snoring.

But it was the epiphany brought about by those images that prompted him to make the biggest decision of his life. One that was life-altering, but there was no other choice. Not if he wanted to have any type of peace and happiness. And not if he wanted to keep the woman he loved.

As she approached him, he extended his hand, eager for that first contact after being without her familiar touch for too long.

"You're the most beautiful sight I've seen in three months," he told her, bringing her hand to his lips.

Victoria bowed. "Thank you, Your Majesty."

Na pari i eychi, she was going to keep it formal and stiff. Like hell. He wasn't having any of that and in about two minutes she'd see just how serious he was about keeping things between them very, very personal.

She'd turned him down in L.A. because he'd been uncertain. Well, after three months of living without her, then finding those damning pictures from the beach and knowing he could indeed have all that was important, he was not going to end this day without getting the one thing in life he could not live without. And his revelation would no doubt shock her. Surprisingly, once he'd made the decision, he wasn't upset about it.

But for the first time in his life he was scared. A ball of nerves settled deep into his stomach. He couldn't lose her. Right now, nothing else mattered but his goal. And that was another first...this goal had absolutely nothing to do with his country.

"Are you ready?" he asked, looking into her blue eyes that never failed to captivate him.

For months he'd had a band around his chest, and seeing her in person only tightened it. The ache for her was unlike anything he'd ever known.

"Do I have a choice?" she whispered, holding his gaze.

Without a word, he wrapped her fingers around his arm and headed toward the closed set of double doors leading to the ballroom. On the other side, hundreds of very important diplomats, presidents and royalty waited to see the crowning of the next king and queen of Galini Isle.

Were they in for a surprise.

Two guards pulled open the tall, arched doors, revealing a ballroom adorned with royal silk the color of his vibrant sash and banners with the Alexander family crest suspended from the ceiling, the balcony and between the windows.

Everyone came to their feet as he and Victoria made their way down the blue satin stretched along the aisle before them, the Archbishop waiting at the end dressed in pristine white robes with a blue sash.

Even Mikos, who was still in a wheelchair but recovering nicely, waited at the end of the aisle. His brother knew exactly what was getting ready to take place. Mikos flashed a knowing smile and gave him a nod of approval.

Stefan swallowed the inkling of fear that kept trying to creep in. This was the right move to make, the only move to make. He had to take this leap and pray it paid off in the end. He wanted Victoria back and would do whatever it took.

Her fingers curled into his forearm and he knew she was nervous, angry, scared. Hopefully after today he could make her happy from here on out. He had to try, at least. What kind of man would he be if he didn't?

Once they reached the end of the aisle, the archbishop gestured for them to step up onto the stage, where two high-back thrones, centuries old, awaited them.

Stefan slid Victoria's hand from his arm and assisted her, careful not to step on the skirt of her gown. Once she was up and seated, he joined her. They faced the crowd, and Stefan knew it was go time.

He'd scaled the death defying rocks of Kalymnos, but that was nothing compared to the anxiety that slid through him, knowing his life and everything he loved was on the line. Every goal he'd ever wanted was within his reach... but he'd give it up in a flash for a lifetime with this woman.

When the archbishop opened his mouth, Stefan held up a hand, cutting the elderly man off.

"I do apologize," Stefan said. "But I have something to say before we proceed, if that's all right."

Obviously shocked, the archbishop stuttered a bit before bowing. "Of course, Your Majesty."

"What are you doing?" Victoria whispered beside him.

"Taking control of my life," he told her before coming to his feet.

Stefan glanced over the crowd, pulling up all his courage and strength. He'd need a great deal of both to get through the next several life-altering moments.

He glanced down to Mikos, who was still smiling. And Stefan knew that if Mikos could practically come back from near death, then Stefan could lay his heart on the line in front of millions of viewers.

"Sorry to interrupt the ceremony before it starts," he said to the crowd of suspicious onlookers. "But I have something important to say and this may change the outcome of today's festivities."

"Stefan," Victoria whispered from behind him. "Stop. Sit down."

Ignoring her, he moved to stand on the other side of her chair because all of this was for her benefit...not the spectators'. He looked down into her eyes and took a deep breath.

"Victoria Dane Alexander, you have been my best friend since we were teens. There's nothing I wouldn't do for you and I've come to learn there's nothing you wouldn't do for me."

Victoria bowed her head, clamping her hands tightly in her lap. He wanted to know what she was thinking, but he had to keep going, had to make her see this wasn't just about a title or a stupid movie.

"I've been using this beautiful woman," he admitted to the crowd. An audible gasp settled over the ballroom. "I needed her to keep this country in my family and become your king. She agreed to marry me, and I promised her after the coronation if she chose to end the marriage, I would step aside."

Stefan couldn't stand it anymore. He reached out, placing a hand over her shoulder and squeezed. She trembled beneath his touch.

"But I can't step aside."

Her head jerked up to meet his. Tears swam in her eyes, ready to fall down at the next blink.

"I can't step aside and let this woman out of my life," he continued. "I don't deserve her or her loyalty. I certainly don't deserve her love for the way I've treated her. But she fell in love with me."

His eyes locked on to hers. "And with no doubts of our future together, I fell in love with her."

Victoria's watery eyes searched his face and Stefan got down on one knee beside her chair. Taking her hand in his, he kissed her knuckles.

"I haven't been honest with Victoria, or all of you. This marriage was a fake, but I do love you, Victoria. And if I can't be your king, then so be it. I couldn't live with myself if I let this woman out of my life."

He took a deep breath as he continued to lay his heart on the line. "Victoria," he said, softer now because nothing else mattered except her response, "I wasn't respectful when I didn't tell you the full truth, but I swear on my life if you let me back into that loving heart of yours, I'll spend the rest of our lives making it up to you. Nothing else matters but you and us…if you'll have me."

She chewed on her bottom lip. "You don't mean this."

Stroking the back of her trembling hand, he smiled. "I've never meant anything more. I'm not sure when I fell in love with you. Maybe it was when I first met you or maybe it was when you were walking down the aisle to become my bride. Looking back, I think I've always been in love with you and I just couldn't admit it to myself. At least I didn't know the level of love I had. It's so much deeper than I ever could've imagined."

Victoria sighed, closed her eyes and let the tears fall.

"Can you say that again?" she asked, lifting her lids to meet his gaze.

Stefan searched her beautiful face. "Which part?"

"The part where you fell in love with me with no doubts of our future."

He chuckled. "I'm a fool not to have realized that I've loved you for years. All this time I wanted to get closer to you, wanted more than a friendship, but I didn't know what. Now I know that what I was searching for was love. And it was there all along."

Her head dipped to her chest as she sniffed. "I'm scared," she whispered. "What if you fall out of love?"

Tipping her chin up with his finger and thumb, he eased in for a gentle, simple kiss. "I've loved you most of my life, Tori. I just didn't have the courage to admit it to myself. There's no way I could ever fall out of love. I've been absolutely miserable without you. Nothing matters, not this title, crown or movie, if you aren't in my life. I'd give it all up for another chance."

"But if you step aside, Galini Isle will go back to Greece."

He smiled. "I found a loophole, finally. When it mattered most, I found a way out."

Her teary eyes searched his. "But how?"

"Mikos will step up if I need him to," he told her.

"I didn't think he could."

He took her hand, kissed it and smiled. "I'll explain later. Can you please put me out of my misery and tell me this marriage will be real from here on out?"

A beautiful, hopeful smile spread across her face. "I don't want you to give up your title or the documentary... though my brothers are pretty upset, but I can talk to them."

Stefan squeezed her hands. "I seriously don't care about anything but being with you. If you're in my future, I can handle whatever comes my way."

She leaned toward him and kissed his lips before whispering in his ear, "Then let's see if we can finish this coronation ceremony and we can celebrate alone wearing only our crowns."

The archbishop stepped forward. "Are the two of you certain this marriage is legitimate now?"

Victoria smiled and nodded. "I'm certain."

Stefan stared into her watery eyes. "Never been more sure of anything in my life."

"Then I approve the continuation of this coronation ceremony," the archbishop declared as the crowd began to clap and cheer.

Stefan hadn't seen Victoria for several minutes and was starting to wonder if she'd changed her mind and run out the palace doors with their last guest.

Midnight had come and gone and the coronation celebration had just calmed down. Dancing, laughing and holding Victoria in his arms nearly the entire evening had been the best moments of his life.

When she could've chosen to turn her back on him, on his title and his beloved country, she hadn't. She'd stood by his side, even when he'd hurt her.

And that gnawing ache would haunt him the rest of his life. Knowing he'd caused her even a second of grief made him ill. But the fact their love overcame his moments of idiocy proved they were meant to be.

"Your Majesty."

Stefan stopped in the corridor leading to his wing and turned to the sound of Hector's voice.

"Yes?"

His loyal assistant and guard smiled. "I'm to give you a message from your queen."

A smile spread across Stefan's face. Yes, she was his queen, his wife, the love of his life.

"And what is it?"

Hector cleared his throat. "I am to tell you, and I quote, 'Tell my king that the last part of his dream is coming true, and he'll know where to find me.'"

Stefan thought for about a half second before he

laughed. "Thank you, Hector. Please make sure the staff stays out of the east wing tonight."

With a faint redness to his wrinkled cheeks, Hector bowed. "As you wish, King Alexander."

As much as he loved hearing that title and knowing it belonged to him, he was loving even more what his sneaky wife had in store for him. He knew just where to find her.

Arousal shot through him fast and hard as his long strides ate up the hallways leading to the destination.

Through the wall of glass, he saw her—his queen wearing her jeweled crown...and nothing else. She hadn't been kidding about the celebration wearing only the crowns. He liked her style of thinking.

Stefan entered the pool area and began undoing the double-breasted buttons of his jacket.

"Queen Alexander, are you aware of the age and expense of that crown upon your head?" he asked, slipping out of the garment.

She smiled, rested her arms on the edge of the pool and peered up at him. "I have a pretty good idea, but I wanted to add a bit to this fantasy, too."

Unlike her, he left his crown sitting on the bench where she'd draped her silk gown.

"And what's your fantasy?"

"Making love while wearing my crown," she told him, a sultry grin inviting him to join her. "I added some pins, so I think we're safe from it falling off."

When he slid off the last of his clothes and turned, he waited until recognition dawned in her eyes.

"Stefan?"

Unable to stop his grin, he took a step closer. "What do you think?"

"I can't believe... When did you get it?"

He glanced down at the new ink on his chest. "A few

weeks ago. I found some of your drawings lying on the desk. I was partial to the one with the crest and our initials. Since I already had the crest, I only had to add your work."

"Come closer and let me see," she told him. "I want to get a better look."

He moved to the edge and hopped in, coming to stand directly beside her. "By all means, feel free to look all you want. Touching is allowed, too."

Her fingertip traced the design that he'd had done in her honor, imagining her face when she finally saw it.

"It's beautiful," she whispered. "I can't believe you took one of my crazy doodles and turned it into something so beautiful. Meaningful."

He grasped her bare shoulders in his hands and pulled her against him. "Everything about you is beautiful and meaningful, Tori. And I think this should be your royal wardrobe," he told her. "The tiara and nothing else."

Soft laughter spilled from her lips. "That's exactly how I want you all the time," she told him.

He nipped at her lips, tilting his hips toward hers. "I'll see about setting that into an order."

"Speaking of orders, how did you manage to find a loophole that would allow Mikos to take your place?"

Not something he wanted to talk about when he was aroused and his wife was wet and in his arms, but he did want her to know the lengths he would go to in order to keep her.

"When I told Mikos that our family would lose control of Galini Isle to Greece because I had to give up the title, he started doing some digging about the rules of divorce and taking the title for himself. Since Karina is pregnant, Mikos could act as ruler until the child became of age, and then that child would take over as ruler."

Tears shimmered in her eyes. "And you were going to step aside?"

"Without a doubt. I would've turned this country over to Satan himself to get you back." His hold tightened on her. "Mikos and I went to the head counsel and stated our case. They were more than willing to let him take the title temporarily until his baby was twenty-one if I chose to step aside."

She searched his eyes. "I didn't know I could ever love like this. Didn't know that someone could love me so unselfishly. God, Stefan, I'm so glad you fought for us."

He ran his hands up her bare, wet back then slid them down to cup her rear. "I wouldn't have let you go, Tori. I can't live without you."

As he claimed his wife, he knew there was nothing he wouldn't do for her. His life was completely perfect, and the girl with braces who'd once captured his teenage attention now held his heart until the day he died.

Epilogue

One year later...

Love surrounded her. Even with the flashbulbs going off like a strobe light outside her limo, Queen Victoria Dane Alexander knew she'd remember this monumental moment forever.

As the car pulled up to the red carpet, Victoria waited for her driver to open the door.

"Are we all ready?" she asked.

Her entire family, Bronson, Mia, Anthony, Charlotte, Olivia and Stefan, all smiled. They'd agreed to ride together to the L.A. premiere of *Legendary Icon*. So much had happened in the past few years, and they wanted to make a united front, to show they were a family first, movie moguls second.

The limo door opened; screams, cameras and the red carpet awaited them. Victoria never tired of the positive attention the media gave to her brothers and mother. They were so talented and she was thrilled to be part of this night, this movie.

The driver helped Olivia out first and the crowd grew even louder.

"She's going to shine tonight," Bronson said with a smile on his face.

Anthony nodded. "She always shines, but she's waited for this for so long. I'm glad we could give this to her."

Emotions overwhelmed Victoria. It wasn't that long ago that Bronson and Anthony were at each other's throats, but now they were family and they loved each other...all because of Olivia Dane.

Anthony and Charlotte exited the limo next, followed by Bronson and Mia. Stefan reached over and took her hand.

"Have I told you how *oraios* you look tonight?"

Victoria had learned over the past year that the Greek term meant "beautiful," but she always loved hearing it come from his lips.

"You've told me." She took a deep breath, ready to really change his life. "I have something to tell you, as well."

He glanced to the open car door. "Shouldn't we be getting out?"

Victoria shrugged. "They're all still dazzled by the rest of my family. I wanted to impress you with my own Greek I've been working on."

One dark brow rose. "Oh, really? And what is that, my love?"

She leaned in and whispered, *"Moro."*

Those dark chocolate eyes widened, dropped to her stomach and back up. "A baby?" he asked. "Tori, my God. Are you serious?"

With tears clogging her throat, she nodded. "Yes. I know we wanted to wait a bit longer, but—"

Stefan took her face in his hands and kissed her, thoroughly, deeply, passionately. Who needed lip gloss for the premiere anyway?

When he leaned back, he was still grinning like she'd never seen before. "I'm thrilled. Are you feeling okay?"

She nodded. "I haven't been sick once, and the doctor said I'm about seven weeks along and very healthy."

He kissed her again. "I love you, Victoria. I can't tell you how much."

She started easing toward the open door, toward the shouts and cameras. "After we celebrate this premiere, you can show me at home."

* * * * *

'Mistress,' Nikolai slotted in cool as ice.

Shock had welded Ella's tongue to the roof of her mouth because
he was sexually propositioning her and nothing could have prepared
her for that. She wasn't drop-dead gorgeous… *he* was! Male heads
didn't swivel when Ella walked down the street because she had
neither the length of leg nor the curves usually deemed necessary
to attract such attention. Why on earth could he be making *her* such
an offer?

'But we don't even know each other,' she framed dazedly. 'You're
a stranger…'

'If you live with me I won't be a stranger for long,' Nikolai pointed out with monumental calm. And the very sound of that inhuman calm and cool forced her to flip round and settle distraught eyes on his lean darkly handsome face.

'You can't be serious about this!'

'I assure you that I am deadly serious. Move in and I'll forget your family's debts.'

'But it's a *crazy* idea!' she gasped.

'It's not crazy to me,' Nikolai asserted. 'When I want anything, I go after it hard and fast.'

Her lashes dipped. Did he want her like that? Enough to track her down, buy up her father's debts, and try and buy rights to her and her body along with those debts? The very idea of that made her dizzy and plunged her brain into even greater turmoil. 'It's immoral… it's blackmail.'

'It's definitely *not* blackmail. I'm giving you the benefit of a choice you didn't have before I came through that door,' Nikolai Drakos fielded with a glittering cool. 'That choice is yours to make.'

'Like hell it is!' Ella fired back. 'It's a complete cheat of a supposed offer!'

Nikolai sent her a gleaming sideways glance. 'No the real cheat was you kissing me the way you did last year and then saying no and acting as if I had grossly insulted you,' he murmured with lethal quietness.

'You *did* insult me!' Ella flung back, her cheeks hot as fire while she wondered if her refusal that night had started off his whole chain reaction. What else could possibly be driving him?

Nikolai straightened lazily as he opened the door. 'If you take offence that easily, maybe it's just as well that the answer is no.'